SWAN LAKE

QUEST FOR THE KINGDOMS

SWAN LAKE

QUEST FOR THE KINGDOMS

REY TERCIERO
MEGAN KEARNEY
COLORS BY MEAGHAN CARTER

HARPER alley

An Imprint of HarperCollinsPublishers

PART I

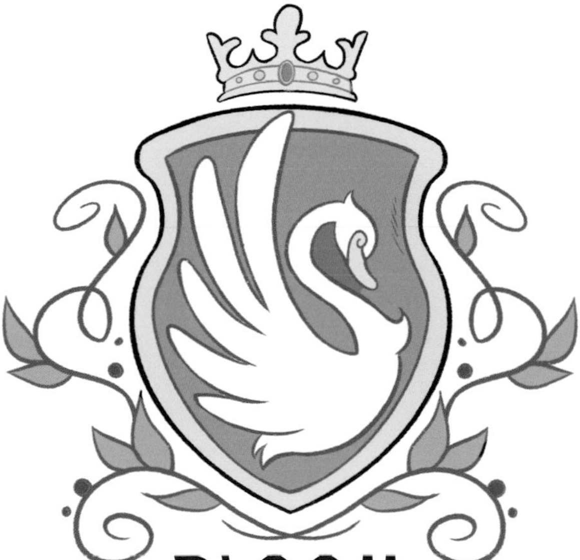

BLOOM

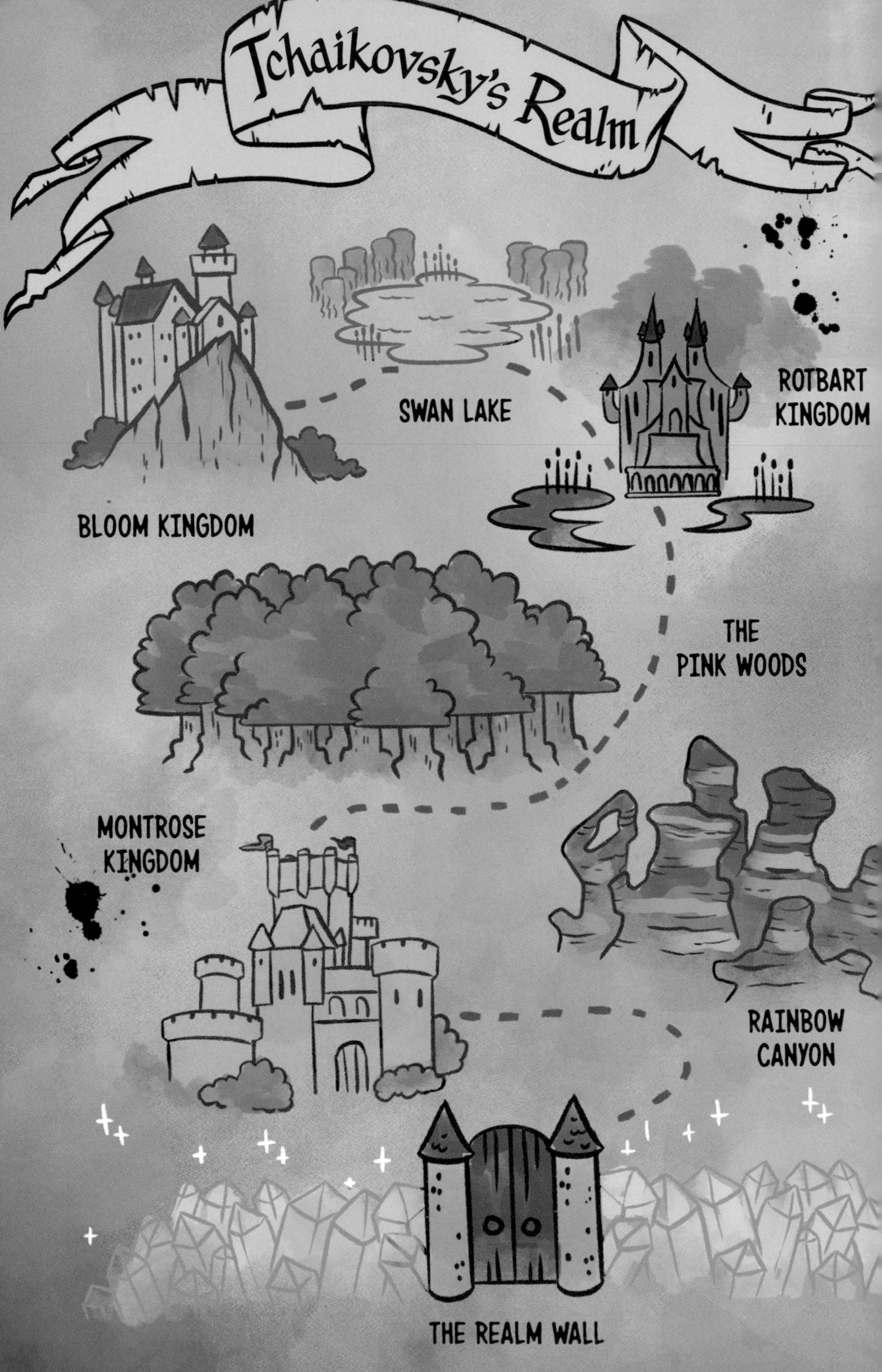
Tchaikovsky's Realm
SWAN LAKE
ROTBART KINGDOM
BLOOM KINGDOM
THE PINK WOODS
MONTROSE KINGDOM
RAINBOW CANYON
THE REALM WALL

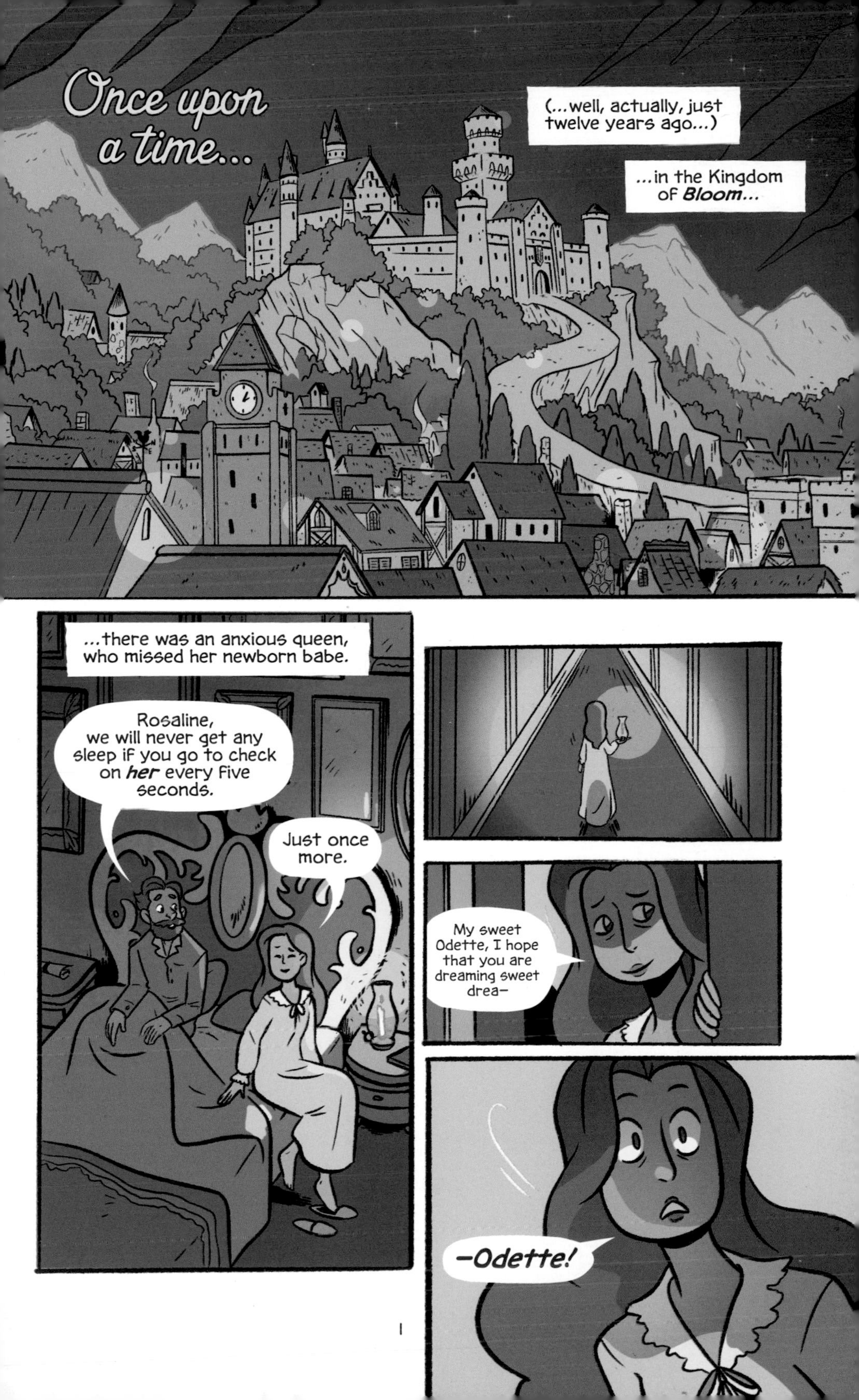
Once upon a time...
(...well, actually, just twelve years ago...)
...in the Kingdom of Bloom...
...there was an anxious queen, who missed her newborn babe.
Rosaline, we will never get any sleep if you go to check on her every five seconds.
Just once more.
My sweet Odette, I hope that you are dreaming sweet drea–
–Odette!

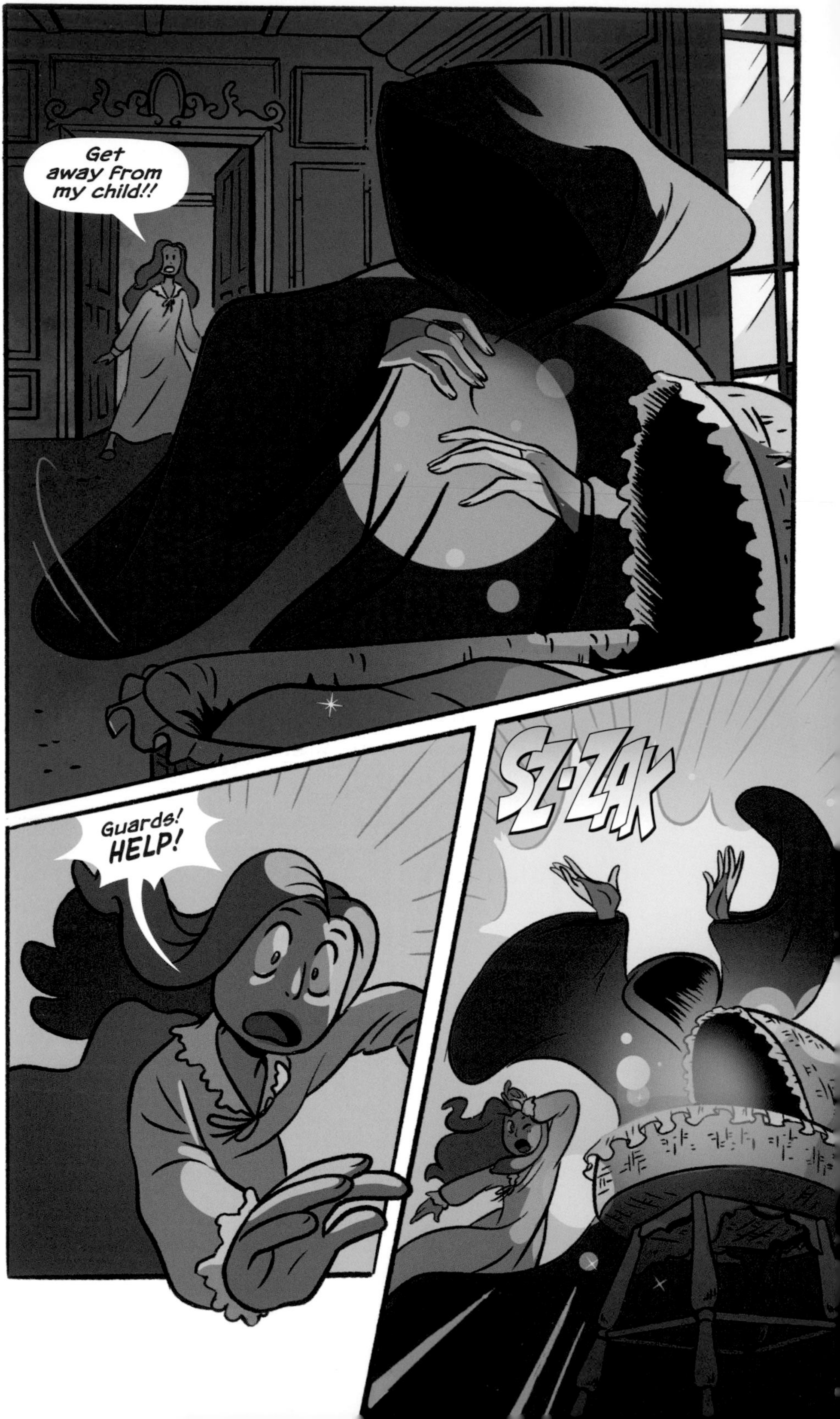
Get away from my child!!
Guards! HELP!
SZ-ZAK

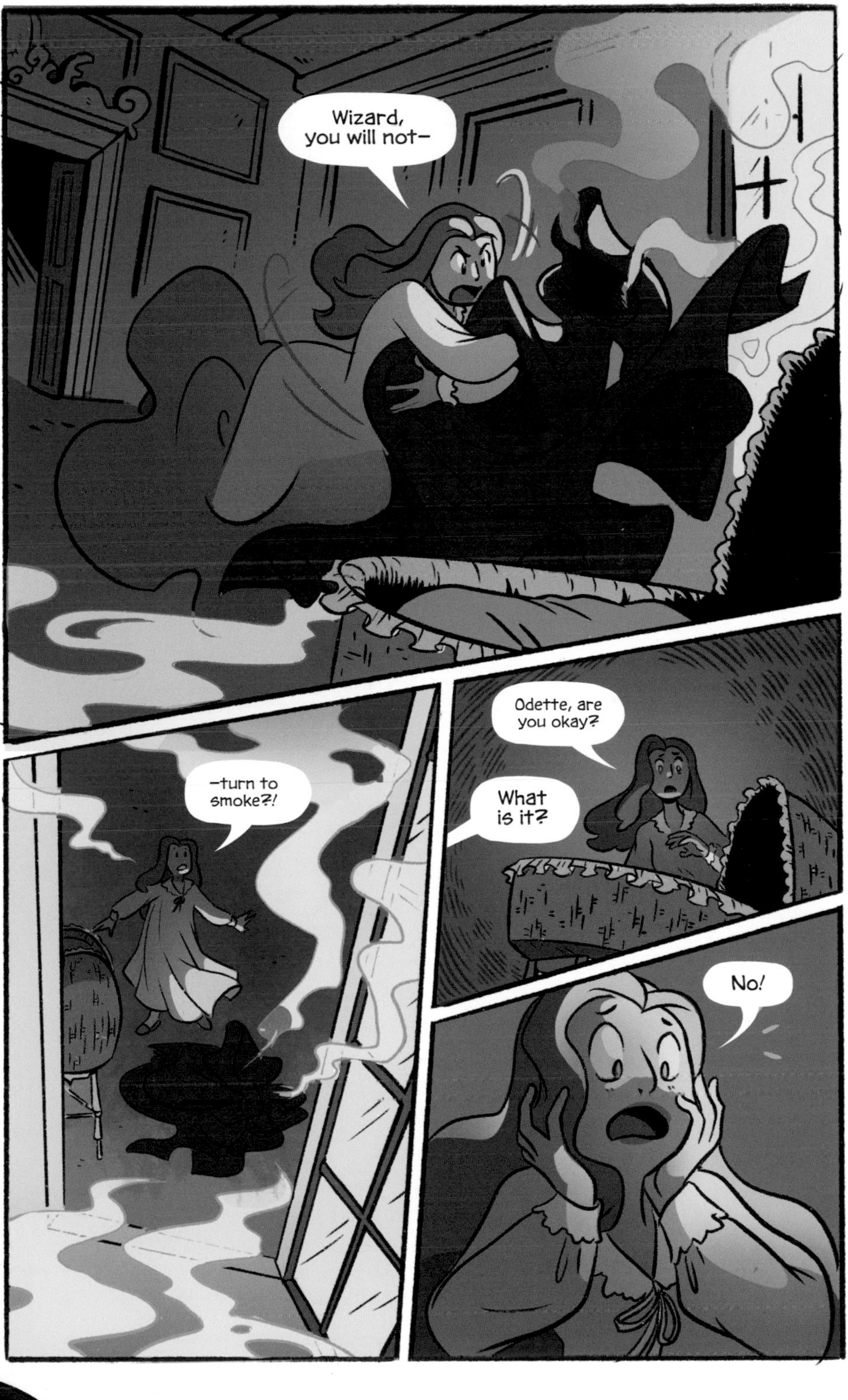
Wizard, you will not–
–turn to smoke?!
Odette, are you okay?
What is it?
No!

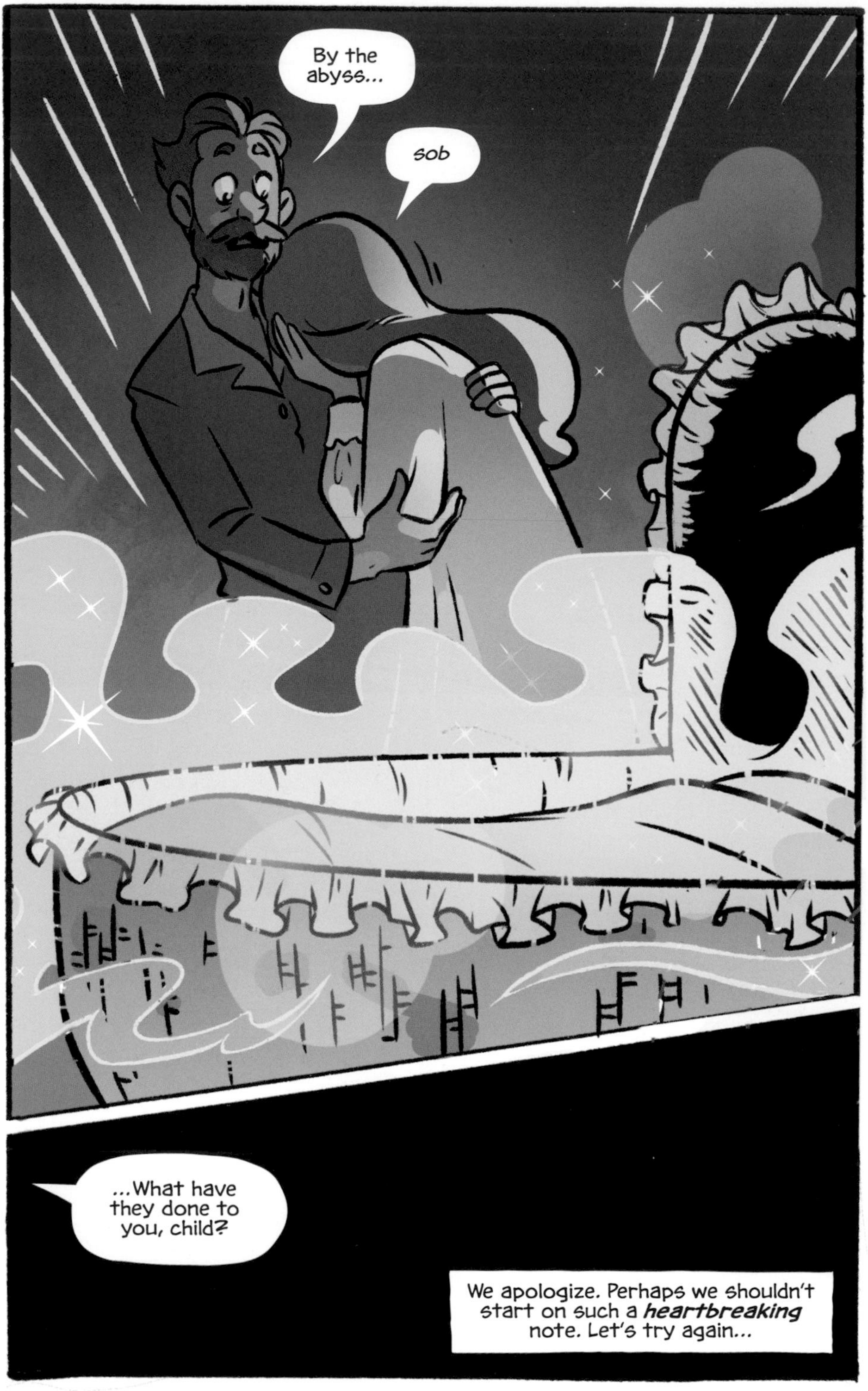
By the abyss...
sob
...What have they done to you, child?
We apologize. Perhaps we shouldn't start on such a ***heartbreaking*** note. Let's try again...

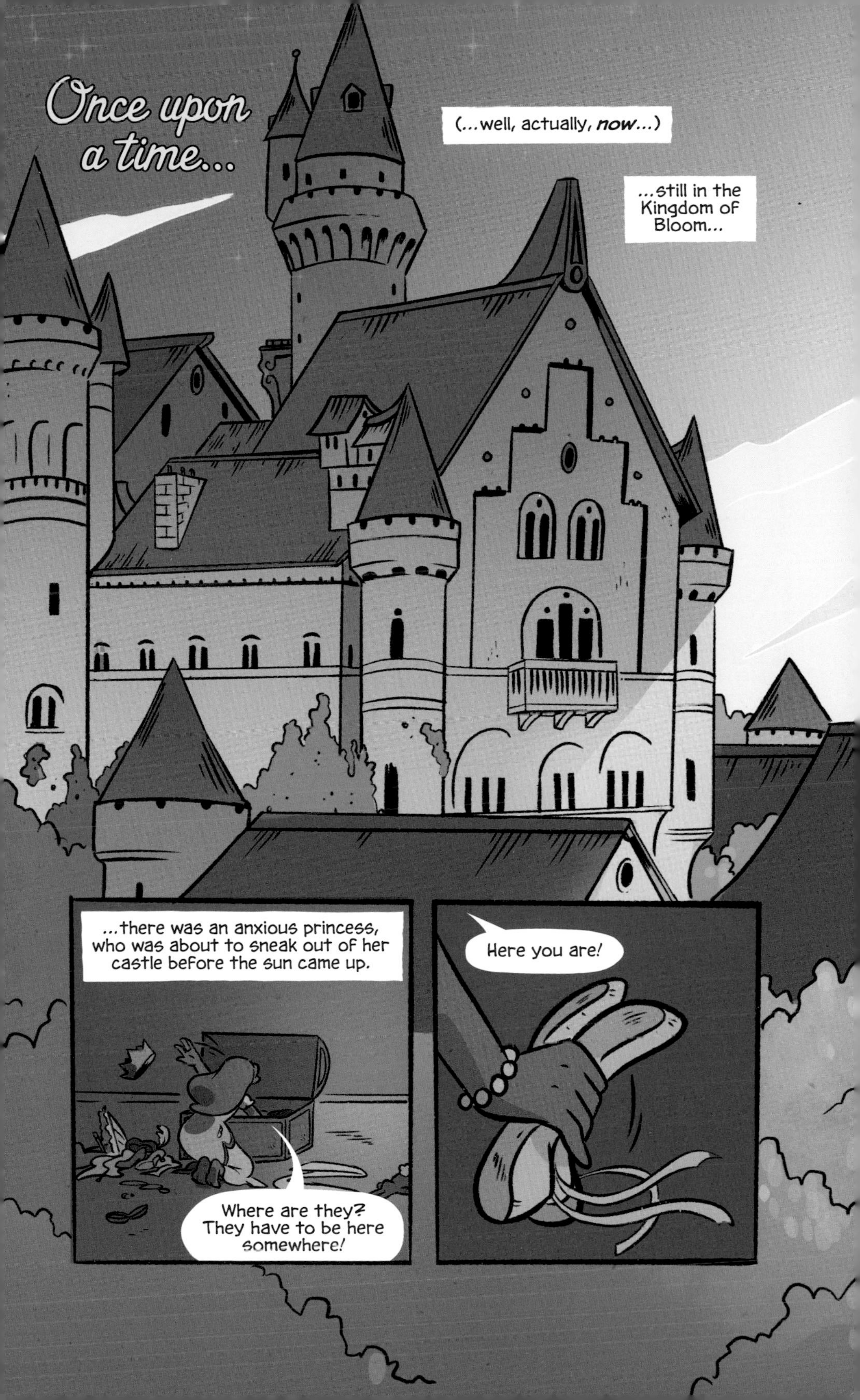
Once upon a time...
(...well, actually, *now*...)
...still in the Kingdom of Bloom...
...there was an anxious princess, who was about to sneak out of her castle before the sun came up.
Where are they? They have to be here somewhere!
Here you are!

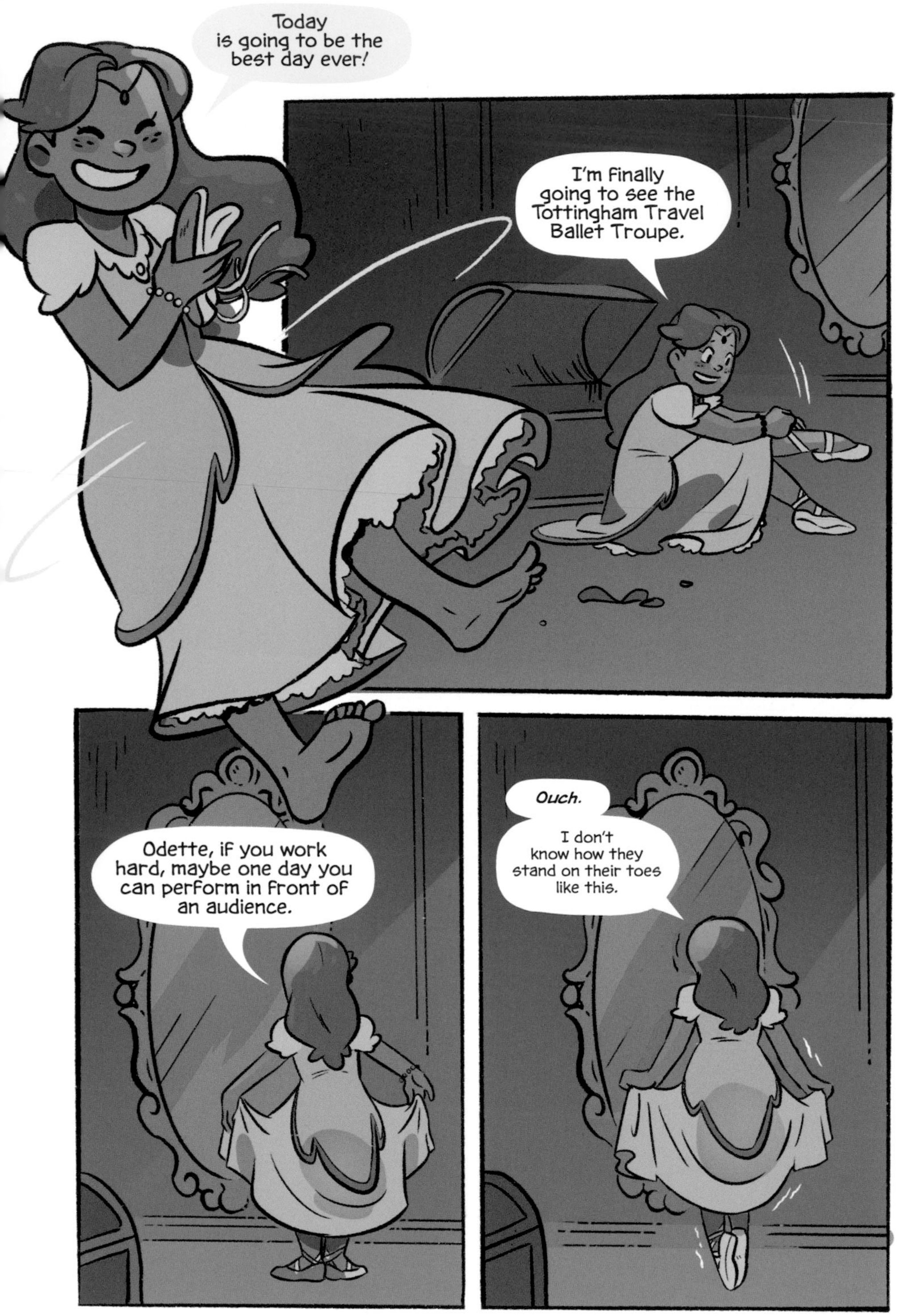
Today is going to be the best day ever!
I'm finally going to see the Tottingham Travel Ballet Troupe.
Odette, if you work hard, maybe one day you can perform in front of an audience.
Ouch.
I don't know how they stand on their toes like this.

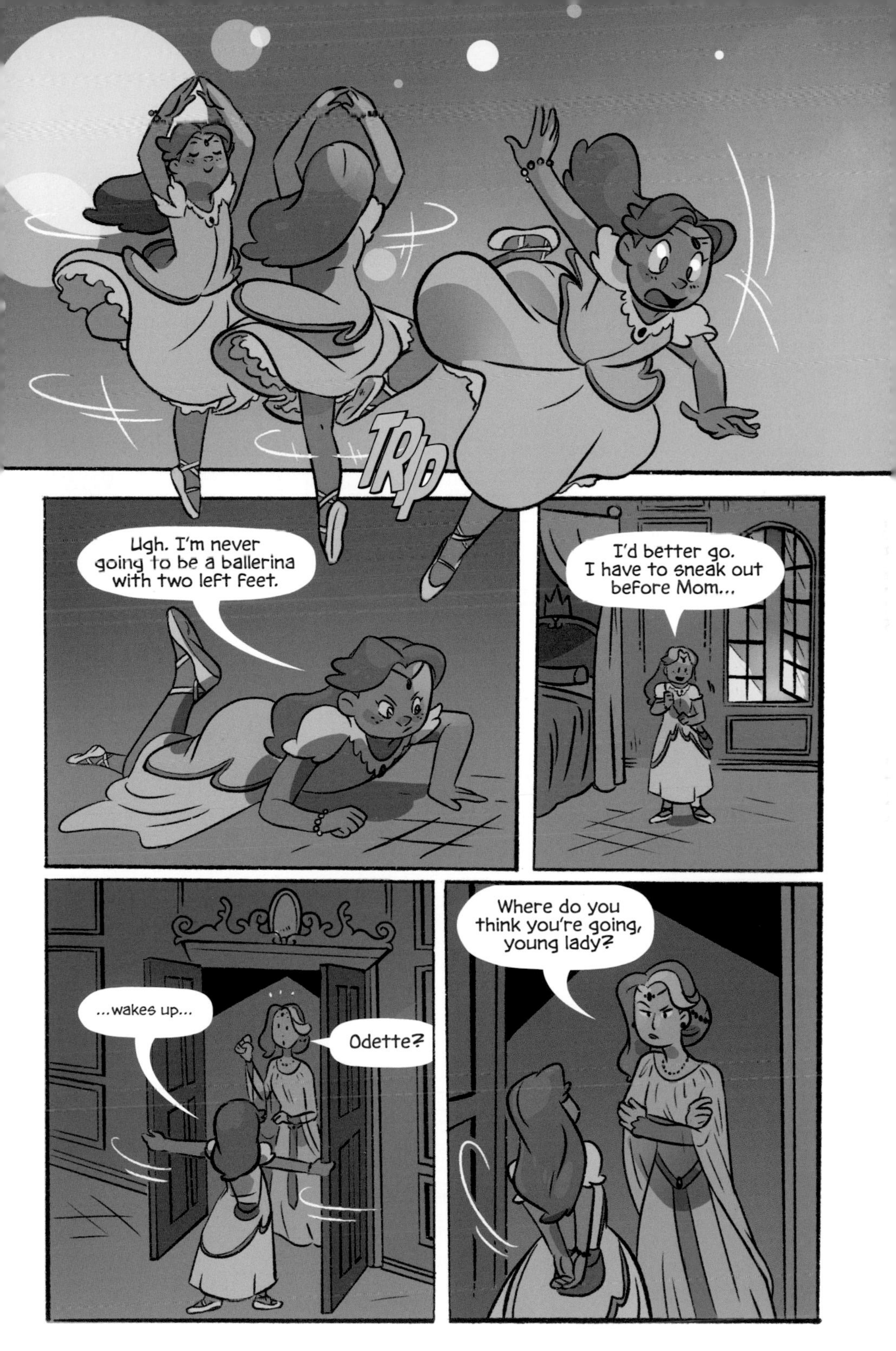
TRIP
Ugh. I'm never going to be a ballerina with two left feet.
I'd better go. I have to sneak out before Mom...
...wakes up...
Odette?
Where do you think you're going, young lady?

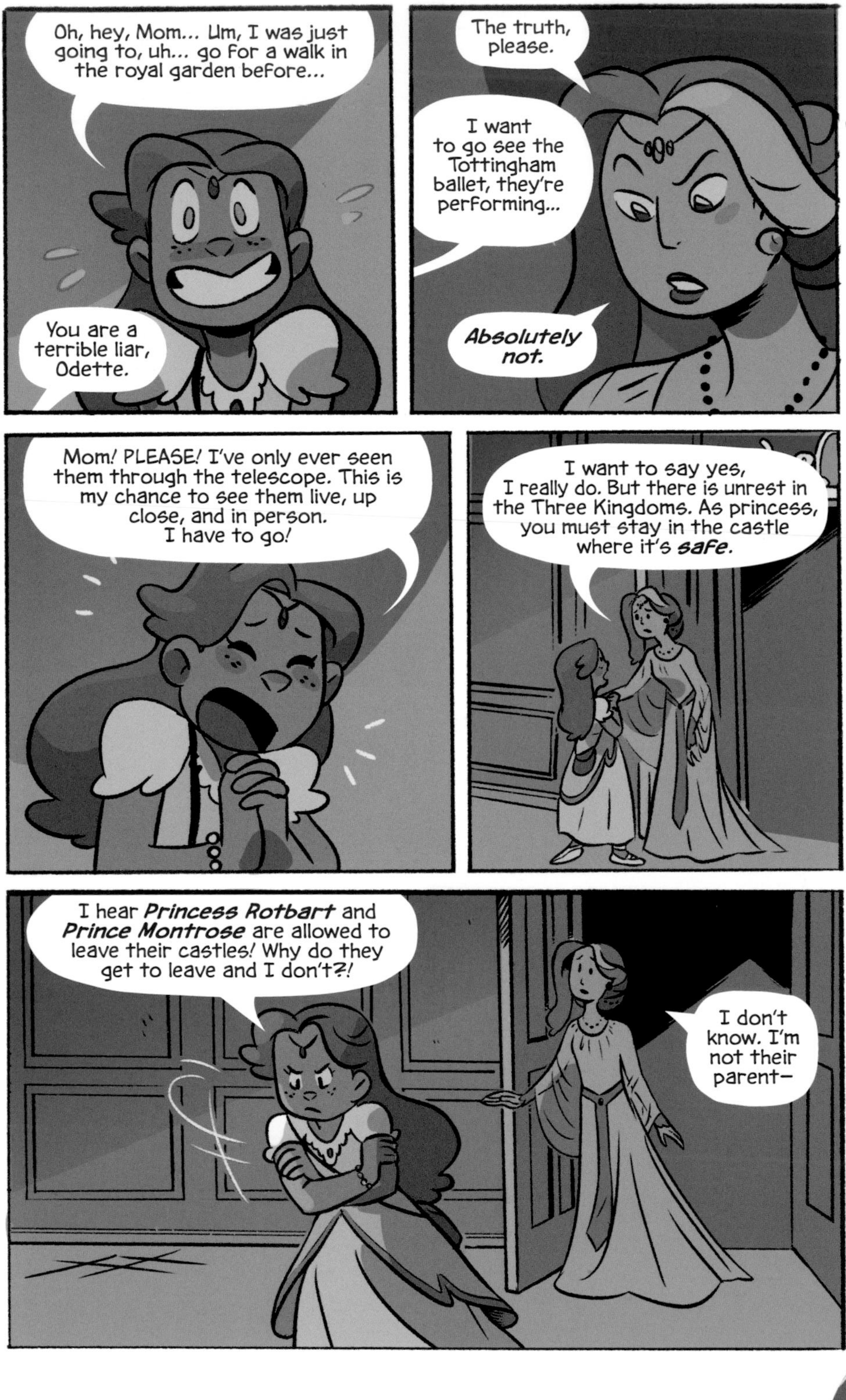
Oh, hey, Mom... Um, I was just going to, uh... go for a walk in the royal garden before...
You are a terrible liar, Odette.
The truth, please.
I want to go see the Tottingham ballet, they're performing...
Absolutely not.
Mom! PLEASE! I've only ever seen them through the telescope. This is my chance to see them live, up close, and in person. I have to go!
I want to say yes, I really do. But there is unrest in the Three Kingdoms. As princess, you must stay in the castle where it's safe.
I hear Princess Rotbart and Prince Montrose are allowed to leave their castles! Why do they get to leave and I don't?!
I don't know. I'm not their parent—

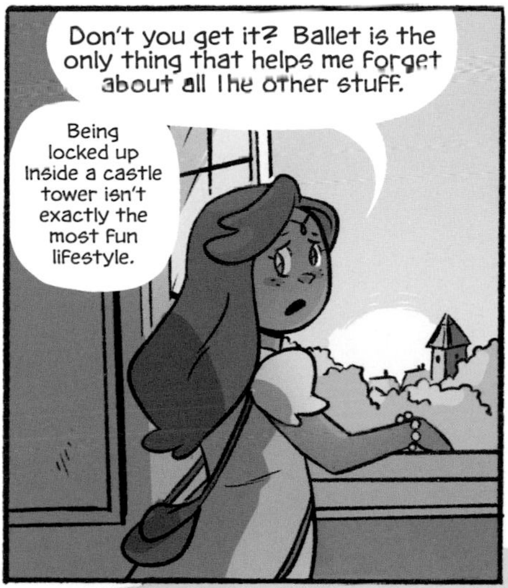
Don't you get it? Ballet is the only thing that helps me forget about all the other stuff.
Being locked up inside a castle tower isn't exactly the most fun lifestyle.

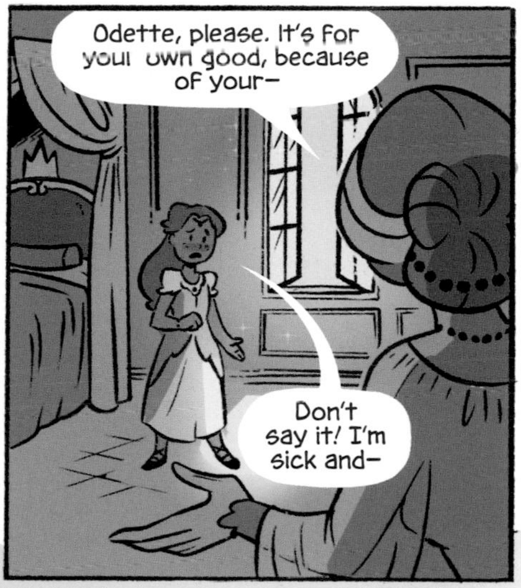
Odette, please. It's for your own good, because of your—
Don't say it! I'm sick and—

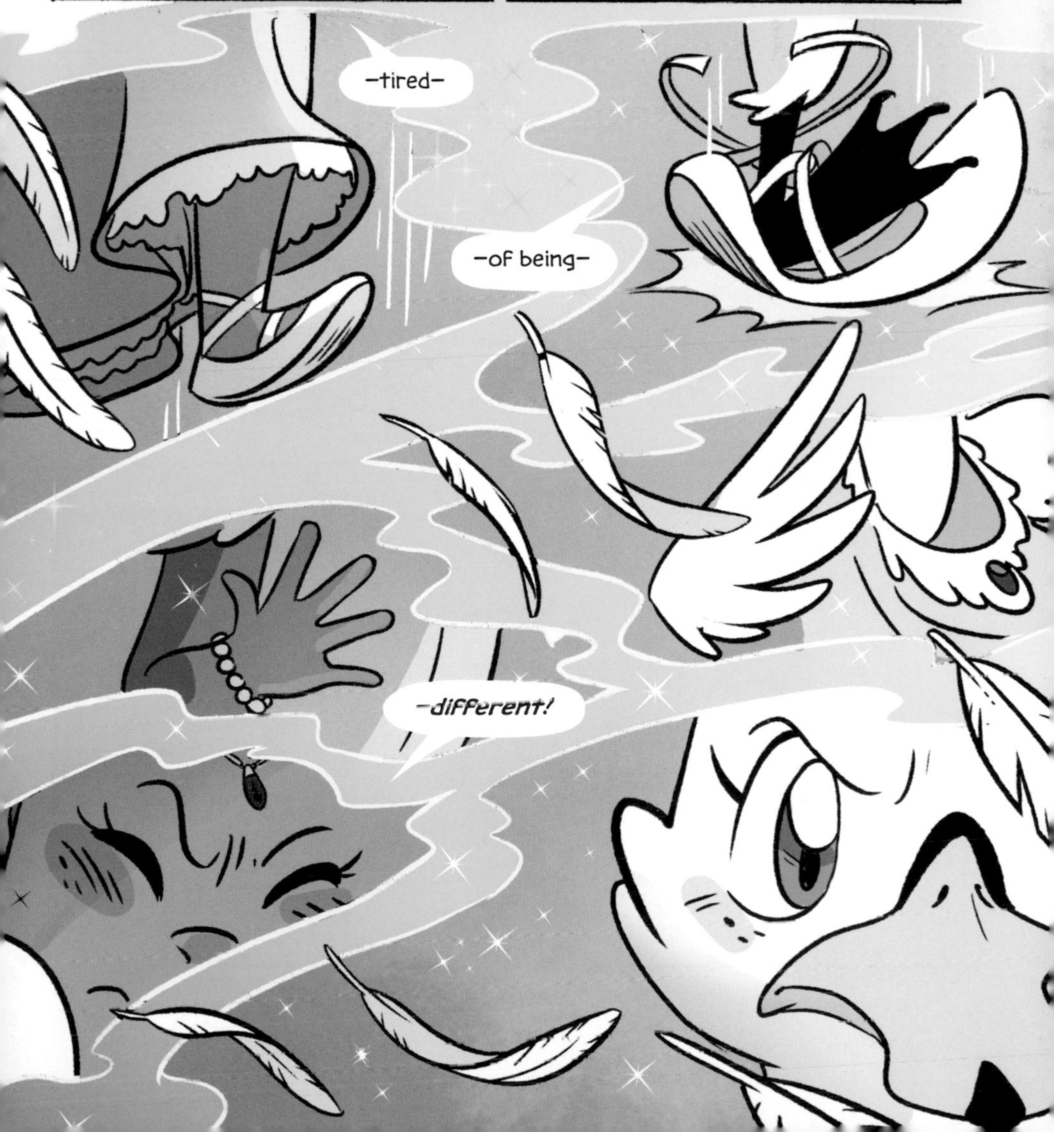
—tired—
—of being—
—different!

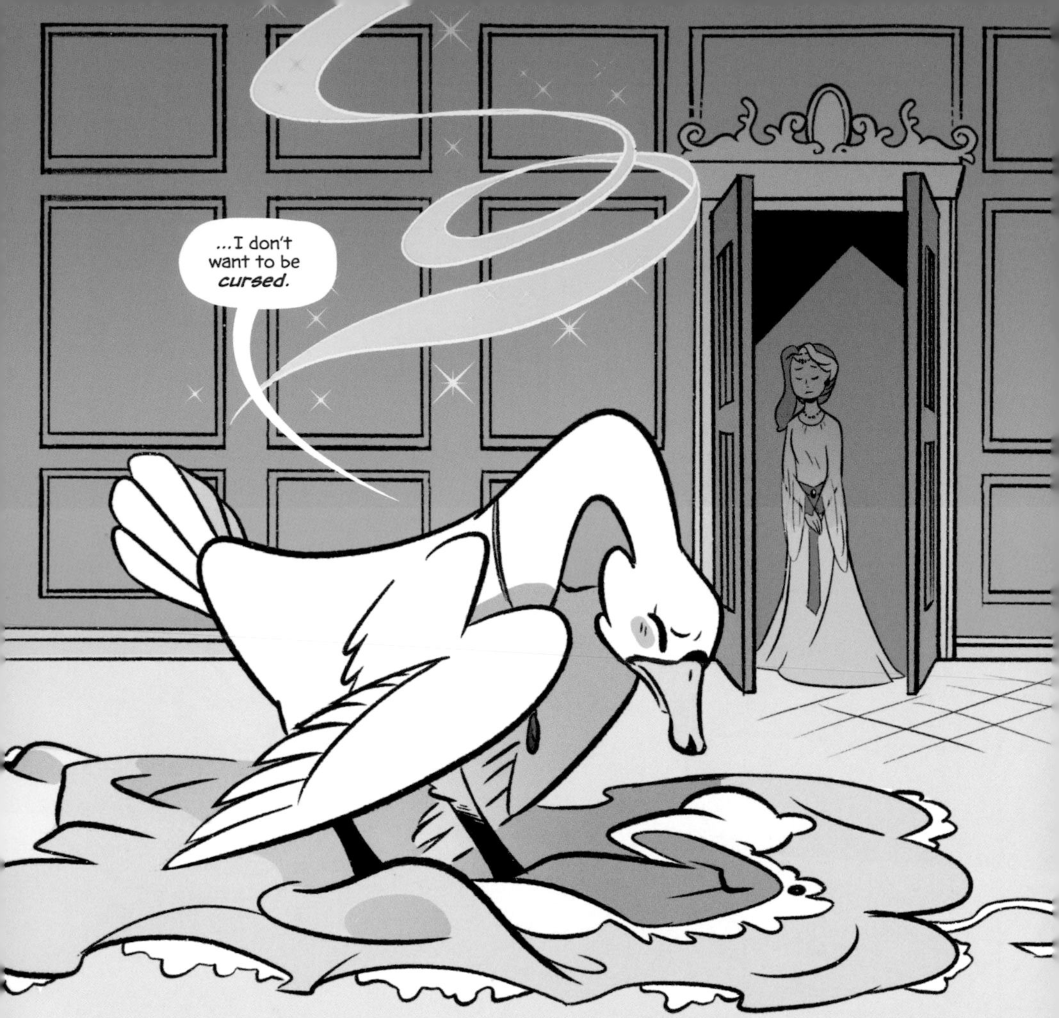
...I don't want to be *cursed.*

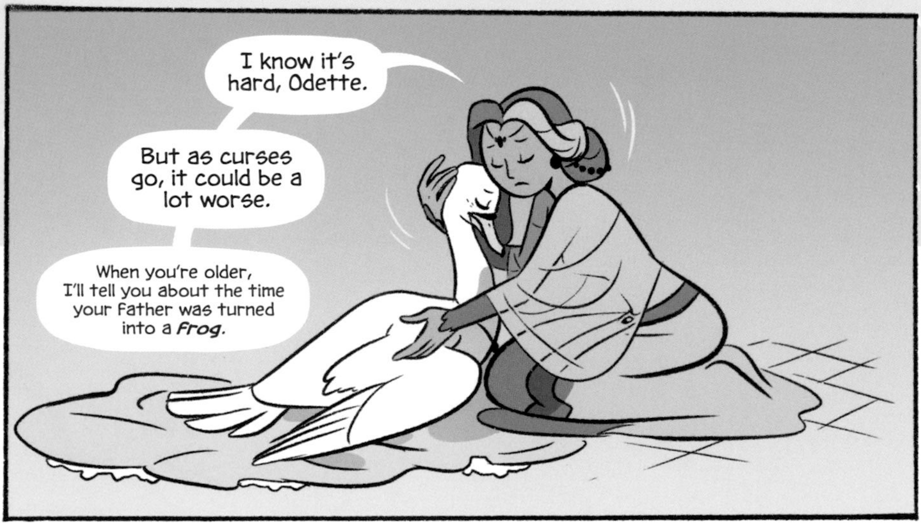
I know it's hard, Odette.
But as curses go, it could be a lot worse.
When you're older, I'll tell you about the time your father was turned into a *frog.*

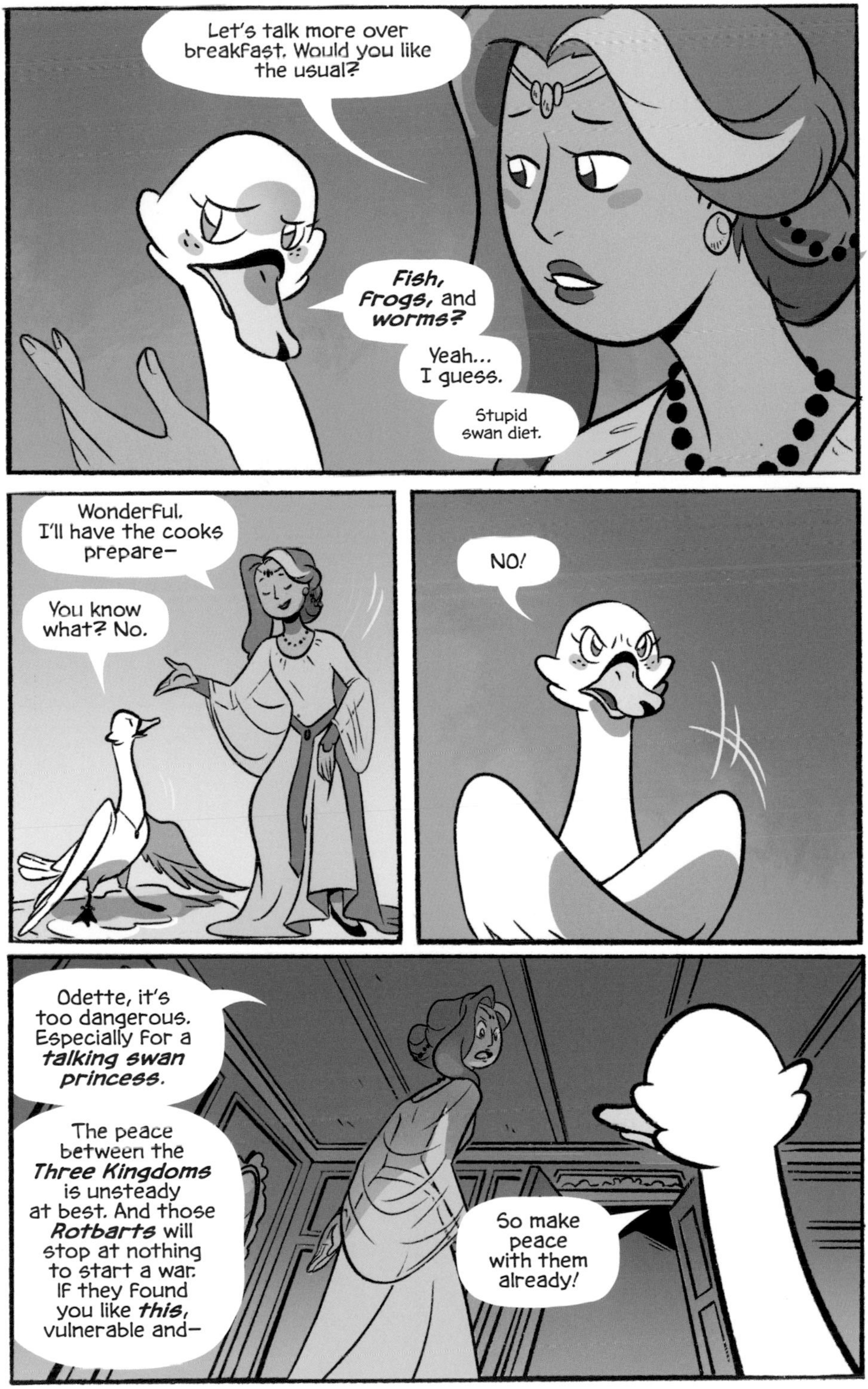
Let's talk more over breakfast. Would you like the usual?
Fish, frogs, and *worms?*
Yeah... I guess.
Stupid swan diet.
Wonderful. I'll have the cooks prepare—
You know what? No.
NO!
Odette, it's too dangerous. Especially for a *talking swan princess.*
The peace between the *Three Kingdoms* is unsteady at best. And those *Rotbarts* will stop at nothing to start a war. If they found you like *this,* vulnerable and—
So make peace with them already!

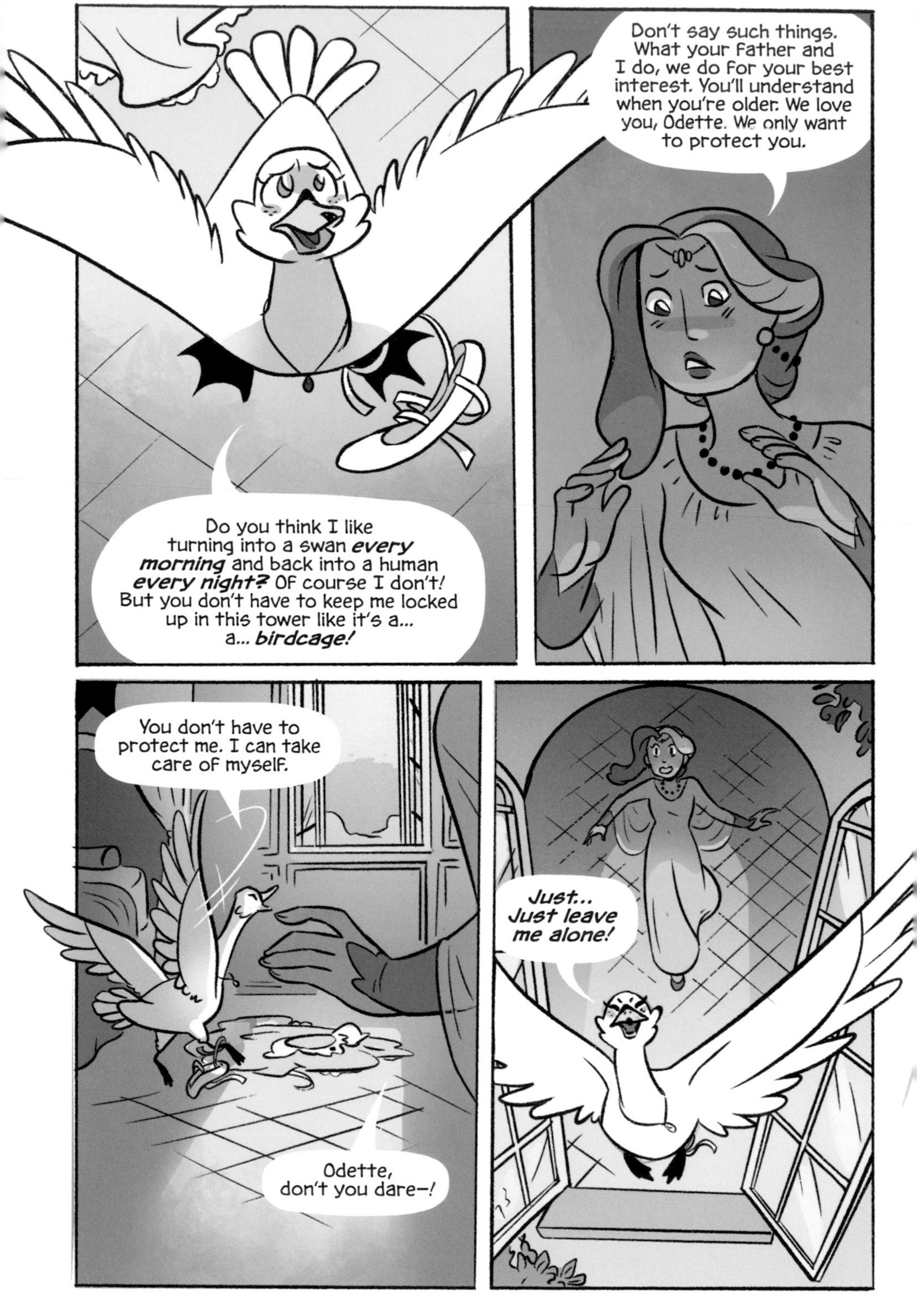
Do you think I like turning into a swan ***every morning*** and back into a human ***every night?*** Of course I don't! But you don't have to keep me locked up in this tower like it's a... a... ***birdcage!***
Don't say such things. What your father and I do, we do for your best interest. You'll understand when you're older. We love you, Odette. We only want to protect you.
You don't have to protect me. I can take care of myself.
Odette, don't you dare–!
Just... Just leave me alone!

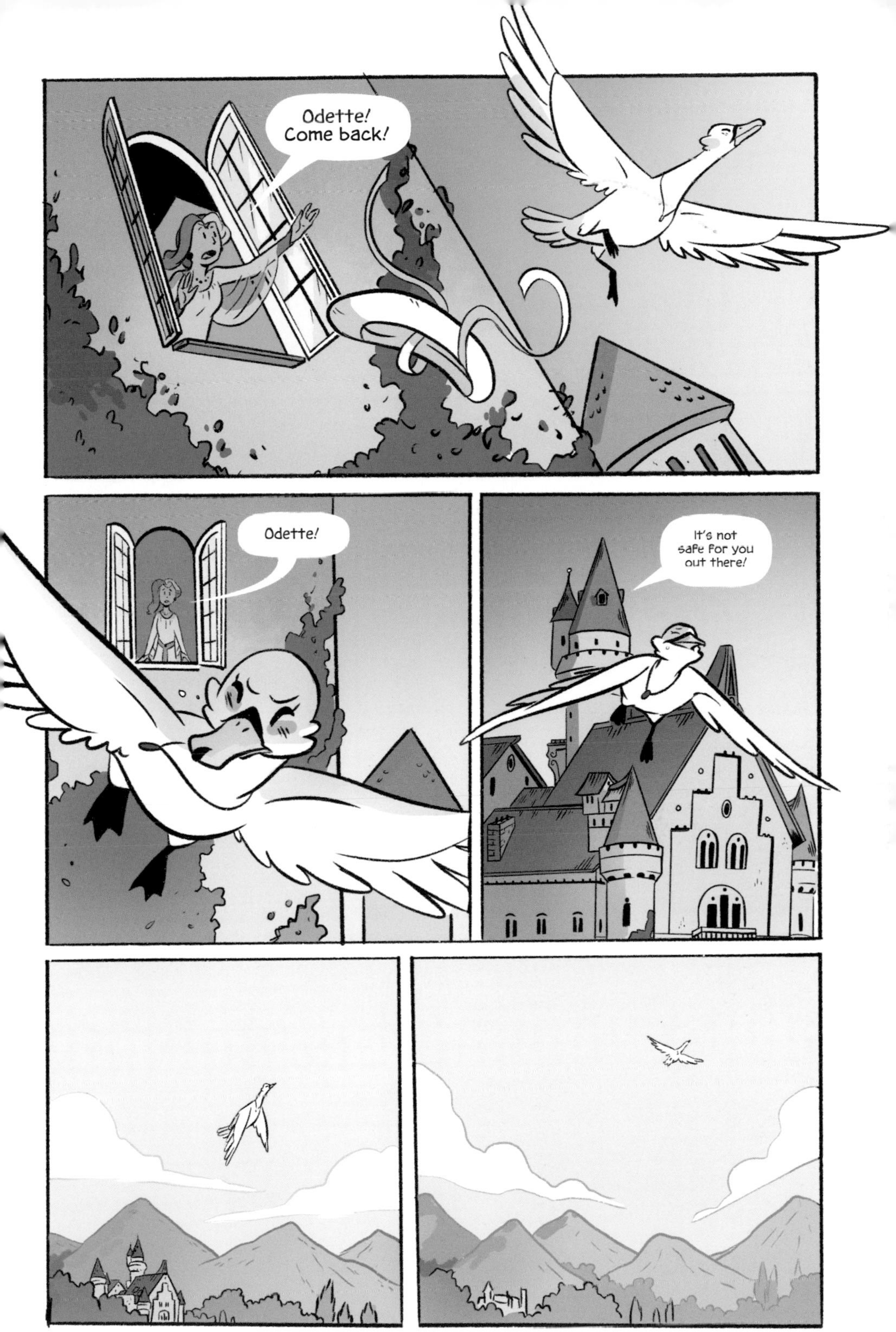
Odette! Come back!
Odette!
It's not safe for you out there!

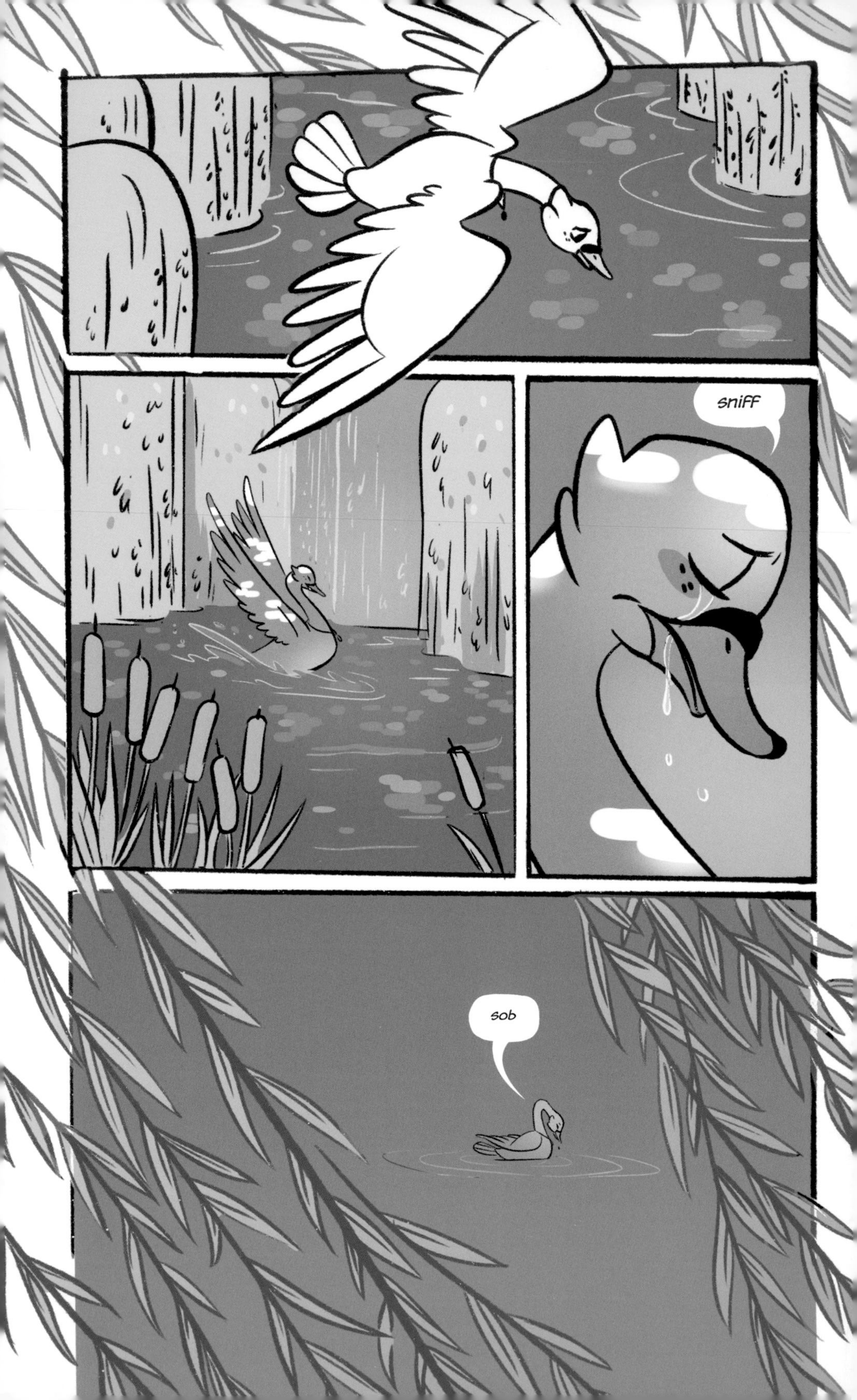
sniff
sob

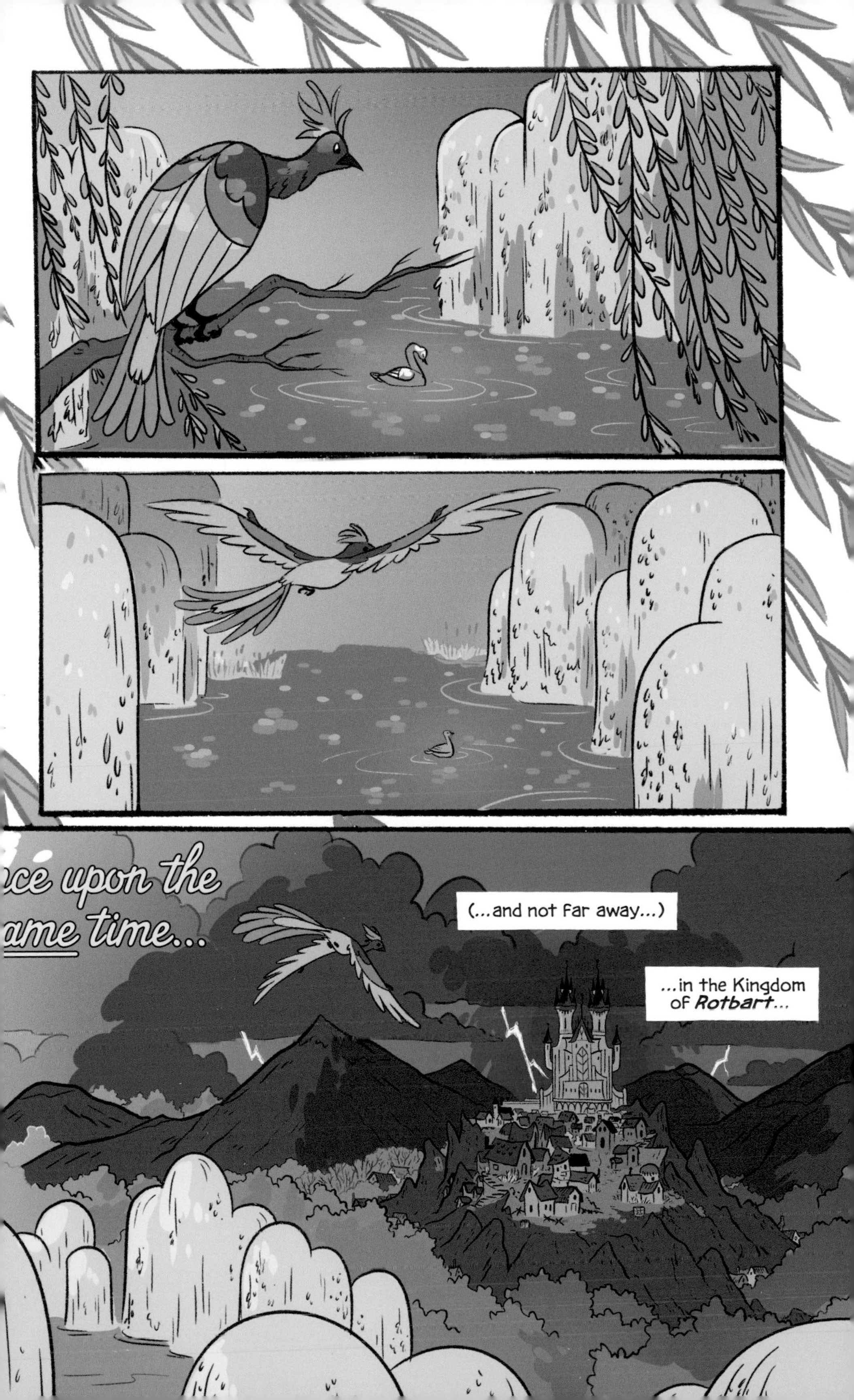

ce upon the
ame time...
(...and not far away...)
...in the Kingdom of Rotbart...

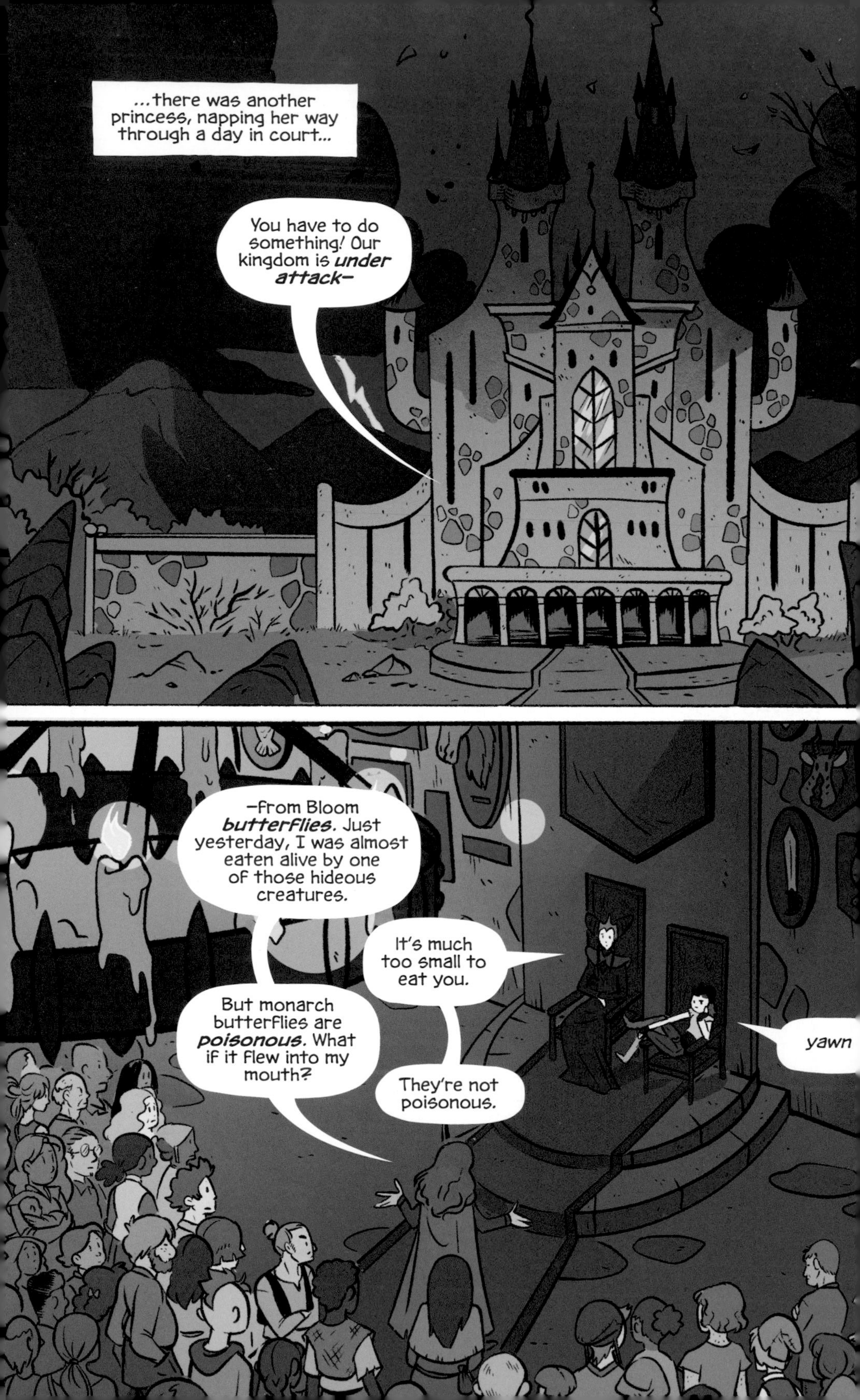
...there was another princess, napping her way through a day in court...
You have to do something! Our kingdom is *under attack*—
—from Bloom *butterflies*. Just yesterday, I was almost eaten alive by one of those hideous creatures.
It's much too small to eat you.
But monarch butterflies are *poisonous*. What if it flew into my mouth?
They're not poisonous.
yawn

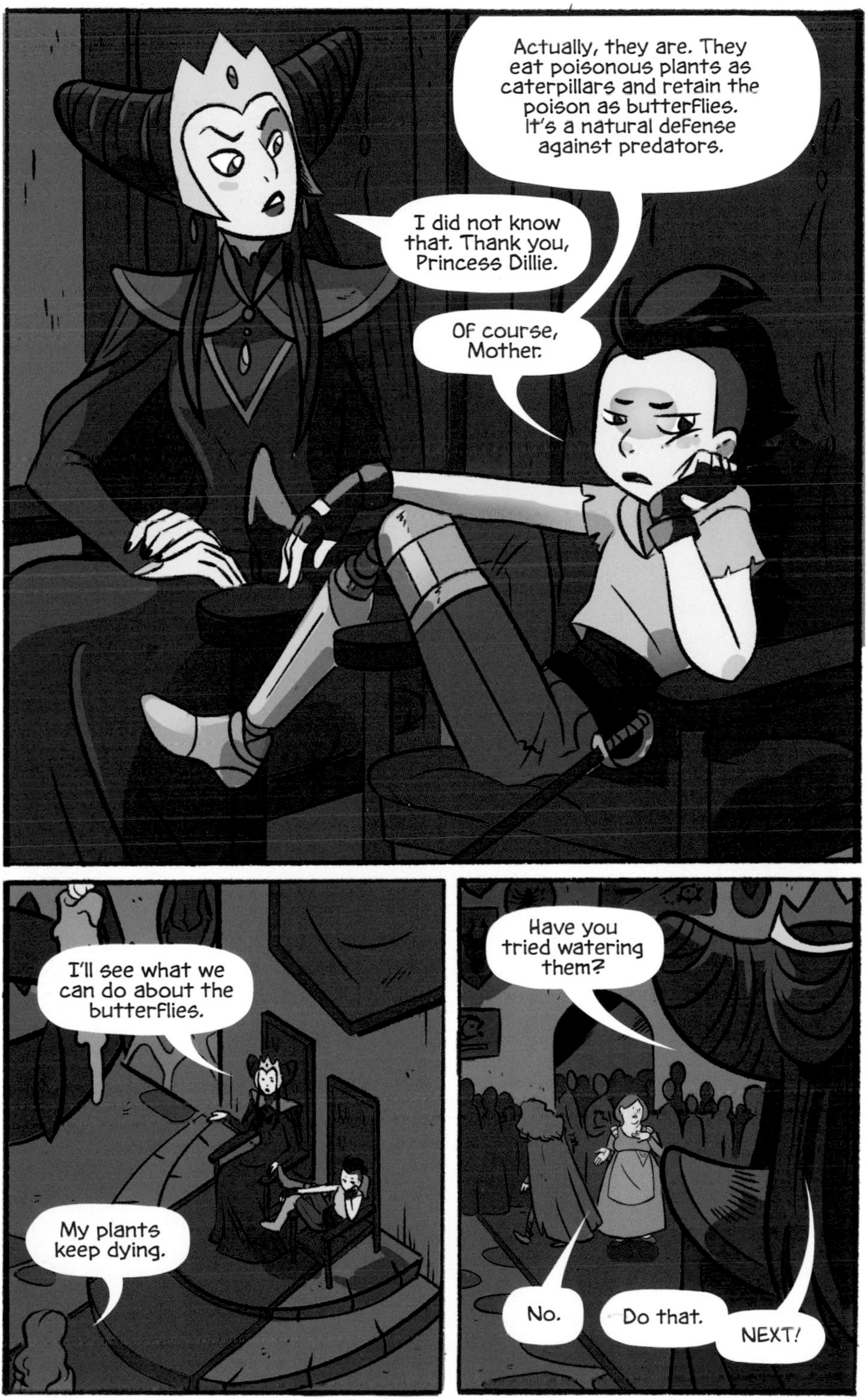
Actually, they are. They eat poisonous plants as caterpillars and retain the poison as butterflies. It's a natural defense against predators.
I did not know that. Thank you, Princess Dillie.
Of course, Mother.
I'll see what we can do about the butterflies.
My plants keep dying.
Have you tried watering them?
No.
Do that.
NEXT!

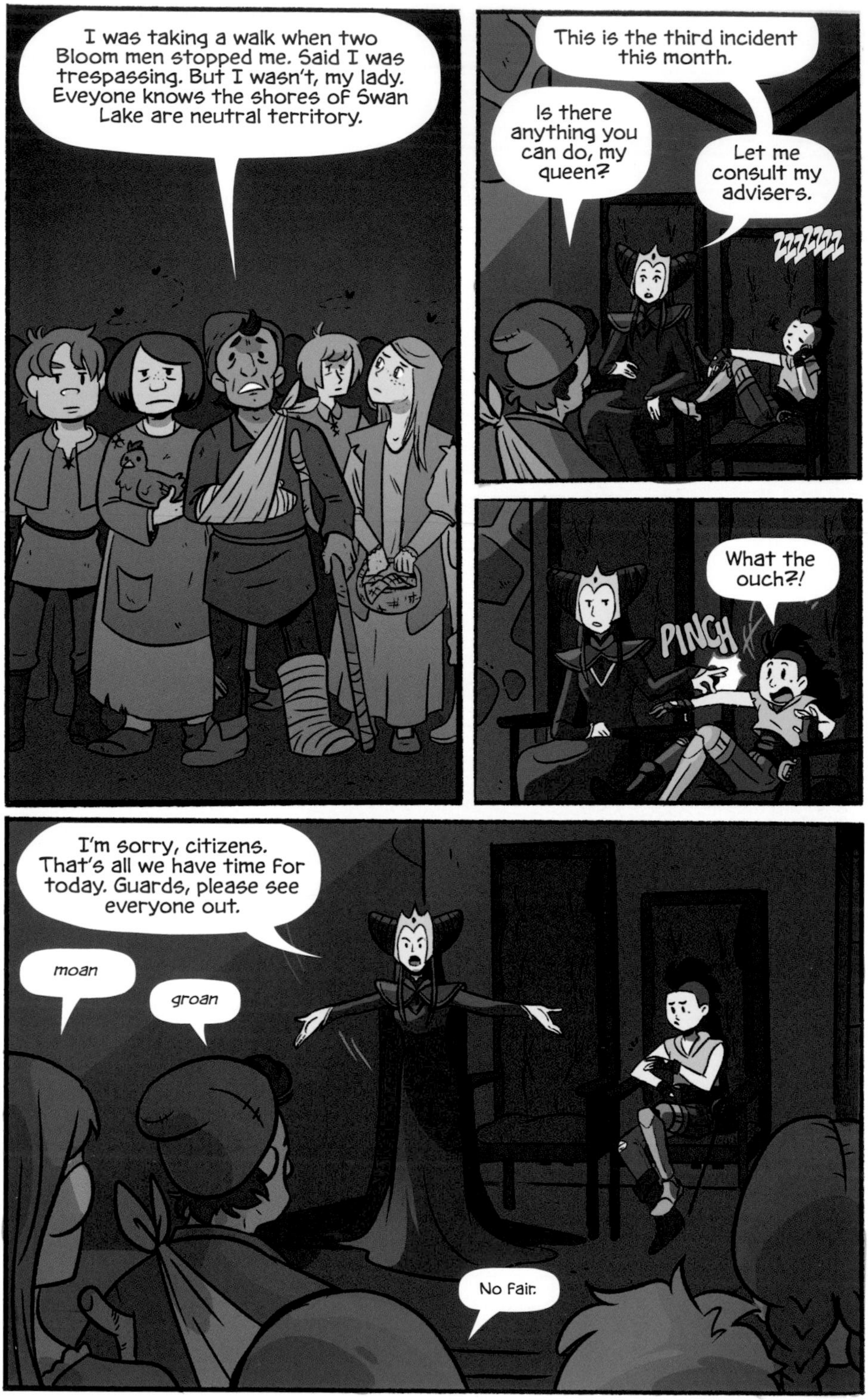
I was taking a walk when two Bloom men stopped me. Said I was trespassing. But I wasn't, my lady. Eveyone knows the shores of Swan Lake are neutral territory.
This is the third incident this month.
Is there anything you can do, my queen?
Let me consult my advisers.
ZZZZZZZ
What the ouch?!
PINCH
I'm sorry, citizens. That's all we have time for today. Guards, please see everyone out.
moan
groan
No fair.

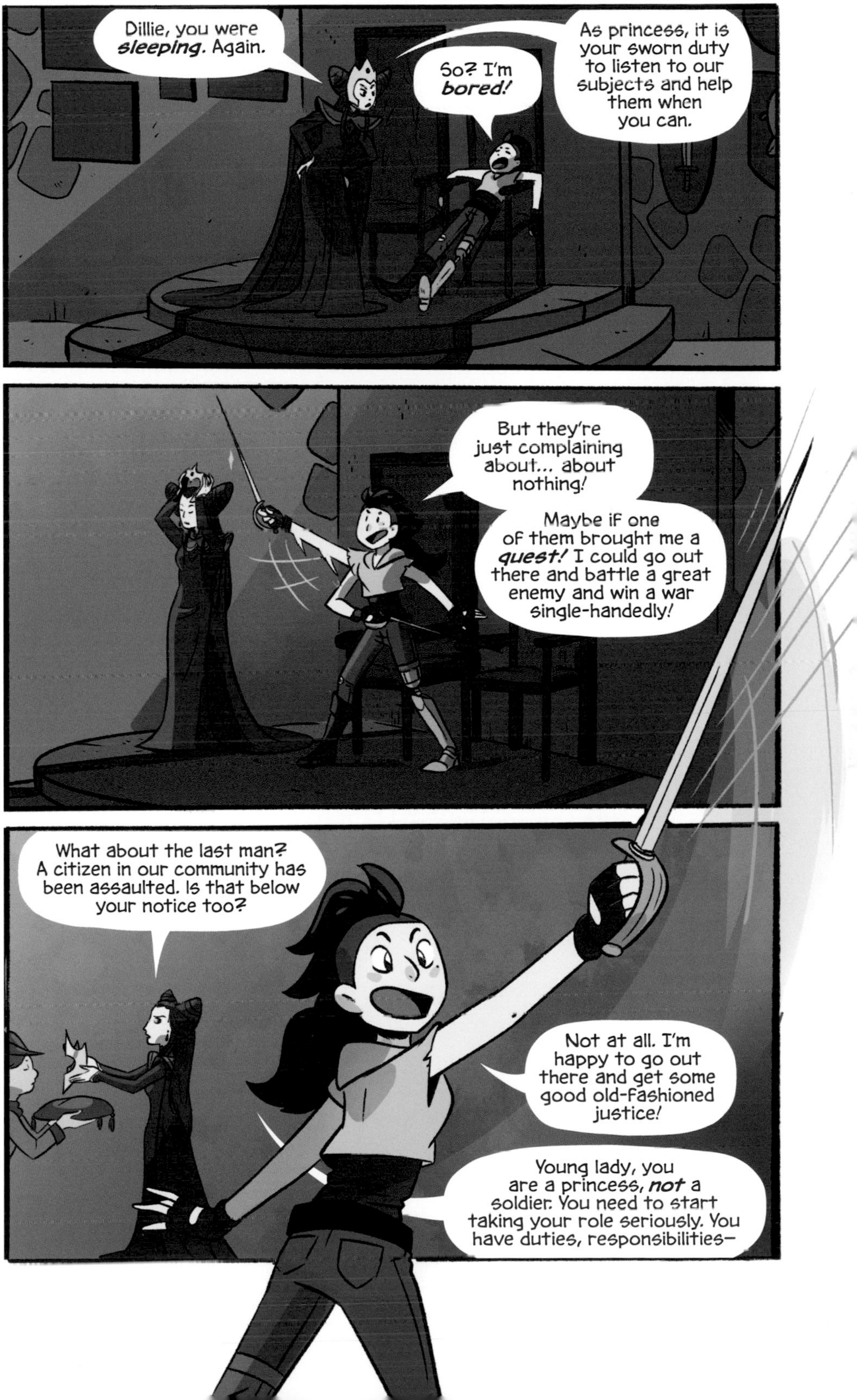

Dillie, you were *sleeping*. Again.
So? I'm *bored!*
As princess, it is your sworn duty to listen to our subjects and help them when you can.
But they're just complaining about... about nothing!
Maybe if one of them brought me a *quest!* I could go out there and battle a great enemy and win a war single-handedly!
What about the last man? A citizen in our community has been assaulted. Is that below your notice too?
Not at all. I'm happy to go out there and get some good old-fashioned justice!
Young lady, you are a princess, *not* a soldier. You need to start taking your role seriously. You have duties, responsibilities—

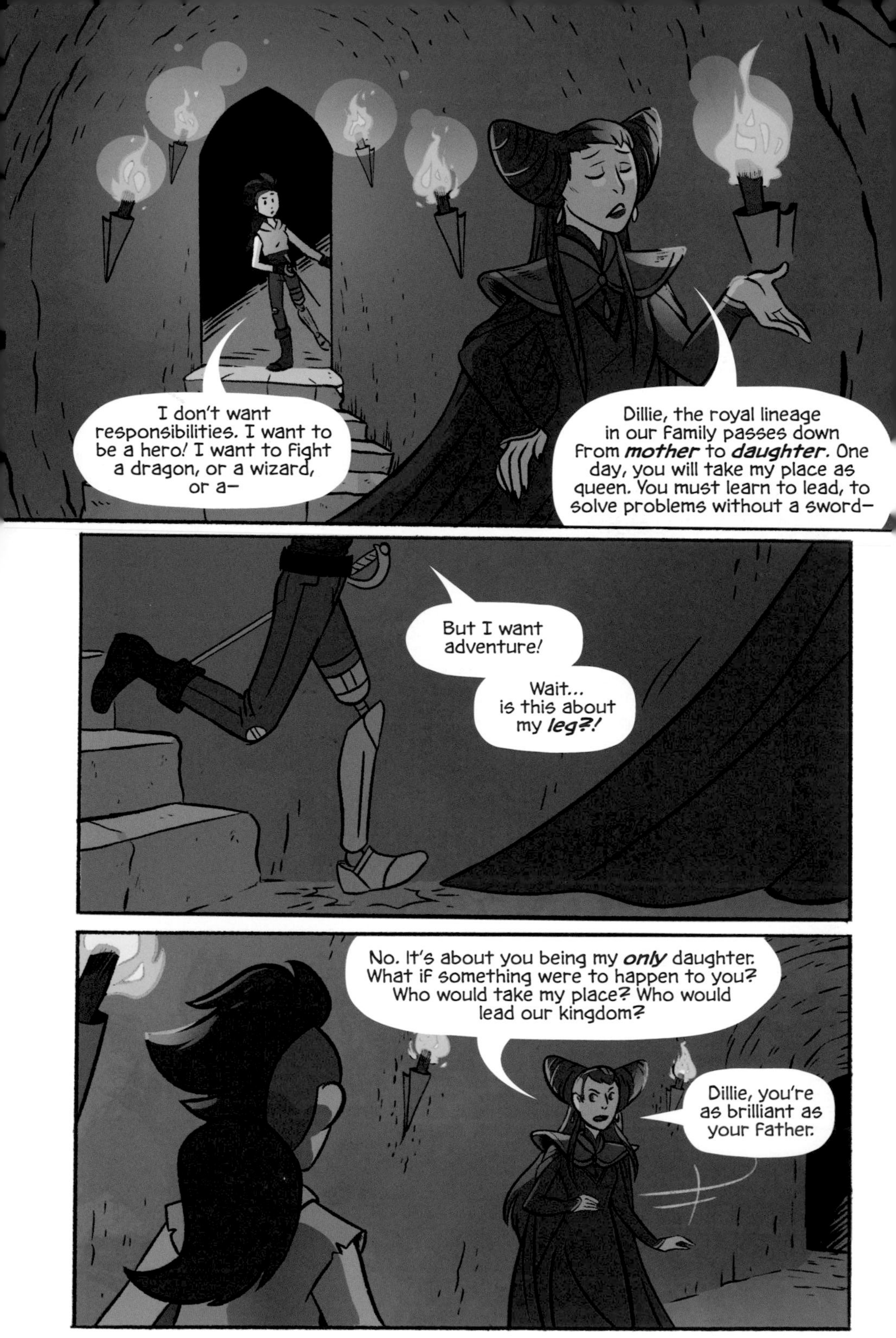
I don't want responsibilities. I want to be a hero! I want to fight a dragon, or a wizard, or a—
Dillie, the royal lineage in our family passes down from *mother* to *daughter*. One day, you will take my place as queen. You must learn to lead, to solve problems without a sword—
But I want adventure!
Wait... is this about my *leg?!*
No. It's about you being my *only* daughter. What if something were to happen to you? Who would take my place? Who would lead our kingdom?
Dillie, you're as brilliant as your father.

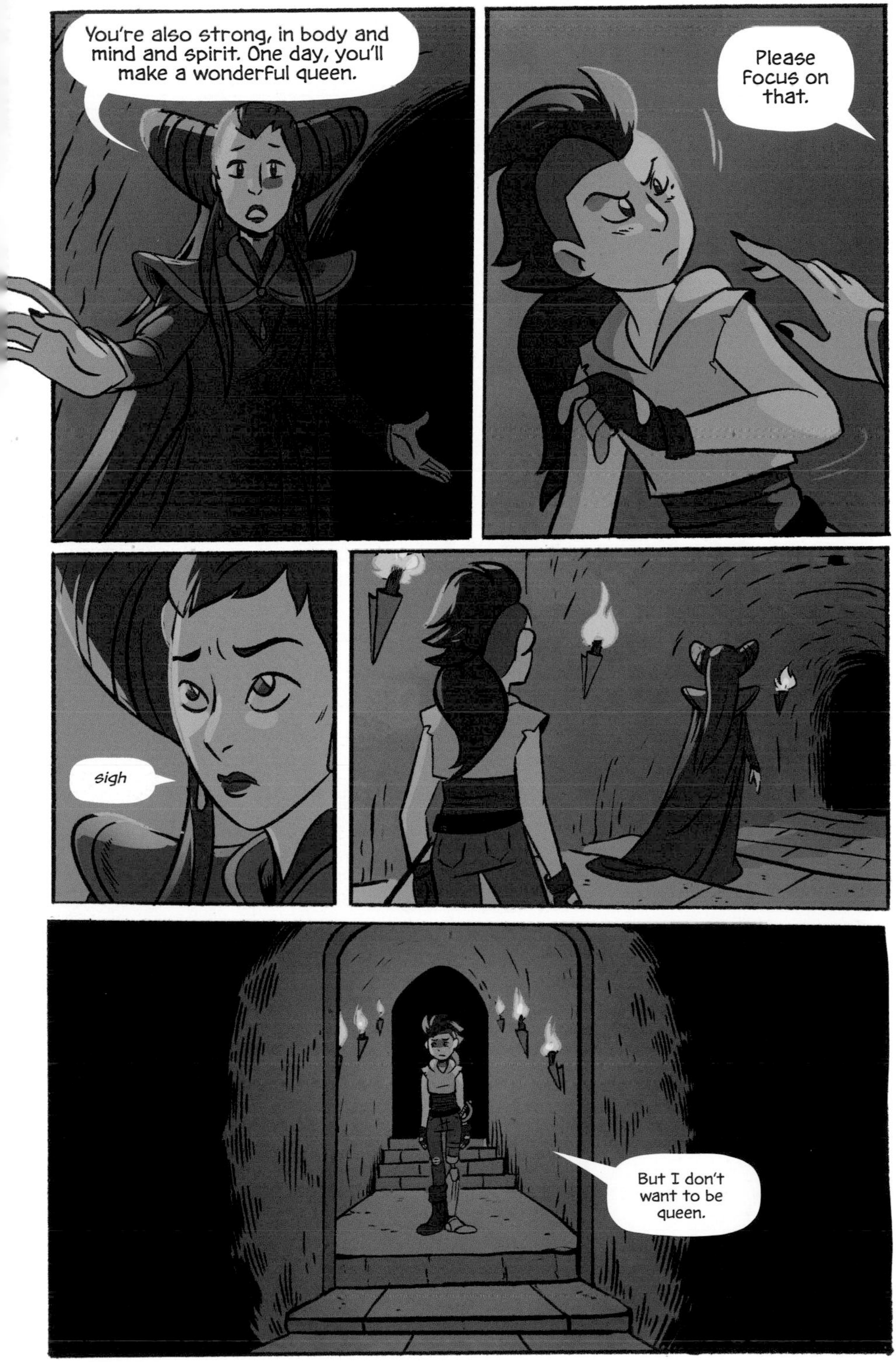
You're also strong, in body and mind and spirit. One day, you'll make a wonderful queen.
Please focus on that.
sigh
But I don't want to be queen.

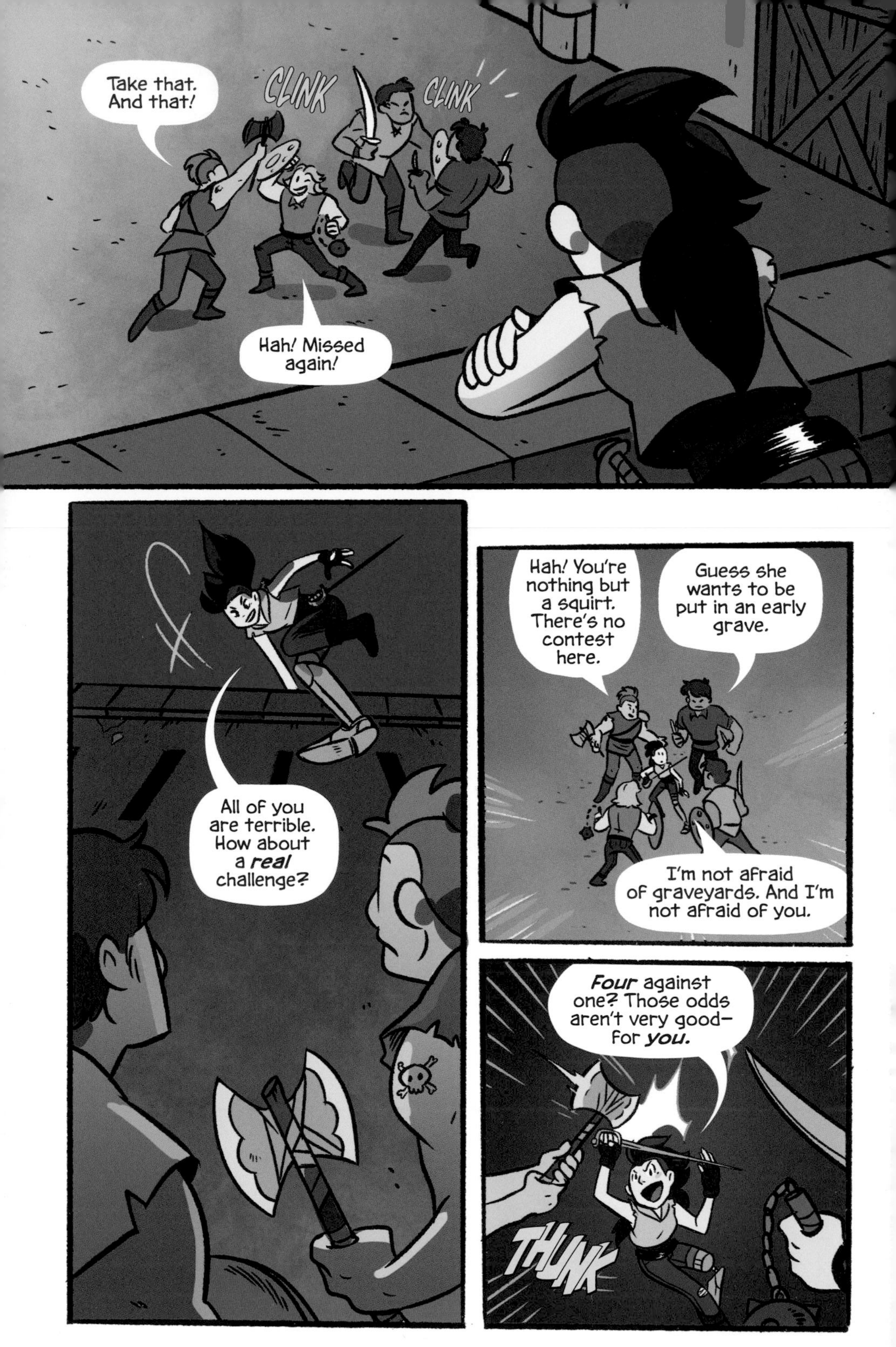
Take that. And that!
CLINK
CLINK
Hah! Missed again!
All of you are terrible. How about a *real* challenge?
Hah! You're nothing but a squirt. There's no contest here.
Guess she wants to be put in an early grave.
I'm not afraid of graveyards. And I'm not afraid of you.
Four against one? Those odds aren't very good—for ***you.***
THUNK

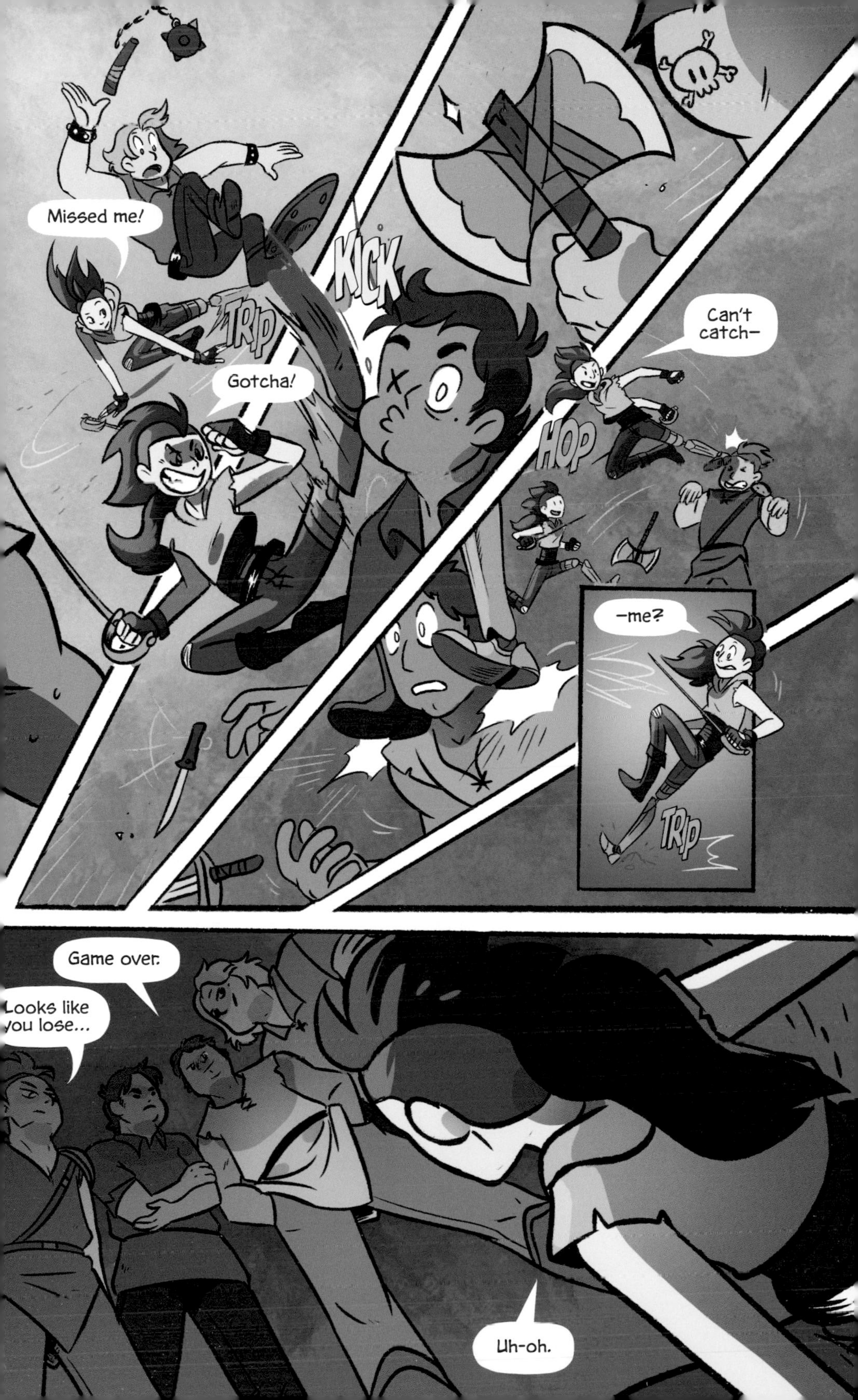
Missed me!
KICK
TRIP
Gotcha!
Can't catch—
HOP
—me?
TRIP
Game over.
Looks like you lose...
Uh-oh.

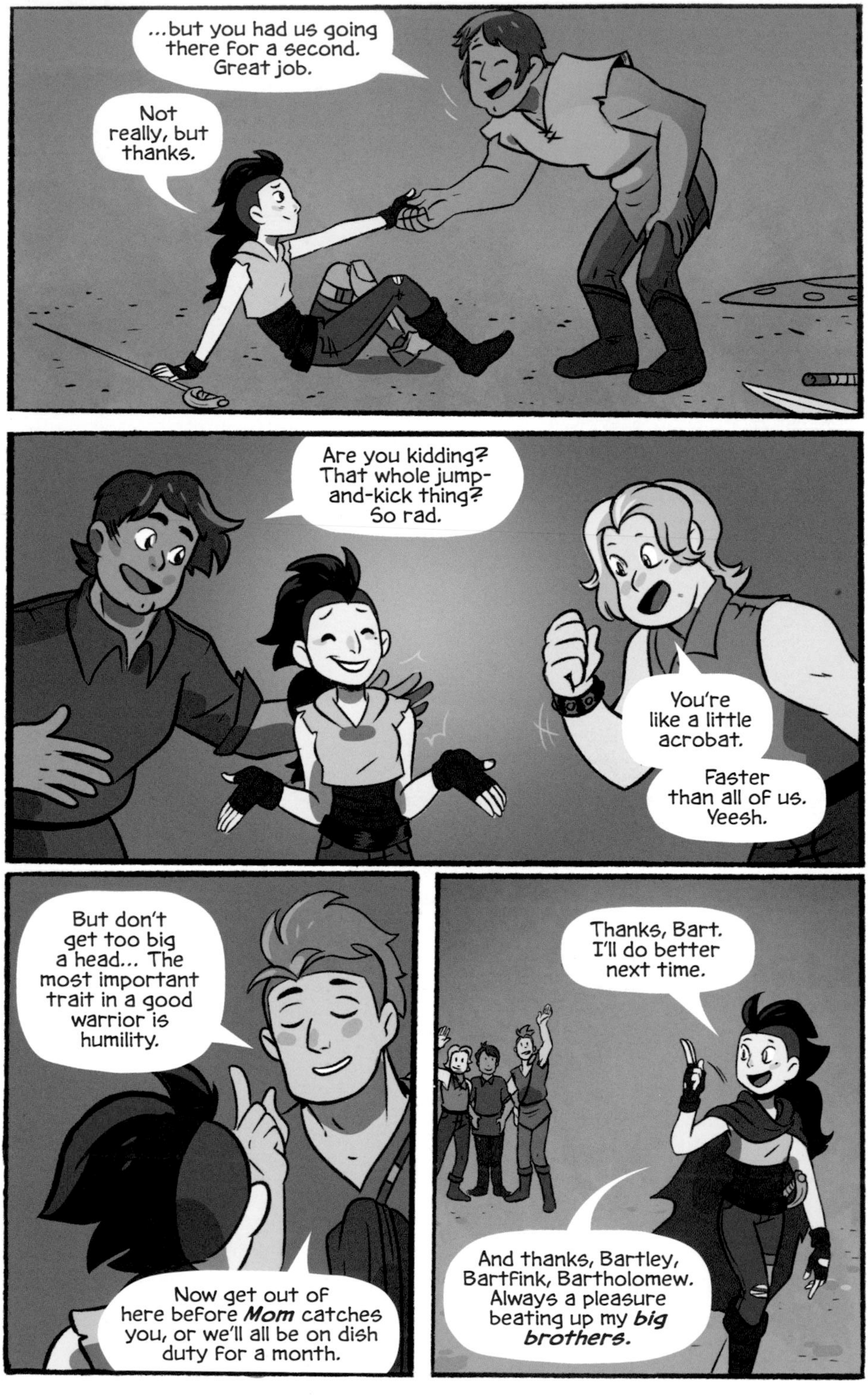
...but you had us going there for a second. Great job.
Not really, but thanks.
Are you kidding? That whole jump-and-kick thing? So rad.
You're like a little acrobat.
Faster than all of us. Yeesh.
But don't get too big a head... The most important trait in a good warrior is humility.
Now get out of here before *Mom* catches you, or we'll all be on dish duty for a month.
Thanks, Bart. I'll do better next time.
And thanks, Bartley, Bartfink, Bartholomew. Always a pleasure beating up my ***big brothers.***

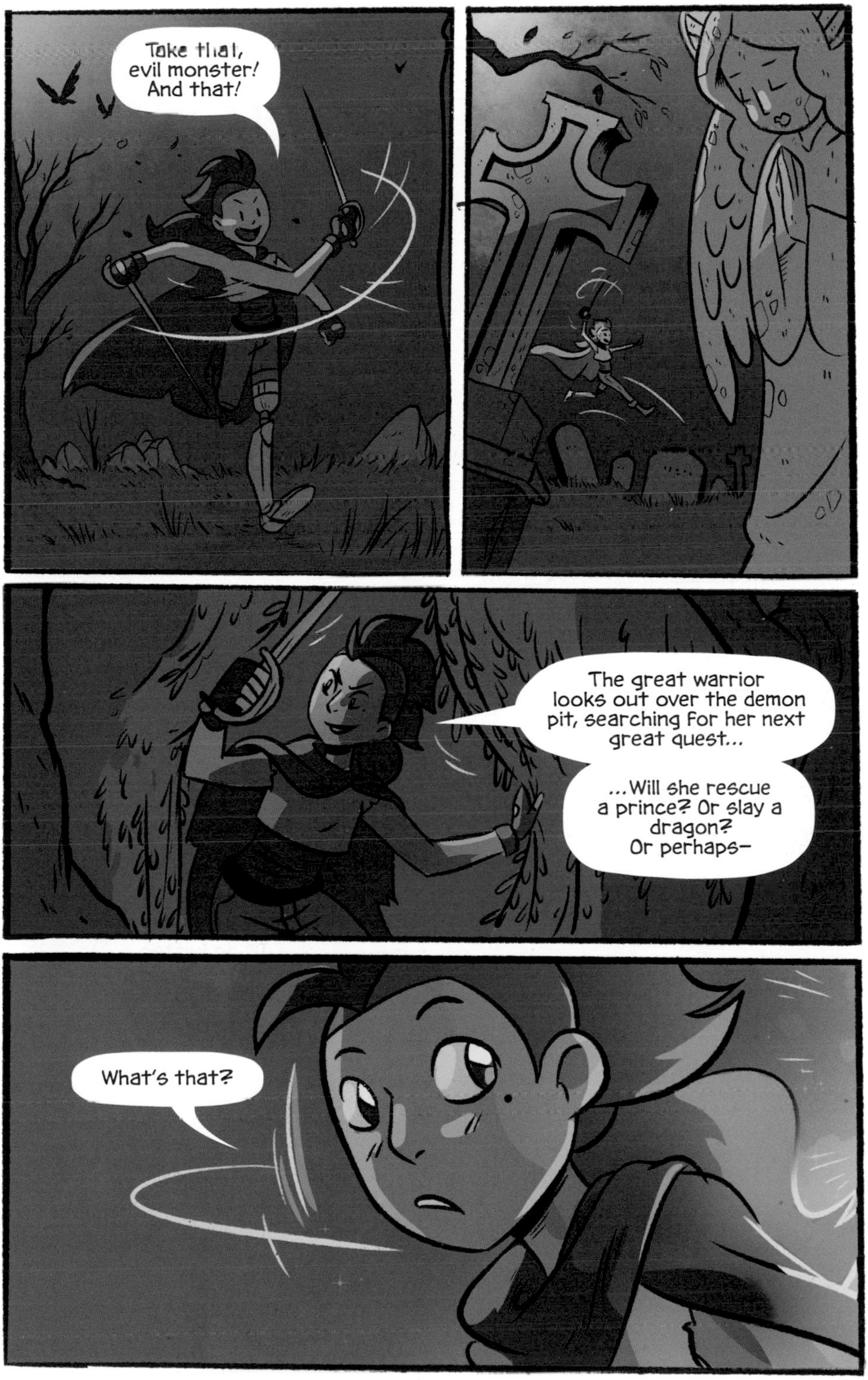
Take that, evil monster! And that!
The great warrior looks out over the demon pit, searching for her next great quest...
...Will she rescue a prince? Or slay a dragon? Or perhaps—
What's that?

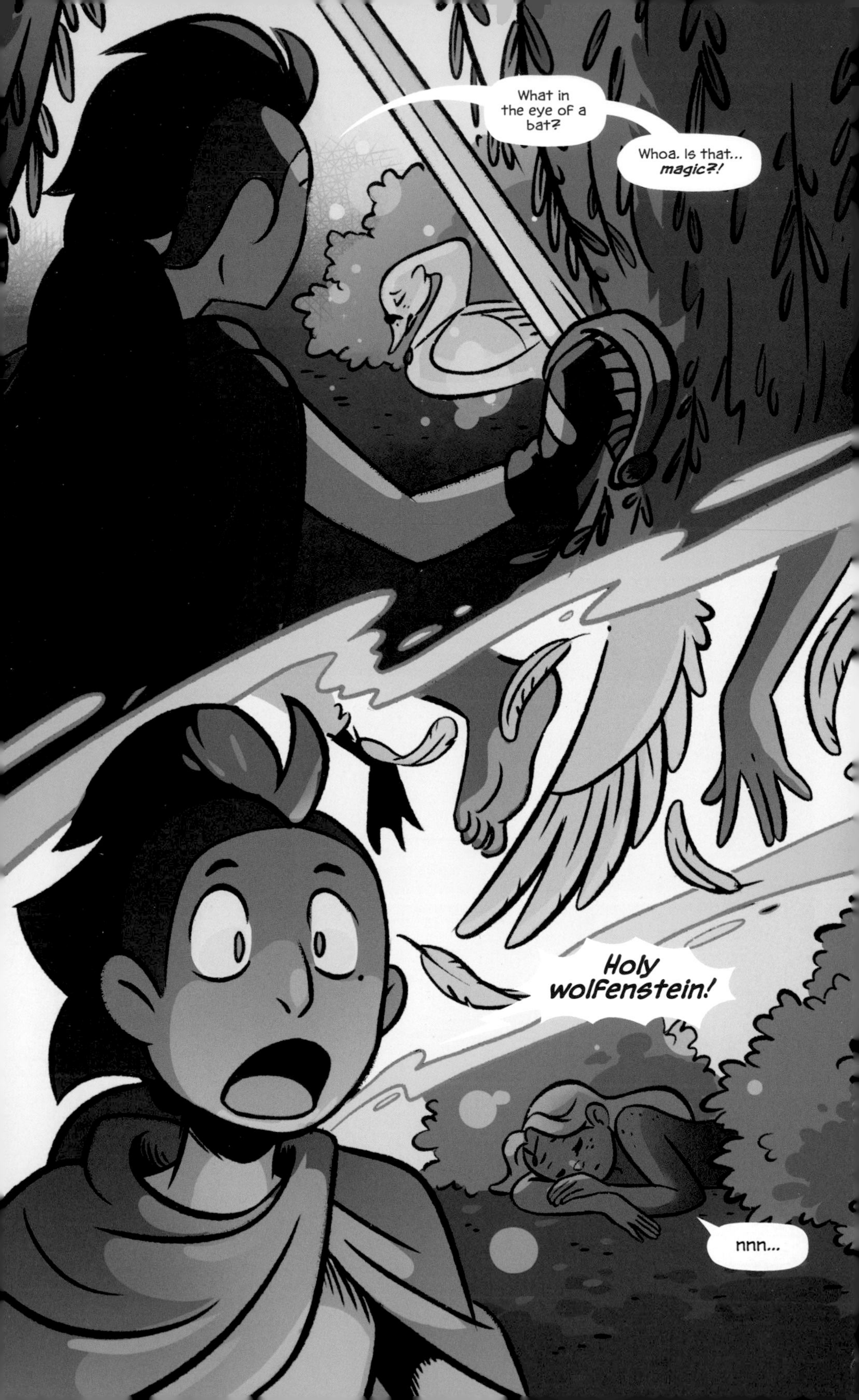
What in the eye of a bat?
Whoa. Is that... *magic?!*
Holy wolfenstein!
nnn...

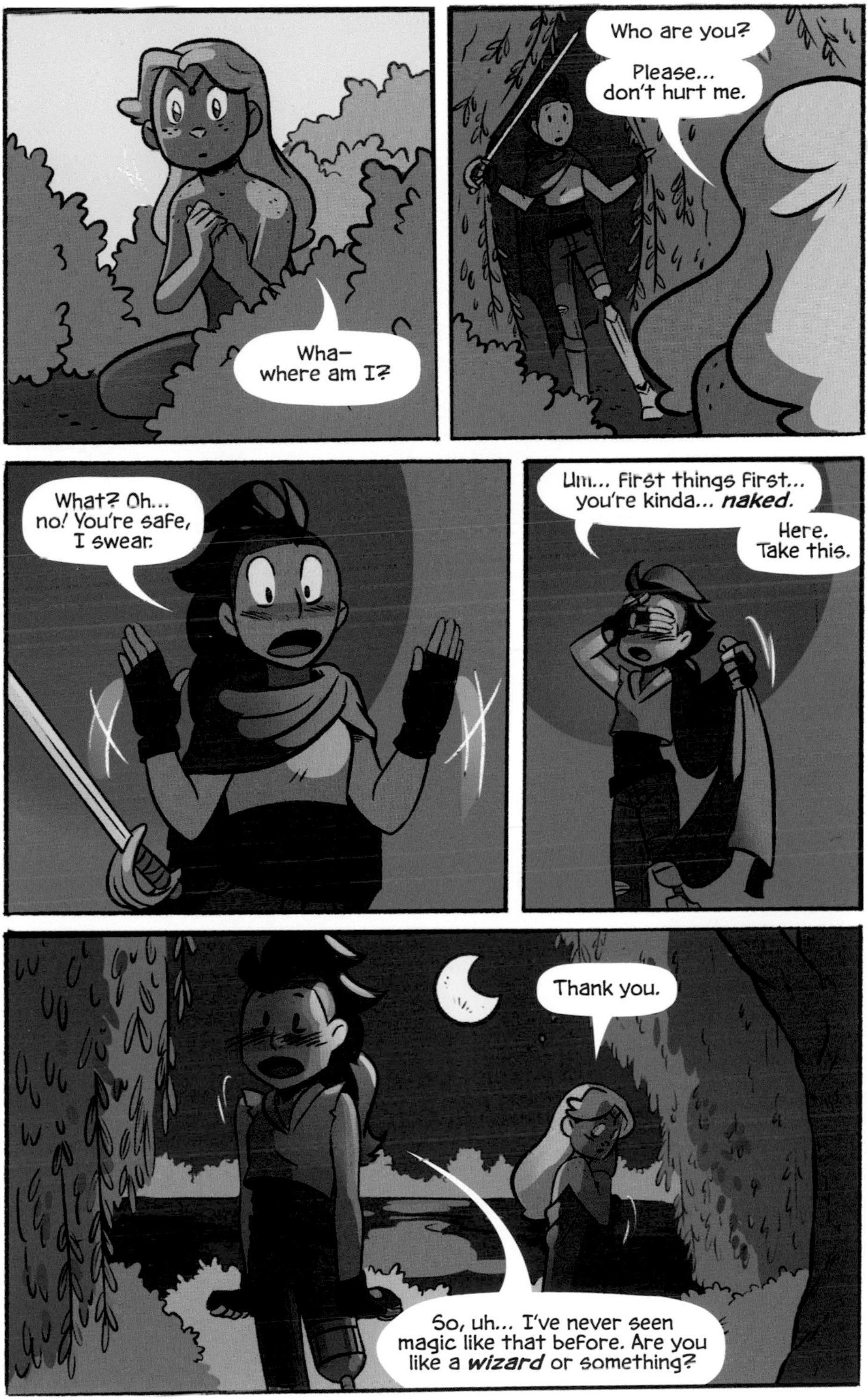
Wha-
where am I?
Who are you?
Please... don't hurt me.
What? Oh... no! You're safe, I swear.
Um... first things first... you're kinda... *naked.*
Here. Take this.
Thank you.
So, uh... I've never seen magic like that before. Are you like a *wizard* or something?

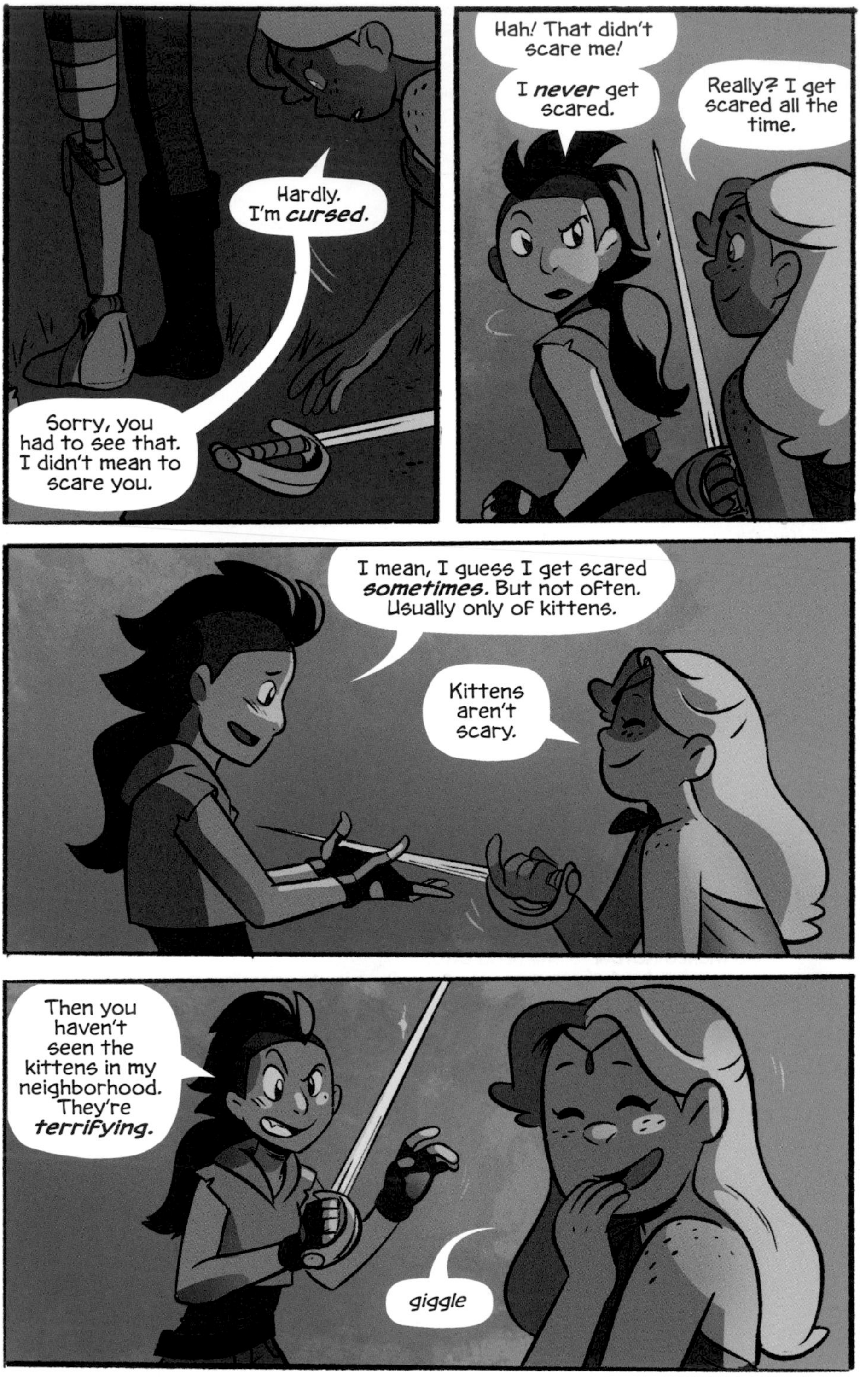
Sorry, you had to see that. I didn't mean to scare you.
Hardly. I'm *cursed.*
Hah! That didn't scare me!
I *never* get scared.
Really? I get scared all the time.
I mean, I guess I get scared *sometimes*. But not often. Usually only of kittens.
Kittens aren't scary.
Then you haven't seen the kittens in my neighborhood. They're *terrifying.*
giggle

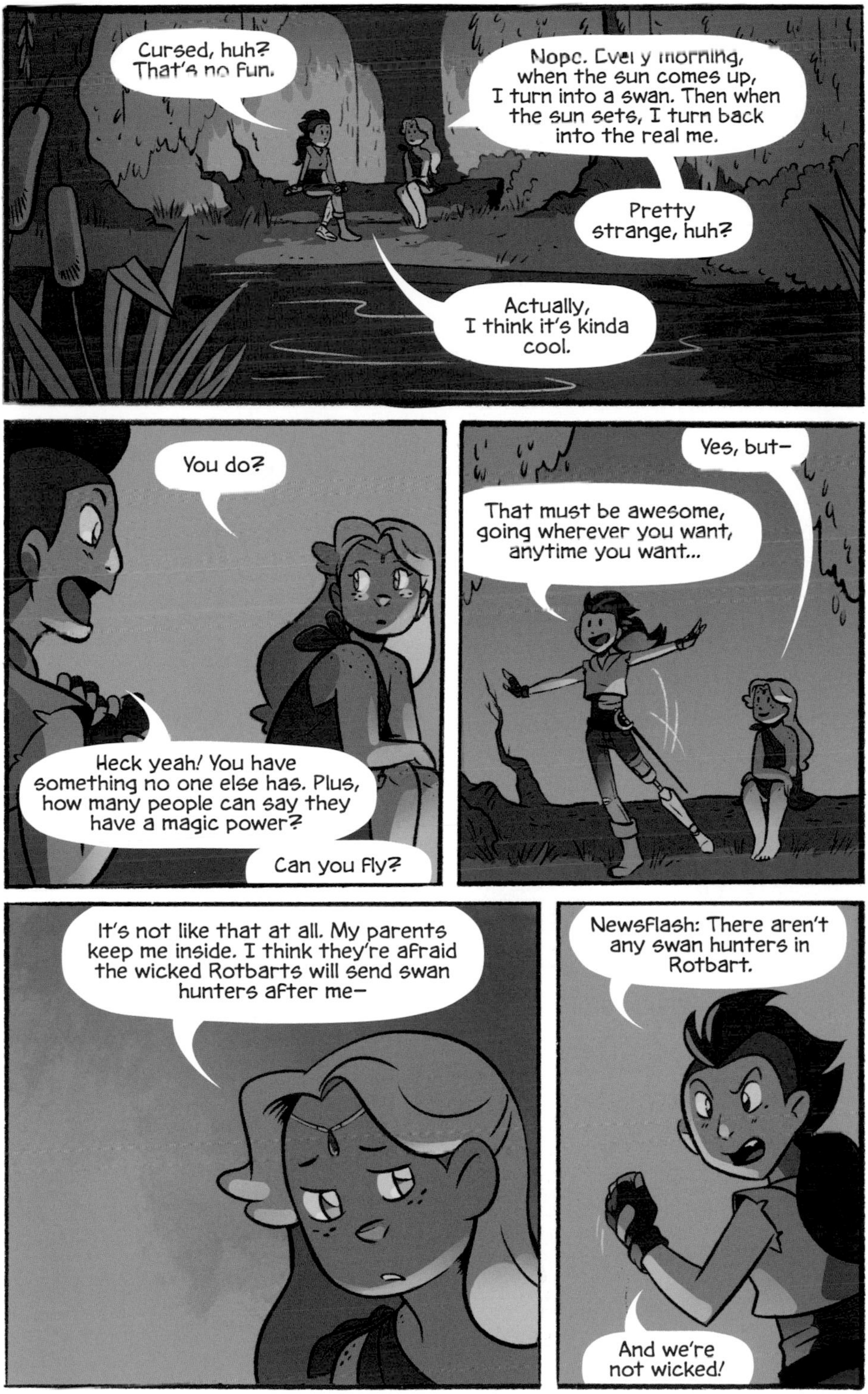
Cursed, huh? That's no fun.
Nope. Every morning, when the sun comes up, I turn into a swan. Then when the sun sets, I turn back into the real me.
Pretty strange, huh?
Actually, I think it's kinda cool.
You do?
Heck yeah! You have something no one else has. Plus, how many people can say they have a magic power?
Can you fly?
That must be awesome, going wherever you want, anytime you want...
Yes, but–
It's not like that at all. My parents keep me inside. I think they're afraid the wicked Rotbarts will send swan hunters after me–
Newsflash: There aren't any swan hunters in Rotbart.
And we're not wicked!

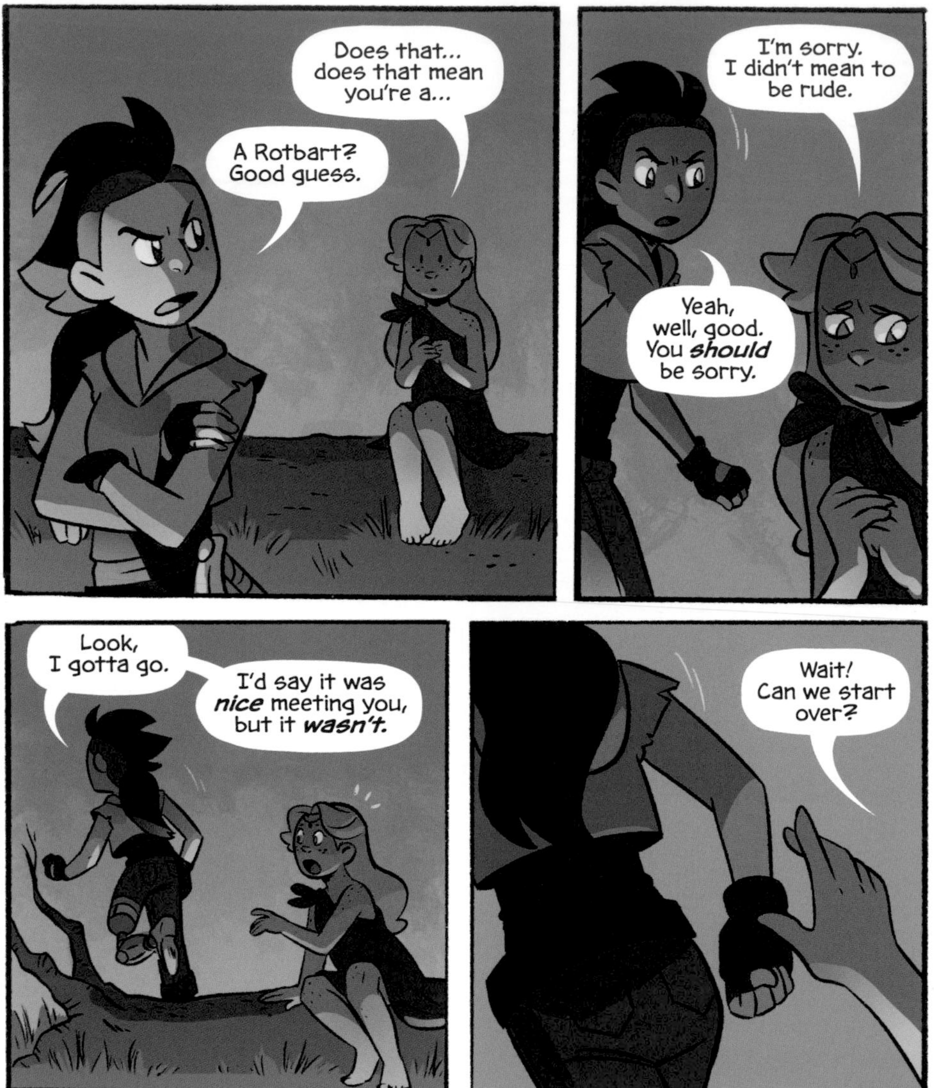
Does that... does that mean you're a...
A Rotbart? Good guess.
I'm sorry. I didn't mean to be rude.
Yeah, well, good. You *should* be sorry.
Look, I gotta go.
I'd say it was *nice* meeting you, but it *wasn't.*
Wait! Can we start over?
Why?

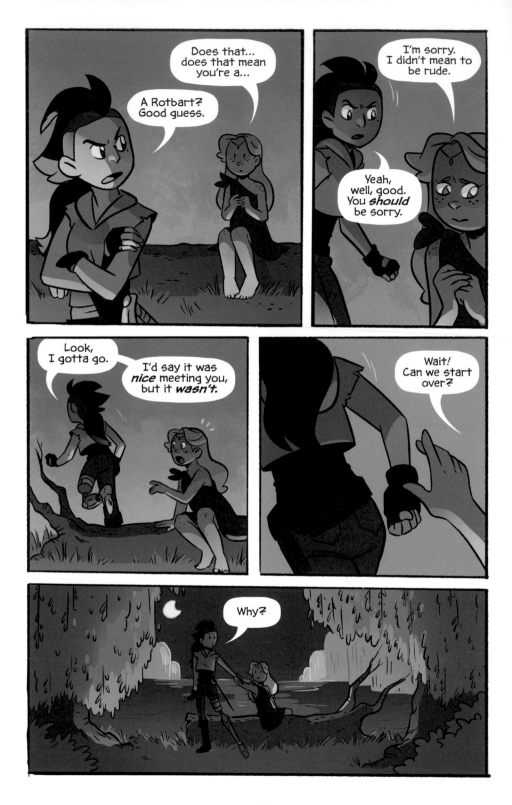

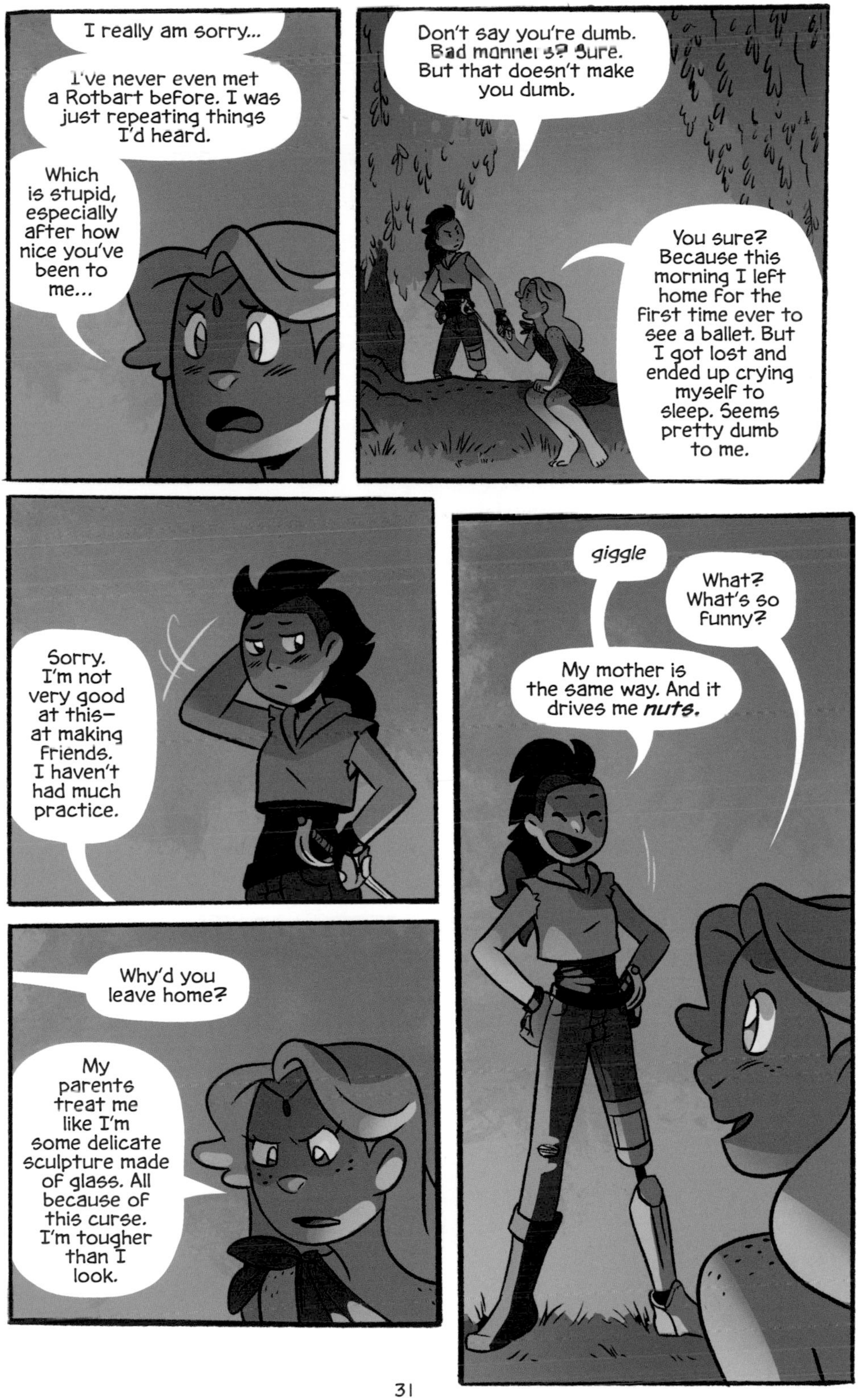
I really am sorry...
I've never even met a Rotbart before. I was just repeating things I'd heard.
Which is stupid, especially after how nice you've been to me...
Don't say you're dumb. Bad manners? Sure. But that doesn't make you dumb.
You sure? Because this morning I left home for the first time ever to see a ballet. But I got lost and ended up crying myself to sleep. Seems pretty dumb to me.
Sorry. I'm not very good at this— at making friends. I haven't had much practice.
Why'd you leave home?
My parents treat me like I'm some delicate sculpture made of glass. All because of this curse. I'm tougher than I look.
giggle
What? What's so funny?
My mother is the same way. And it drives me ***nuts.***

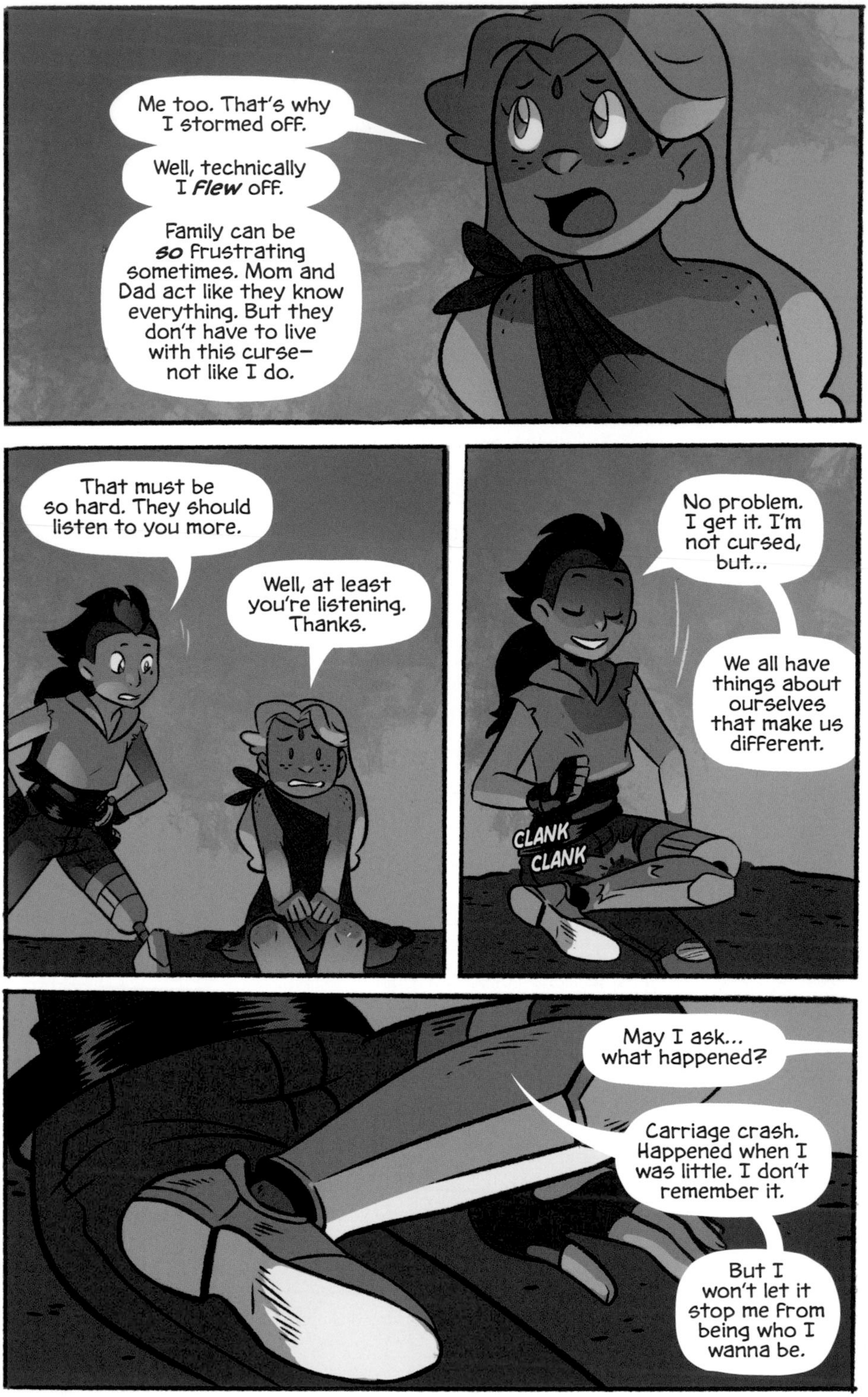
Me too. That's why I stormed off.
Well, technically I *flew* off.
Family can be *so* frustrating sometimes. Mom and Dad act like they know everything. But they don't have to live with this curse— not like I do.
That must be so hard. They should listen to you more.
Well, at least you're listening. Thanks.
No problem. I get it. I'm not cursed, but...
We all have things about ourselves that make us different.
CLANK
CLANK
May I ask... what happened?
Carriage crash. Happened when I was little. I don't remember it.
But I won't let it stop me from being who I wanna be.

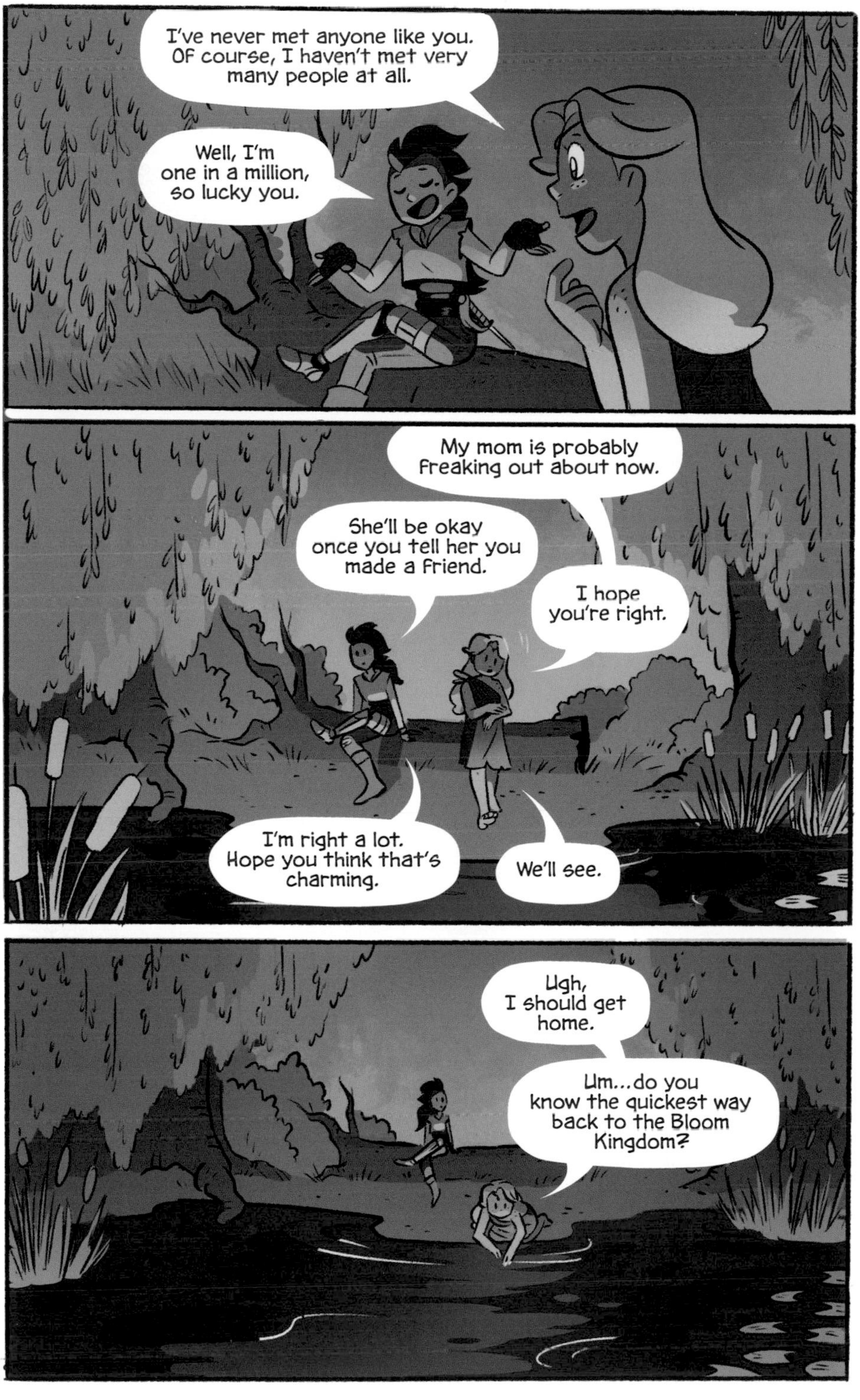
I've never met anyone like you. Of course, I haven't met very many people at all.
Well, I'm one in a million, so lucky you.
My mom is probably freaking out about now.
She'll be okay once you tell her you made a friend.
I hope you're right.
I'm right a lot. Hope you think that's charming.
We'll see.
Ugh, I should get home.
Um...do you know the quickest way back to the Bloom Kingdom?

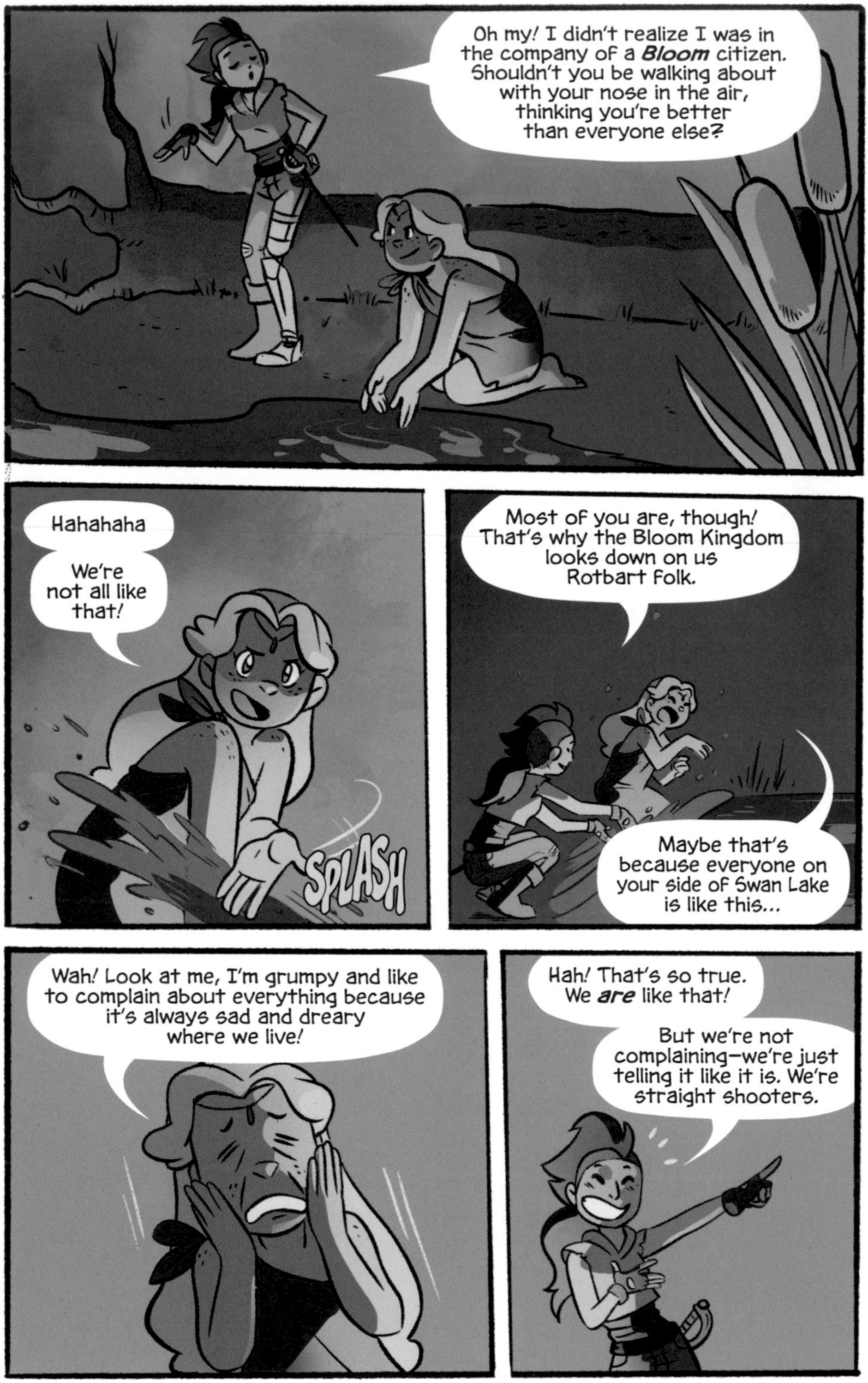

Oh my! I didn't realize I was in the company of a *Bloom* citizen. Shouldn't you be walking about with your nose in the air, thinking you're better than everyone else?
Hahahaha
We're not all like that!
SPLASH
Most of you are, though! That's why the Bloom Kingdom looks down on us Rotbart Folk.
Maybe that's because everyone on your side of Swan Lake is like this...
Wah! Look at me, I'm grumpy and like to complain about everything because it's always sad and dreary where we live!
Hah! That's so true. We *are* like that!
But we're not complaining—we're just telling it like it is. We're straight shooters.

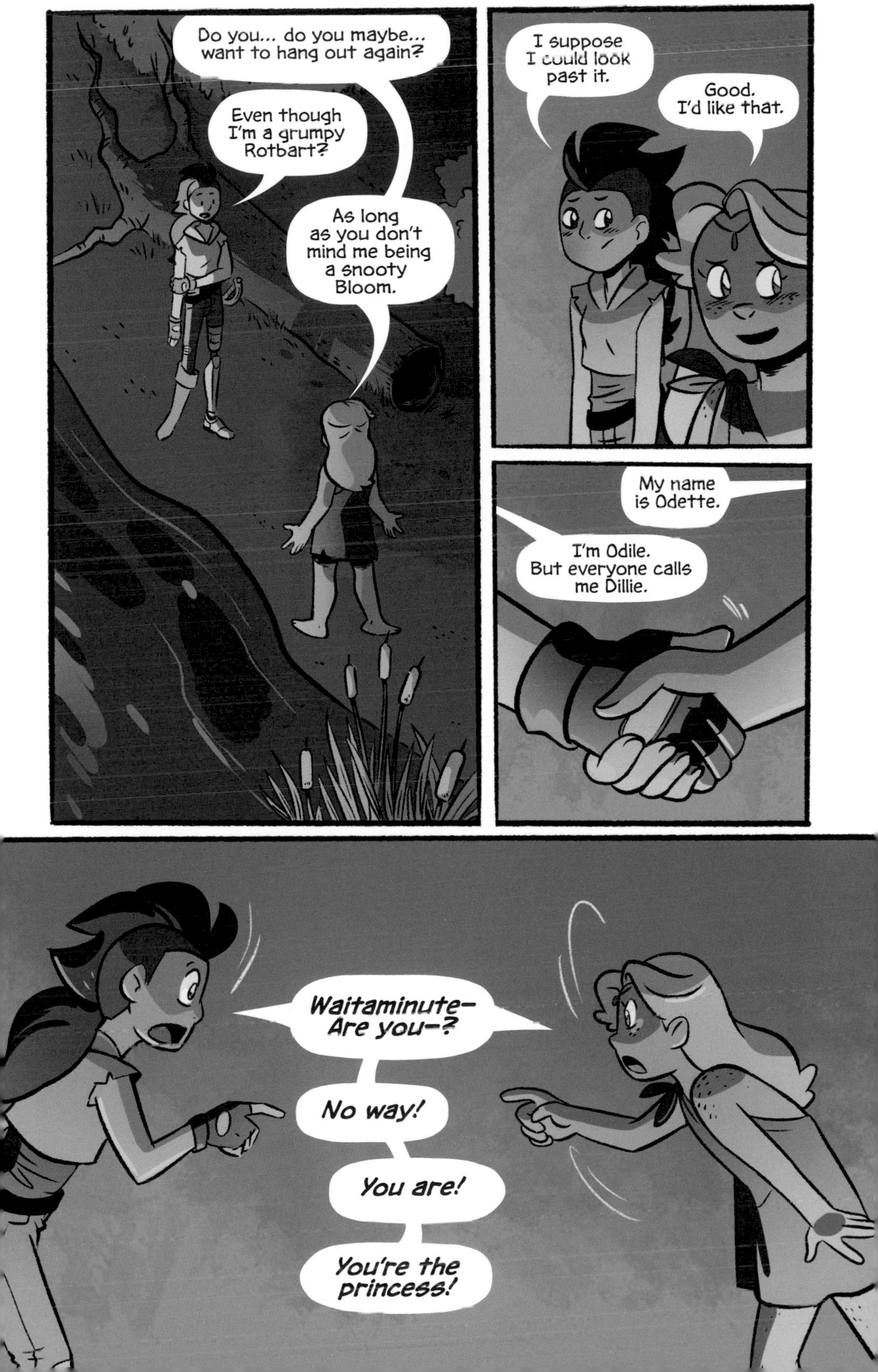
Do you... do you maybe... want to hang out again?
Even though I'm a grumpy Rotbart?
As long as you don't mind me being a snooty Bloom.
I suppose I could look past it.
Good. I'd like that.
My name is Odette.
I'm Odile. But everyone calls me Dillie.
Waitaminute- Are you-?
No way!
You are!
You're the princess!

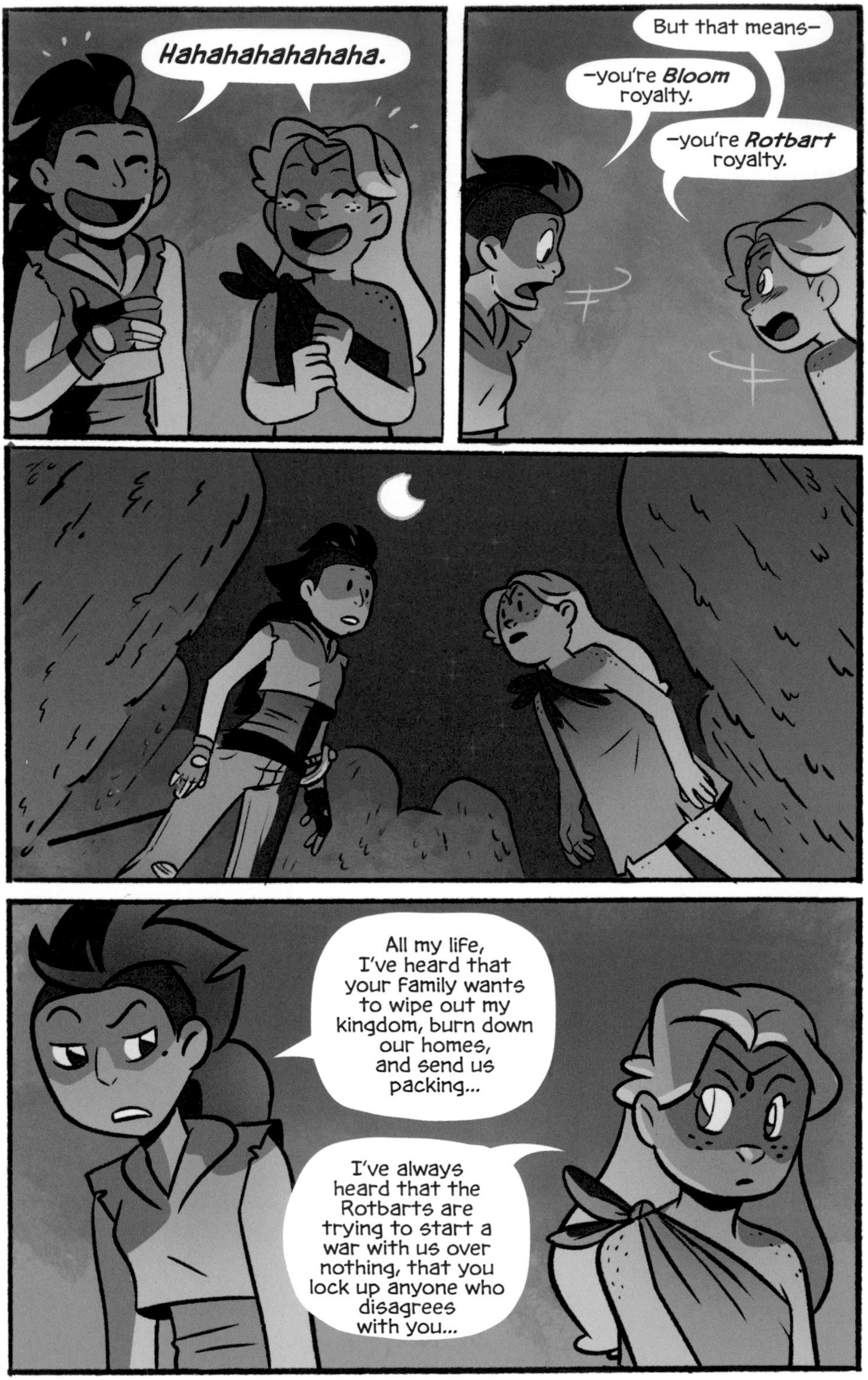

Hahahahahahaha.
But that means—
—you're *Bloom* royalty.
—you're *Rotbart* royalty.
All my life, I've heard that your family wants to wipe out my kingdom, burn down our homes, and send us packing...
I've always heard that the Rotbarts are trying to start a war with us over nothing, that you lock up anyone who disagrees with you...

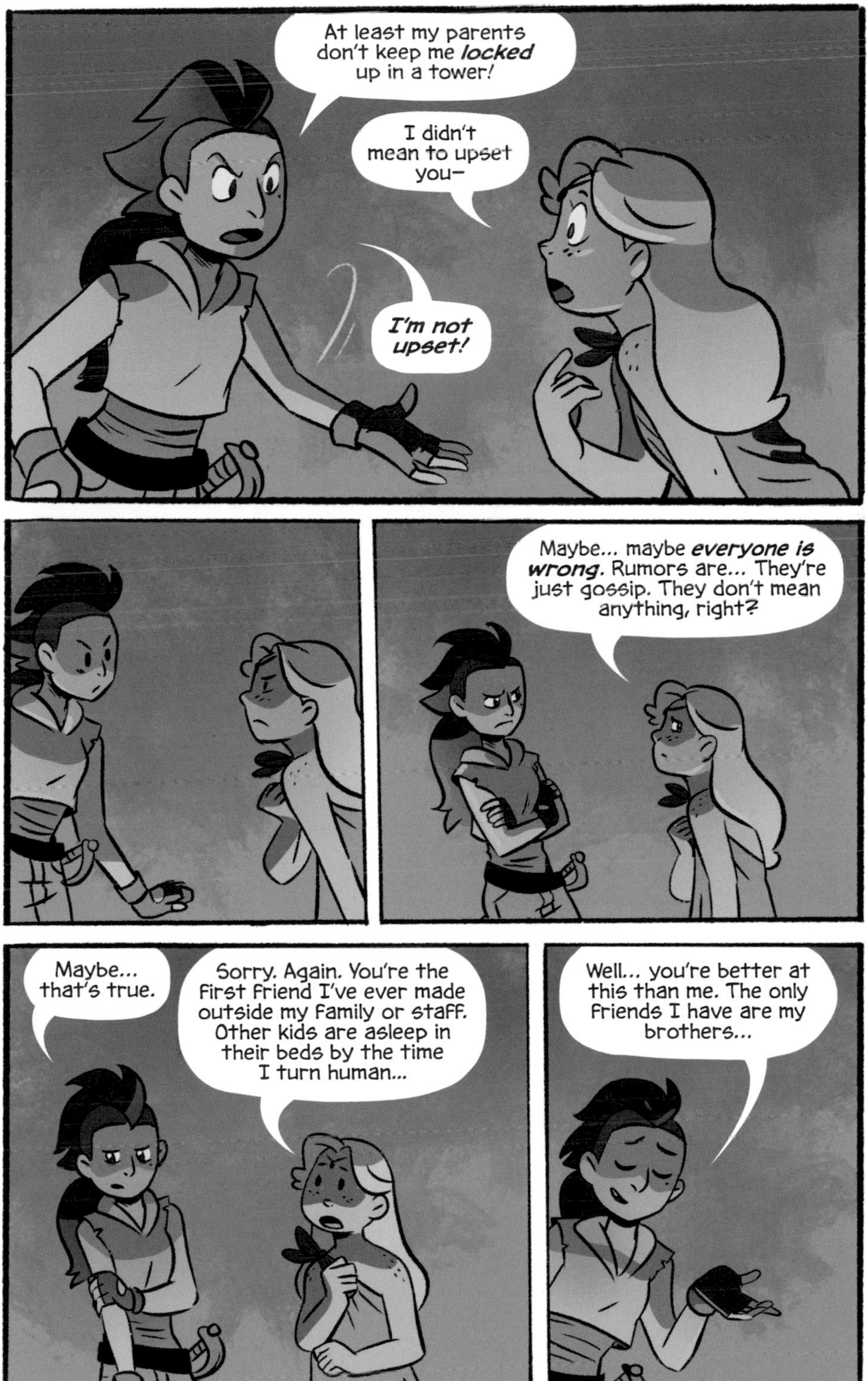
At least my parents don't keep me *locked* up in a tower!
I didn't mean to upset you—
I'm not upset!
Maybe... maybe *everyone is wrong.* Rumors are... They're just gossip. They don't mean anything, right?
Maybe... that's true.
Sorry. Again. You're the first friend I've ever made outside my family or staff. Other kids are asleep in their beds by the time I turn human...
Well... you're better at this than me. The only friends I have are my brothers...

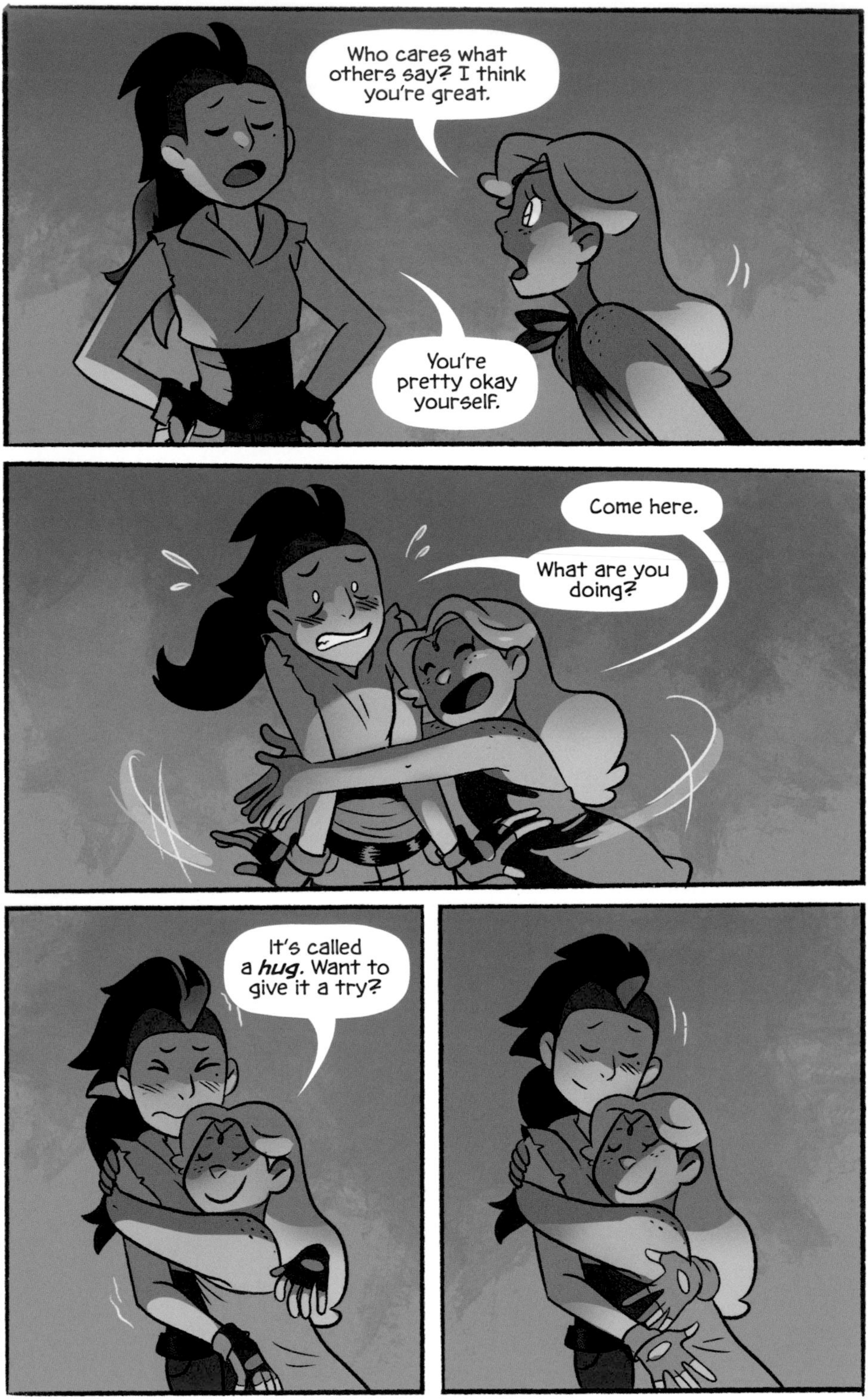
Who cares what others say? I think you're great.
You're pretty okay yourself.
Come here.
What are you doing?
It's called a *hug*. Want to give it a try?

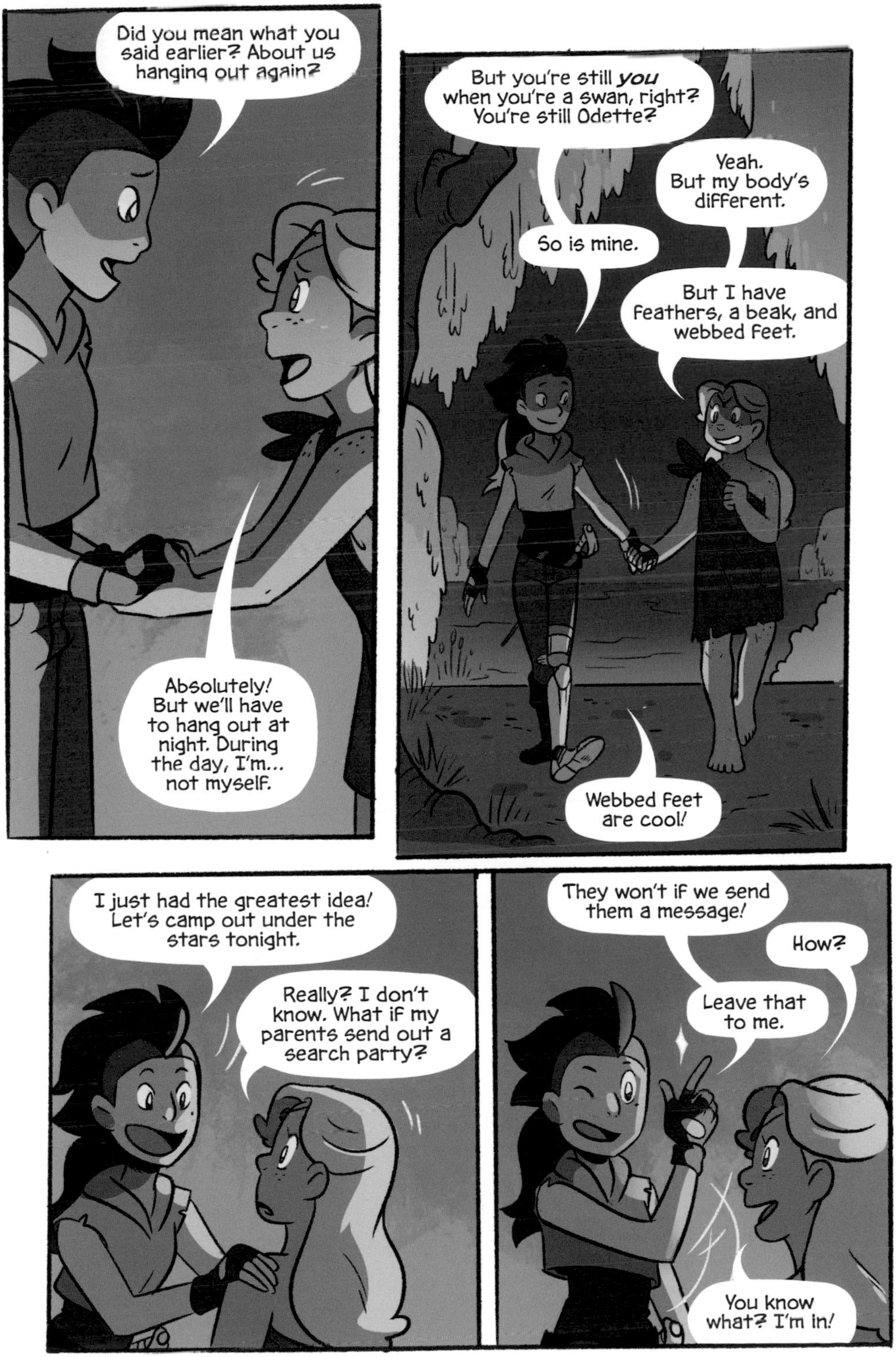
Did you mean what you said earlier? About us hanging out again?
Absolutely! But we'll have to hang out at night. During the day, I'm... not myself.
But you're still *you* when you're a swan, right? You're still Odette?
Yeah. But my body's different.
So is mine.
But I have feathers, a beak, and webbed feet.
Webbed feet are cool!
I just had the greatest idea! Let's camp out under the stars tonight.
Really? I don't know. What if my parents send out a search party?
They won't if we send them a message!
How?
Leave that to me.
You know what? I'm in!

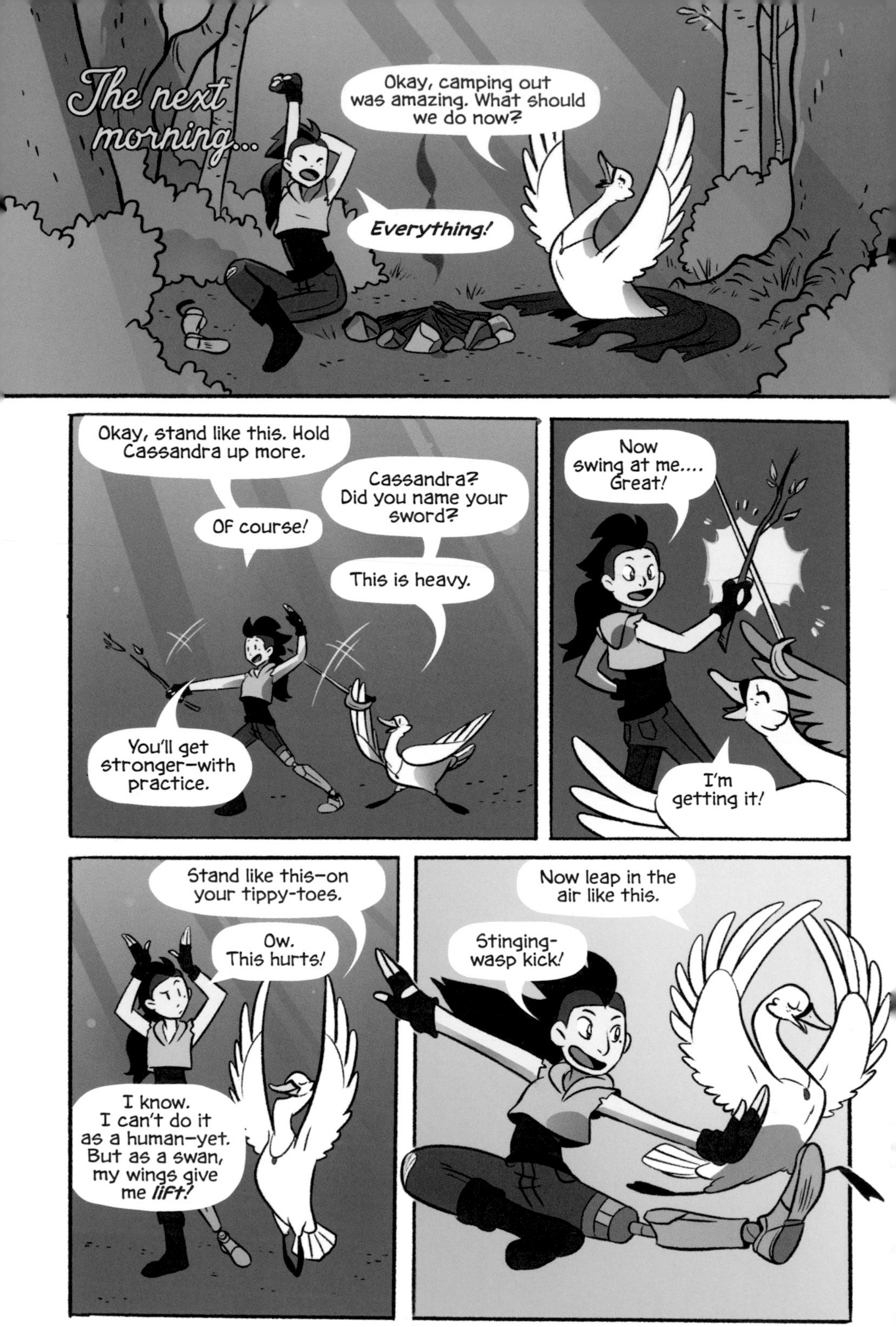
The next morning...
Okay, camping out was amazing. What should we do now?
Everything!
Okay, stand like this. Hold Cassandra up more.
Cassandra? Did you name your sword?
Of course!
This is heavy.
You'll get stronger—with practice.
Now swing at me.... Great!
I'm getting it!
Stand like this—on your tippy-toes.
Ow. This hurts!
I know. I can't do it as a human—yet. But as a swan, my wings give me *lift!*
Now leap in the air like this.
Stinging-wasp kick!

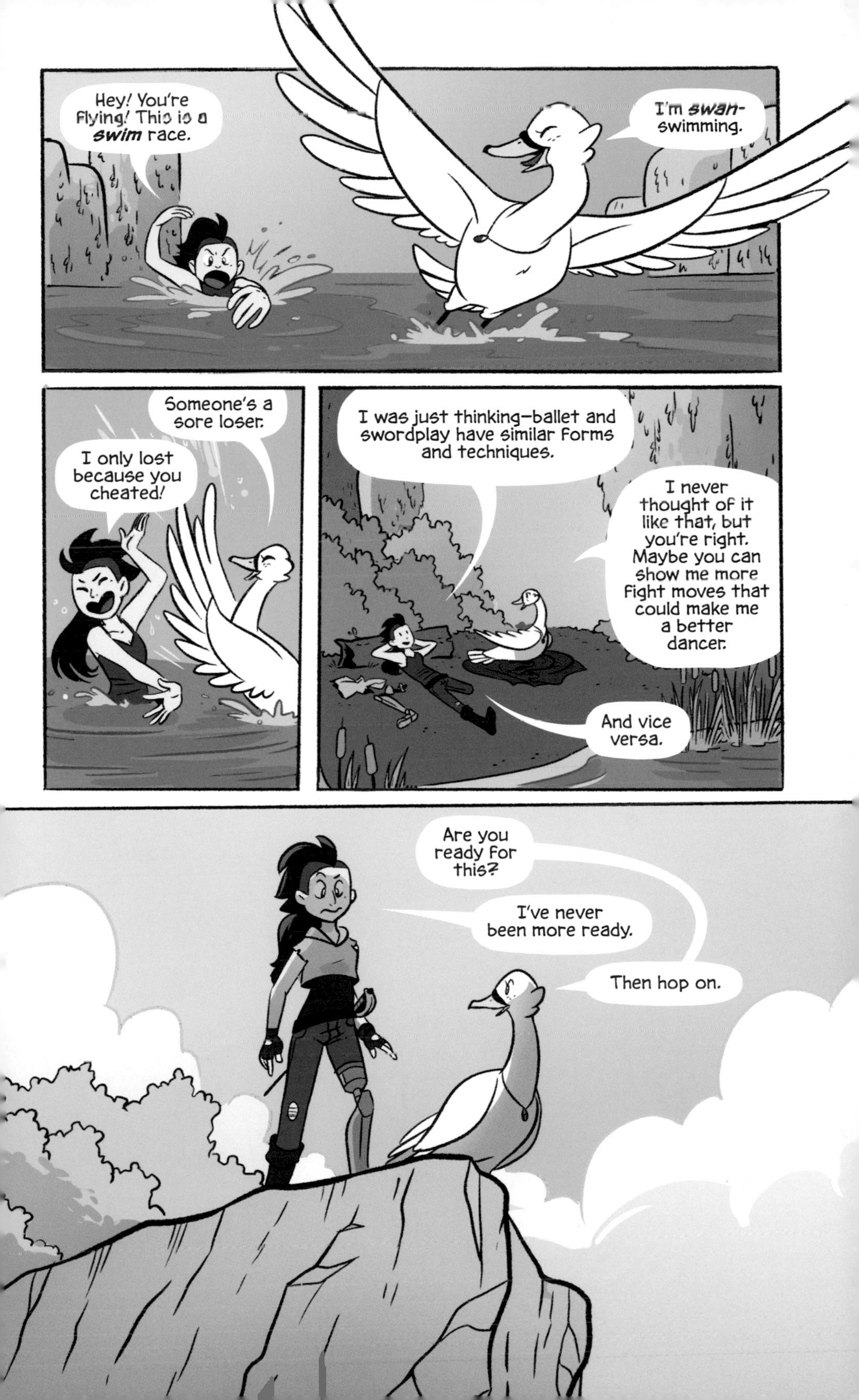
Hey! You're flying! This is a *swim* race.
I'm *swan*-swimming.
Someone's a sore loser.
I only lost because you cheated!
I was just thinking—ballet and swordplay have similar forms and techniques.
I never thought of it like that, but you're right. Maybe you can show me more fight moves that could make me a better dancer.
And vice versa.
Are you ready for this?
I've never been more ready.
Then hop on.

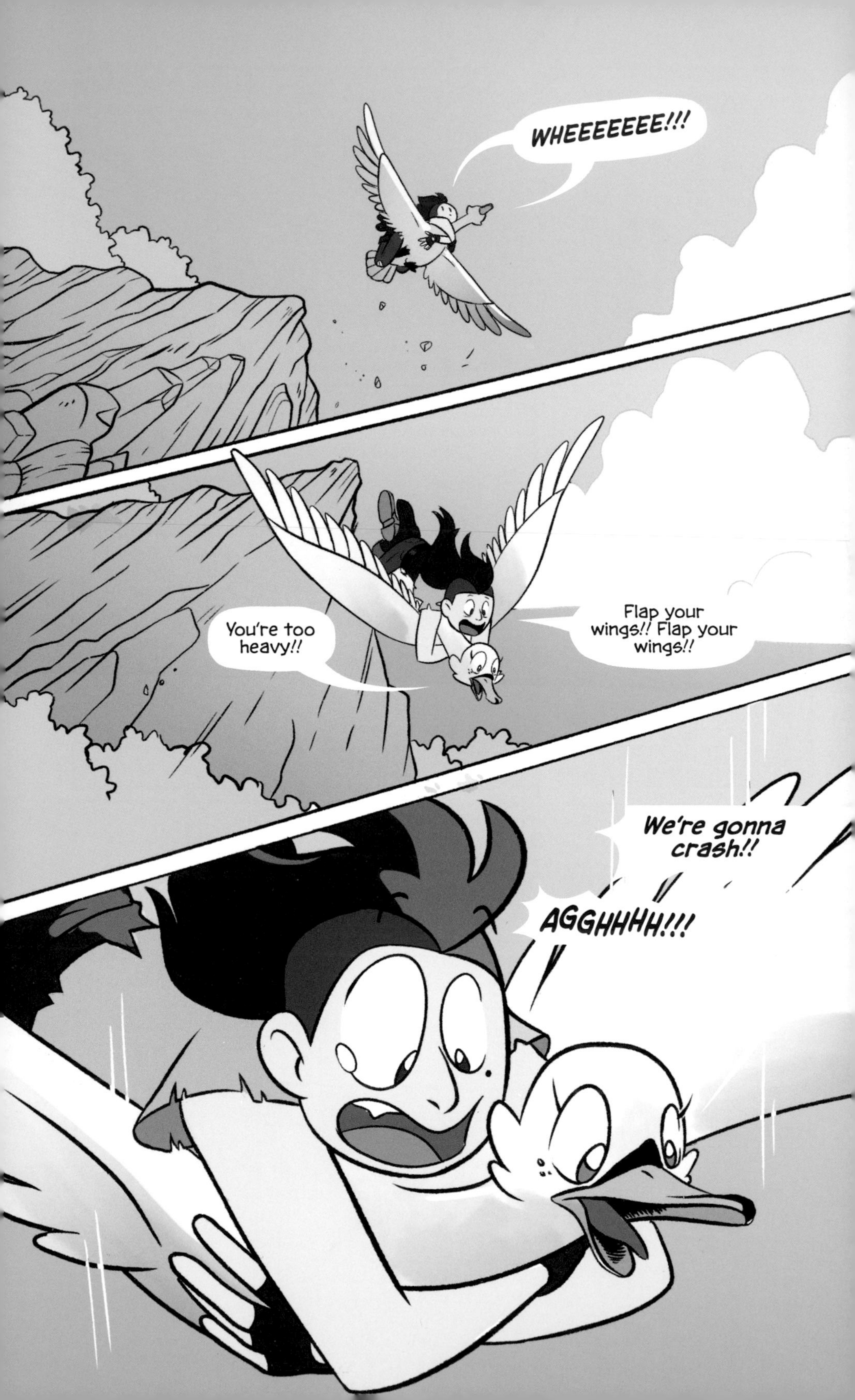
WHEEEEEEE!!!
Flap your wings!! Flap your wings!!
You're too heavy!!
We're gonna crash!!
AGGHHHH!!!

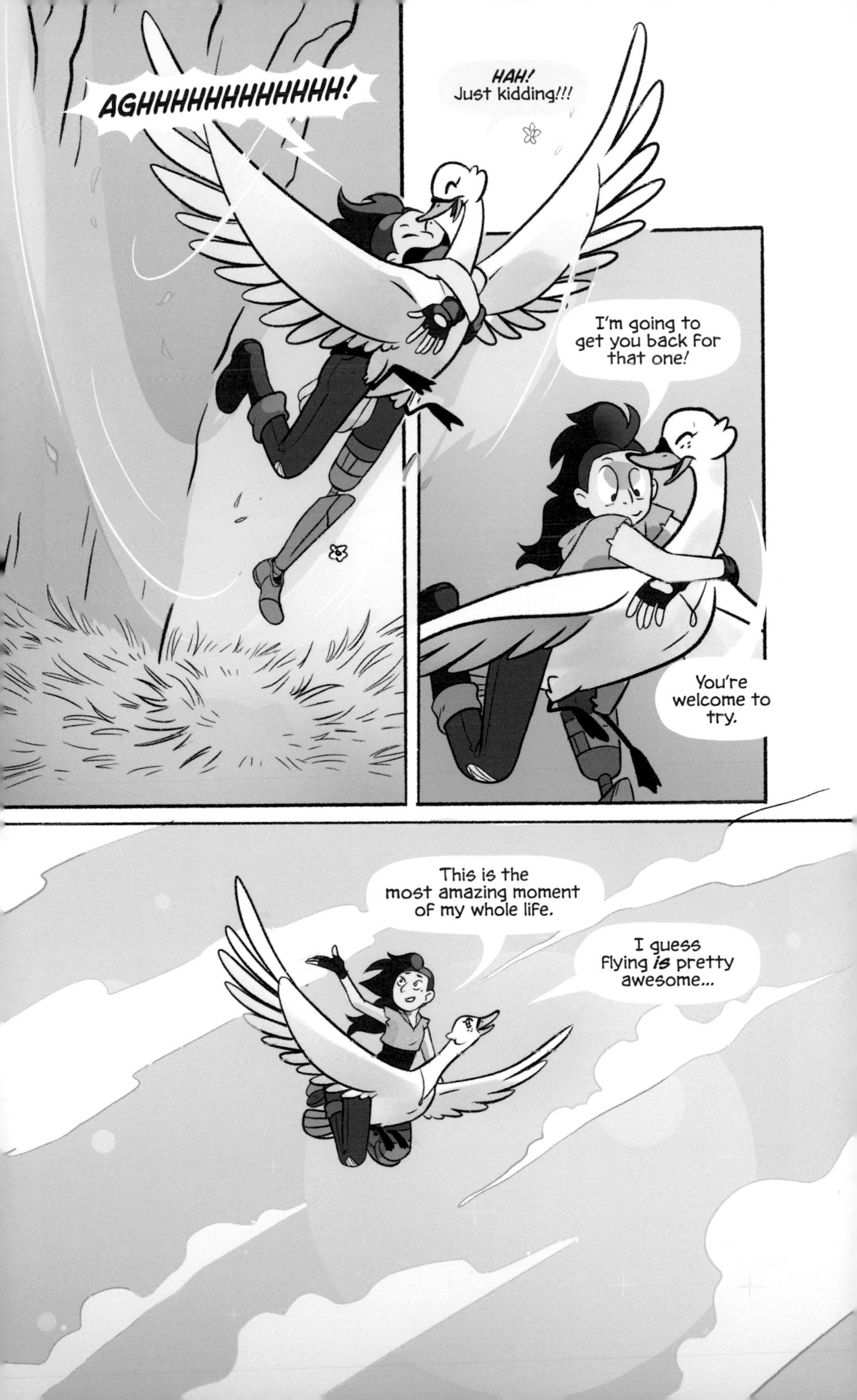
AGHHHHHHHHHHHH!
HAH!
Just kidding!!!
I'm going to get you back for that one!
You're welcome to try.
This is the most amazing moment of my whole life.
I guess flying *is* pretty awesome...

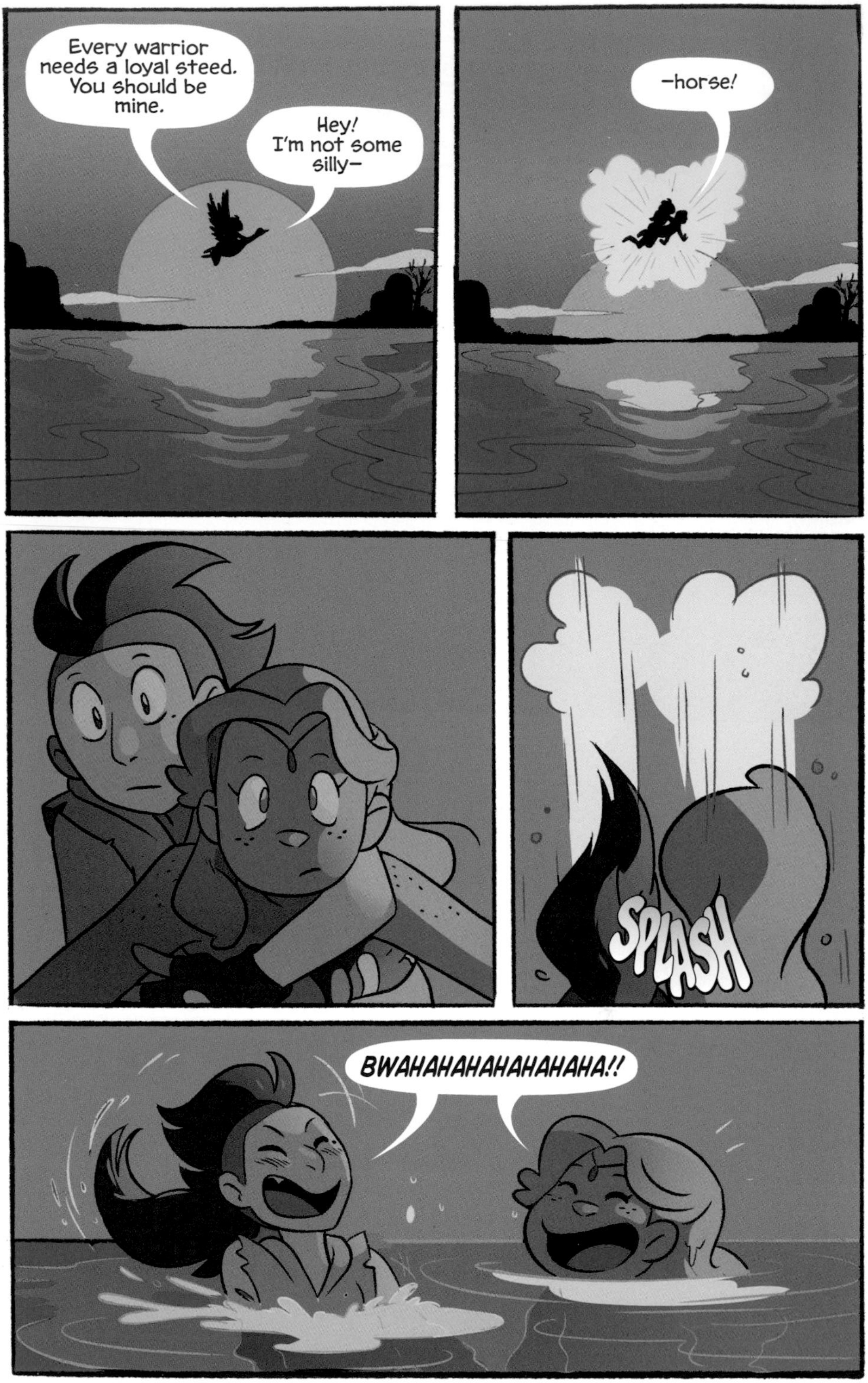
Every warrior needs a loyal steed. You should be mine.
Hey! I'm not some silly–
–horse!
SPLASH
BWAHAHAHAHAHAHAHA!!

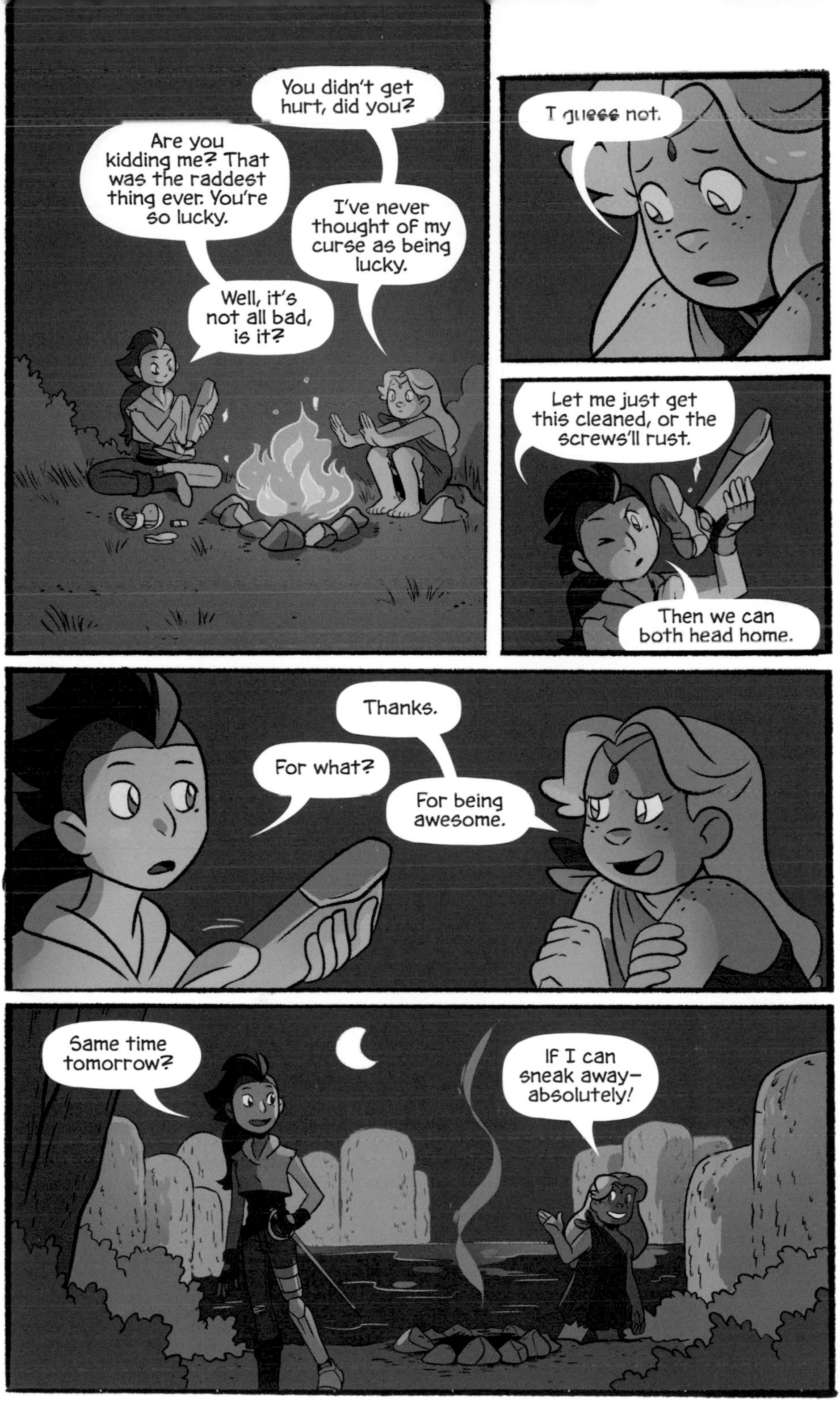
You didn't get hurt, did you?
Are you kidding me? That was the raddest thing ever. You're so lucky.
I've never thought of my curse as being lucky.
Well, it's not all bad, is it?
I guess not.
Let me just get this cleaned, or the screws'll rust.
Then we can both head home.
Thanks.
For what?
For being awesome.
Same time tomorrow?
If I can sneak away—absolutely!

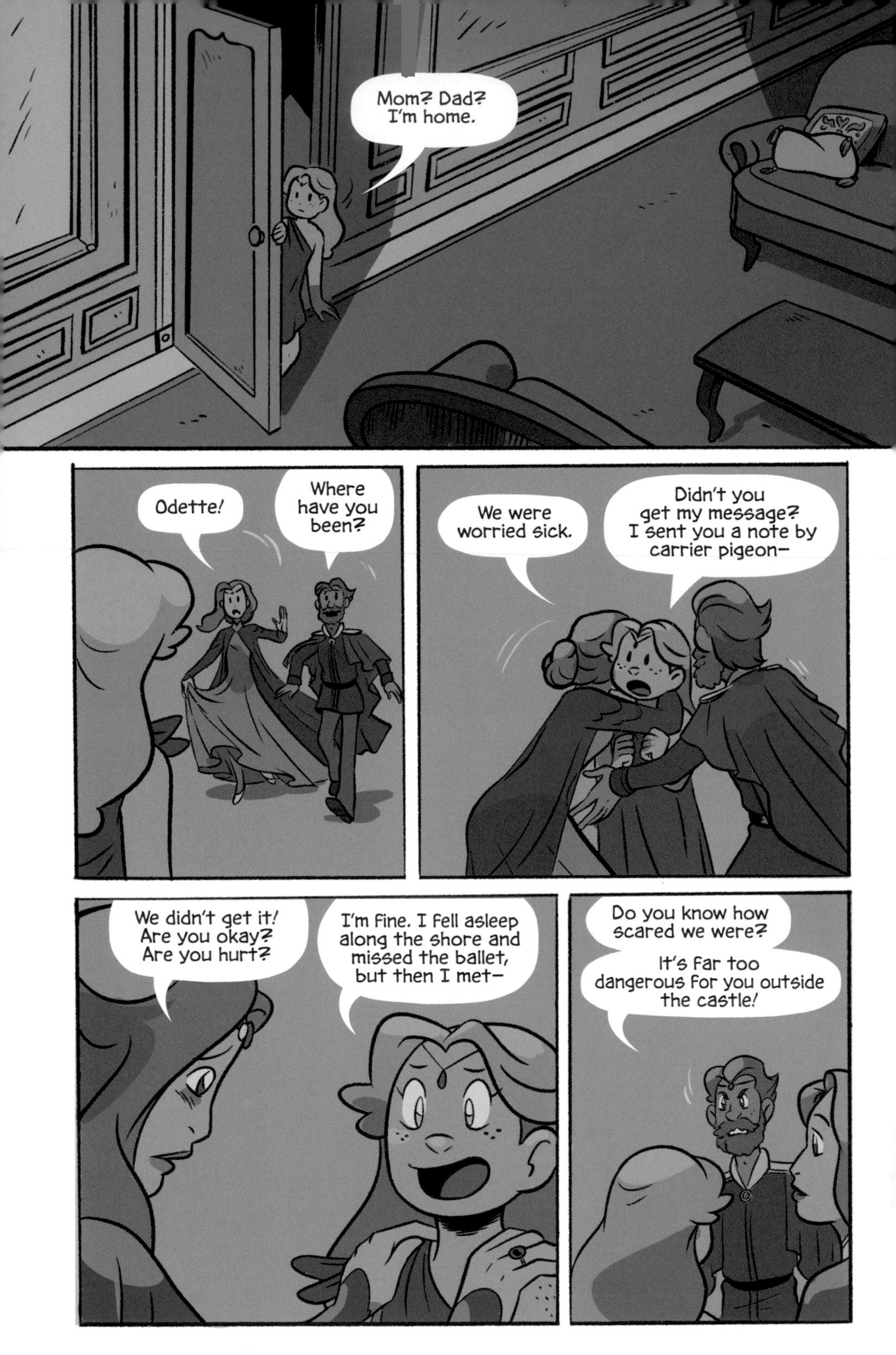
Mom? Dad? I'm home.
Odette!
Where have you been?
We were worried sick.
Didn't you get my message? I sent you a note by carrier pigeon—
We didn't get it! Are you okay? Are you hurt?
I'm fine. I fell asleep along the shore and missed the ballet, but then I met—
Do you know how scared we were?
It's far too dangerous for you outside the castle!

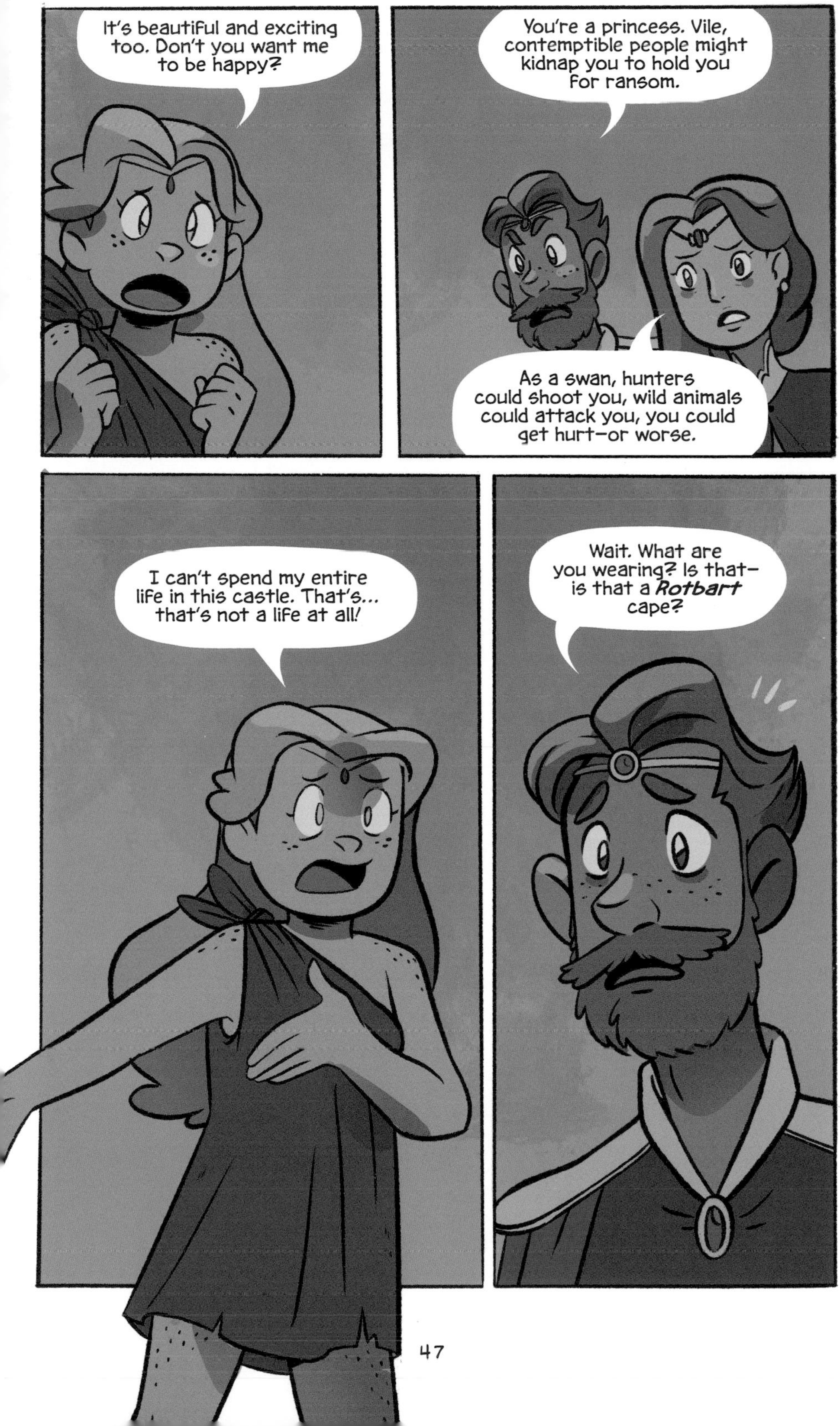
It's beautiful and exciting too. Don't you want me to be happy?
You're a princess. Vile, contemptible people might kidnap you to hold you for ransom.
As a swan, hunters could shoot you, wild animals could attack you, you could get hurt—or worse.
I can't spend my entire life in this castle. That's... that's not a life at all!
Wait. What are you wearing? Is that—is that a *Rotbart* cape?

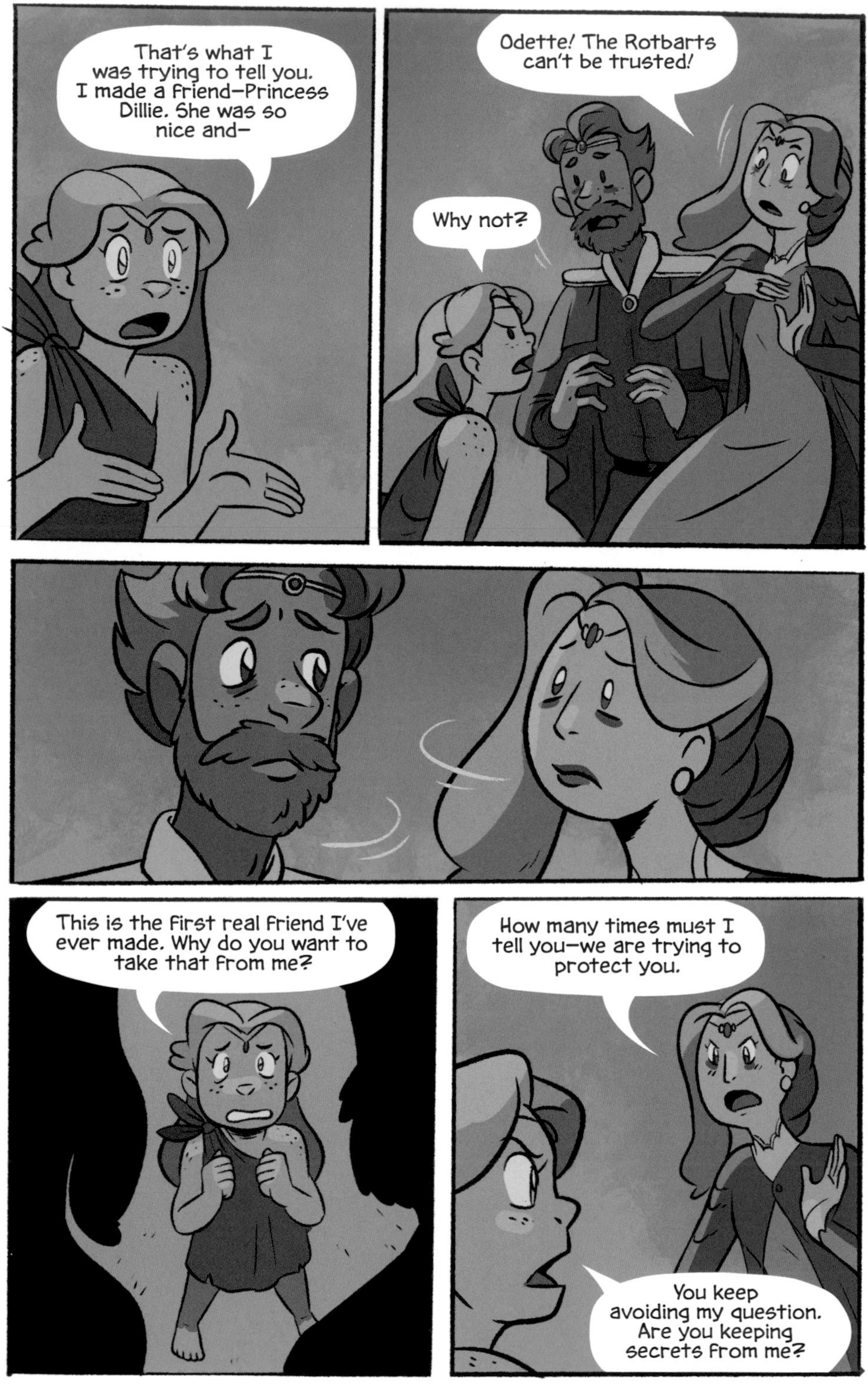
That's what I was trying to tell you. I made a friend—Princess Dillie. She was so nice and—
Odette! The Rotbarts can't be trusted!
Why not?
This is the first real friend I've ever made. Why do you want to take that from me?
How many times must I tell you—we are trying to protect you.
You keep avoiding my question. Are you keeping secrets from me?

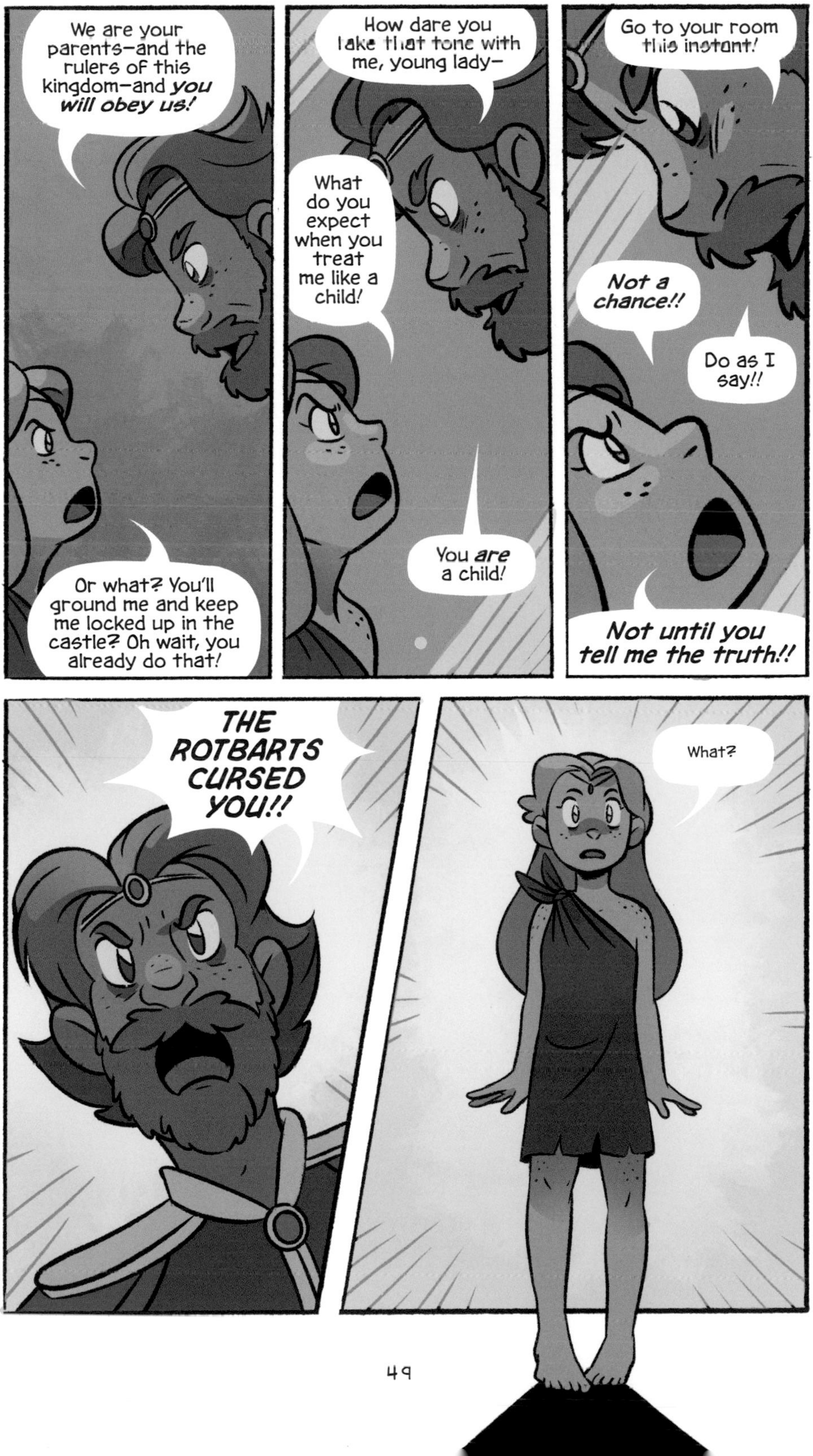
We are your parents—and the rulers of this kingdom—and *you will obey us!*
Or what? You'll ground me and keep me locked up in the castle? Oh wait, you already do that!
How dare you take that tone with me, young lady—
What do you expect when you treat me like a child!
You *are* a child!
Go to your room this instant!
Not a chance!!
Do as I say!!
Not until you tell me the truth!!
THE ROTBARTS CURSED YOU!!
What?

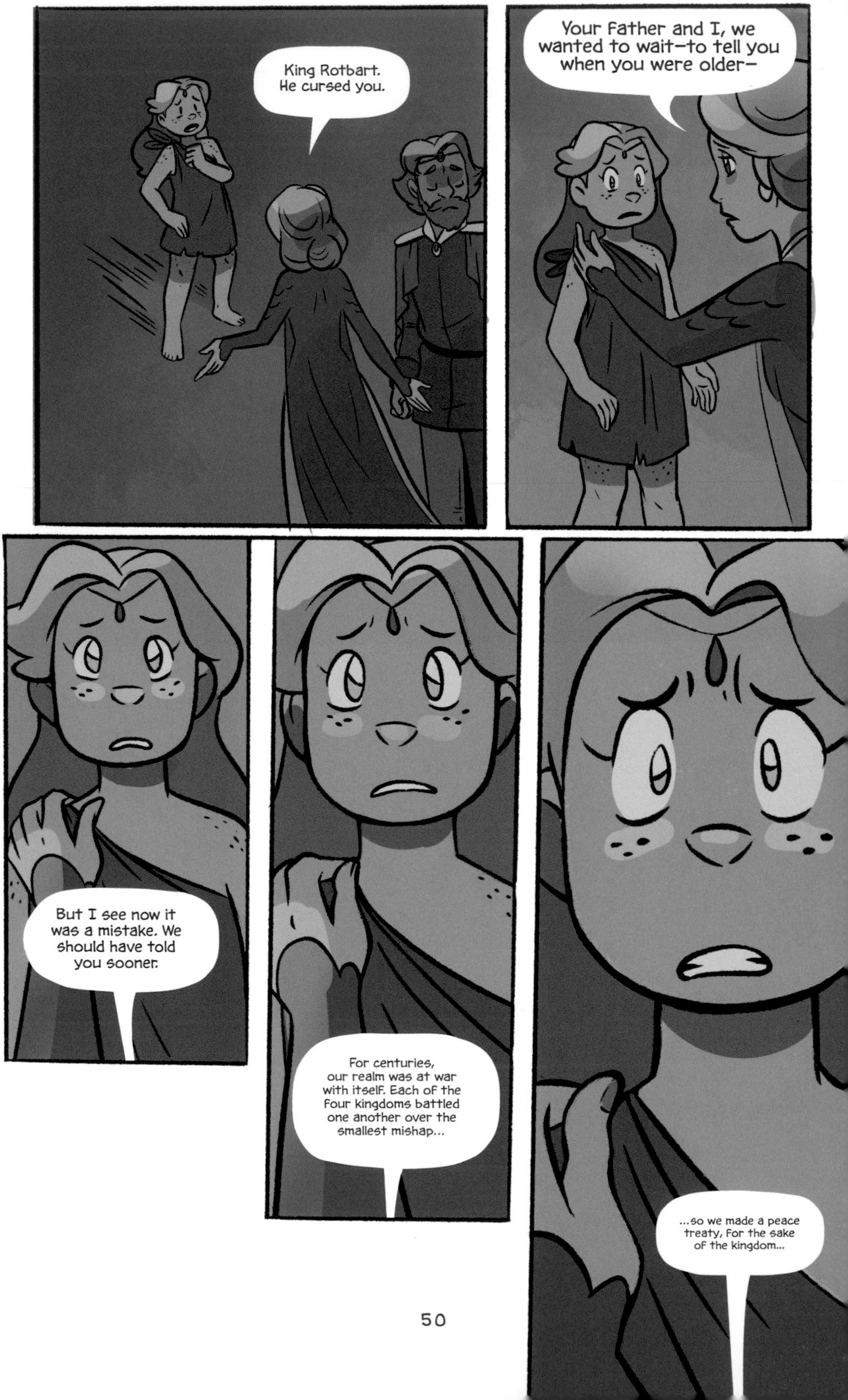
King Rotbart. He cursed you.
Your father and I, we wanted to wait—to tell you when you were older—
But I see now it was a mistake. We should have told you sooner.
For centuries, our realm was at war with itself. Each of the four kingdoms battled one another over the smallest mishap...
...so we made a peace treaty, for the sake of the kingdom...

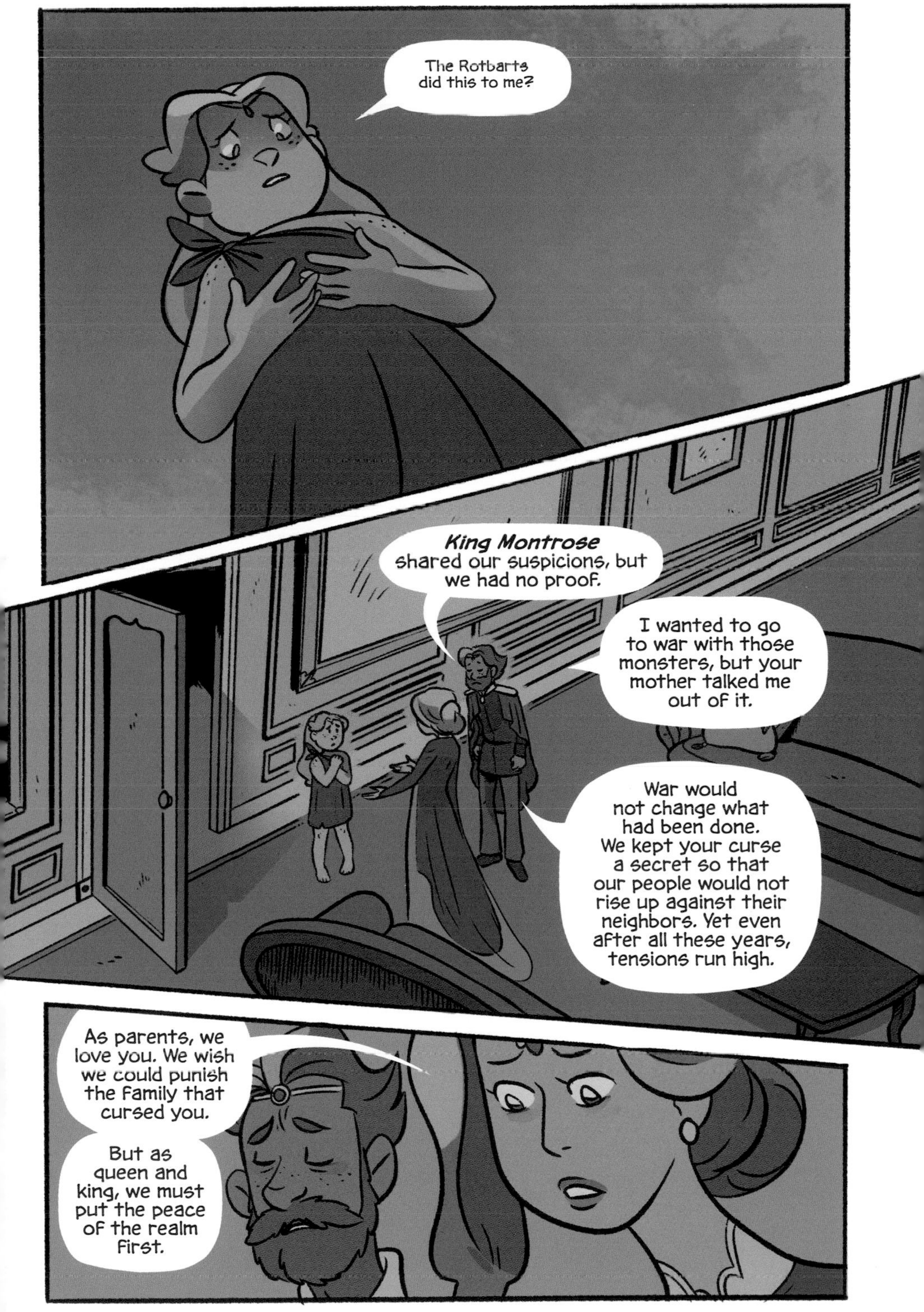

The Rotbarts did this to me?
King Montrose shared our suspicions, but we had no proof.
I wanted to go to war with those monsters, but your mother talked me out of it.
War would not change what had been done. We kept your curse a secret so that our people would not rise up against their neighbors. Yet even after all these years, tensions run high.
As parents, we love you. We wish we could punish the family that cursed you.
But as queen and king, we must put the peace of the realm first.

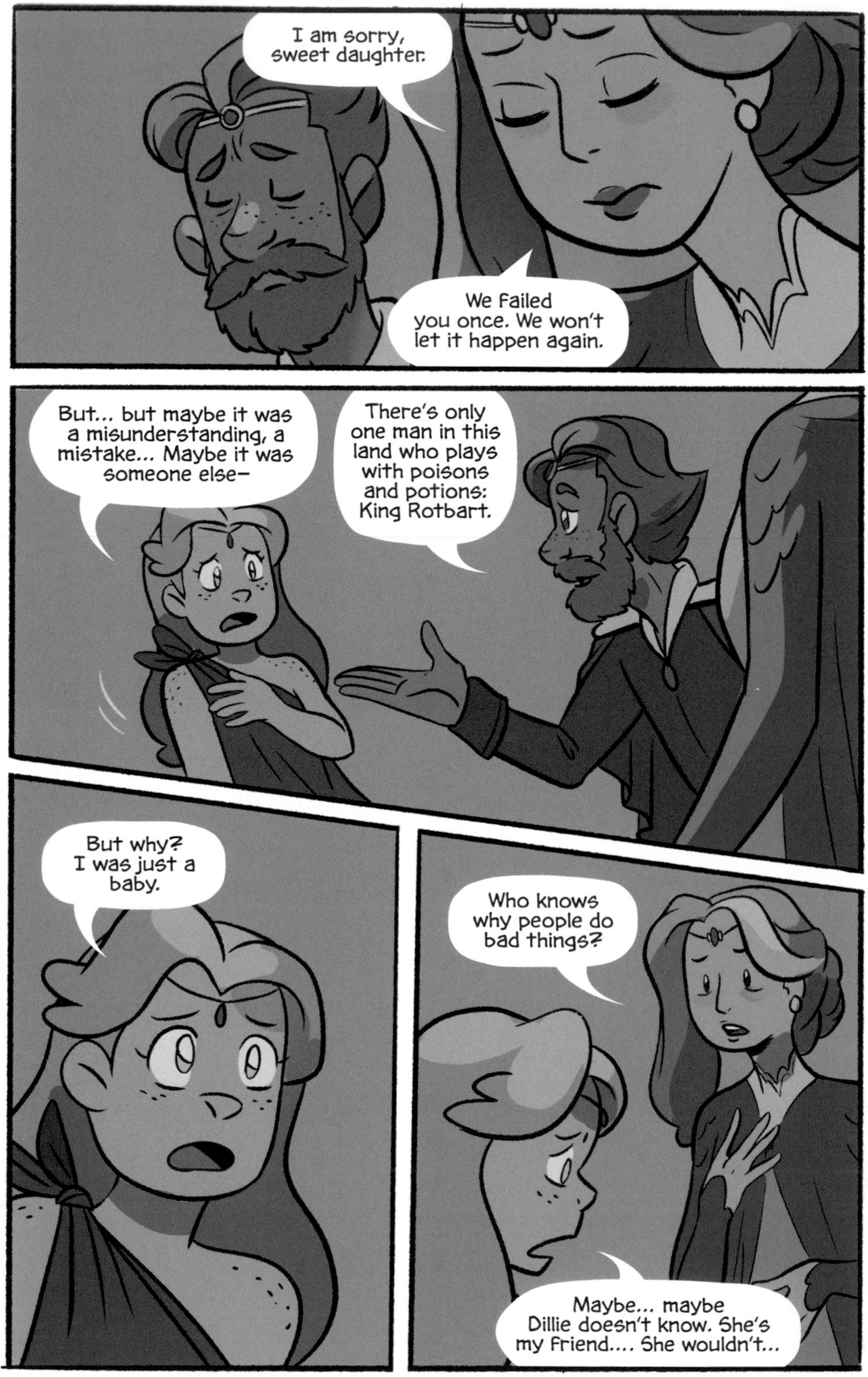
I am sorry, sweet daughter.
We failed you once. We won't let it happen again.
But... but maybe it was a misunderstanding, a mistake... Maybe it was someone else—
There's only one man in this land who plays with poisons and potions: King Rotbart.
But why? I was just a baby.
Who knows why people do bad things?
Maybe... maybe Dillie doesn't know. She's my friend.... She wouldn't...

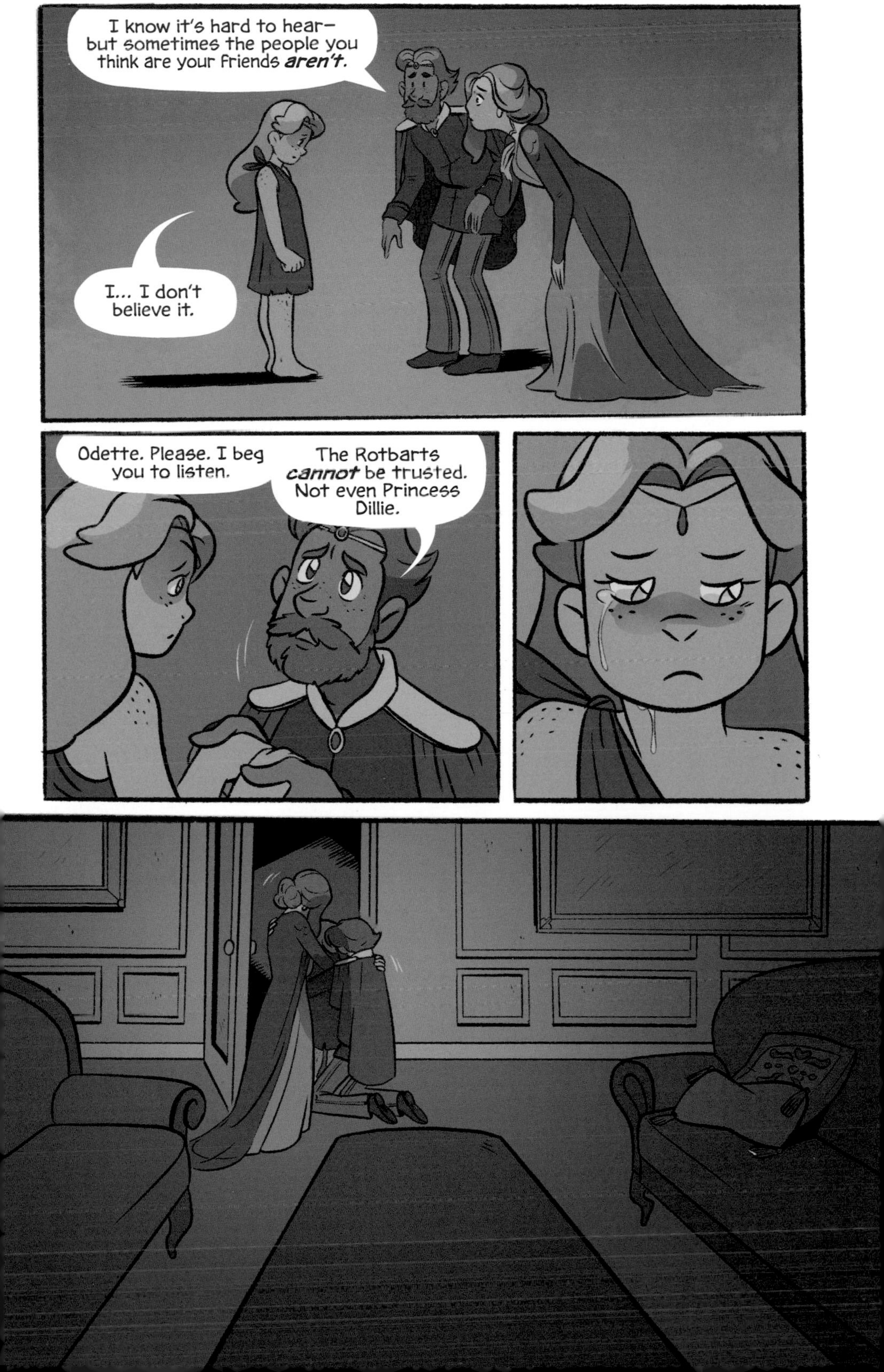
I know it's hard to hear—but sometimes the people you think are your friends *aren't*.
I... I don't believe it.
Odette. Please. I beg you to listen.
The Rotbarts *cannot* be trusted. Not even Princess Dillie.

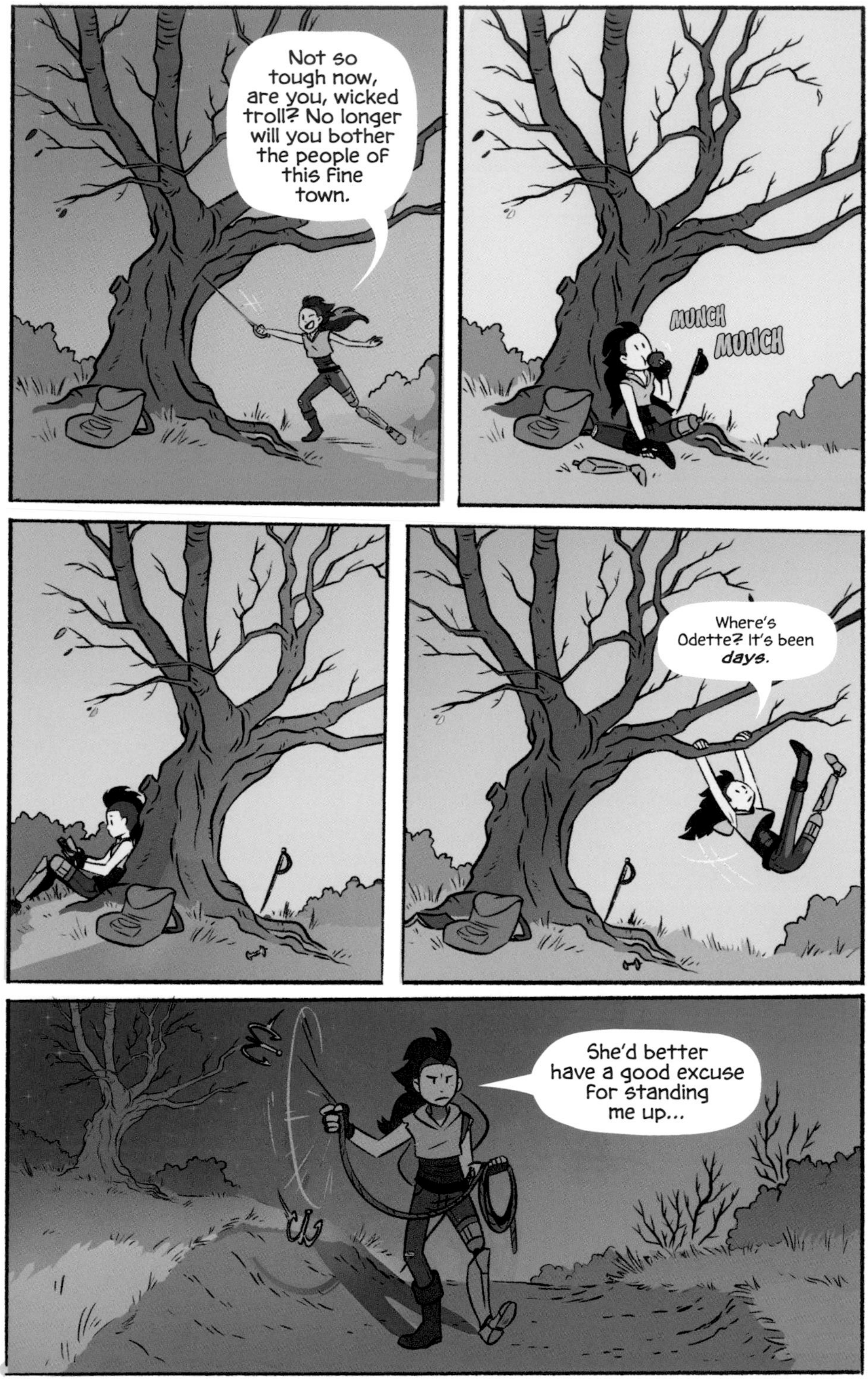

Not so tough now, are you, wicked troll? No longer will you bother the people of this fine town.
MUNCH
MUNCH
Where's Odette? It's been *days*.
She'd better have a good excuse for standing me up...

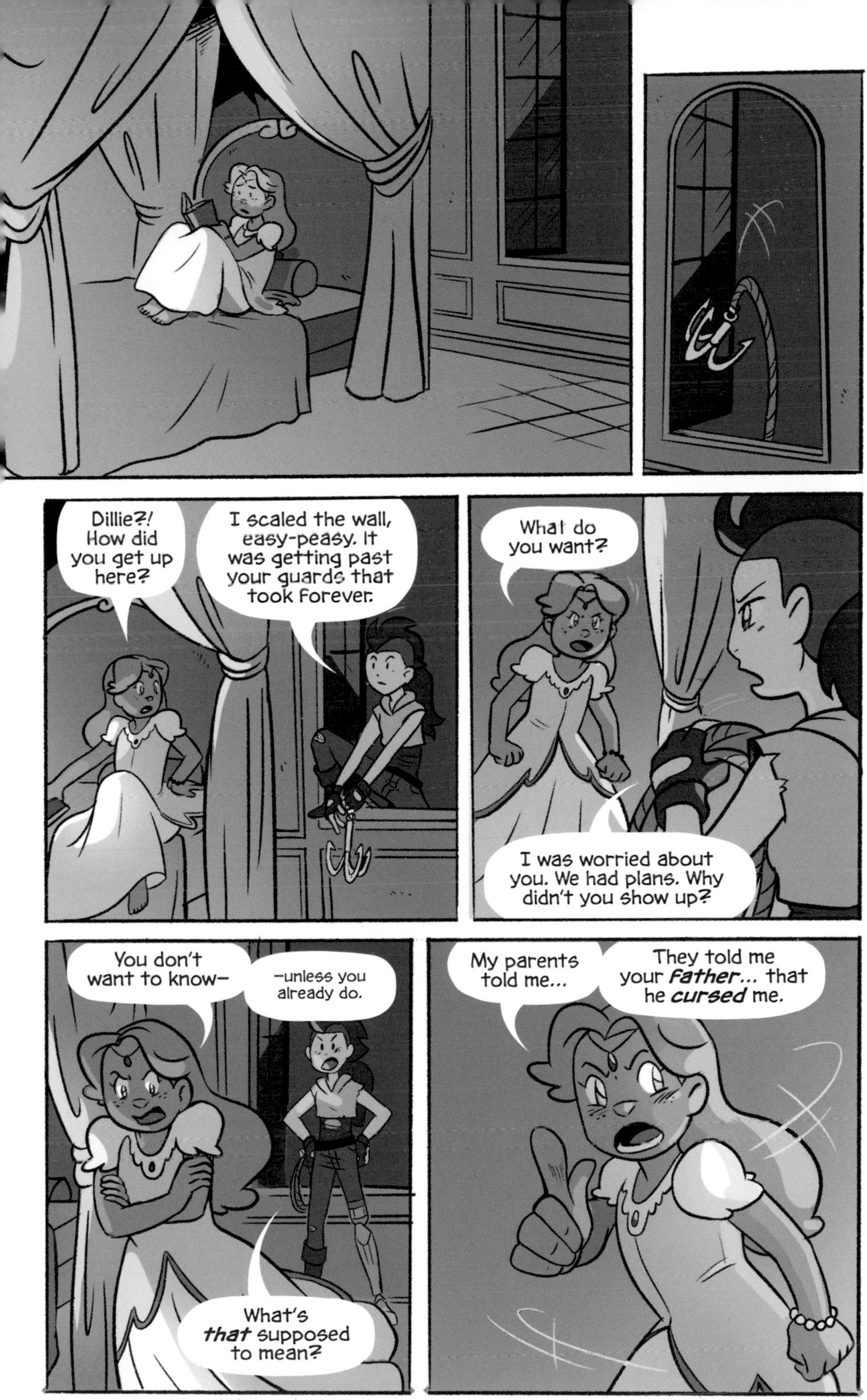
Dillie?! How did you get up here?
I scaled the wall, easy-peasy. It was getting past your guards that took forever.
What do you want?
I was worried about you. We had plans. Why didn't you show up?
You don't want to know—
—unless you already do.
What's *that* supposed to mean?
My parents told me...
They told me your ***father***... that he ***cursed*** me.

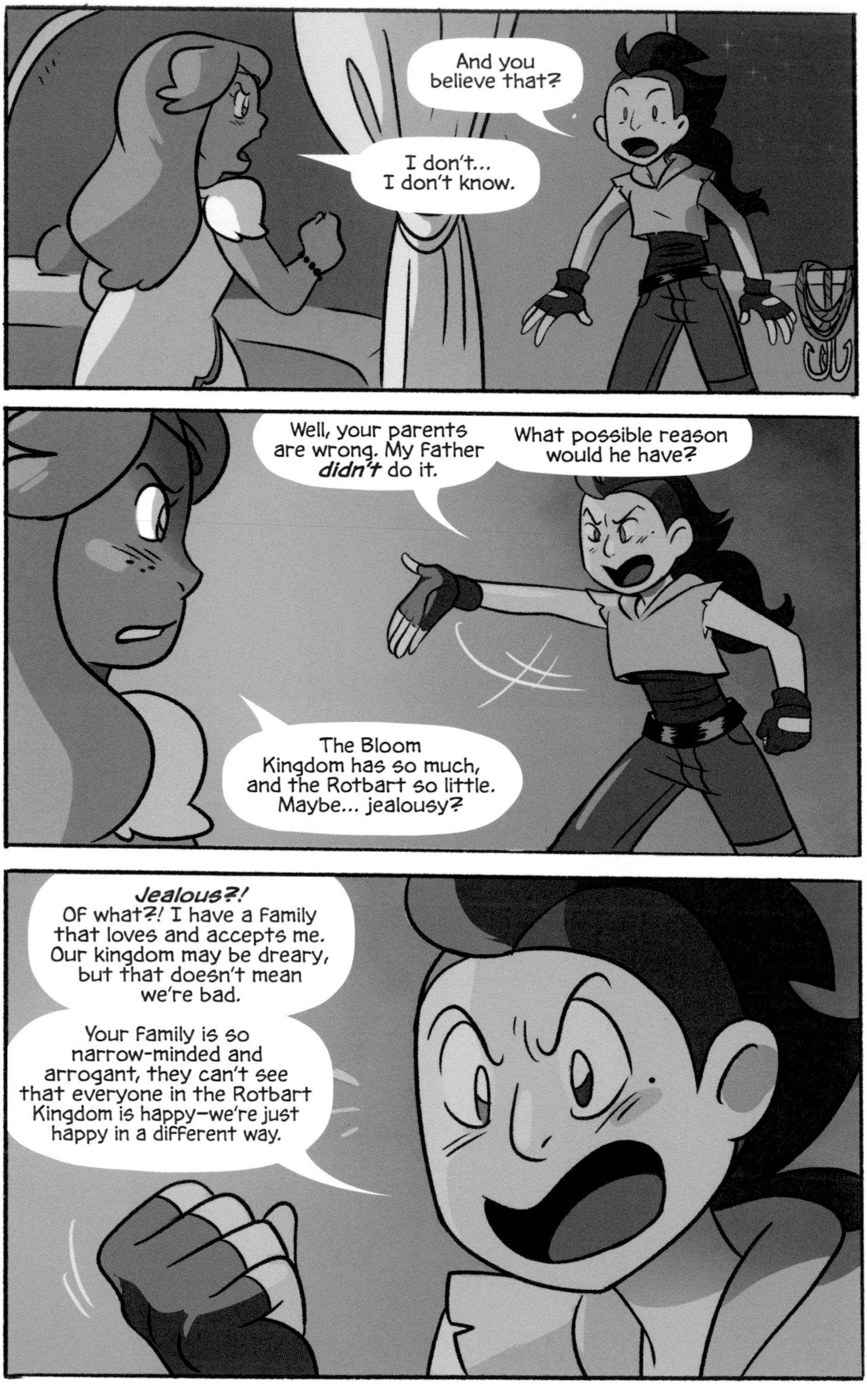
And you believe that?
I don't... I don't know.
Well, your parents are wrong. My father *didn't* do it.
What possible reason would he have?
The Bloom Kingdom has so much, and the Rotbart so little. Maybe... jealousy?
Jealous?! Of what?! I have a family that loves and accepts me. Our kingdom may be dreary, but that doesn't mean we're bad.
Your family is so narrow-minded and arrogant, they can't see that everyone in the Rotbart Kingdom is happy—we're just happy in a different way.

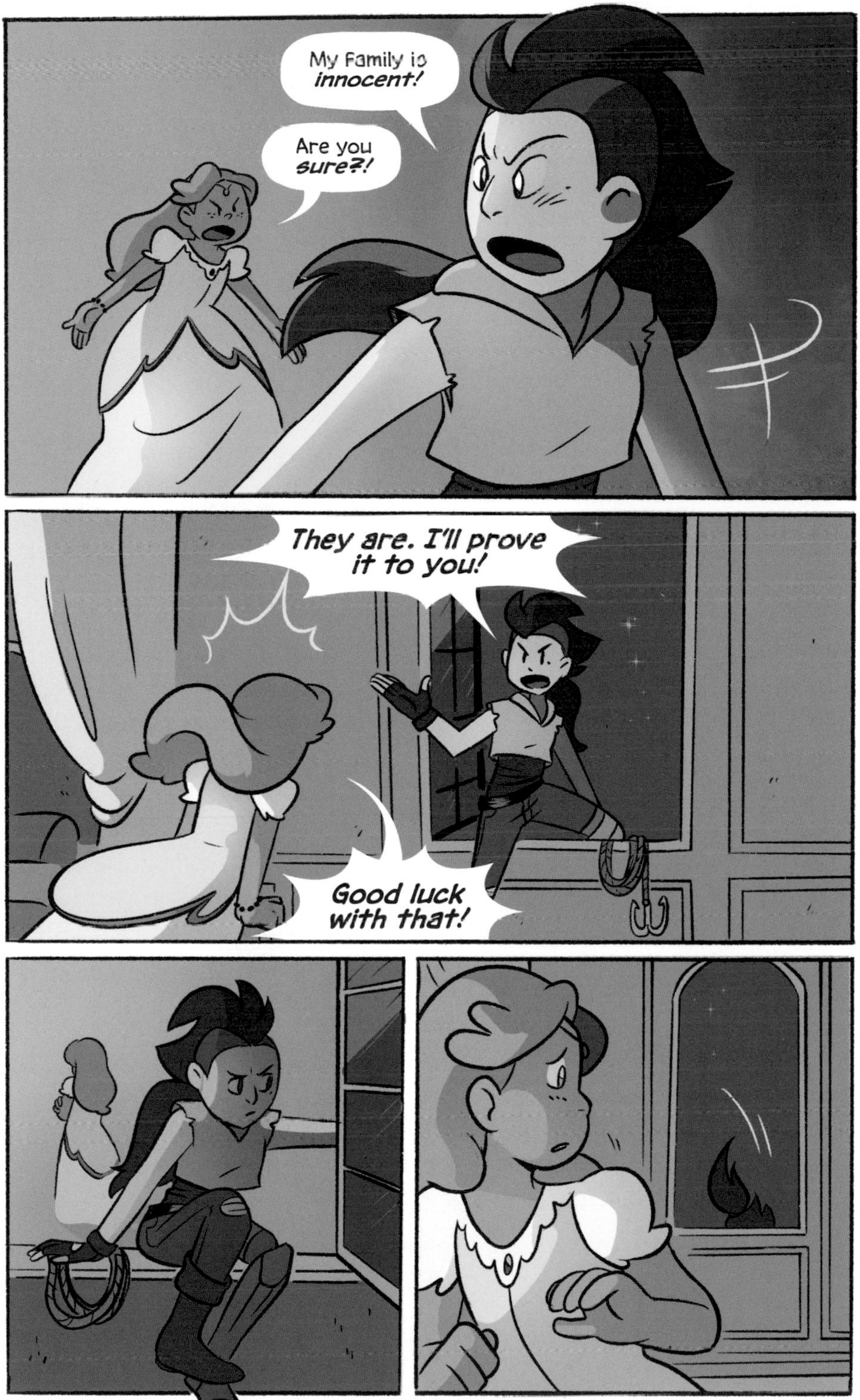
My family is innocent!
Are you sure?!
They are. I'll prove it to you!
Good luck with that!

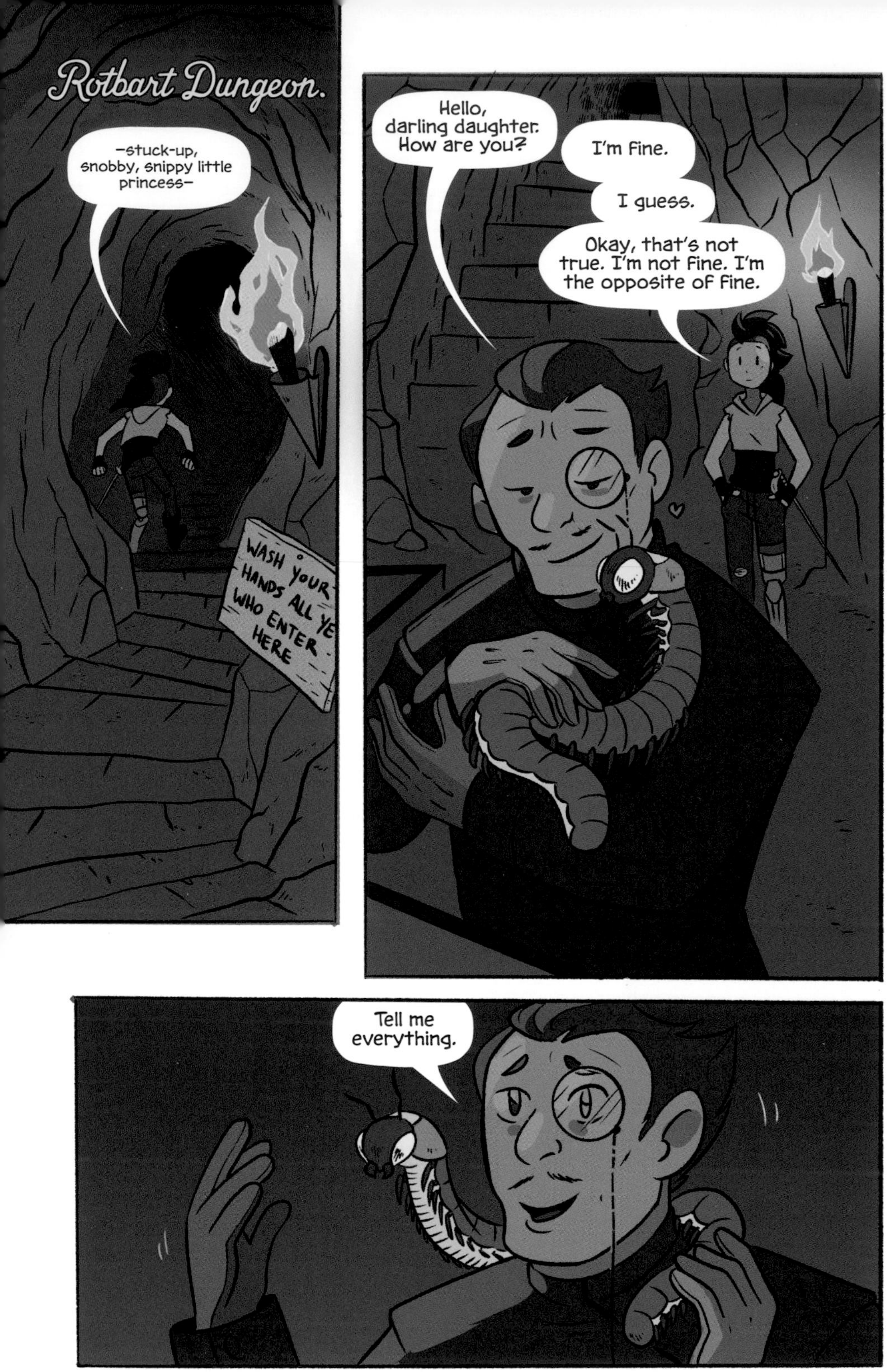
Rotbart Dungeon.
—stuck-up, snobby, snippy little princess—
WASH YOUR HANDS ALL YE WHO ENTER HERE
Hello, darling daughter. How are you?
I'm fine.
I guess.
Okay, that's not true. I'm not fine. I'm the opposite of fine.
Tell me everything.

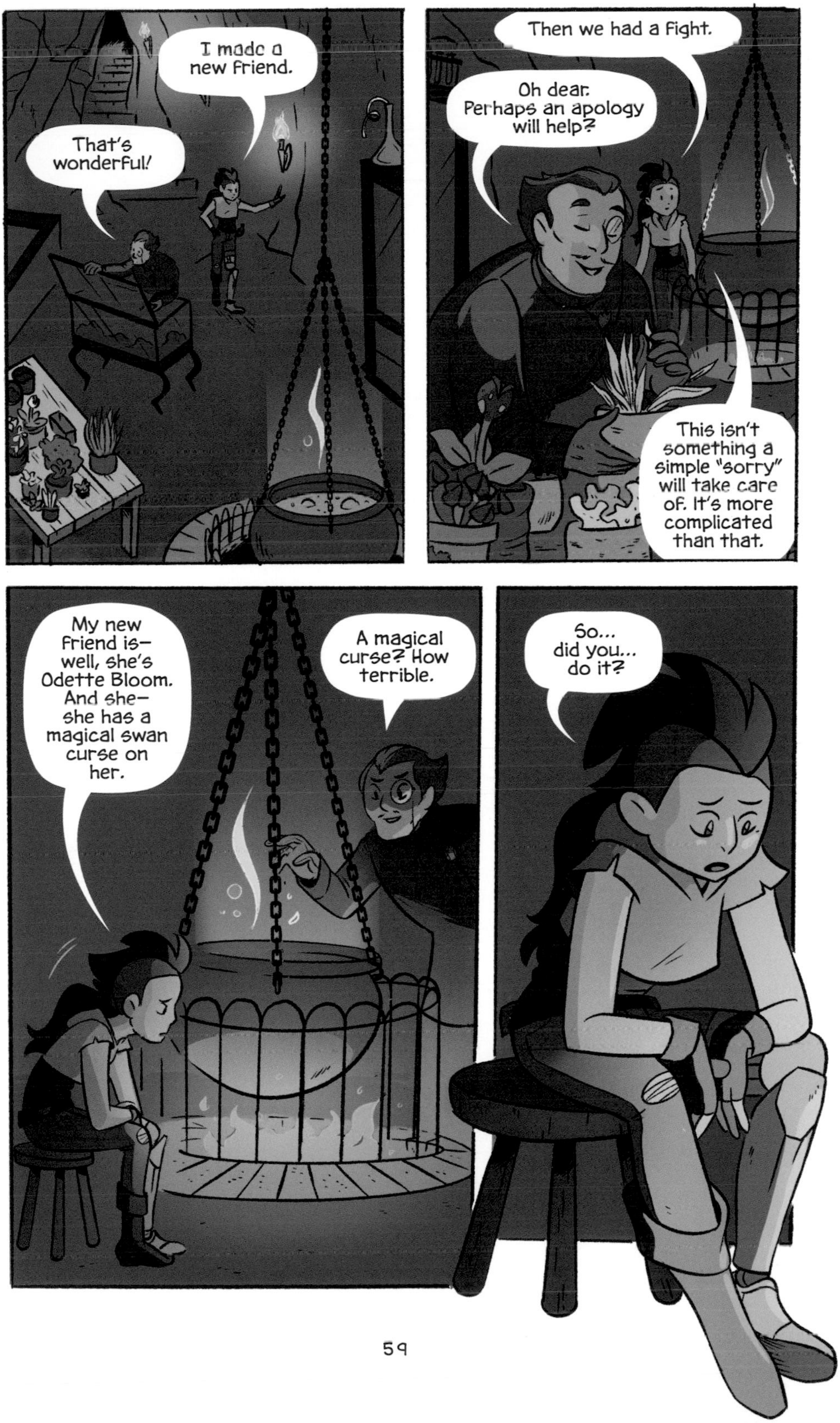
I made a new friend.
That's wonderful!
Then we had a fight.
Oh dear. Perhaps an apology will help?
This isn't something a simple "sorry" will take care of. It's more complicated than that.
My new friend is— well, she's Odette Bloom. And she— she has a magical swan curse on her.
A magical curse? How terrible.
So... did you... do it?

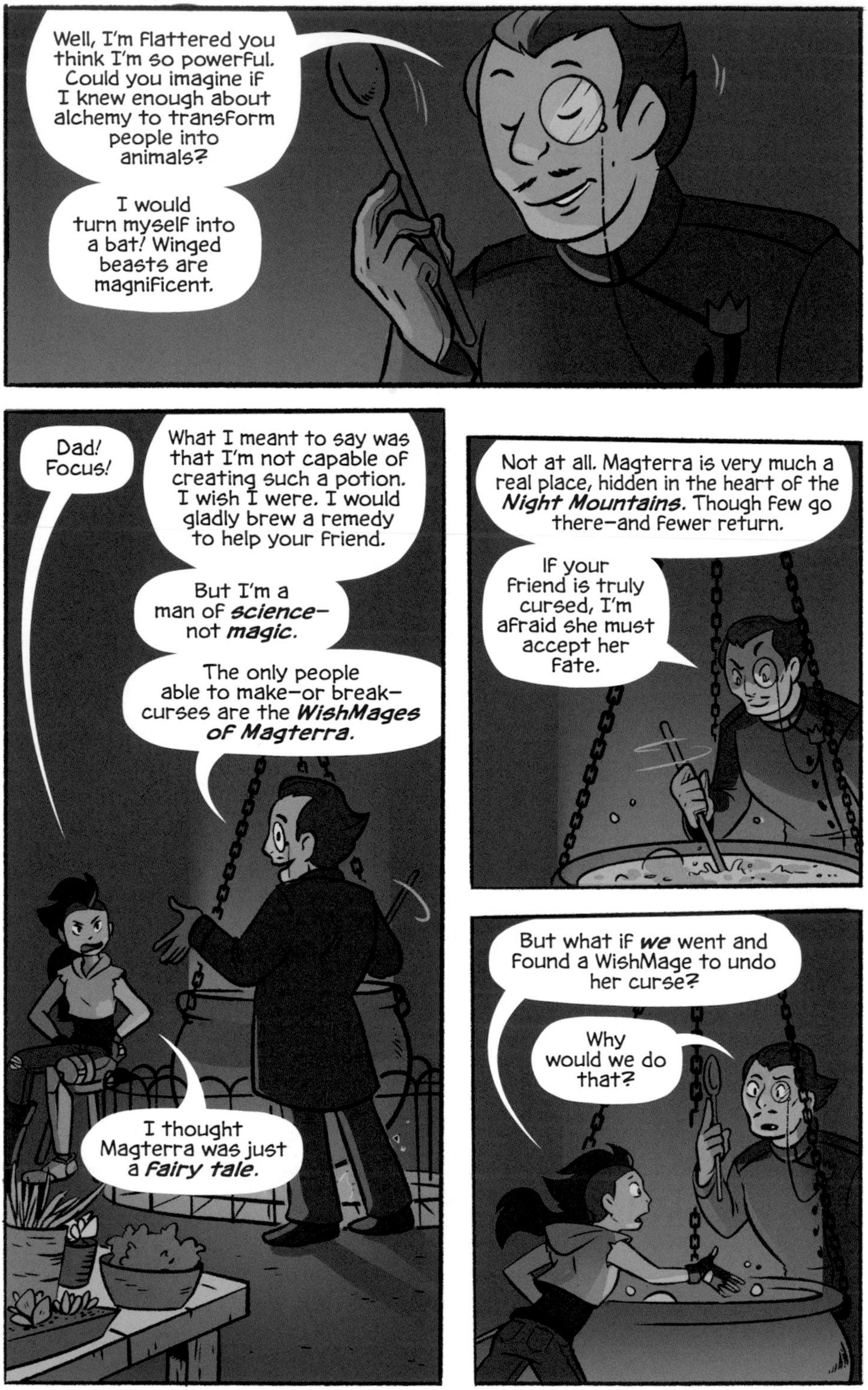

Well, I'm flattered you think I'm so powerful. Could you imagine if I knew enough about alchemy to transform people into animals?
I would turn myself into a bat! Winged beasts are magnificent.
Dad! Focus!
What I meant to say was that I'm not capable of creating such a potion. I wish I were. I would gladly brew a remedy to help your friend.
But I'm a man of *science*–not *magic*.
The only people able to make–or break–curses are the ***WishMages of Magterra***.
I thought Magterra was just a *fairy tale*.
Not at all. Magterra is very much a real place, hidden in the heart of the ***Night Mountains***. Though few go there–and fewer return.
If your friend is truly cursed, I'm afraid she must accept her fate.
But what if *we* went and found a WishMage to undo her curse?
Why would we do that?

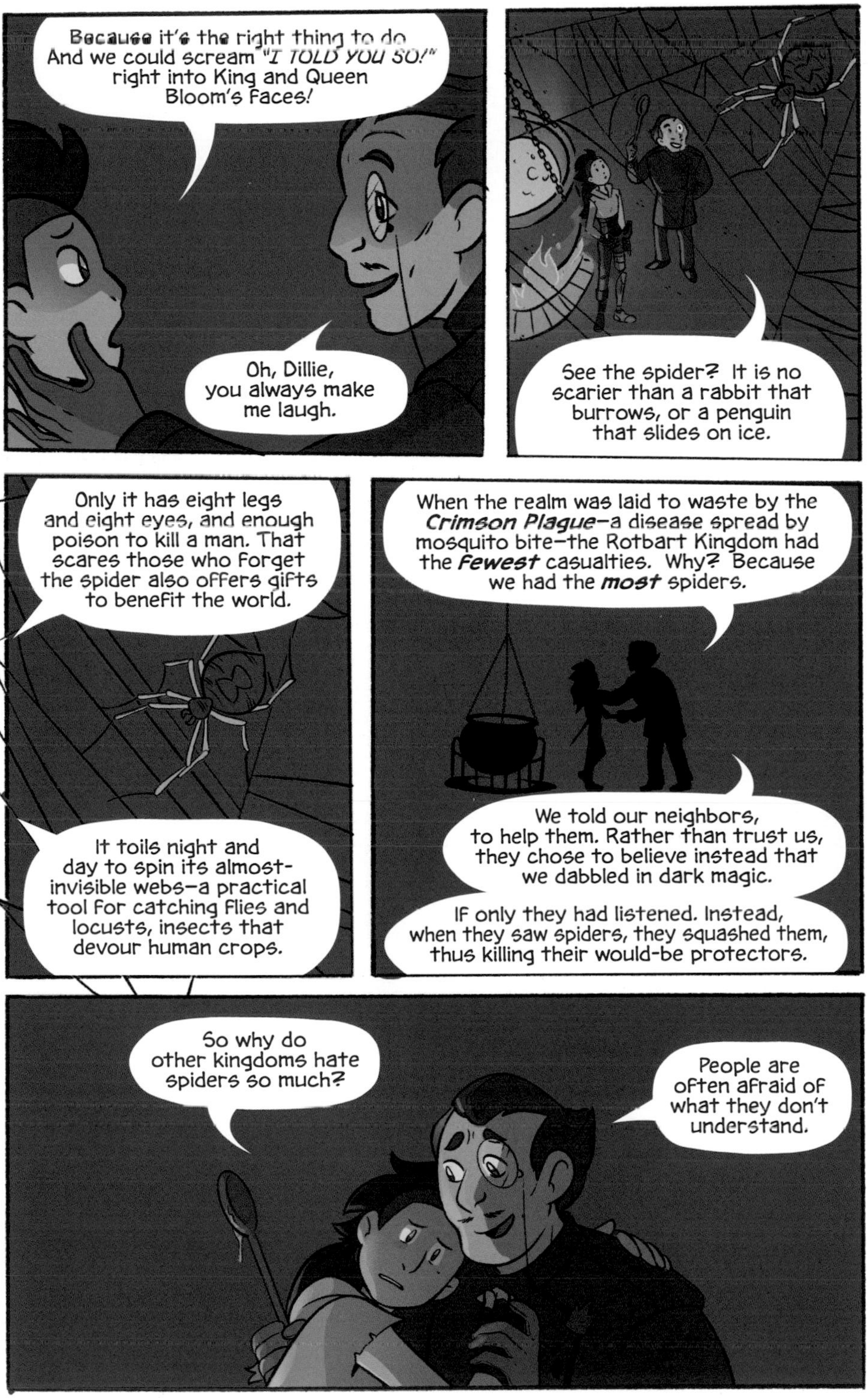
Because it's the right thing to do. And we could scream "I TOLD YOU SO!" right into King and Queen Bloom's faces!
Oh, Dillie, you always make me laugh.
See the spider? It is no scarier than a rabbit that burrows, or a penguin that slides on ice.
Only it has eight legs and eight eyes, and enough poison to kill a man. That scares those who forget the spider also offers gifts to benefit the world.
It toils night and day to spin its almost-invisible webs—a practical tool for catching flies and locusts, insects that devour human crops.
When the realm was laid to waste by the *Crimson Plague*—a disease spread by mosquito bite—the Rotbart Kingdom had the *fewest* casualties. Why? Because we had the *most* spiders.
We told our neighbors, to help them. Rather than trust us, they chose to believe instead that we dabbled in dark magic.
If only they had listened. Instead, when they saw spiders, they squashed them, thus killing their would-be protectors.
So why do other kingdoms hate spiders so much?
People are often afraid of what they don't understand.

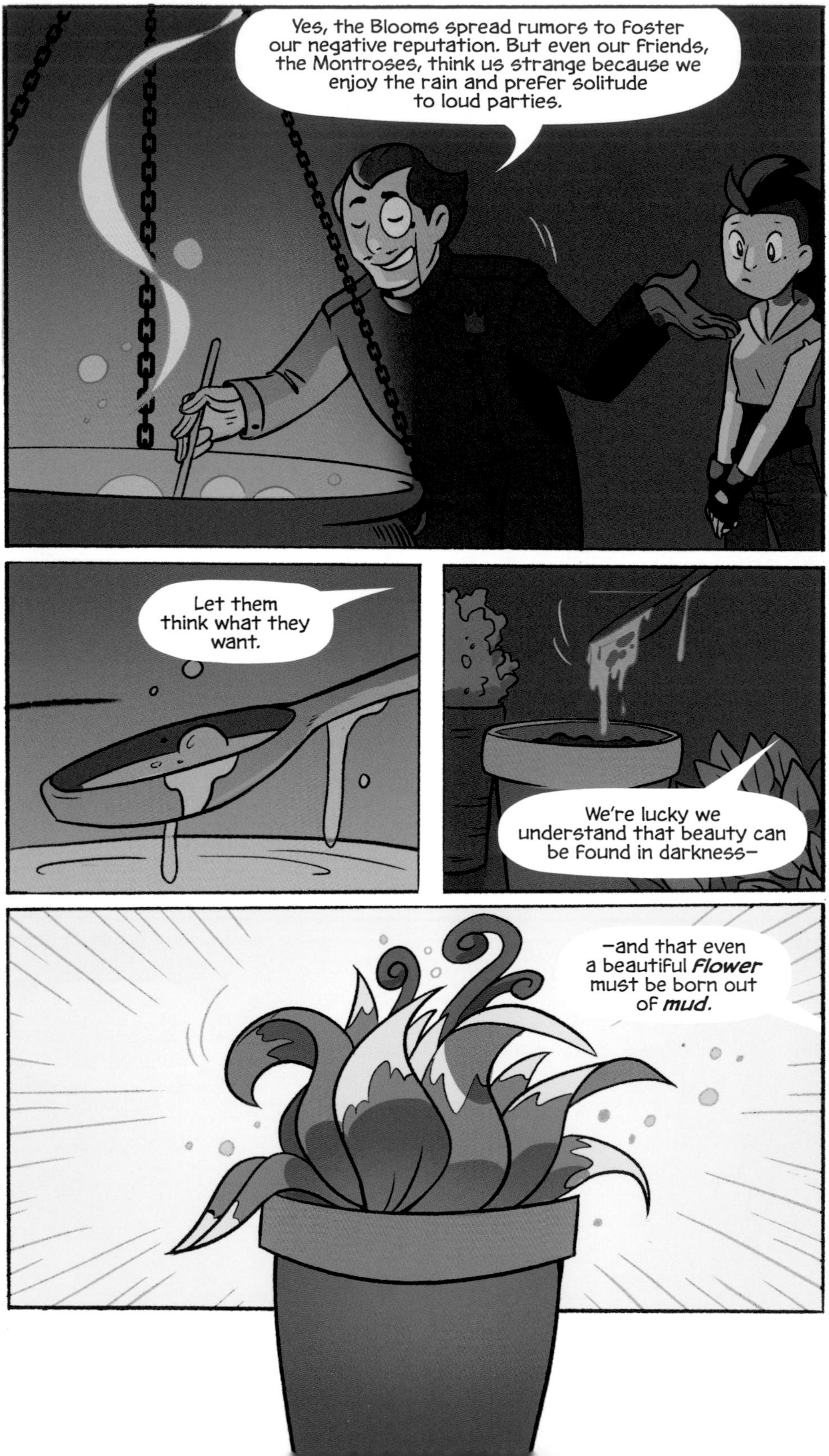
Yes, the Blooms spread rumors to foster our negative reputation. But even our friends, the Montroses, think us strange because we enjoy the rain and prefer solitude to loud parties.
Let them think what they want.
We're lucky we understand that beauty can be found in darkness—
—and that even a beautiful *flower* must be born out of *mud.*

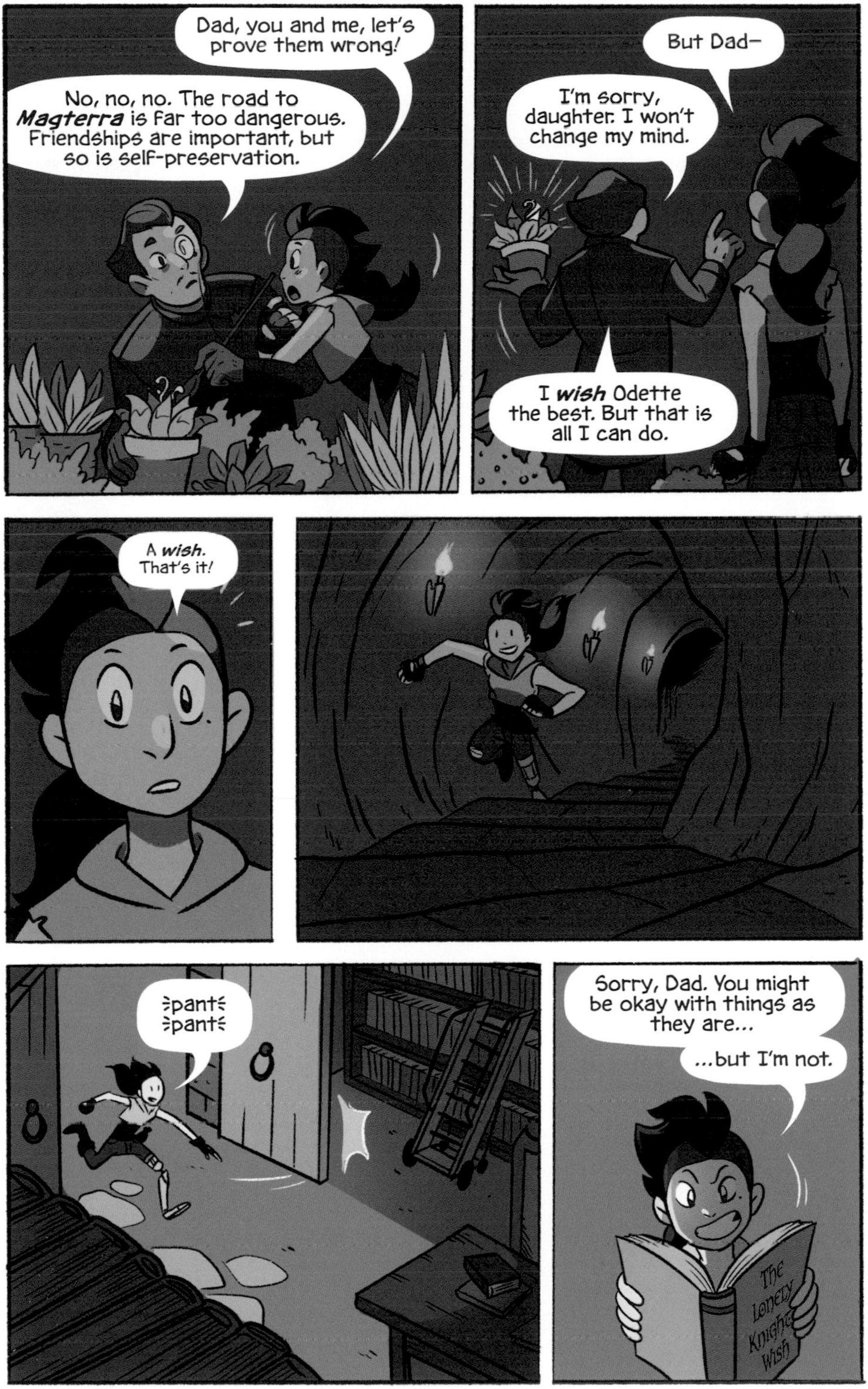
Dad, you and me, let's prove them wrong!
No, no, no. The road to *Magterra* is far too dangerous. Friendships are important, but so is self-preservation.
But Dad—
I'm sorry, daughter. I won't change my mind.
I *wish* Odette the best. But that is all I can do.
A *wish*. That's it!
⁝pant⁝ ⁝pant⁝
Sorry, Dad. You might be okay with things as they are...
...but I'm not.
The Lonely Knight's Wish

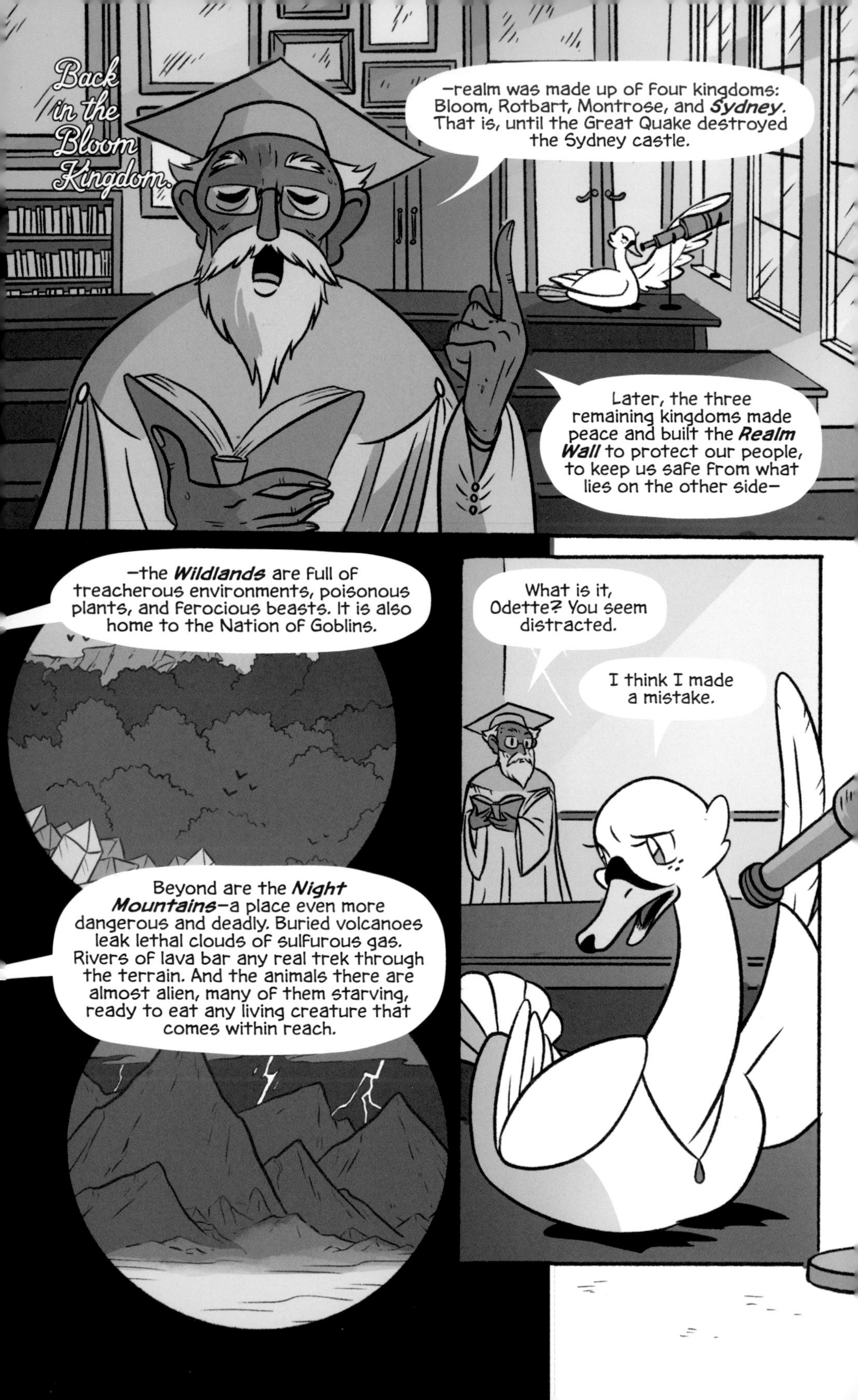
Back in the Bloom Kingdom.
—realm was made up of four kingdoms: Bloom, Rotbart, Montrose, and Sydney. That is, until the Great Quake destroyed the Sydney castle.
Later, the three remaining kingdoms made peace and built the Realm Wall to protect our people, to keep us safe from what lies on the other side—
—the Wildlands are full of treacherous environments, poisonous plants, and ferocious beasts. It is also home to the Nation of Goblins.
Beyond are the Night Mountains—a place even more dangerous and deadly. Buried volcanoes leak lethal clouds of sulfurous gas. Rivers of lava bar any real trek through the terrain. And the animals there are almost alien, many of them starving, ready to eat any living creature that comes within reach.
What is it, Odette? You seem distracted.
I think I made a mistake.

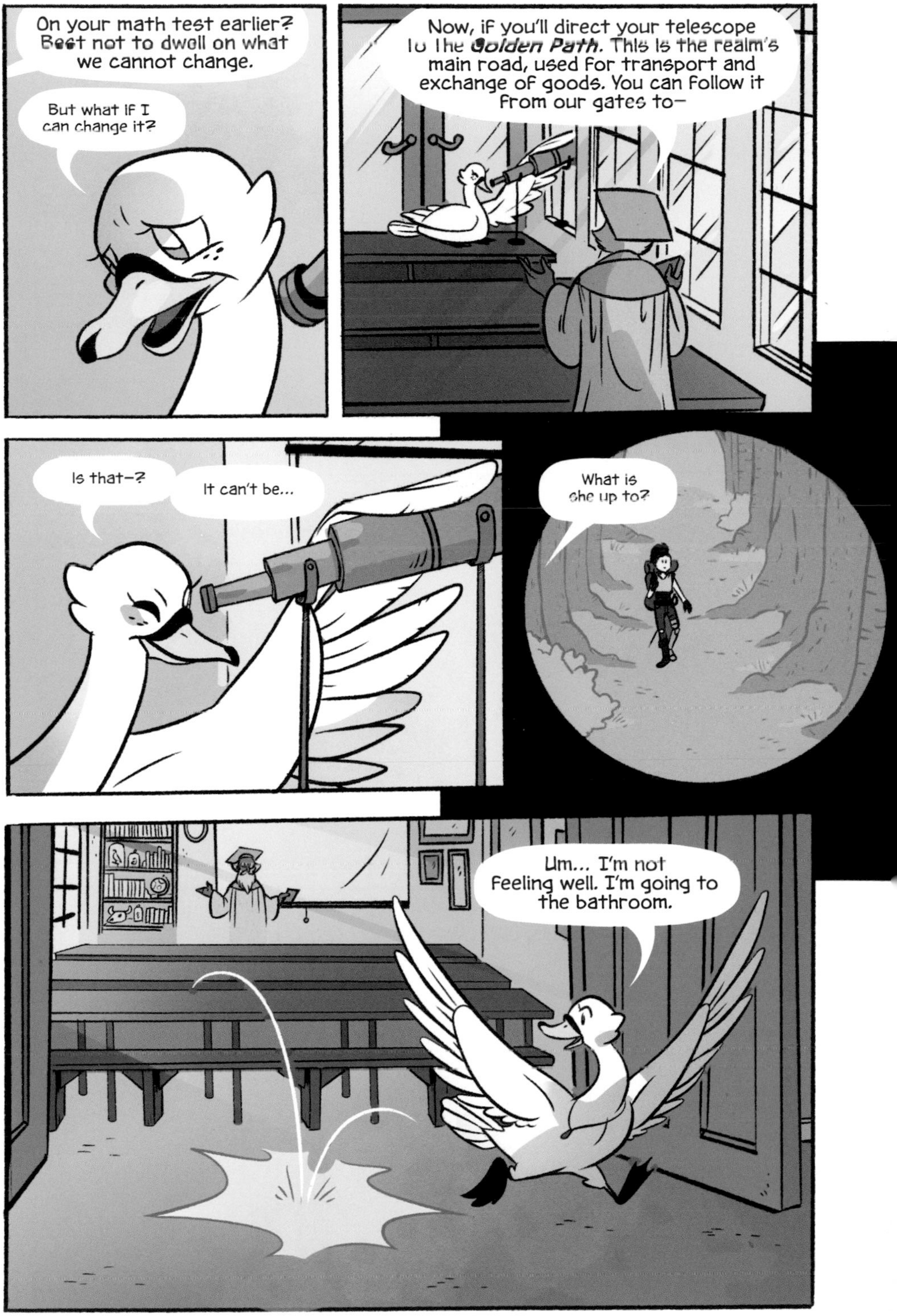
On your math test earlier? Best not to dwell on what we cannot change.
But what if I can change it?
Now, if you'll direct your telescope to the Golden Path. This is the realm's main road, used for transport and exchange of goods. You can follow it from our gates to—
Is that—?
It can't be...
What is she up to?
Um... I'm not feeling well. I'm going to the bathroom.

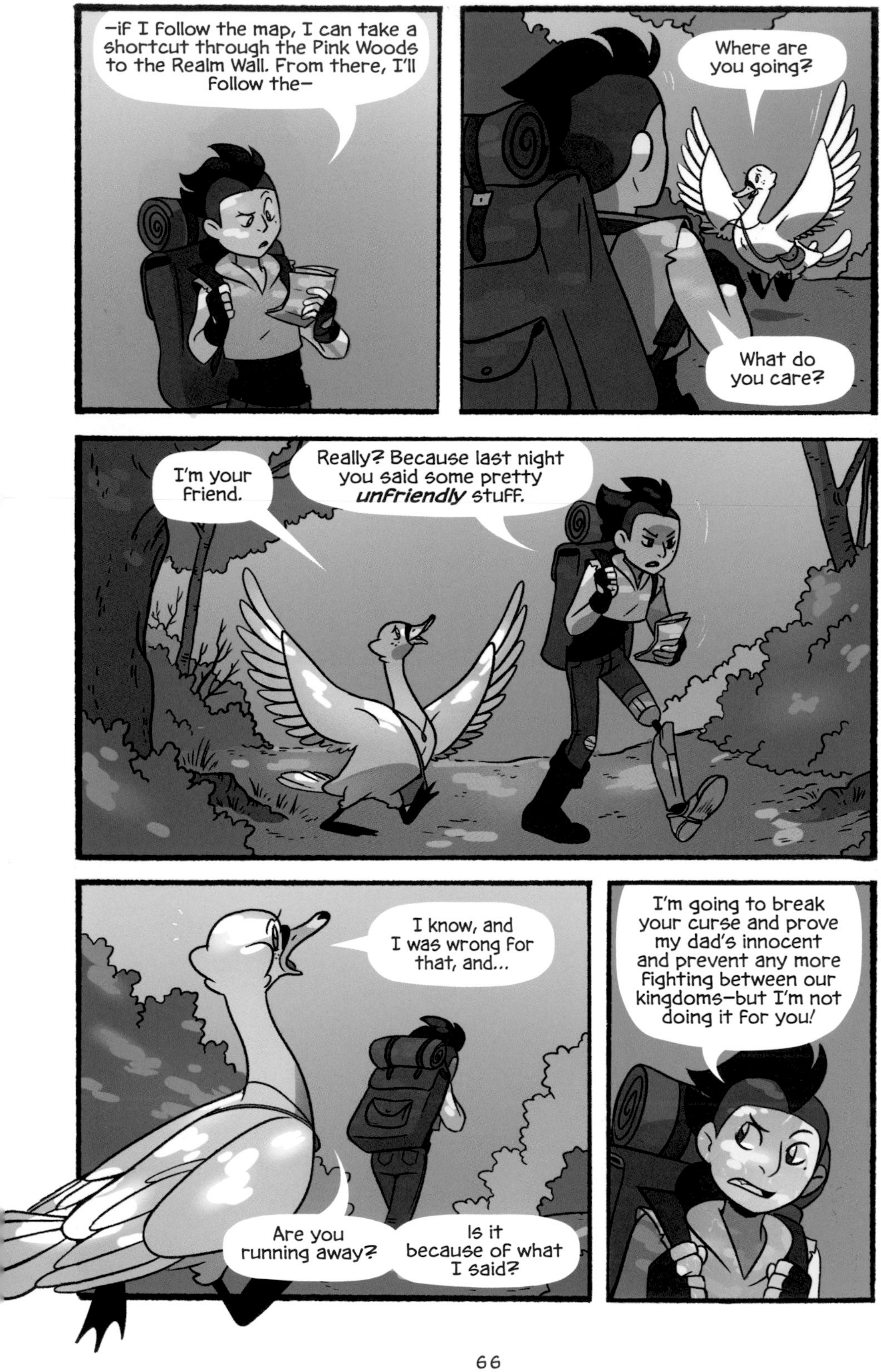
—if I follow the map, I can take a shortcut through the Pink Woods to the Realm Wall. From there, I'll follow the—
Where are you going?
What do you care?
I'm your friend.
Really? Because last night you said some pretty *unfriendly* stuff.
I know, and I was wrong for that, and...
Are you running away?
Is it because of what I said?
I'm going to break your curse and prove my dad's innocent and prevent any more fighting between our kingdoms—but I'm not doing it for you!

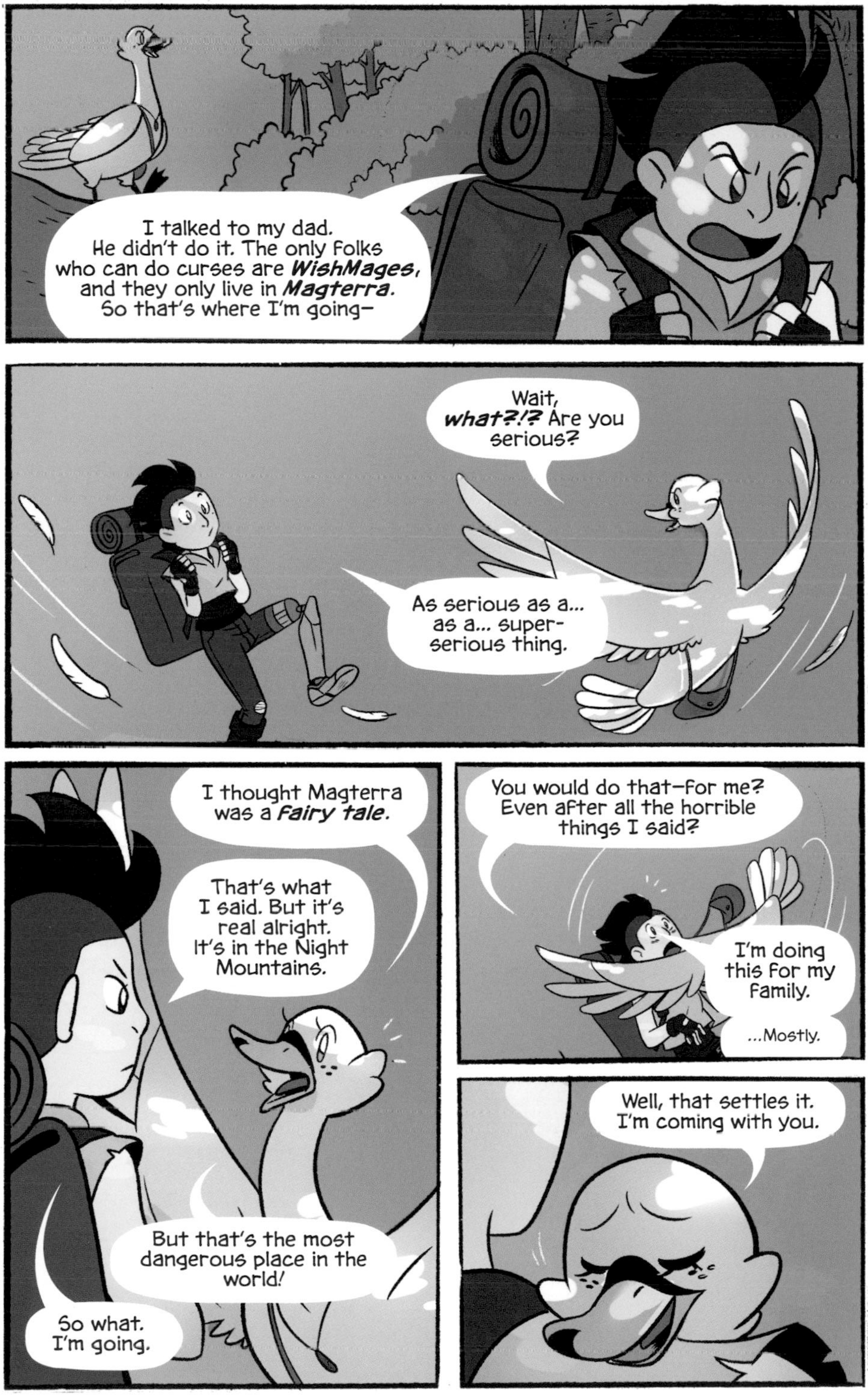
I talked to my dad. He didn't do it. The only folks who can do curses are *WishMages*, and they only live in *Magterra*. So that's where I'm going—
Wait, *what?!?* Are you serious?
As serious as a... as a... super-serious thing.
I thought Magterra was a *fairy tale*.
That's what I said. But it's real alright. It's in the Night Mountains.
But that's the most dangerous place in the world!
So what. I'm going.
You would do that—for me? Even after all the horrible things I said?
I'm doing this for my family.
...Mostly.
Well, that settles it. I'm coming with you.

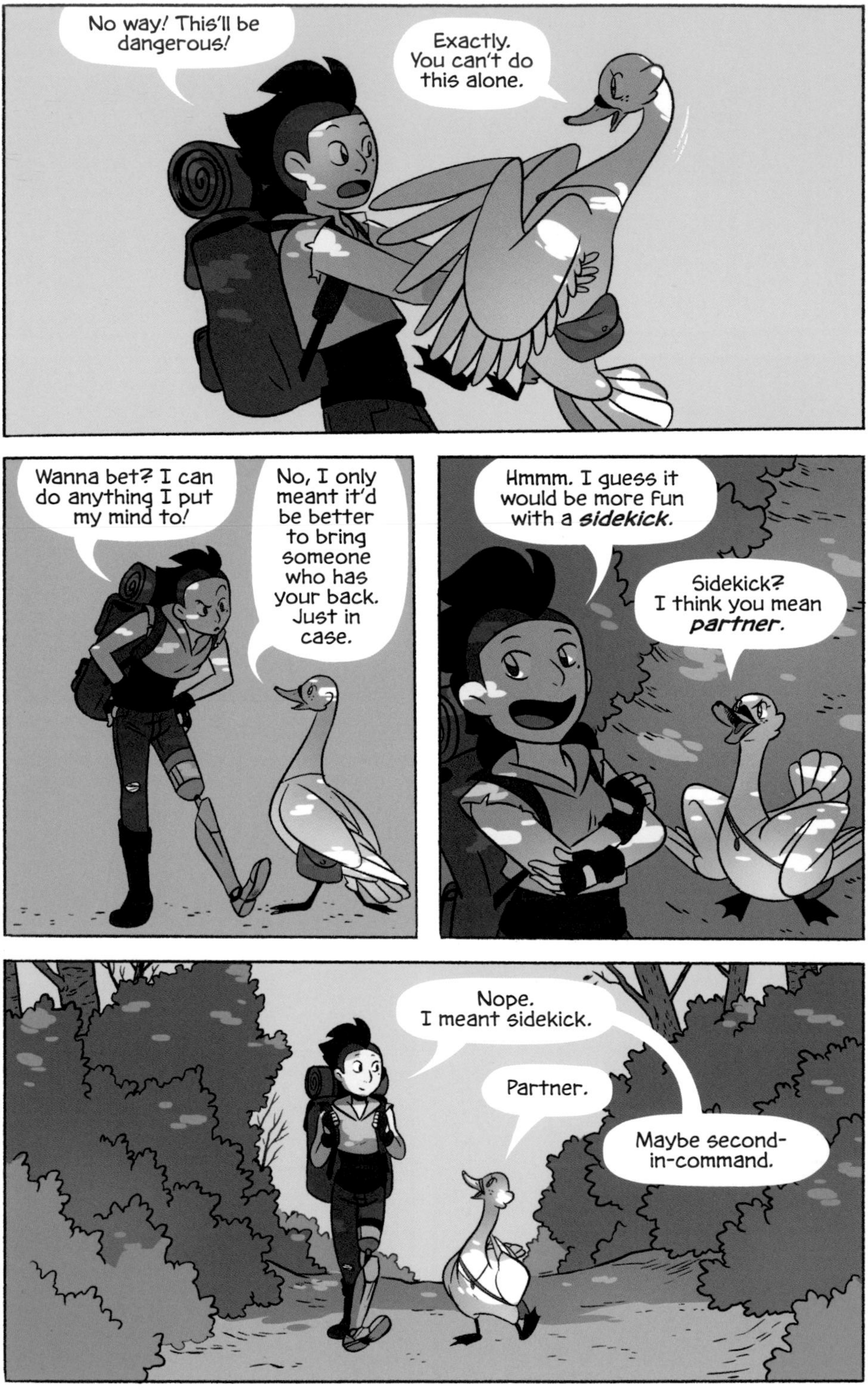
No way! This'll be dangerous!
Exactly. You can't do this alone.
Wanna bet? I can do anything I put my mind to!
No, I only meant it'd be better to bring someone who has your back. Just in case.
Hmmm. I guess it would be more fun with a **sidekick**.
Sidekick? I think you mean **partner**.
Nope. I meant sidekick.
Partner.
Maybe second-in-command.

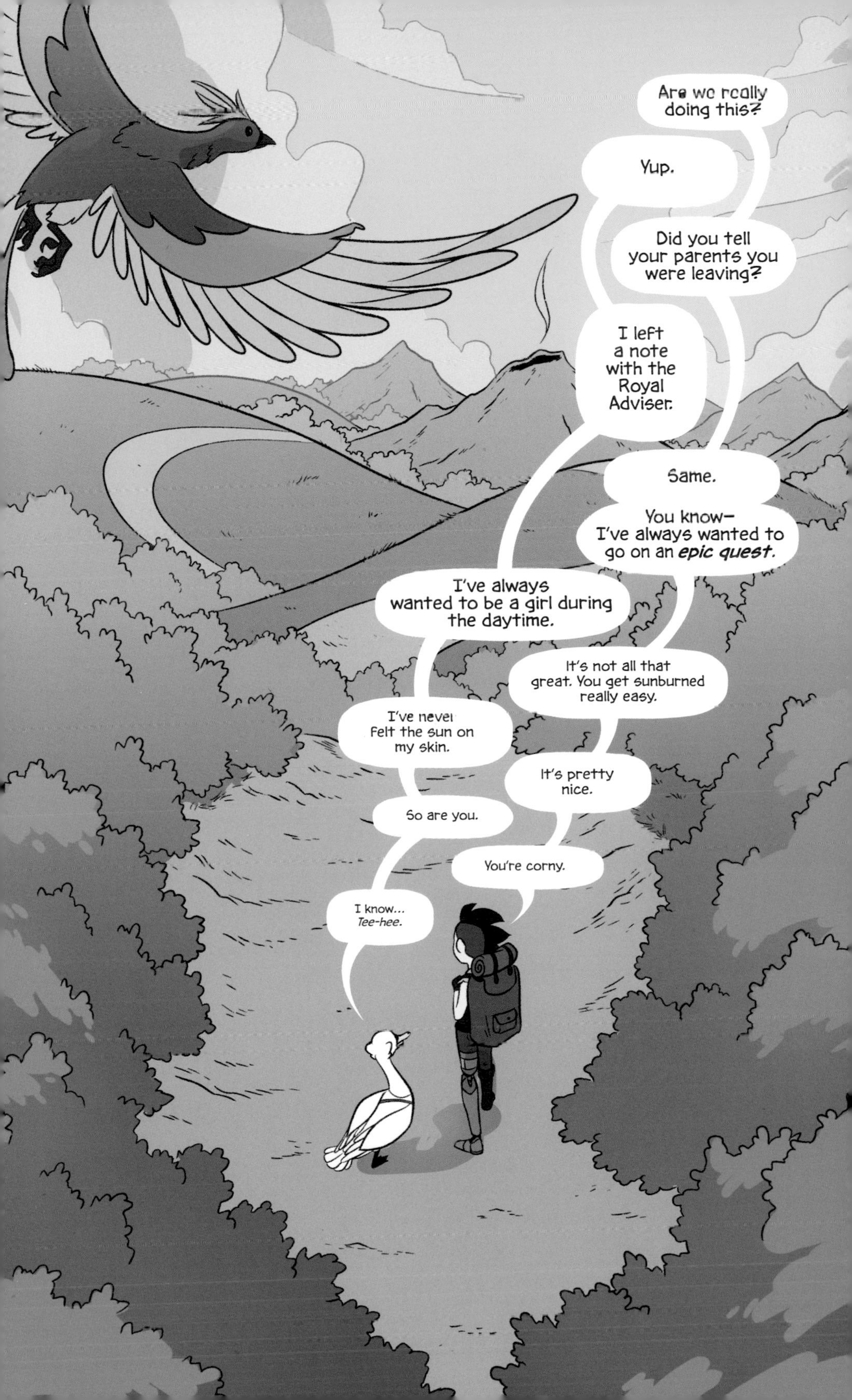
Are we really doing this?
Yup.
Did you tell your parents you were leaving?
I left a note with the Royal Adviser.
Same.
You know— I've always wanted to go on an *epic quest*.
I've always wanted to be a girl during the daytime.
It's not all that great. You get sunburned really easy.
I've never felt the sun on my skin.
It's pretty nice.
So are you.
You're corny.
I know... *Tee-hee.*

PART II

ROTBART

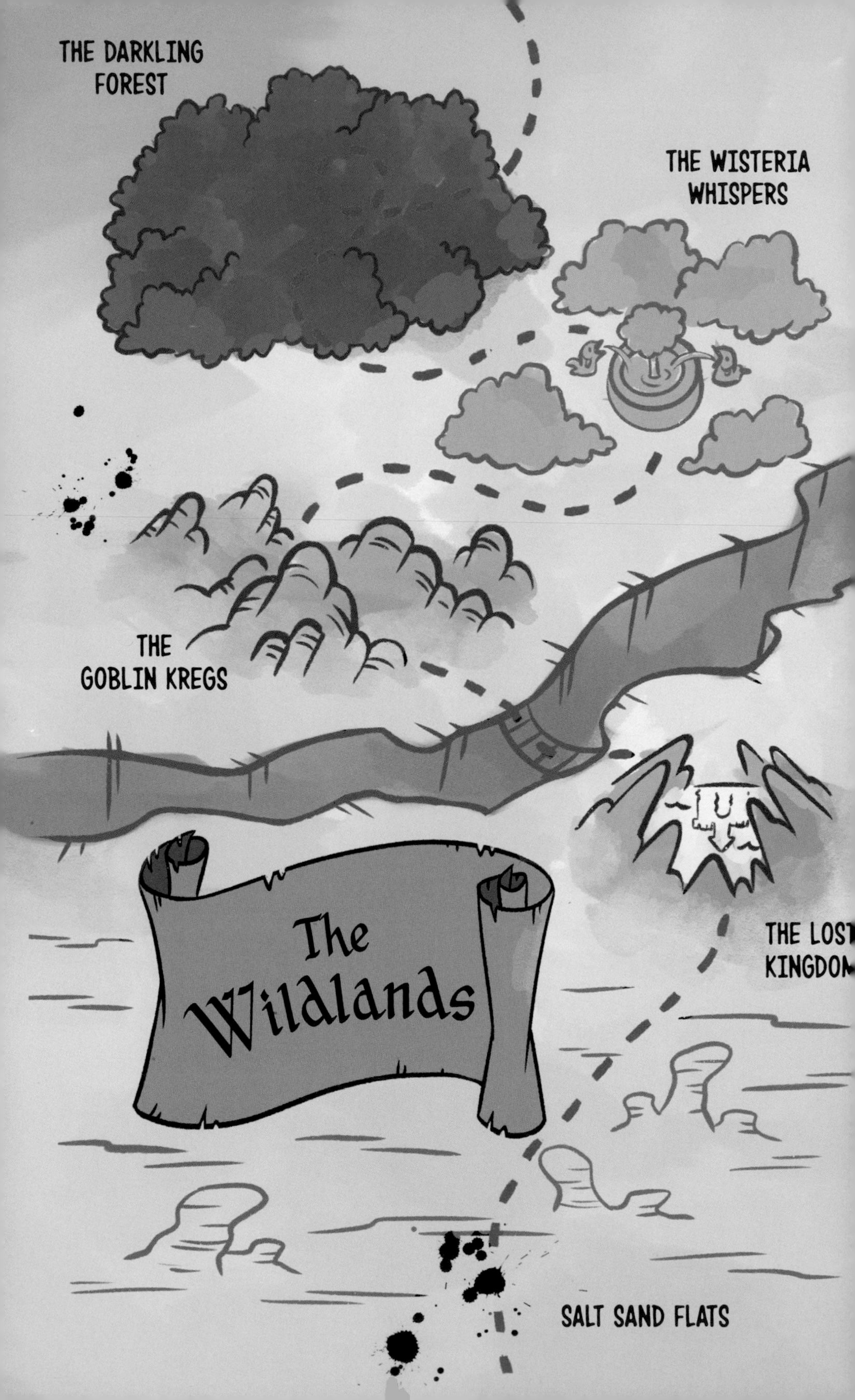
THE DARKLING FOREST
THE WISTERIA WHISPERS
THE GOBLIN KREGS
The Wildlands
THE LOST KINGDOM
SALT SAND FLATS

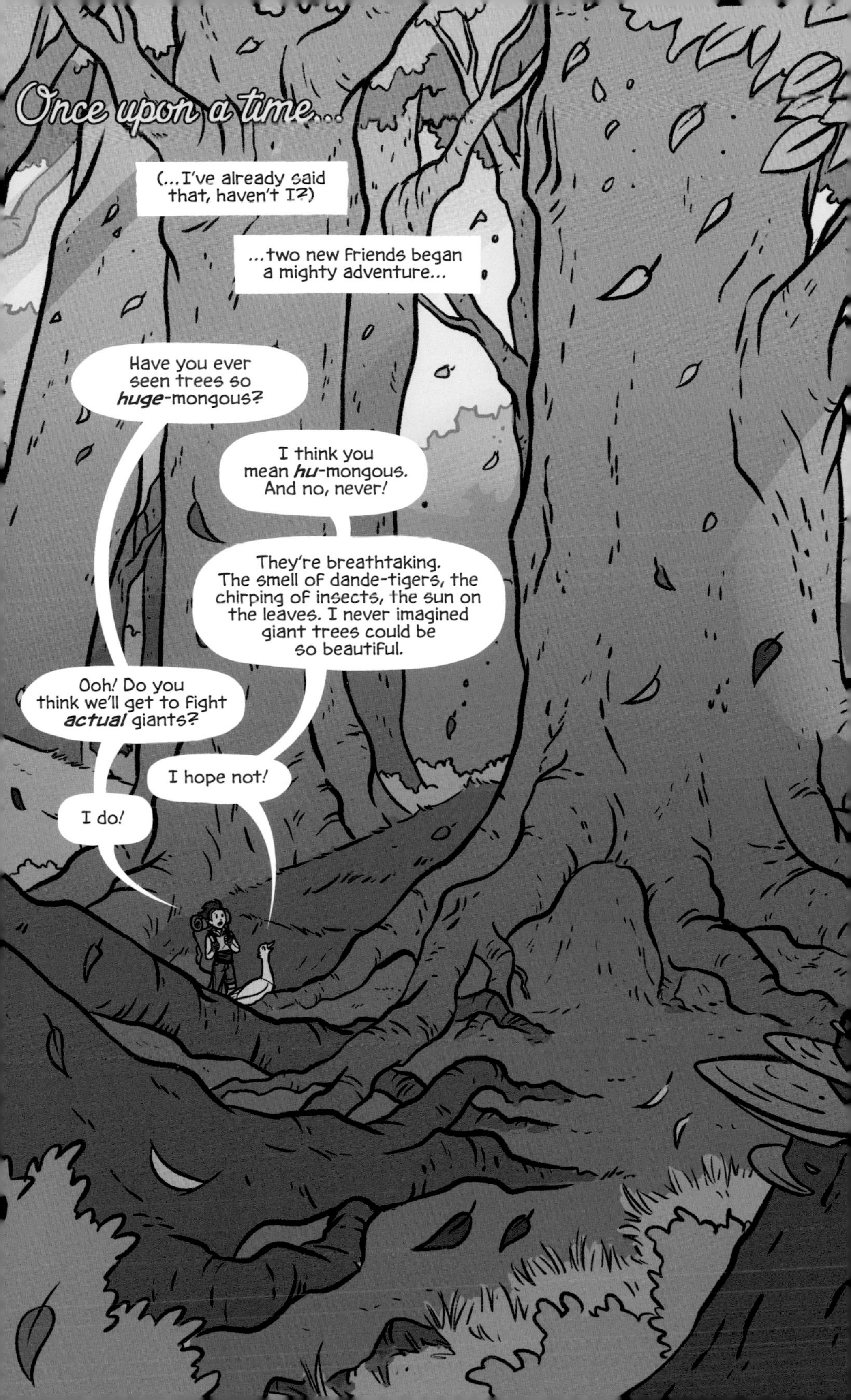
Once upon a time...
(...I've already said that, haven't I?)
...two new friends began a mighty adventure...
Have you ever seen trees so huge-mongous?
I think you mean hu-mongous. And no, never!
They're breathtaking. The smell of dande-tigers, the chirping of insects, the sun on the leaves. I never imagined giant trees could be so beautiful.
Ooh! Do you think we'll get to fight actual giants?
I hope not!
I do!

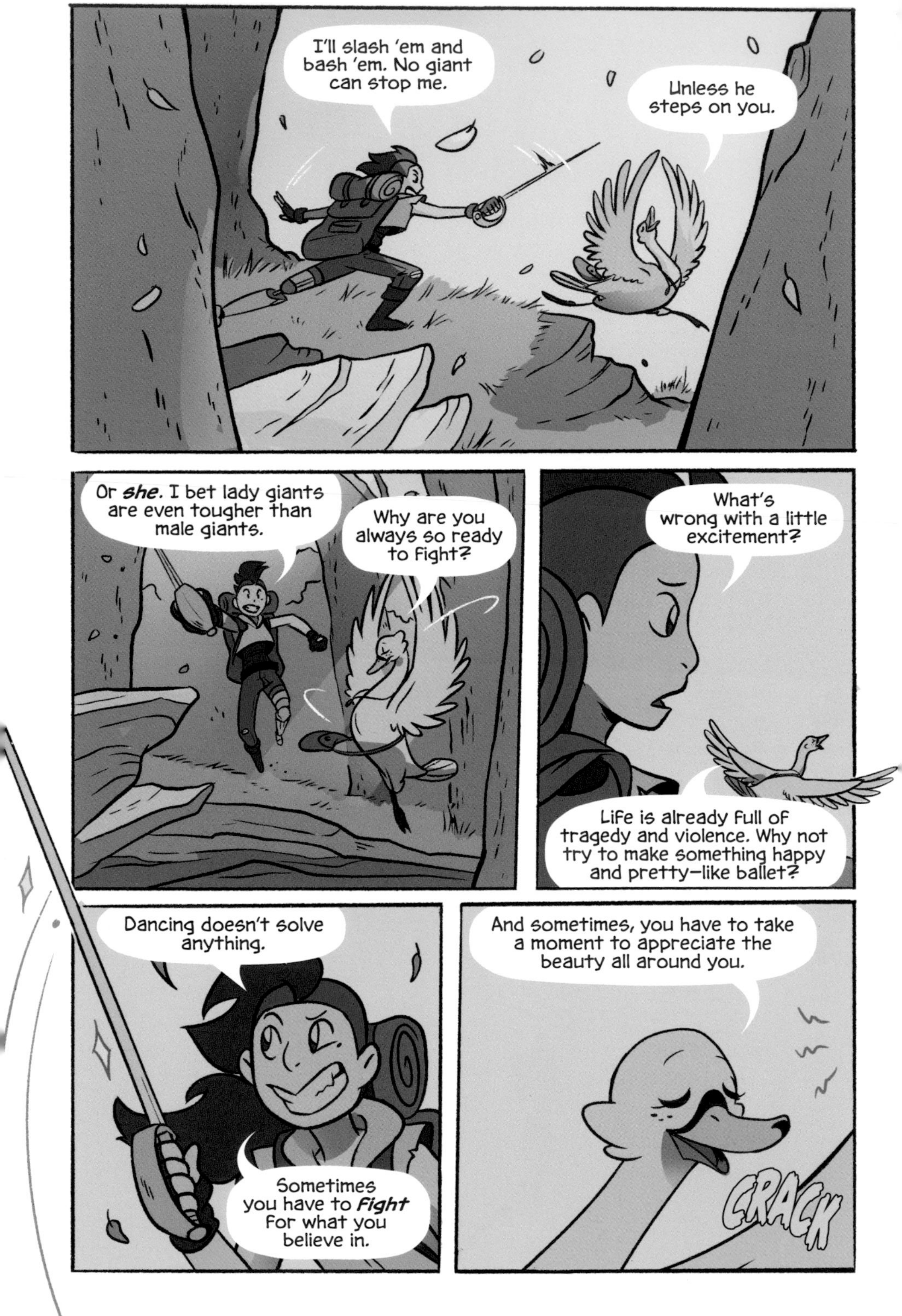
I'll slash 'em and bash 'em. No giant can stop me.
Unless he steps on you.
Or *she*. I bet lady giants are even tougher than male giants.
Why are you always so ready to fight?
What's wrong with a little excitement?
Life is already full of tragedy and violence. Why not try to make something happy and pretty—like ballet?
Dancing doesn't solve anything.
Sometimes you have to ***fight*** for what you believe in.
And sometimes, you have to take a moment to appreciate the beauty all around you.
CRACK

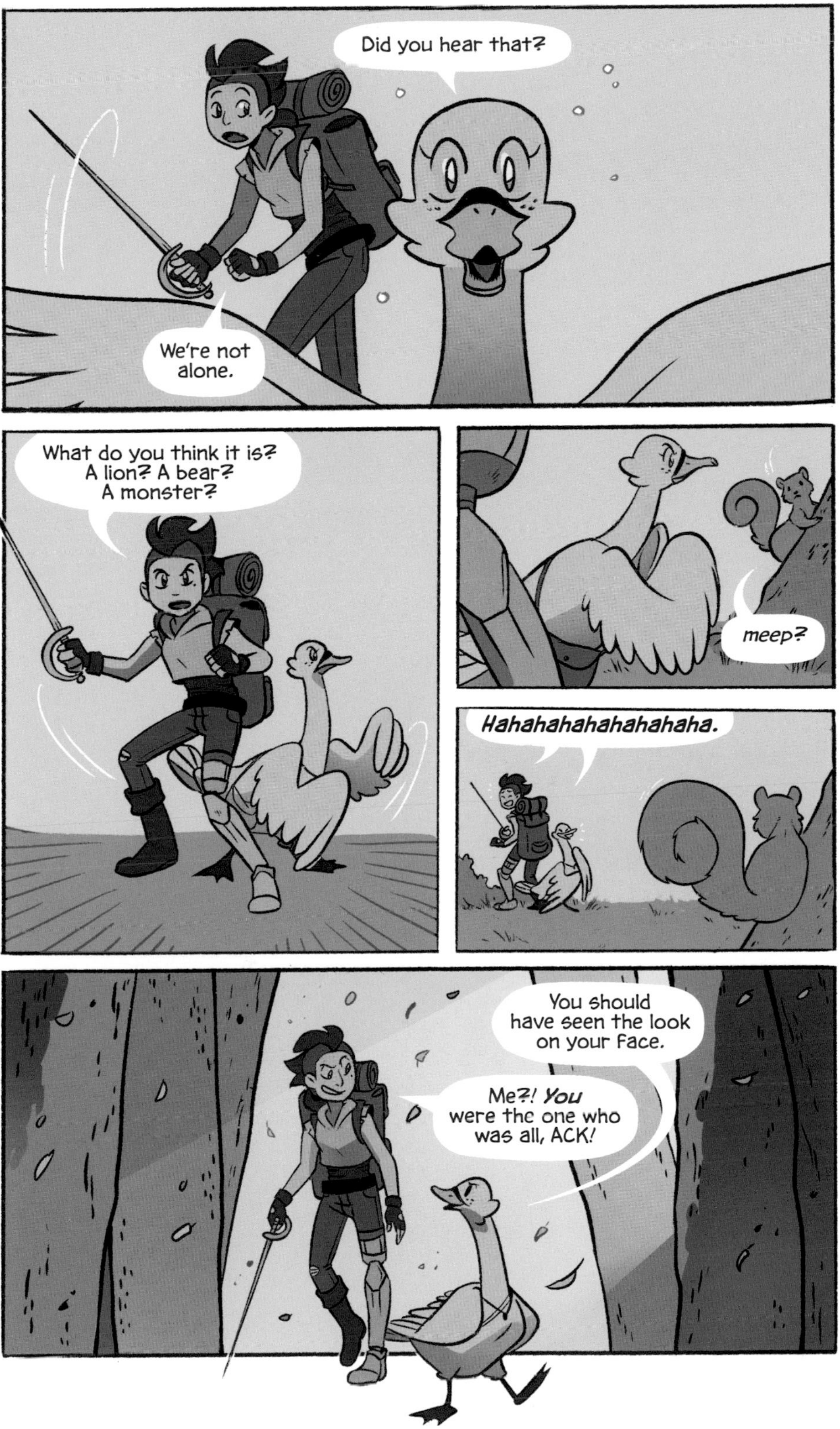
Did you hear that?
We're not alone.
What do you think it is? A lion? A bear? A monster?
meep?
Hahahahahahahahaha.
You should have seen the look on your face.
Me?! You were the one who was all, ACK!

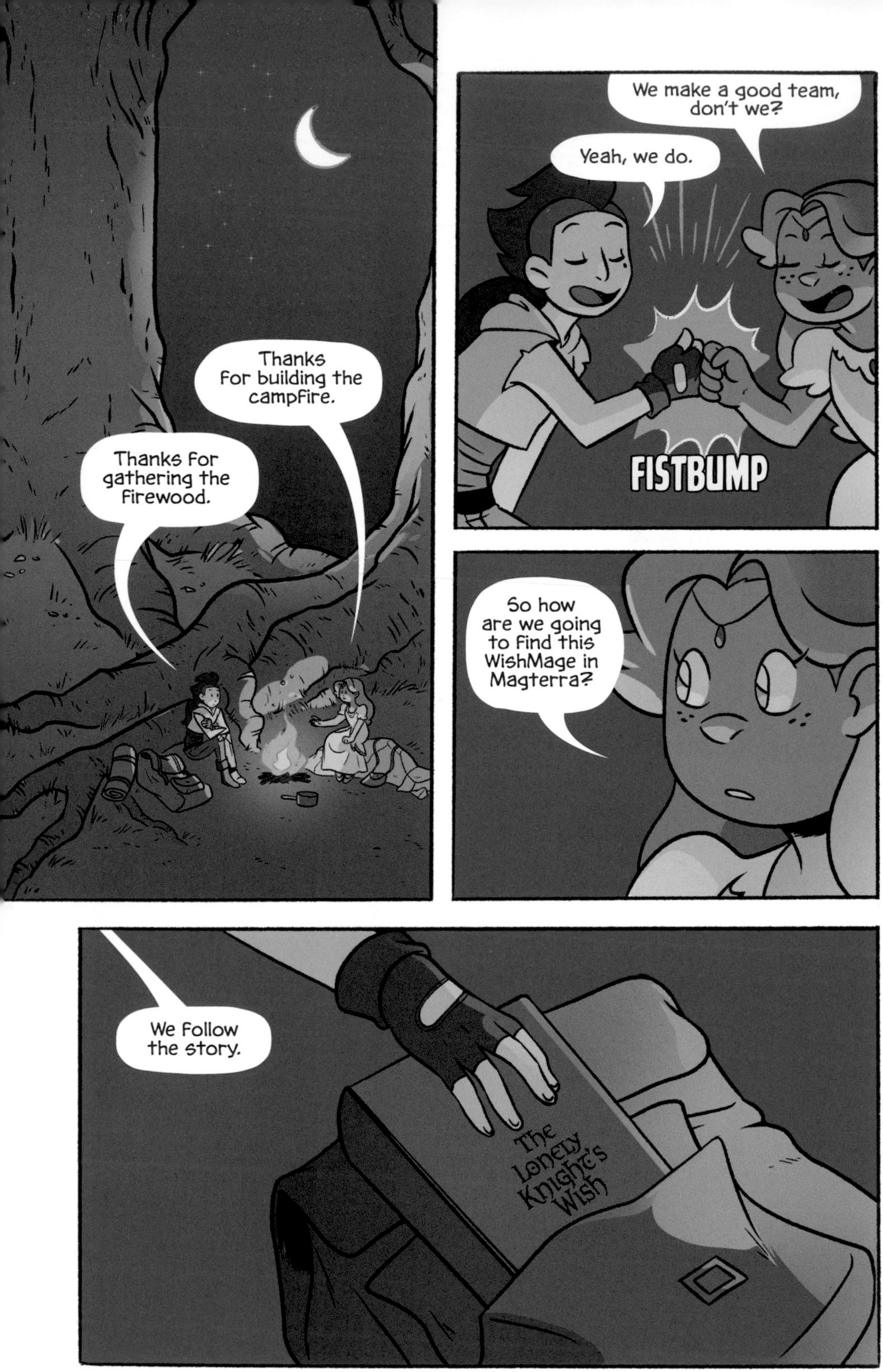
Thanks for gathering the firewood.
Thanks for building the campfire.
We make a good team, don't we?
Yeah, we do.
FISTBUMP
So how are we going to find this WishMage in Magterra?
We follow the story.
The Lonely Knight's Wish

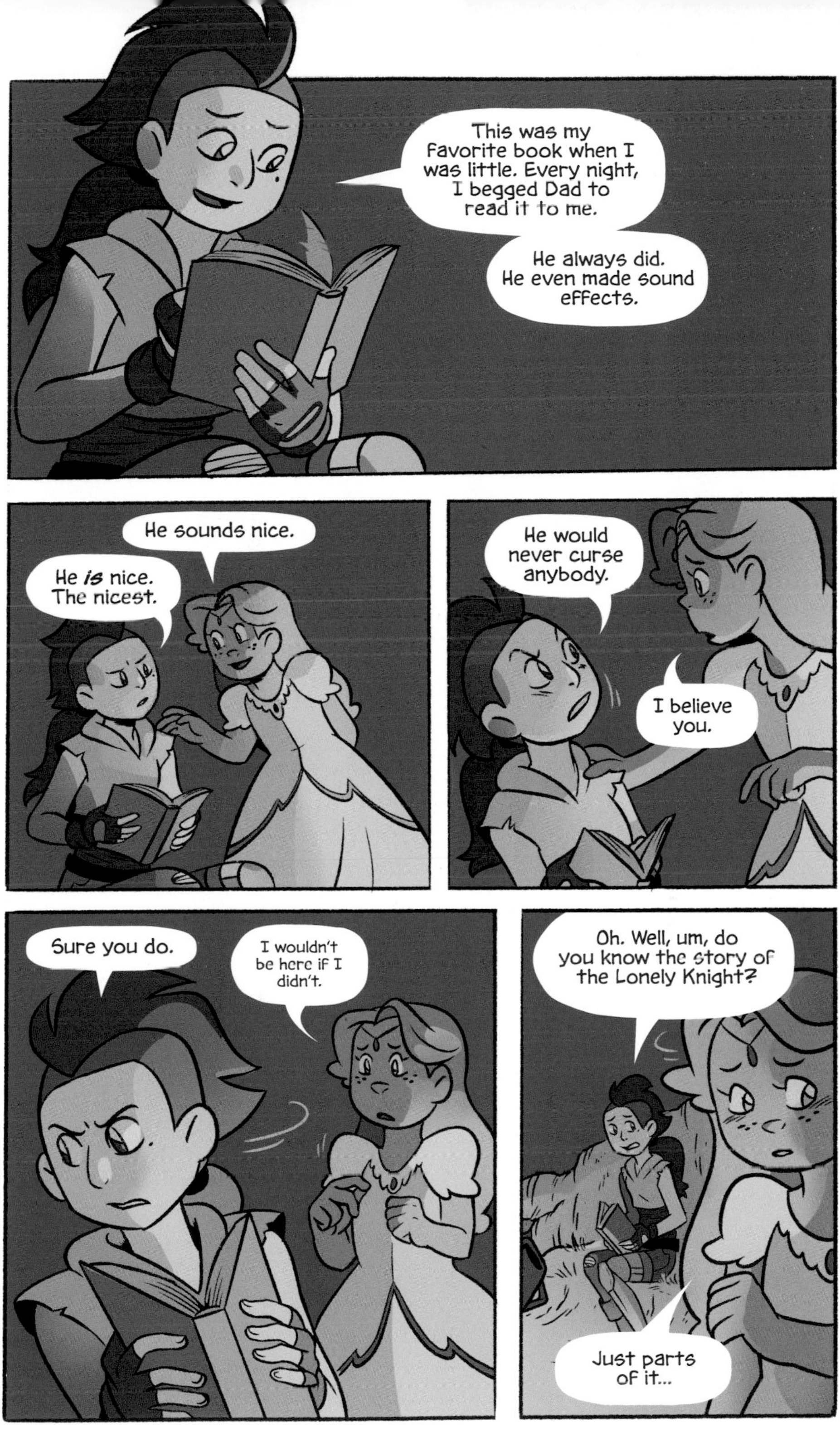
This was my favorite book when I was little. Every night, I begged Dad to read it to me.
He always did. He even made sound effects.
He sounds nice.
He *is* nice. The nicest.
He would never curse anybody.
I believe you.
Sure you do.
I wouldn't be here if I didn't.
Oh. Well, um, do you know the story of the Lonely Knight?
Just parts of it...

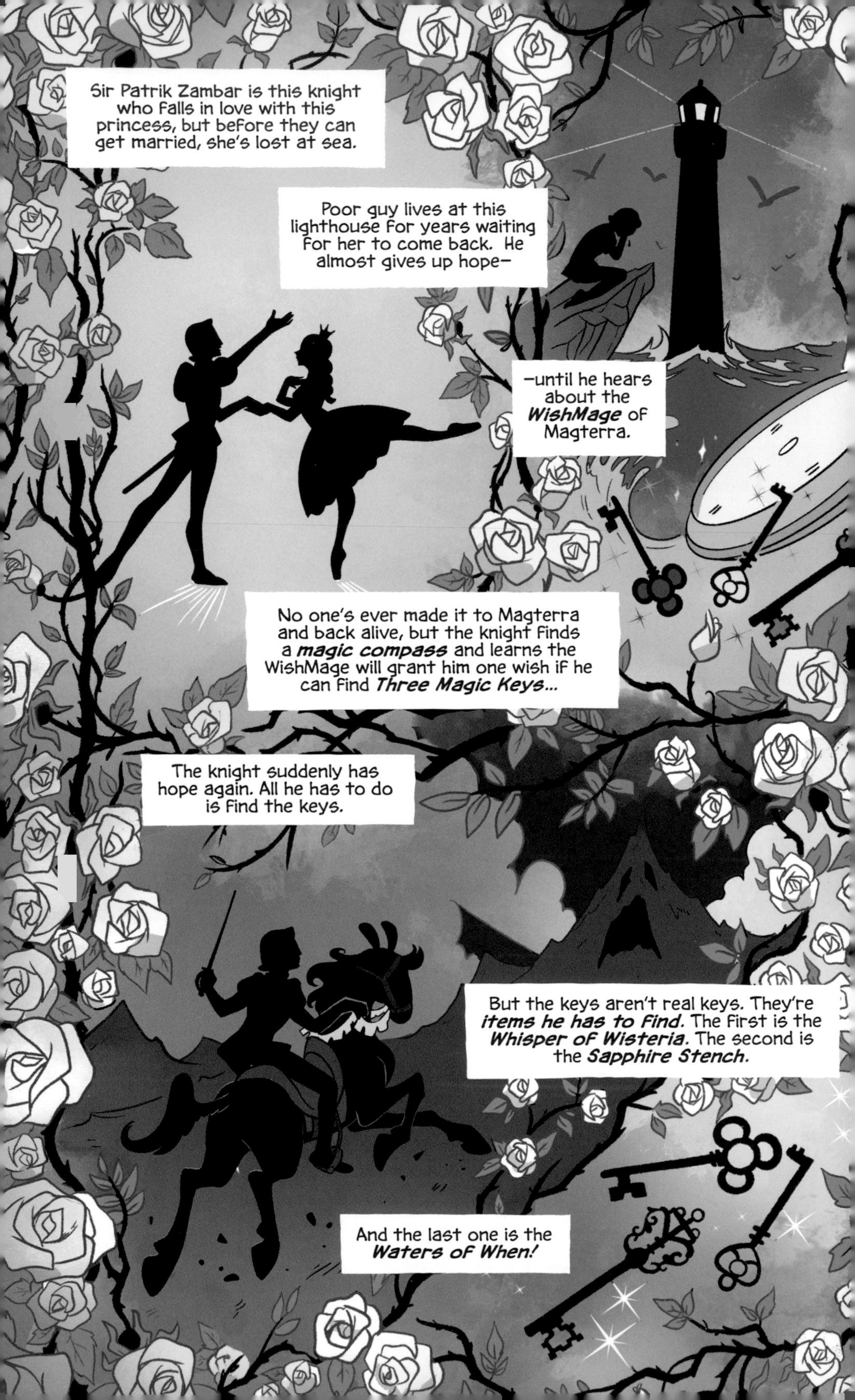

Sir Patrik Zambar is this knight who falls in love with this princess, but before they can get married, she's lost at sea.
Poor guy lives at this lighthouse for years waiting for her to come back. He almost gives up hope—
—until he hears about the ***WishMage*** of Magterra.
No one's ever made it to Magterra and back alive, but the knight finds a ***magic compass*** and learns the WishMage will grant him one wish if he can find ***Three Magic Keys...***
The knight suddenly has hope again. All he has to do is find the keys.
But the keys aren't real keys. They're ***items he has to find***. The first is the ***Whisper of Wisteria***. The second is the ***Sapphire Stench***.
And the last one is the ***Waters of When!***

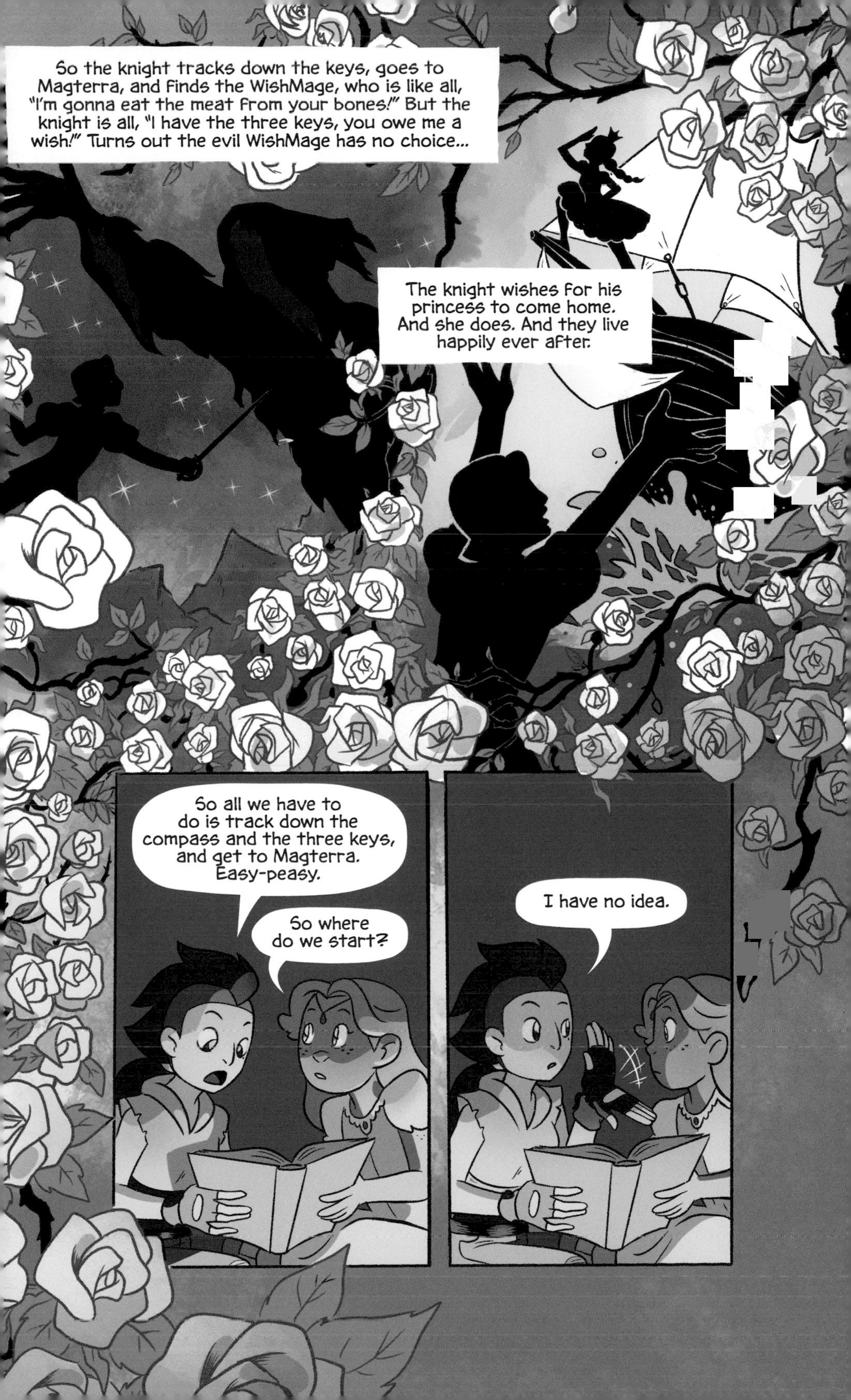
So the knight tracks down the keys, goes to Magterra, and finds the WishMage, who is like all, "I'm gonna eat the meat from your bones!" But the knight is all, "I have the three keys, you owe me a wish!" Turns out the evil WishMage has no choice...
The knight wishes for his princess to come home. And she does. And they live happily ever after.
So all we have to do is track down the compass and the three keys, and get to Magterra. Easy-peasy.
So where do we start?
I have no idea.

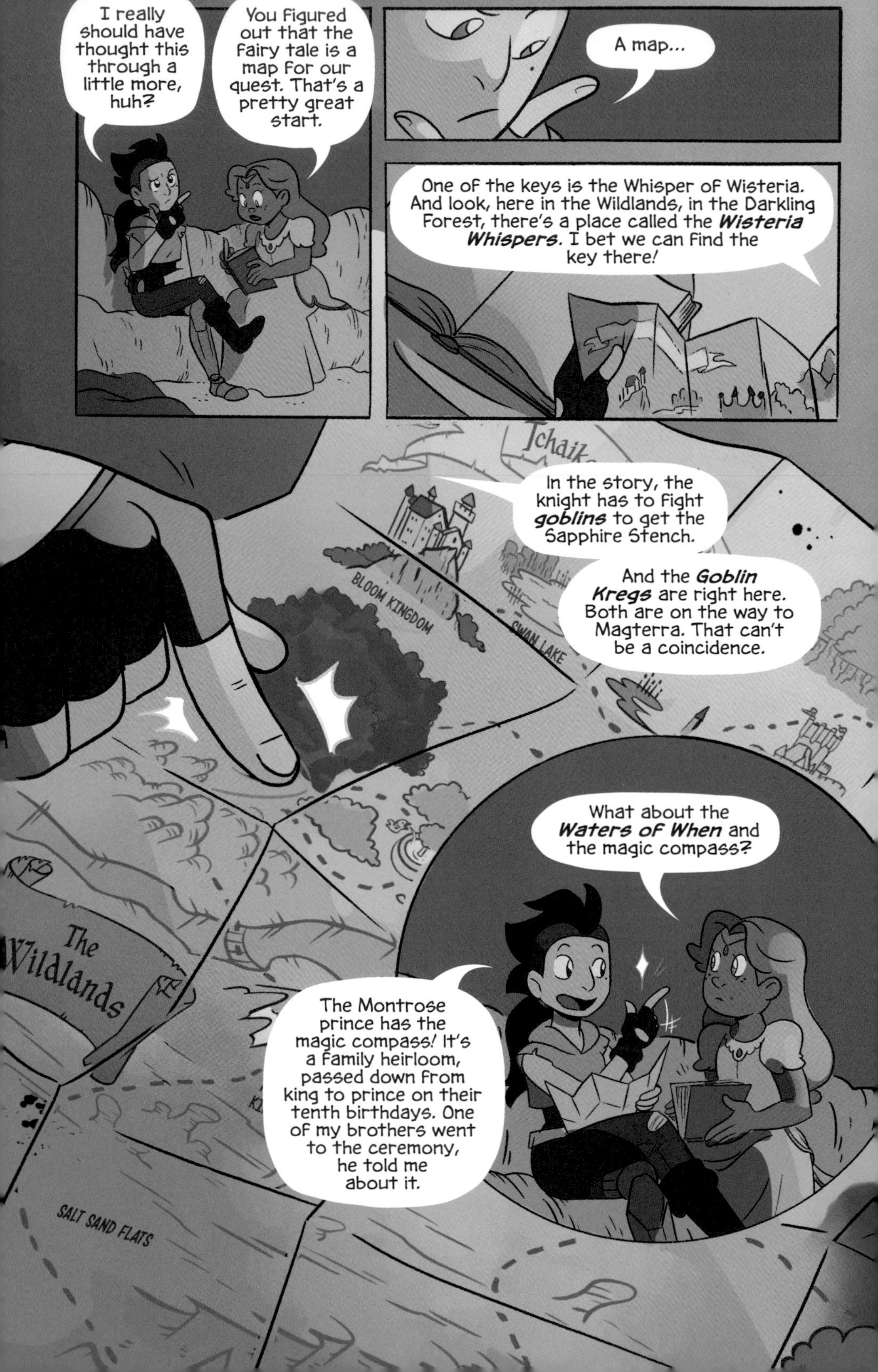
I really should have thought this through a little more, huh?
You figured out that the fairy tale is a map for our quest. That's a pretty great start.
A map...
One of the keys is the Whisper of Wisteria. And look, here in the Wildlands, in the Darkling Forest, there's a place called the ***Wisteria Whispers.*** I bet we can find the key there!
In the story, the knight has to fight ***goblins*** to get the Sapphire Stench.
And the ***Goblin Kregs*** are right here. Both are on the way to Magterra. That can't be a coincidence.
BLOOM KINGDOM
SWAN LAKE
What about the ***Waters of When*** and the magic compass?
The Wildlands
The Montrose prince has the magic compass! It's a family heirloom, passed down from king to prince on their tenth birthdays. One of my brothers went to the ceremony, he told me about it.
SALT SAND FLATS

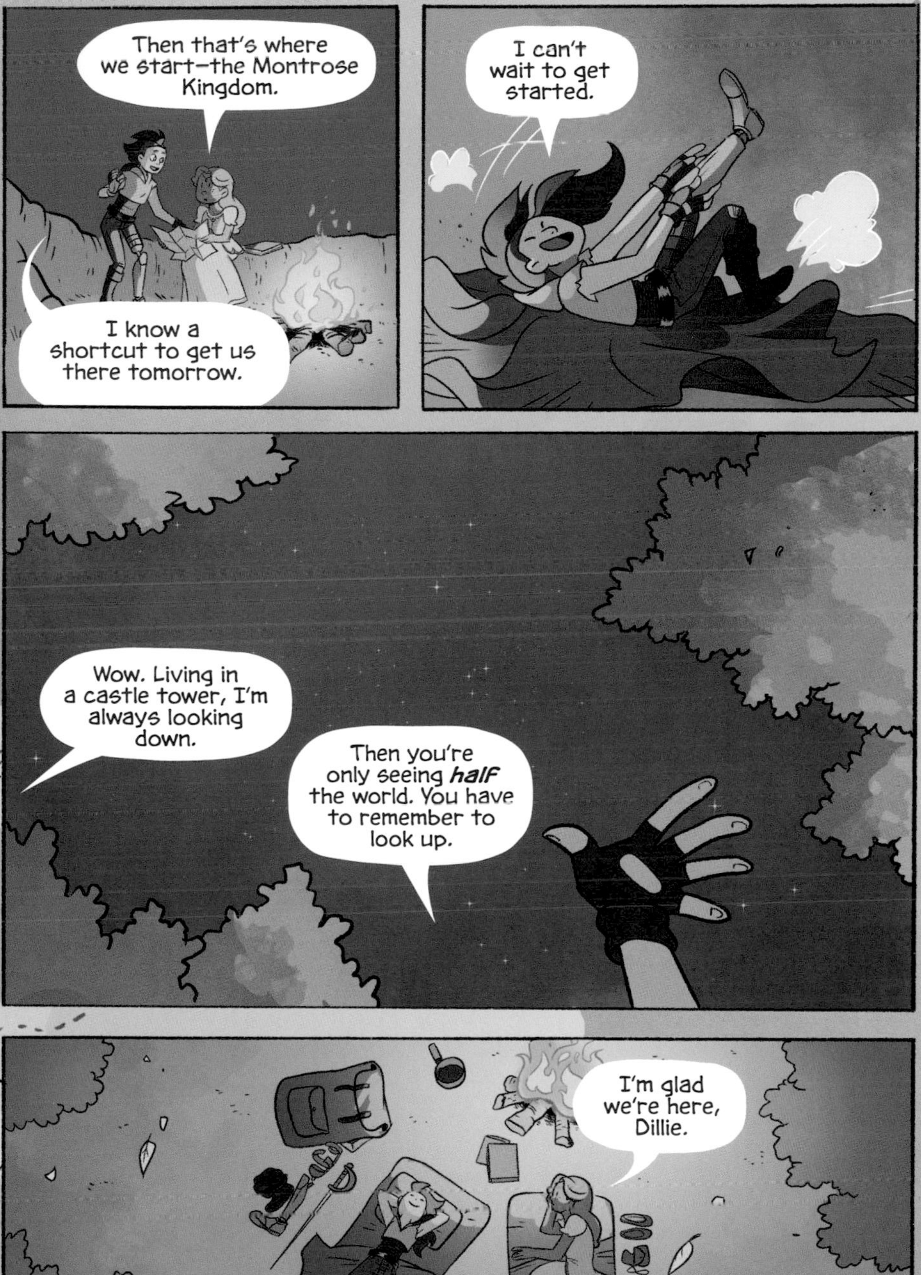
Then that's where we start—the Montrose Kingdom.
I know a shortcut to get us there tomorrow.
I can't wait to get started.
Wow. Living in a castle tower, I'm always looking down.
Then you're only seeing ***half*** the world. You have to remember to look up.
I'm glad we're here, Dillie.
Me too, O. Me too.

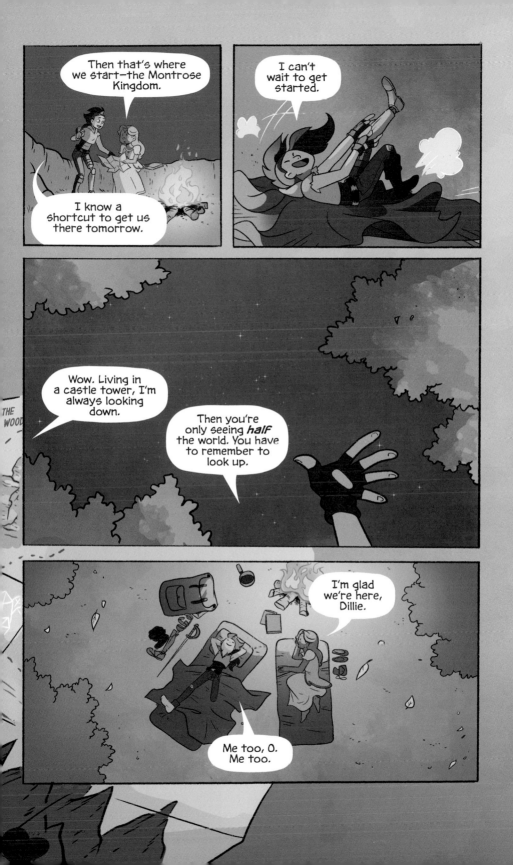

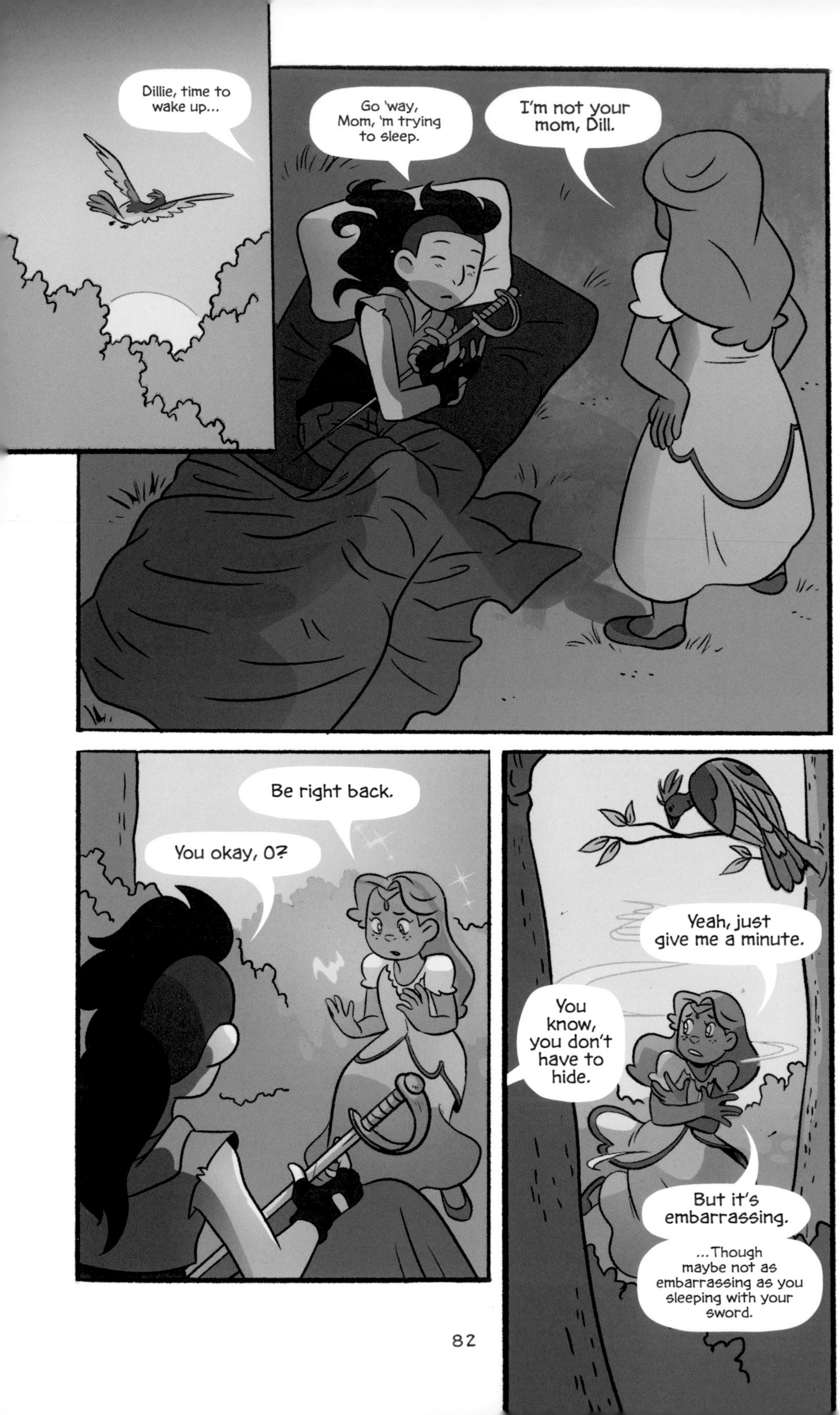
Dillie, time to wake up...
Go 'way, Mom, 'm trying to sleep.
I'm not your mom, Dill.
Be right back.
You okay, O?
Yeah, just give me a minute.
You know, you don't have to hide.
But it's embarrassing.
...Though maybe not as embarrassing as you sleeping with your sword.

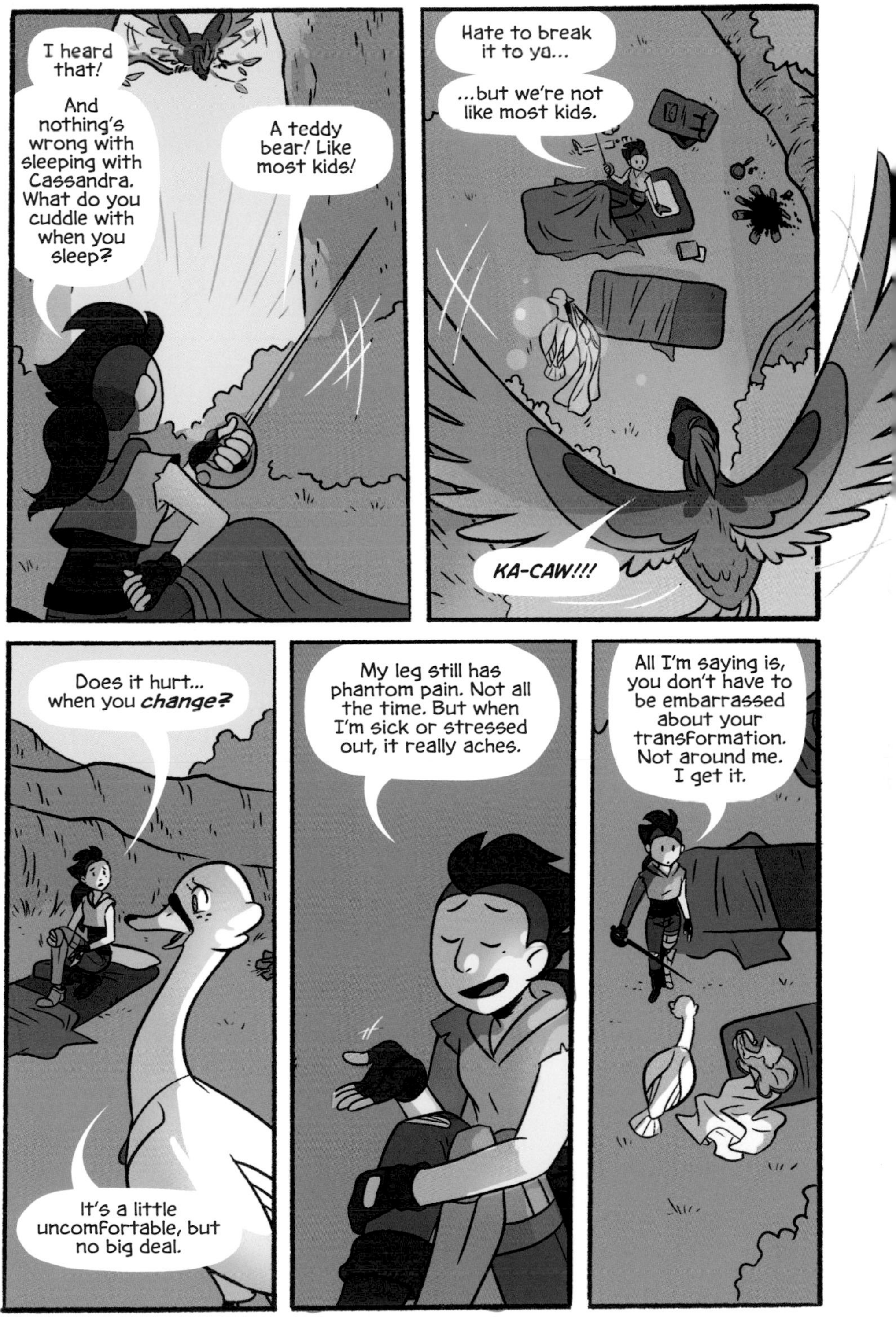
I heard that!
And nothing's wrong with sleeping with Cassandra. What do you cuddle with when you sleep?
A teddy bear! Like most kids!
Hate to break it to ya...
...but we're not like most kids.
KA-CAW!!!
Does it hurt... when you *change?*
It's a little uncomfortable, but no big deal.
My leg still has phantom pain. Not all the time. But when I'm sick or stressed out, it really aches.
All I'm saying is, you don't have to be embarrassed about your transformation. Not around me. I get it.

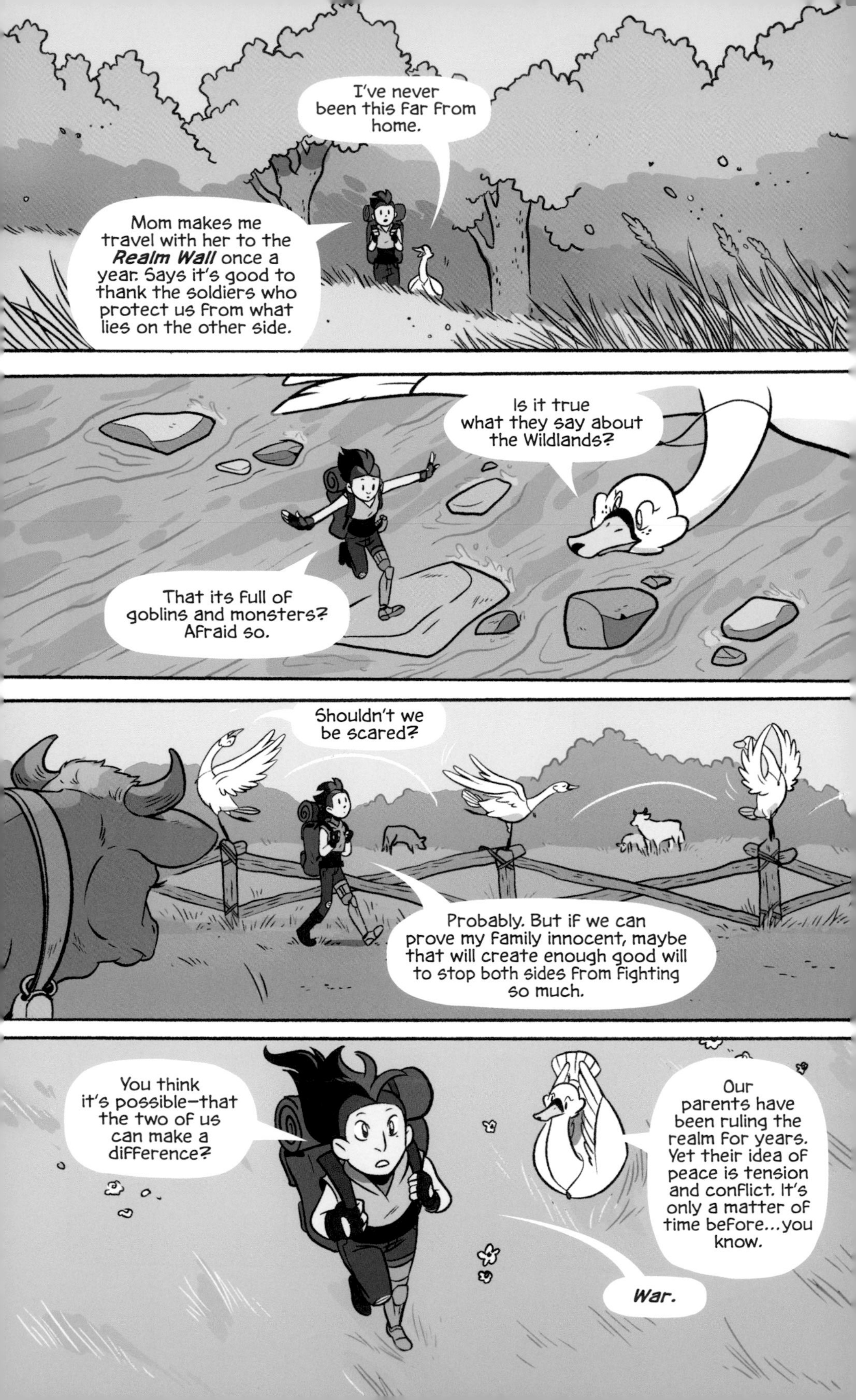
I've never been this far from home.
Mom makes me travel with her to the *Realm Wall* once a year. Says it's good to thank the soldiers who protect us from what lies on the other side.
Is it true what they say about the Wildlands?
That its full of goblins and monsters? Afraid so.
Shouldn't we be scared?
Probably. But if we can prove my family innocent, maybe that will create enough good will to stop both sides from fighting so much.
You think it's possible—that the two of us can make a difference?
Our parents have been ruling the realm for years. Yet their idea of peace is tension and conflict. It's only a matter of time before...you know.
War.

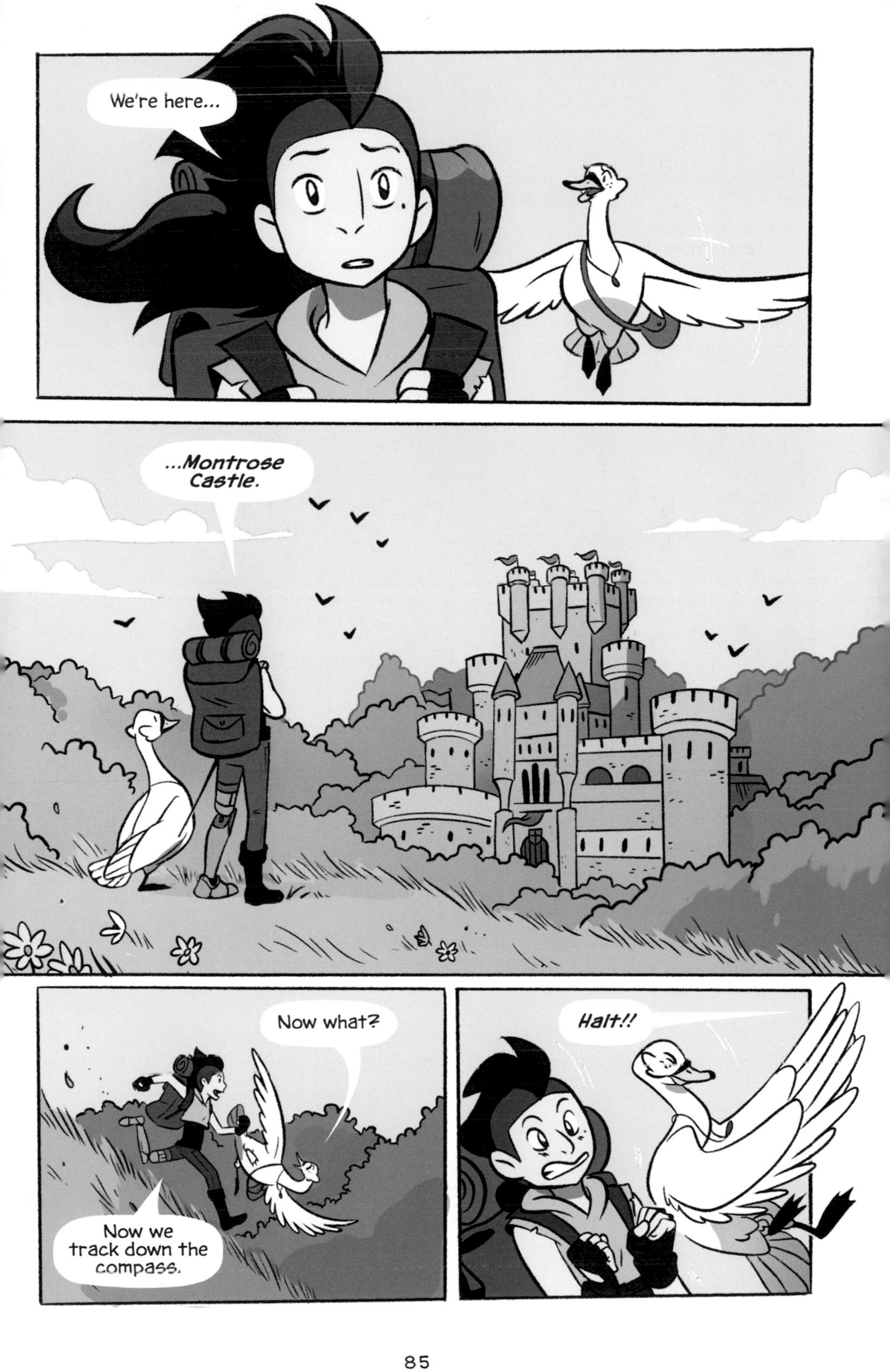
We're here...
...Montrose Castle.
Now what?
Now we track down the compass.
Halt!!

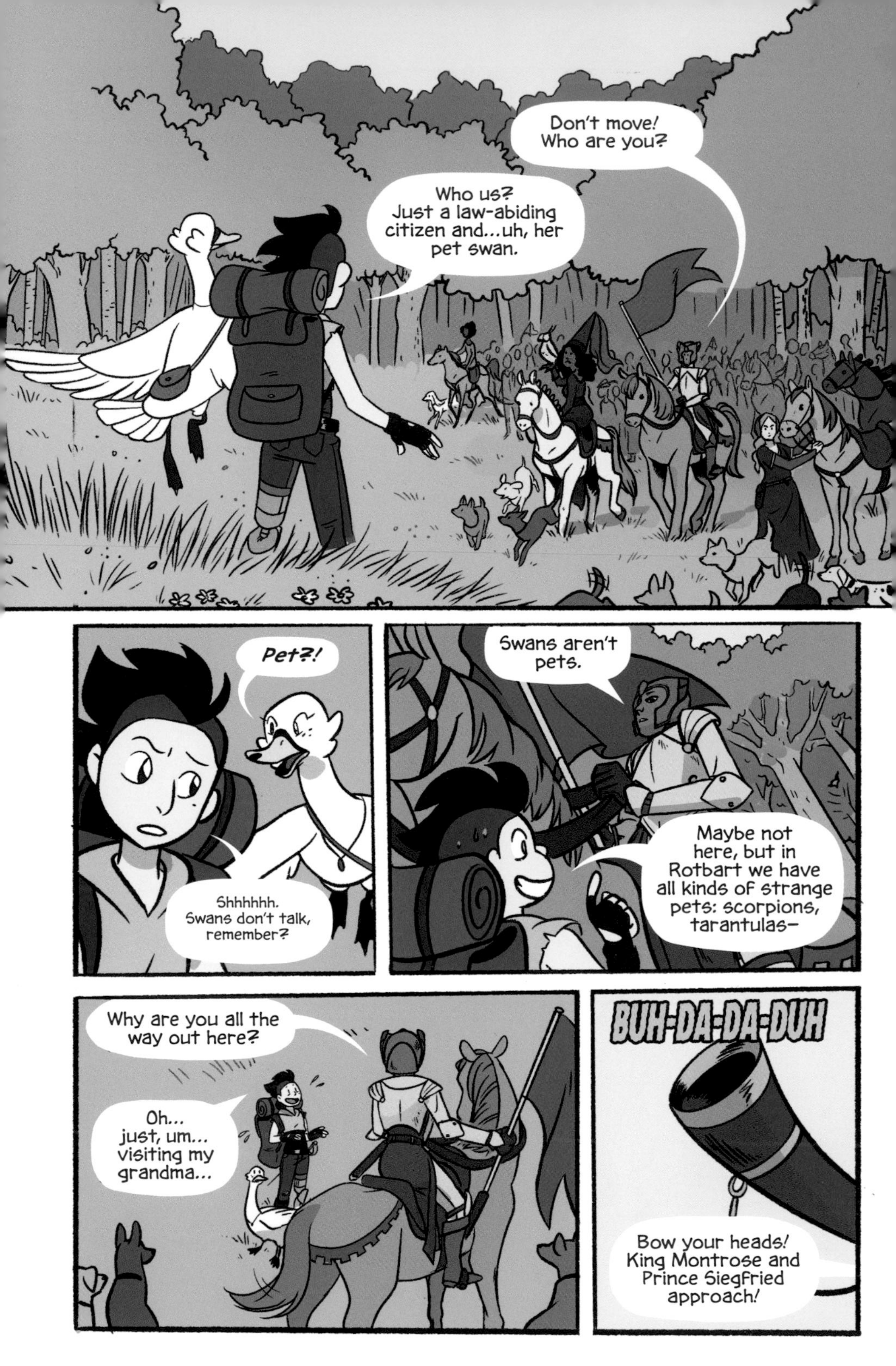
Don't move! Who are you?
Who us? Just a law-abiding citizen and...uh, her pet swan.
Pet?!
Shhhhhh. Swans don't talk, remember?
Swans aren't pets.
Maybe not here, but in Rotbart we have all kinds of strange pets: scorpions, tarantulas—
Why are you all the way out here?
Oh... just, um... visiting my grandma...
BUH-DA-DA-DUH
Bow your heads! King Montrose and Prince Siegfried approach!

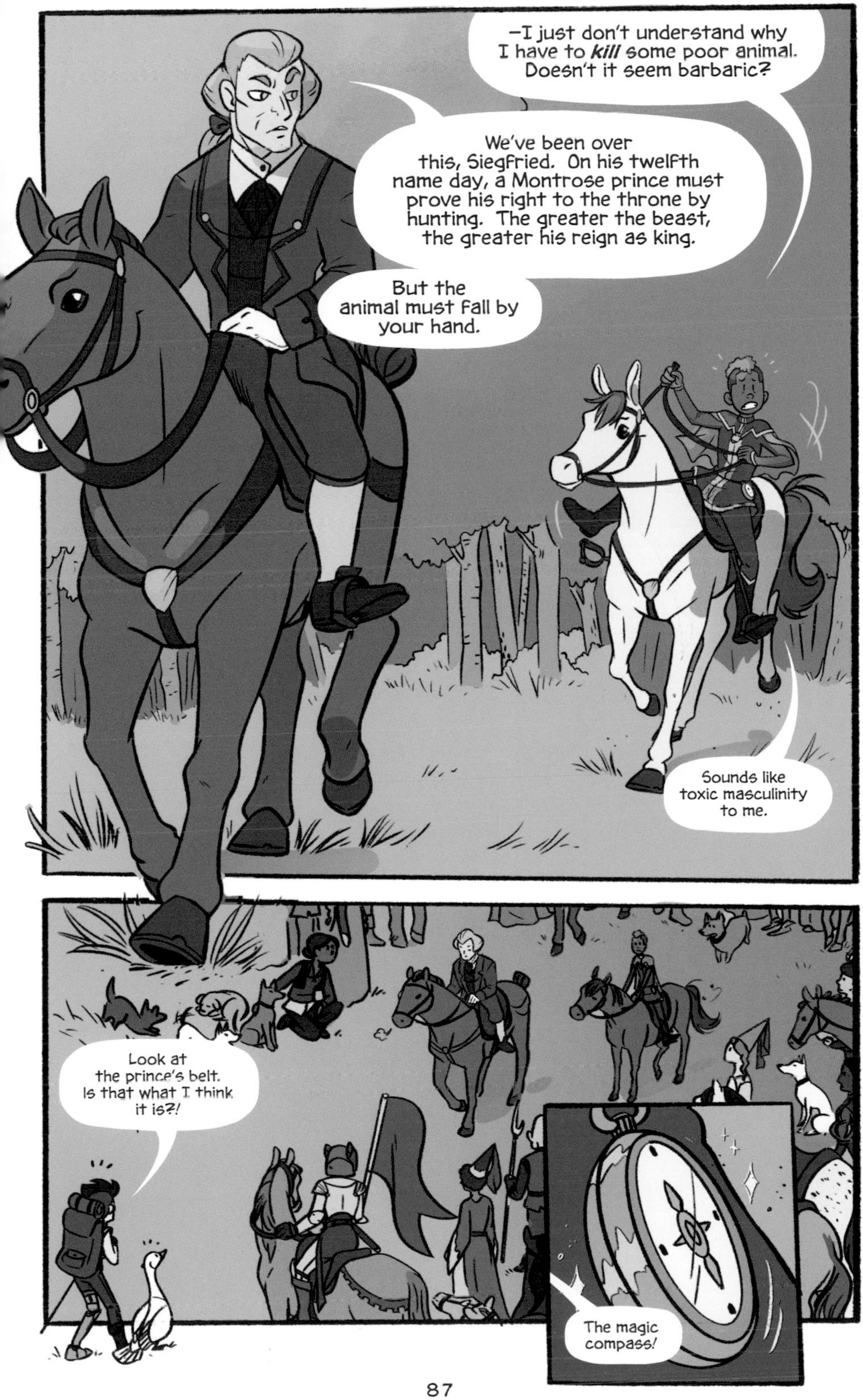
—I just don't understand why I have to *kill* some poor animal. Doesn't it seem barbaric?
We've been over this, Siegfried. On his twelfth name day, a Montrose prince must prove his right to the throne by hunting. The greater the beast, the greater his reign as king.
But the animal must fall by your hand.
Sounds like toxic masculinity to me.
Look at the prince's belt. Is that what I think it is?!
The magic compass!

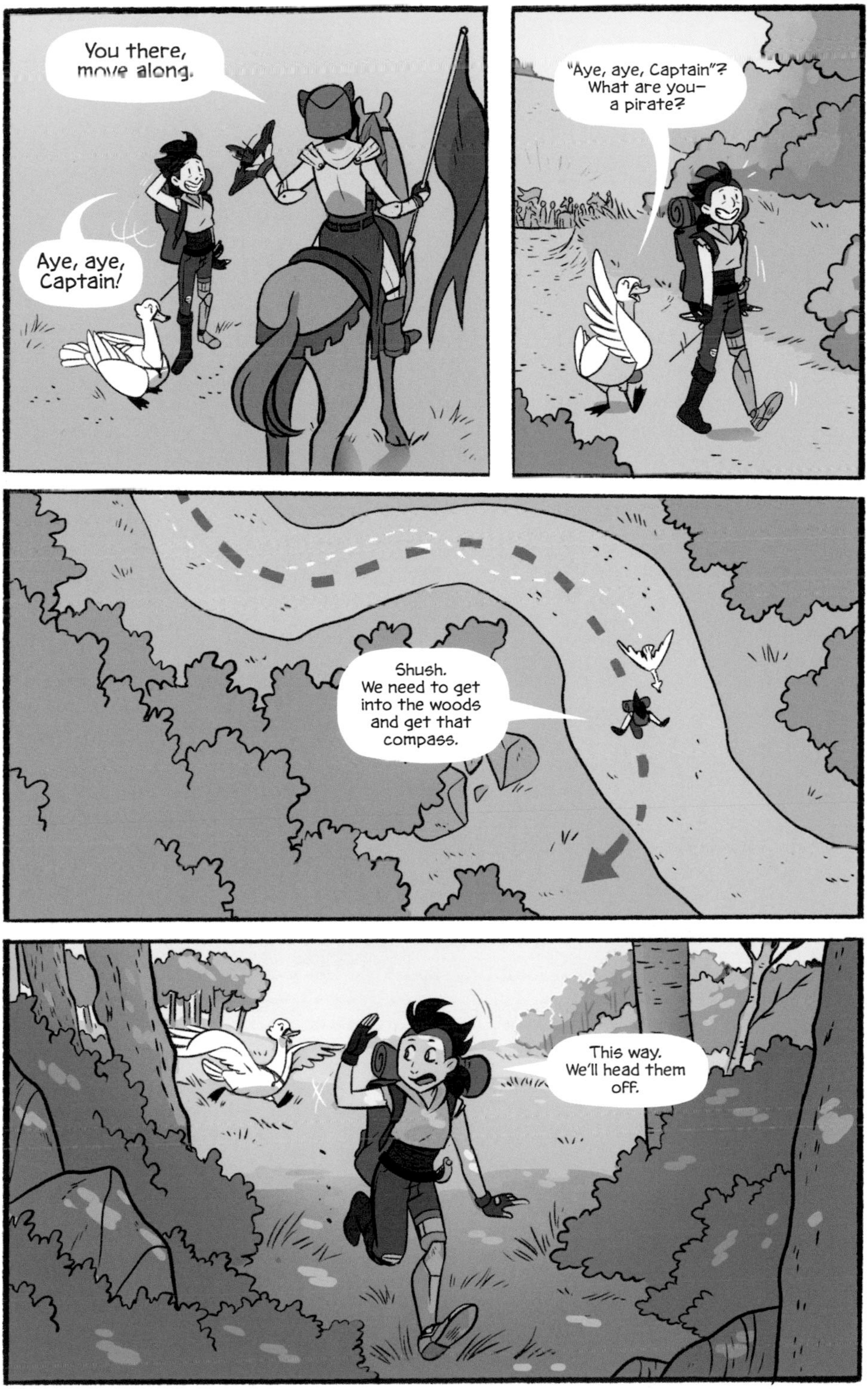
You there, move along.
Aye, aye, Captain!
"Aye, aye, Captain"? What are you— a pirate?
Shush. We need to get into the woods and get that compass.
This way. We'll head them off.

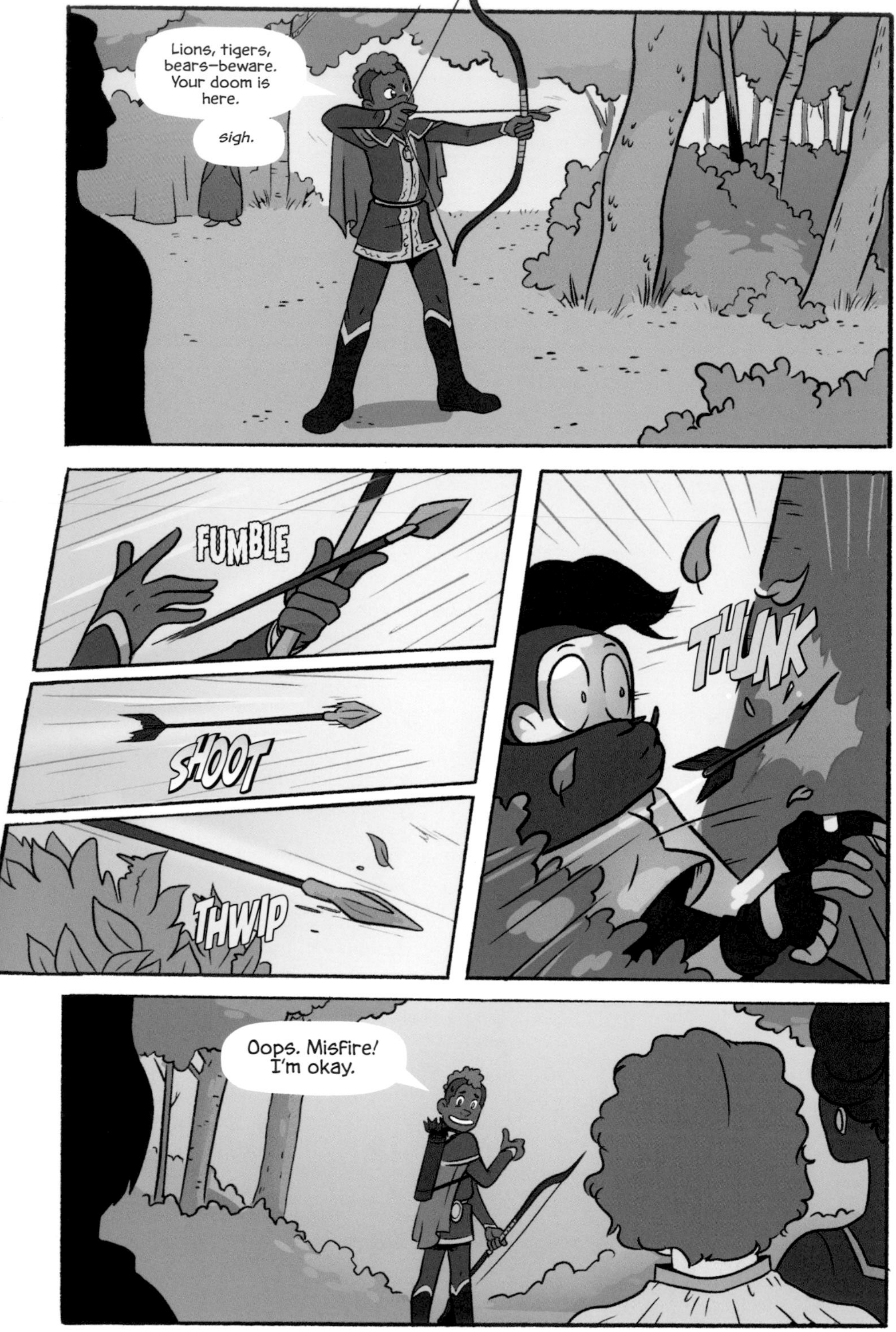
Lions, tigers, bears—beware. Your doom is here.
sigh.
FUMBLE
SHOOT
THWIP
THUNK
Oops. Misfire! I'm okay.

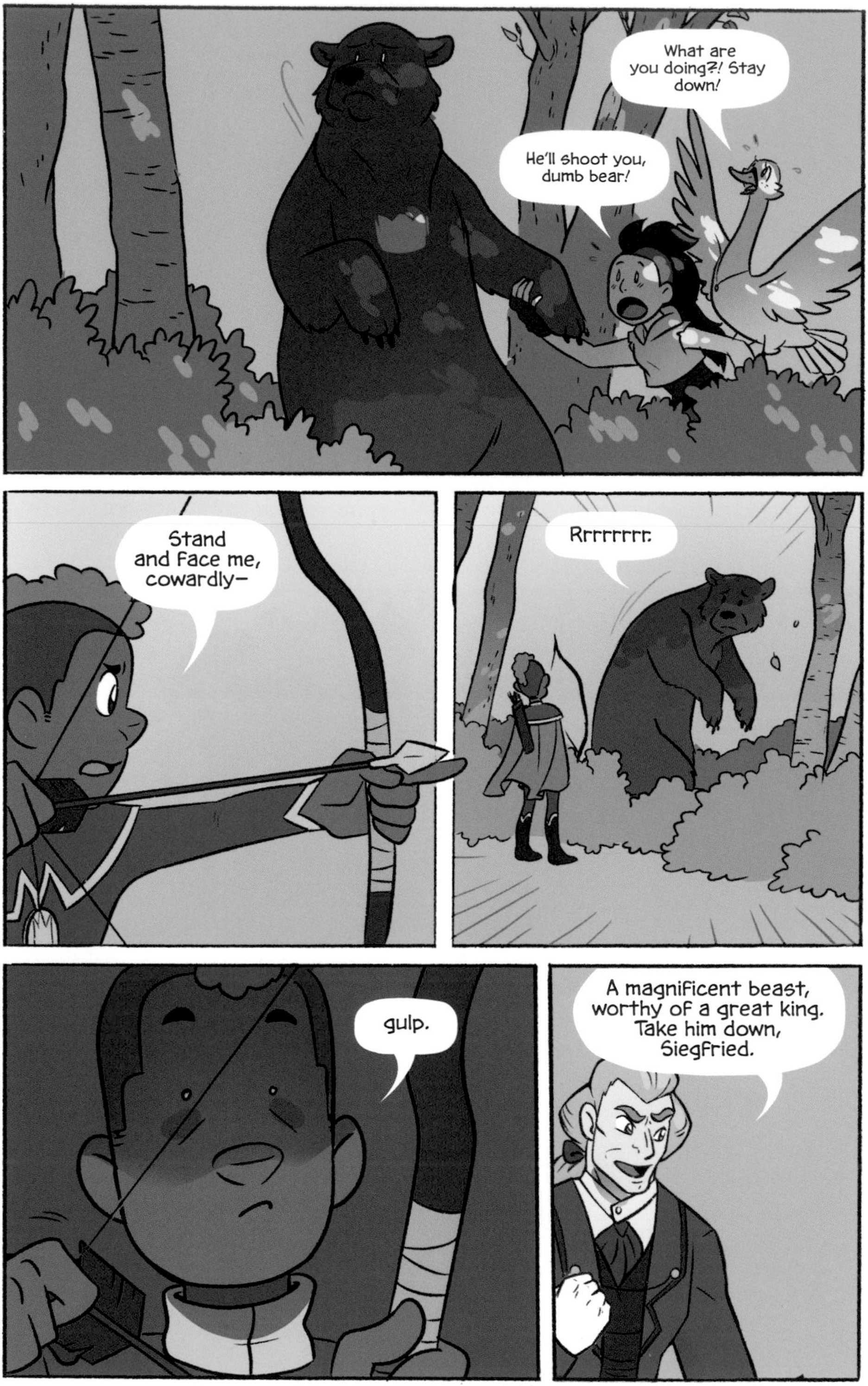
What are you doing?! Stay down!
He'll shoot you, dumb bear!
Stand and face me, cowardly—
Rrrrrrrr.
gulp.
A magnificent beast, worthy of a great king. Take him down, Siegfried.

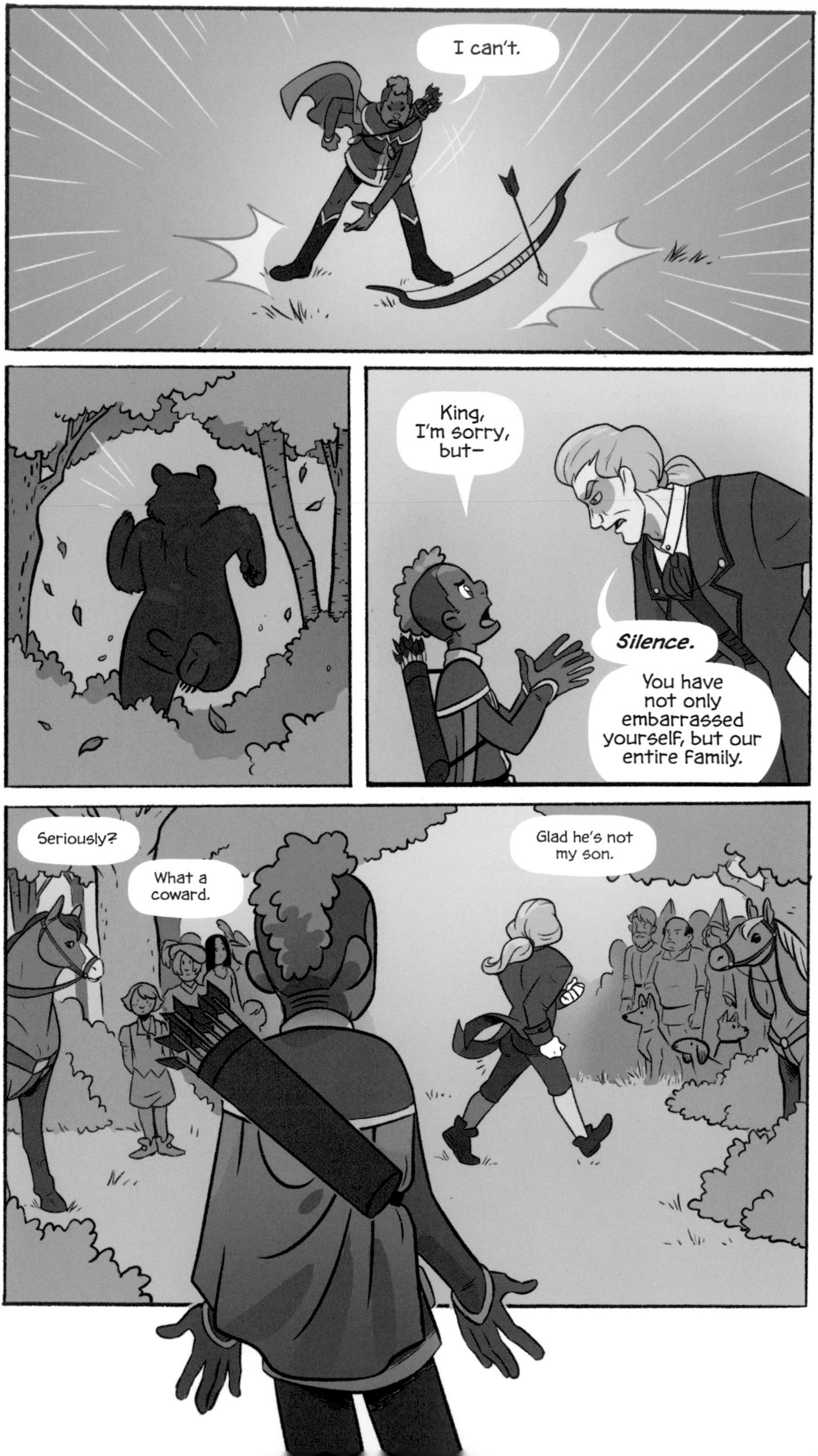
I can't.
King, I'm sorry, but–
Silence.
You have not only embarrassed yourself, but our entire family.
Seriously?
What a coward.
Glad he's not my son.

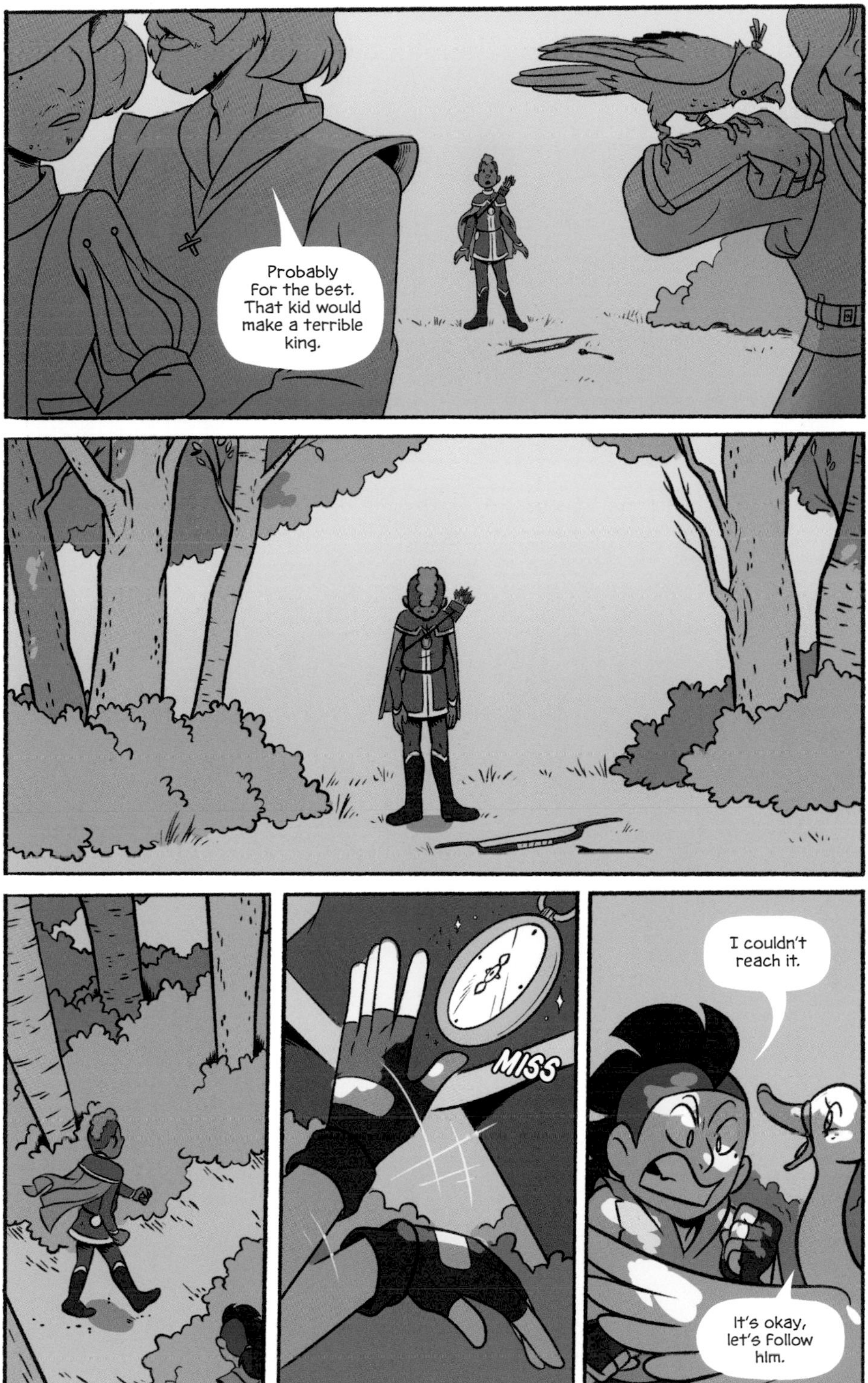
Probably for the best. That kid would make a terrible king.
MISS
I couldn't reach it.
It's okay, let's follow him.

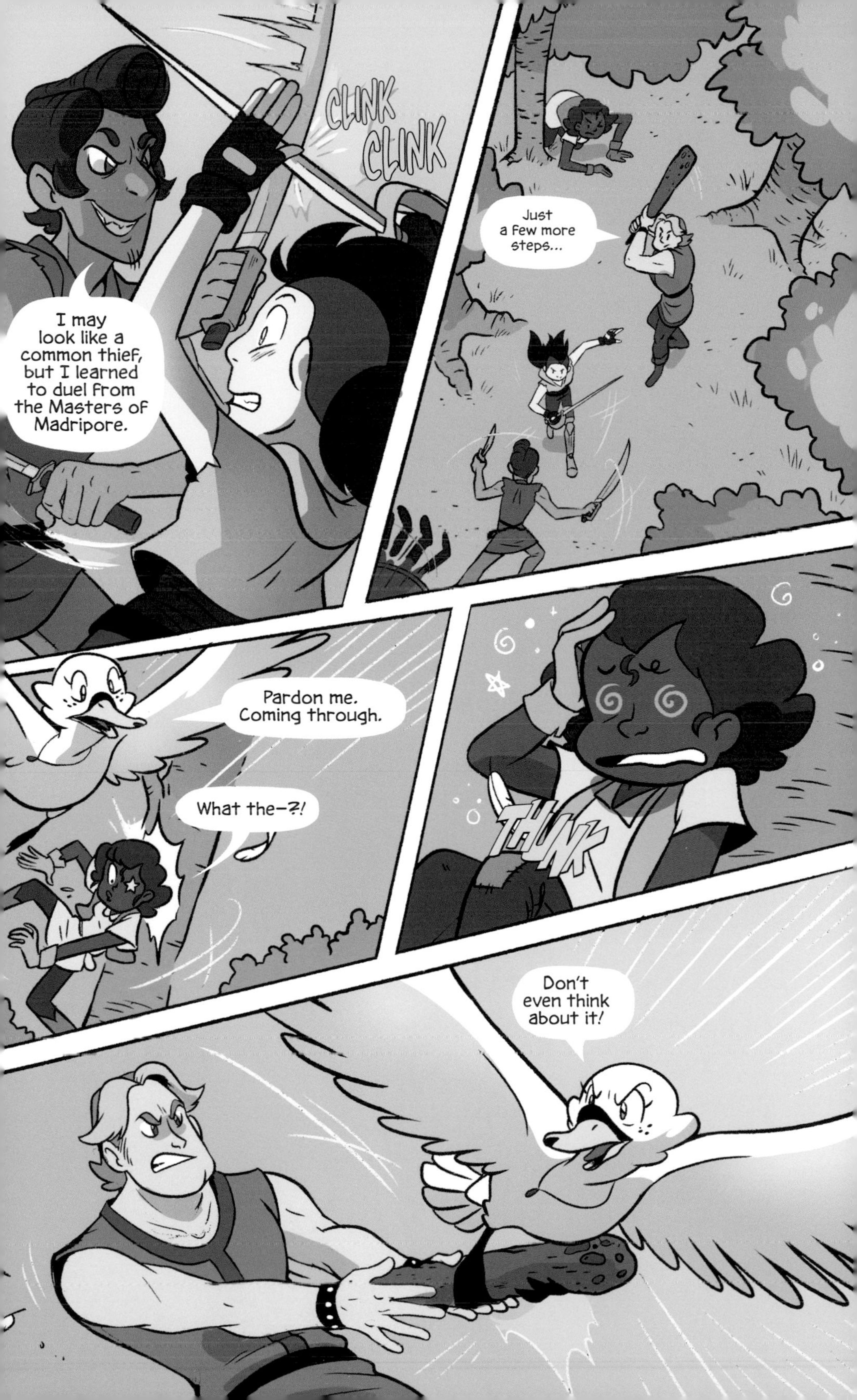
CLINK
CLINK
I may look like a common thief, but I learned to duel from the Masters of Madripore.
Just a few more steps...
Pardon me. Coming through.
What the—?!
THUNK
Don't even think about it!

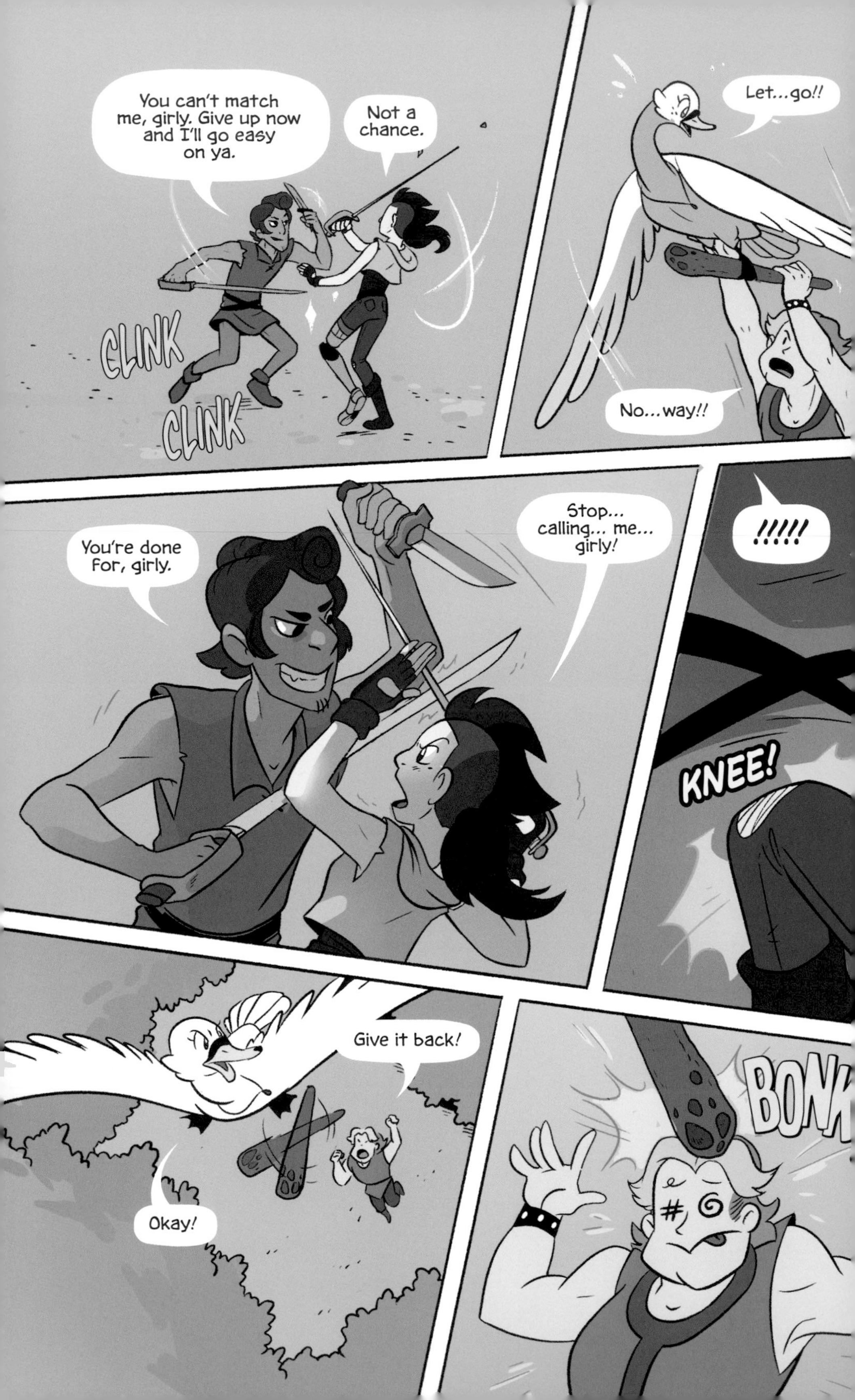
You can't match me, girly. Give up now and I'll go easy on ya.
Not a chance.
CLINK
CLINK
Let...go!!
No...way!!
You're done for, girly.
Stop... calling... me... girly!
!!!!!
KNEE!
Give it back!
Okay!
BONK

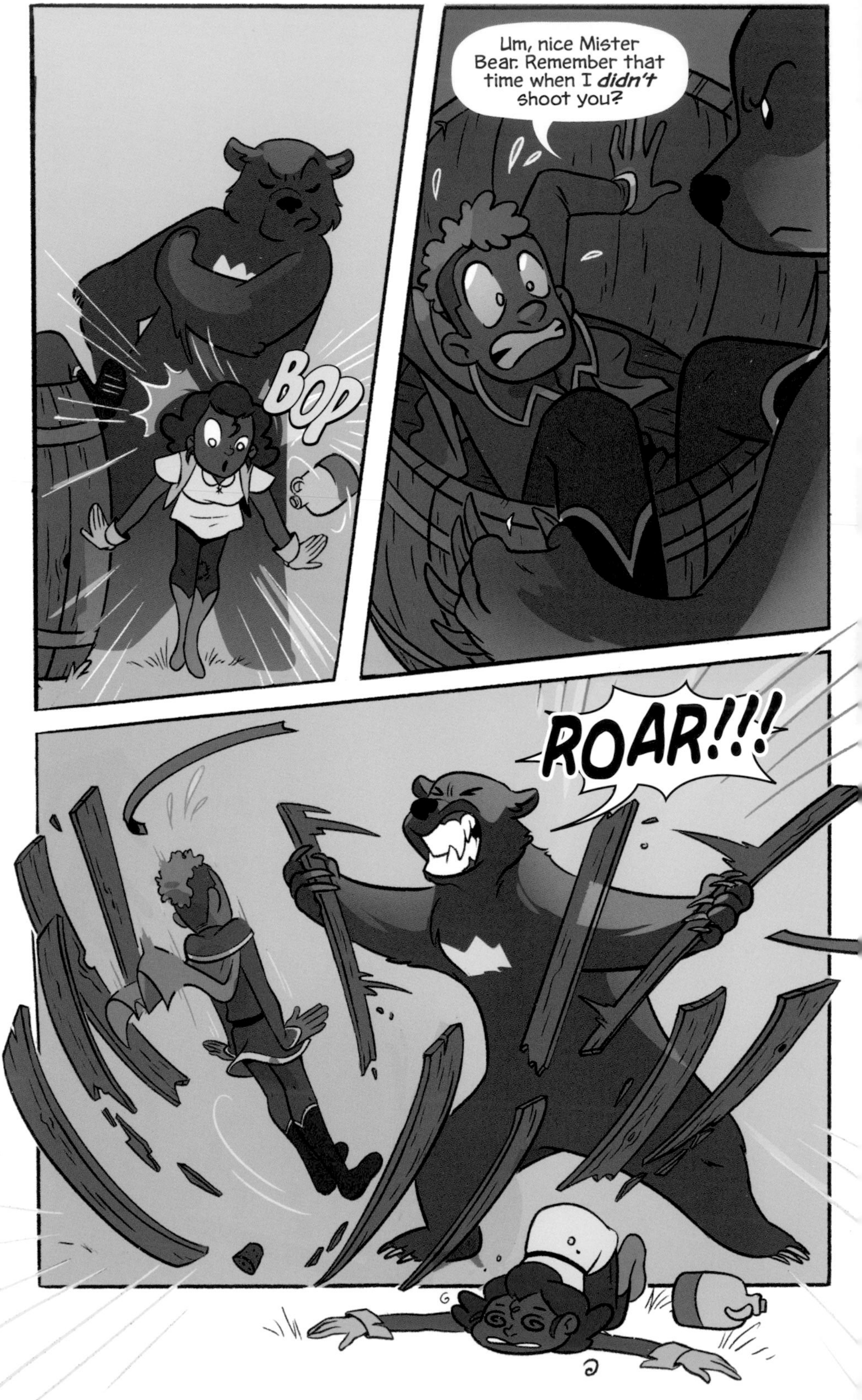
BOP
Um, nice Mister Bear. Remember that time when I *didn't* shoot you?
ROAR!!!

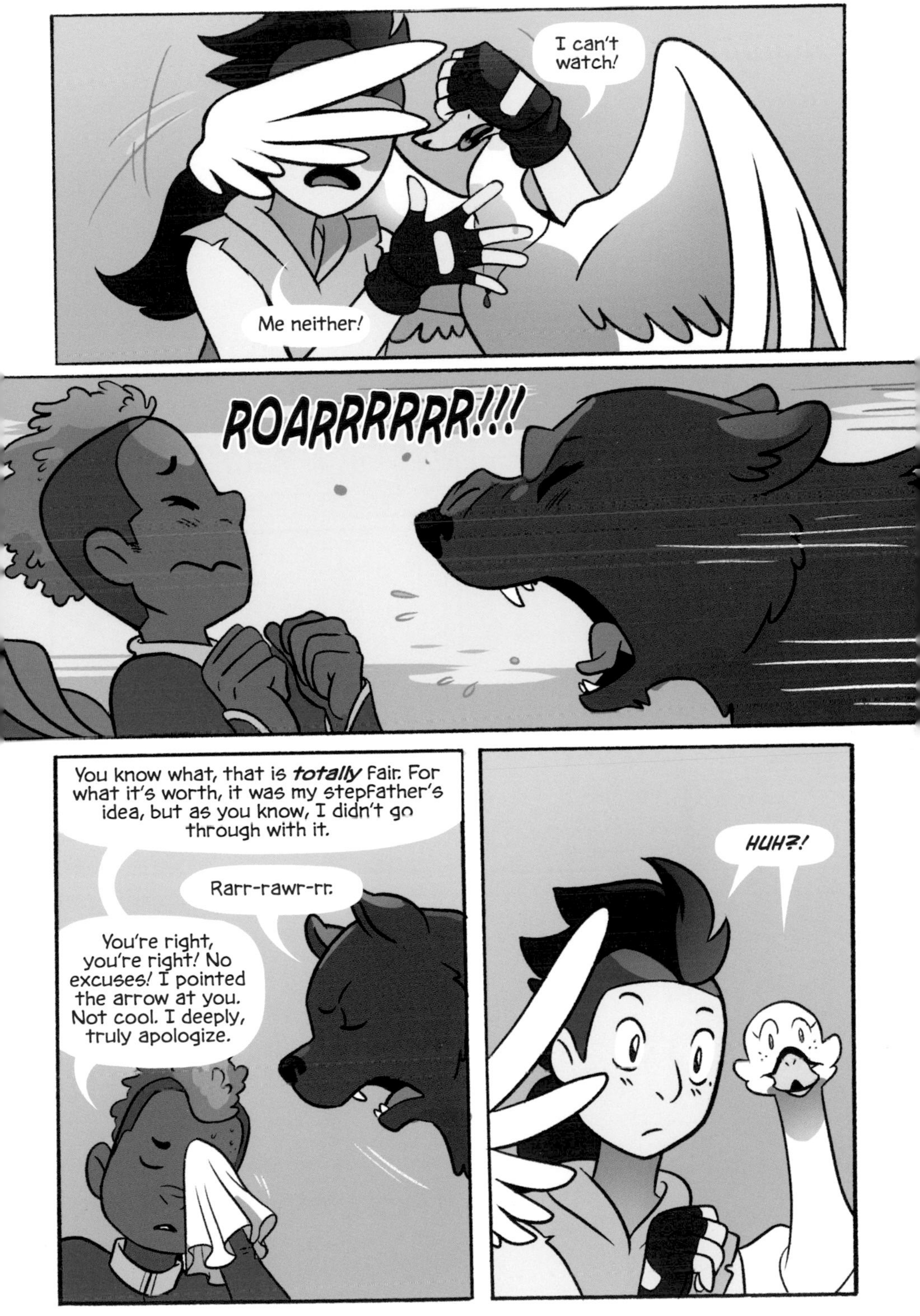
I can't watch!
Me neither!
ROARRRRRR!!!
You know what, that is *totally* fair. For what it's worth, it was my stepfather's idea, but as you know, I didn't go through with it.
Rarr-rawr-rr.
You're right, you're right! No excuses! I pointed the arrow at you. Not cool. I deeply, truly apologize.
HUH?!

108

112

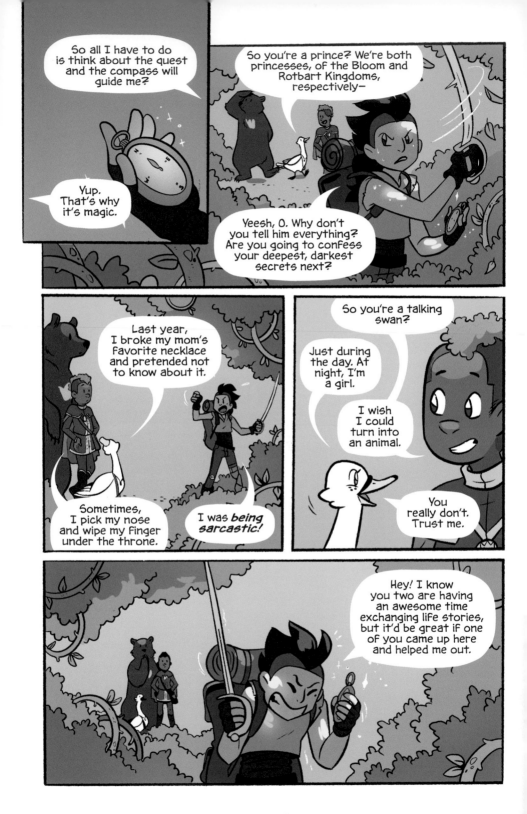

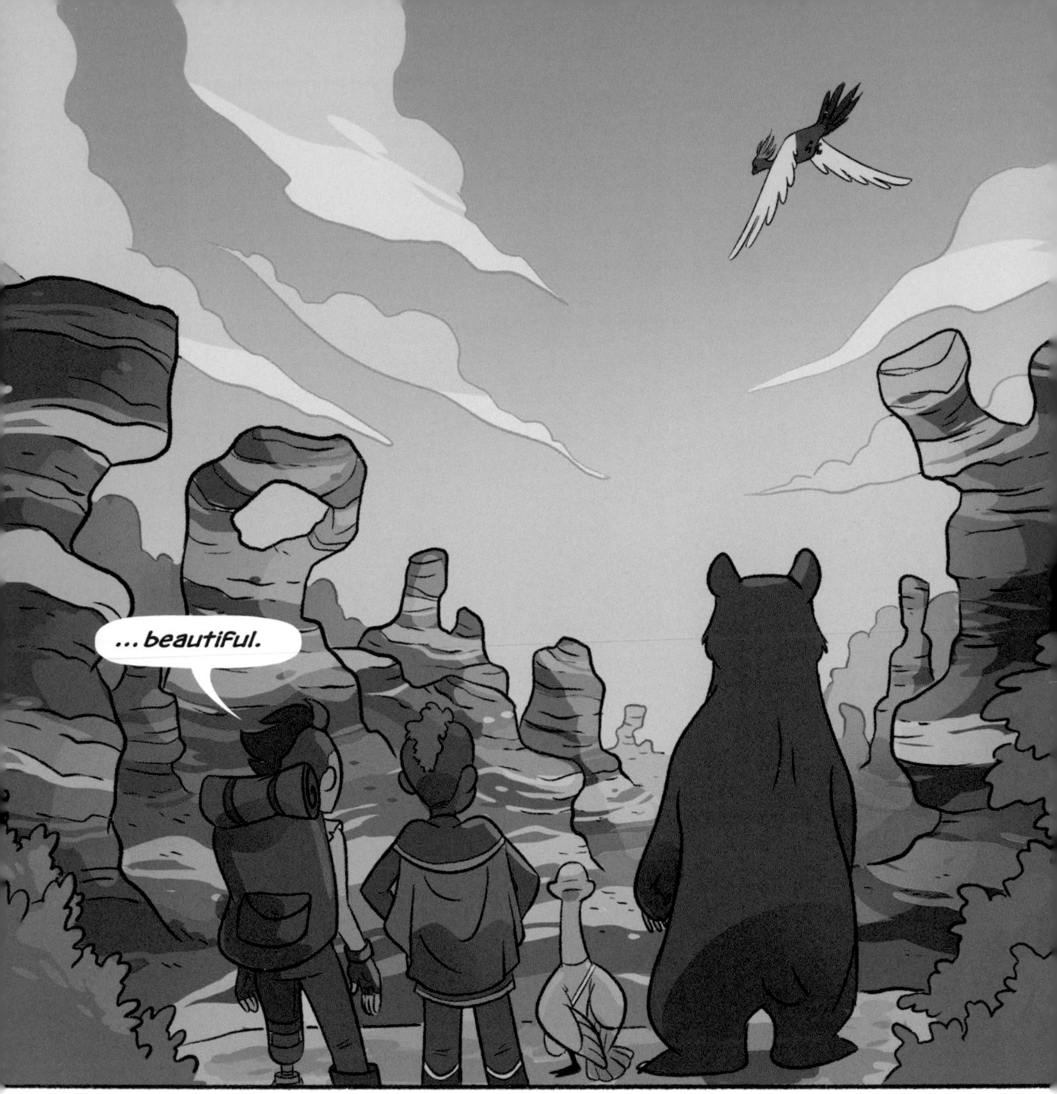
...beautiful.

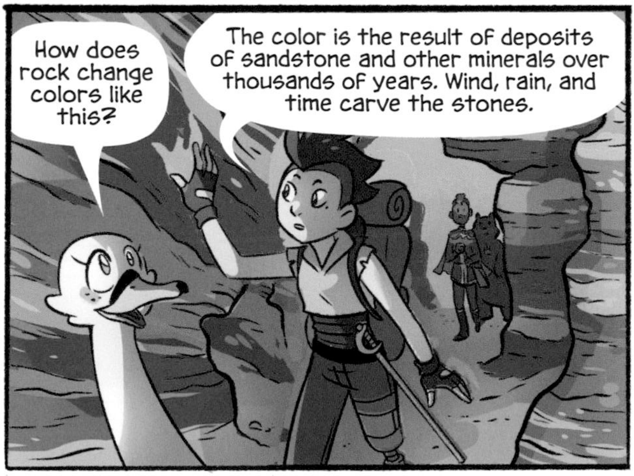
How does rock change colors like this?
The color is the result of deposits of sandstone and other minerals over thousands of years. Wind, rain, and time carve the stones.

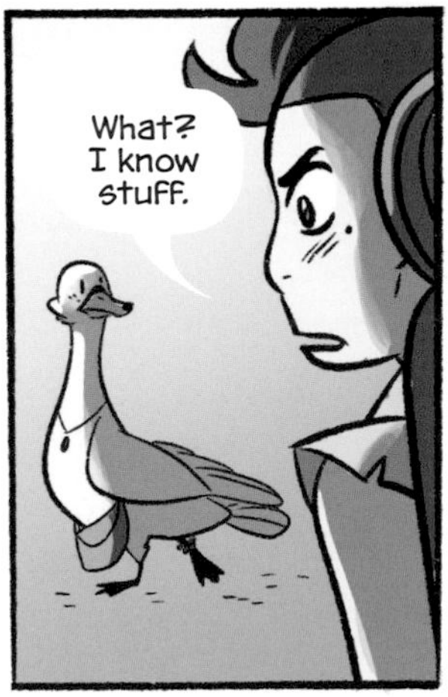
What? I know stuff.

118

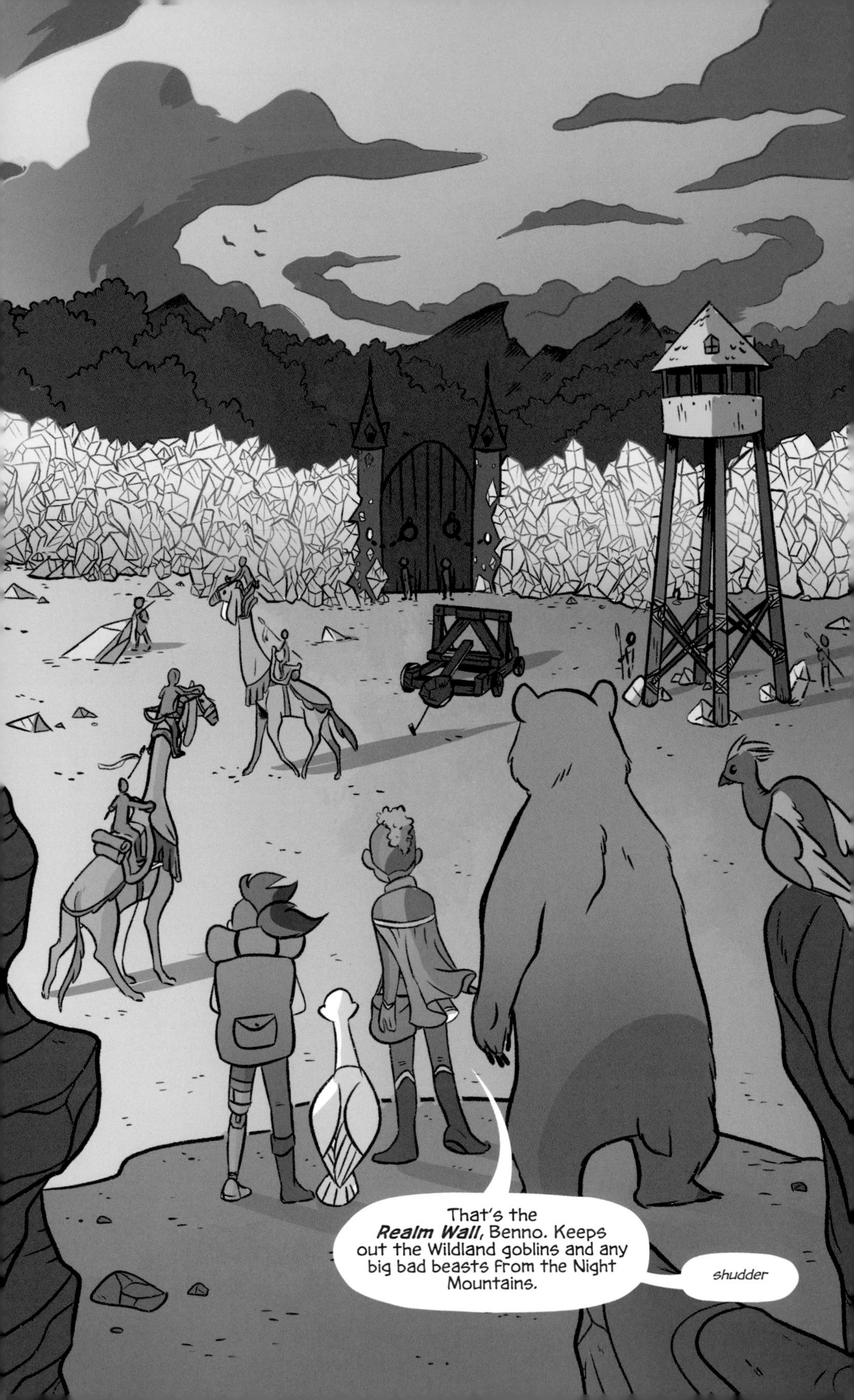

That's the **Realm Wall**, Benno. Keeps out the Wildland goblins and any big bad beasts from the Night Mountains.
shudder

121

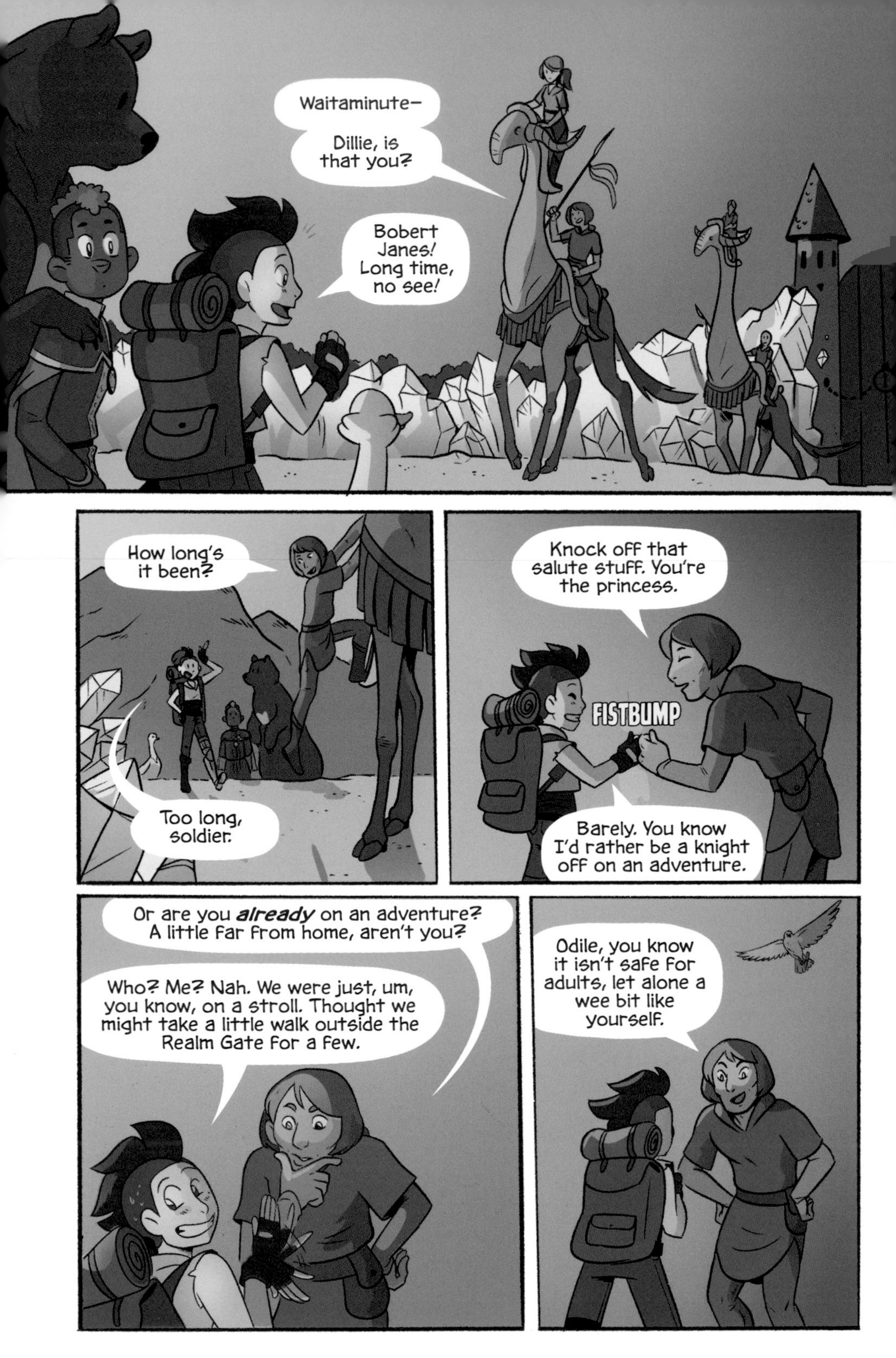
Waitaminute—
Dillie, is that you?
Bobert Janes! Long time, no see!
How long's it been?
Too long, soldier.
Knock off that salute stuff. You're the princess.
FISTBUMP
Barely. You know I'd rather be a knight off on an adventure.
Or are you *already* on an adventure? A little far from home, aren't you?
Who? Me? Nah. We were just, um, you know, on a stroll. Thought we might take a little walk outside the Realm Gate for a few.
Odile, you know it isn't safe for adults, let alone a wee bit like yourself.

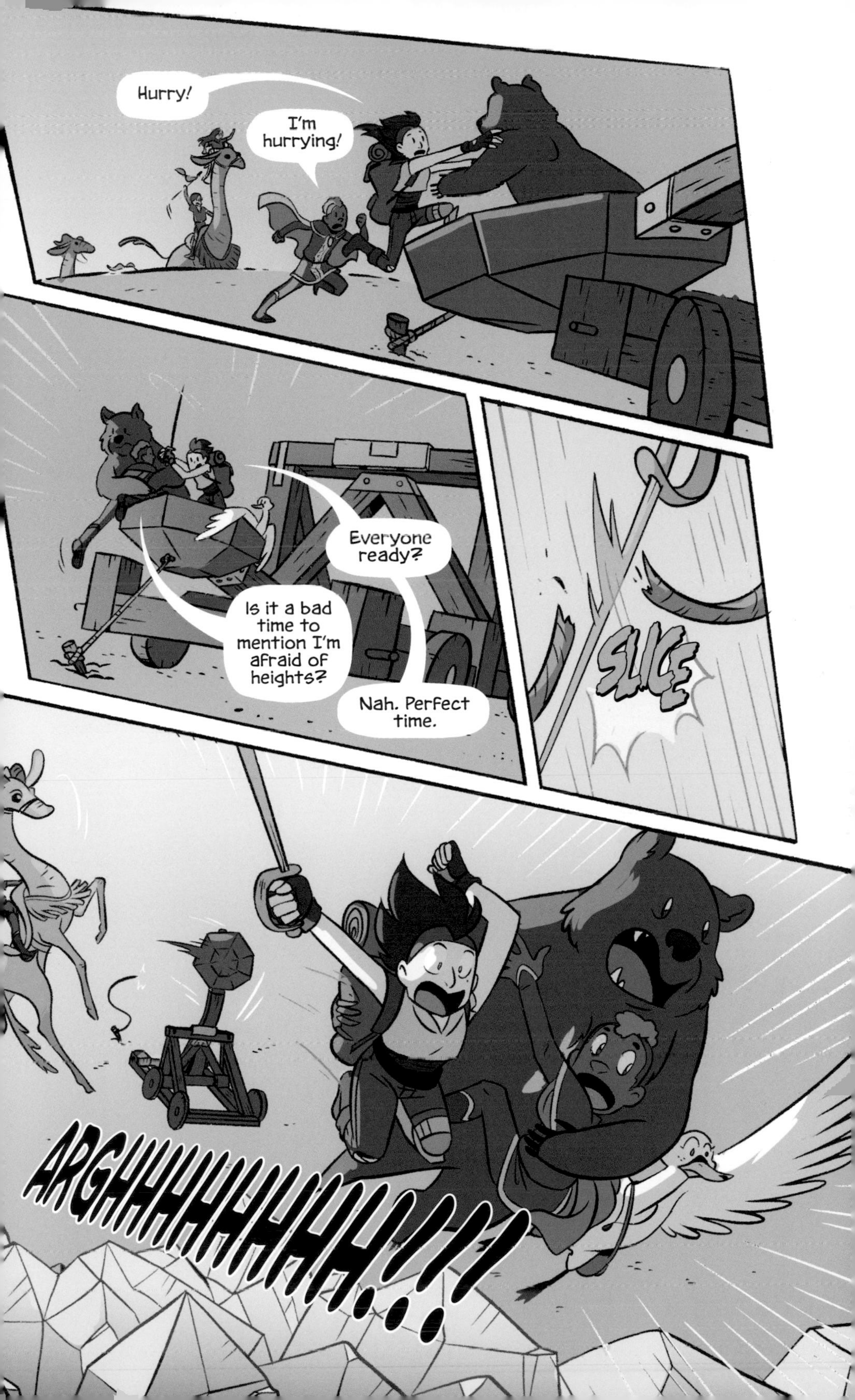
Hurry!
I'm hurrying!
Everyone ready?
Is it a bad time to mention I'm afraid of heights?
Nah. Perfect time.
SLICE
ARGHHHHHHH!!!!

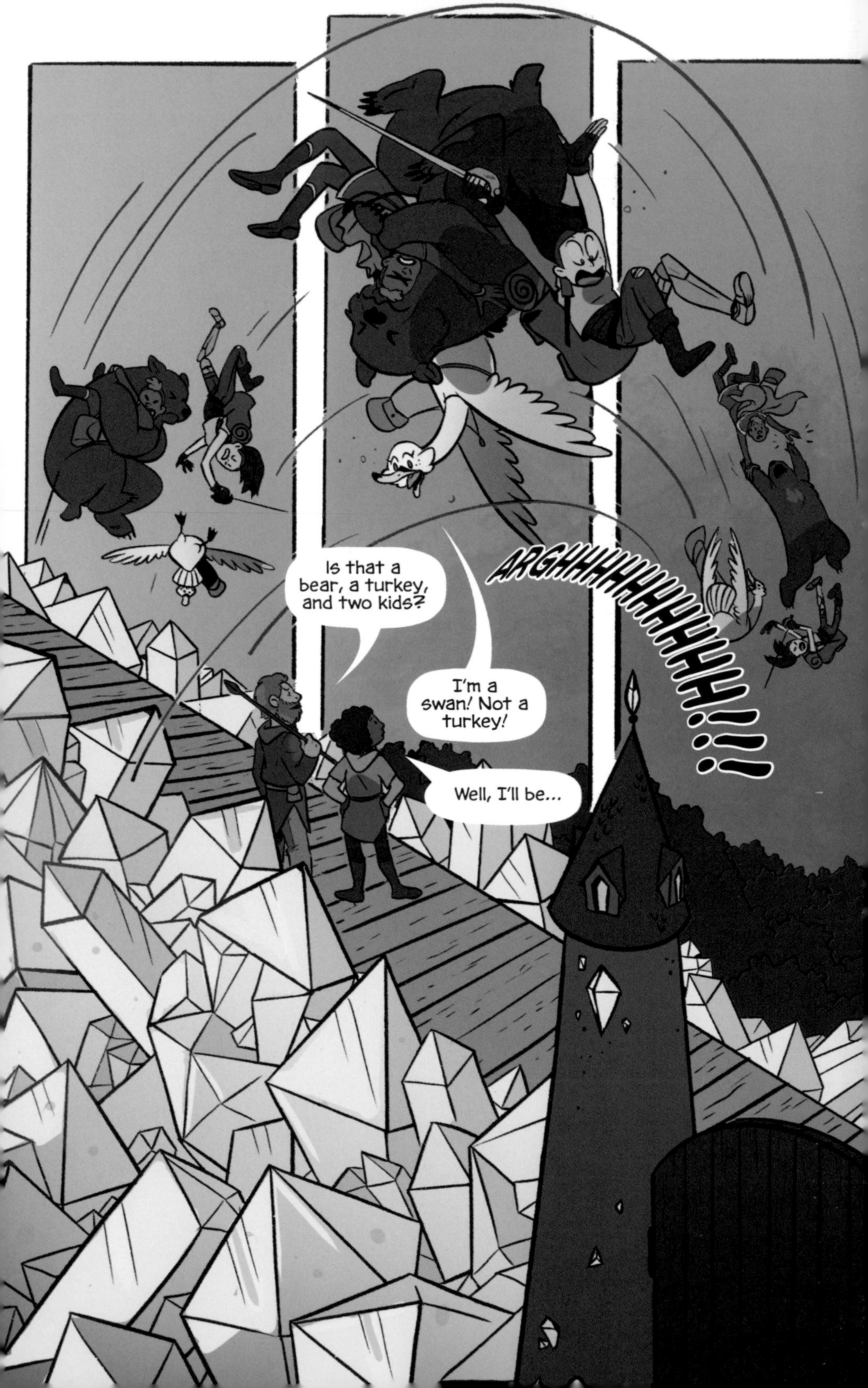
Is that a bear, a turkey, and two kids?
I'm a swan! Not a turkey!
ARGHHHHHHHHHHHH!!!!
Well, I'll be...

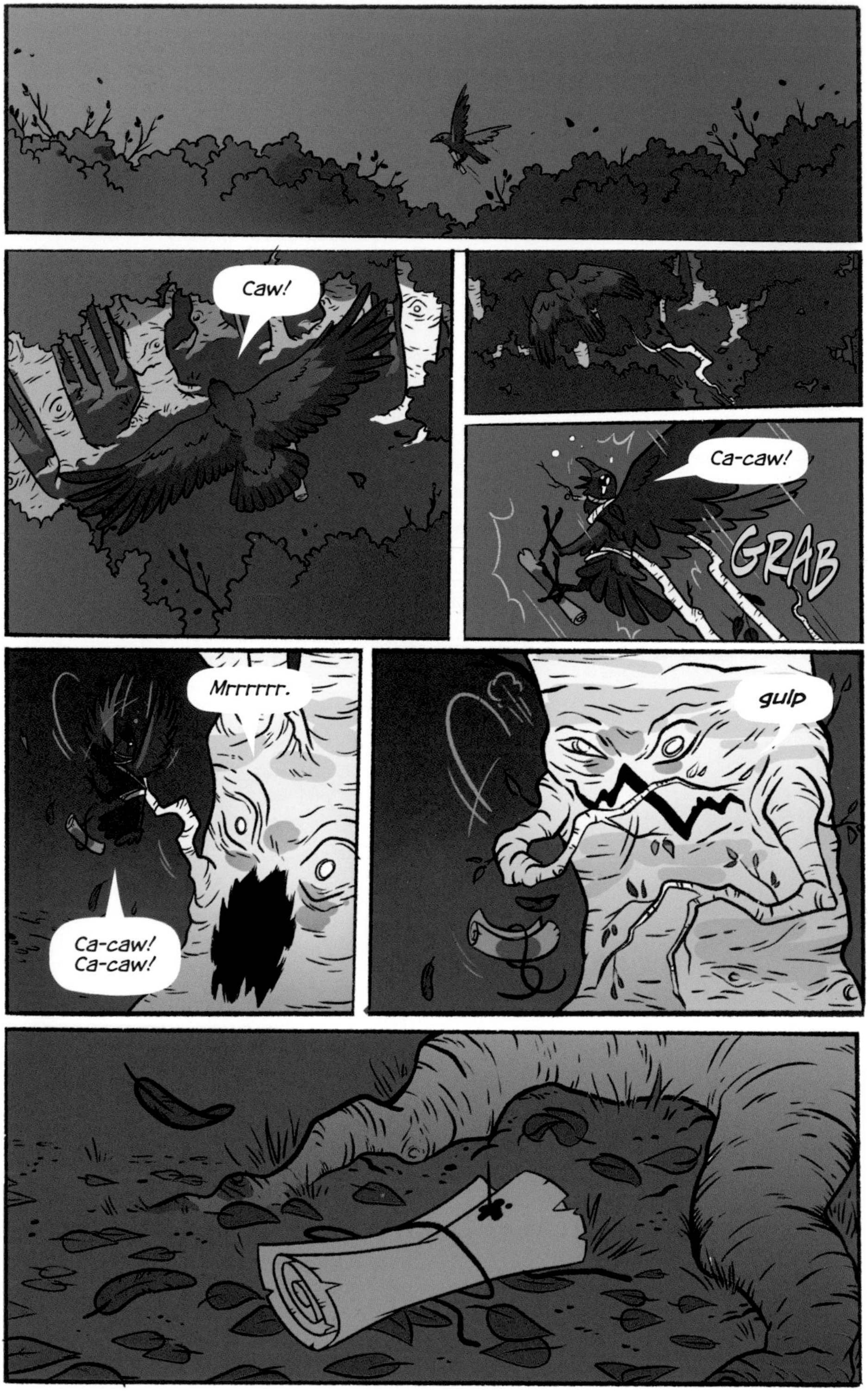
Caw!
Ca-caw!
GRAB
Mrrrrrr.
Ca-caw! Ca-caw!
gulp

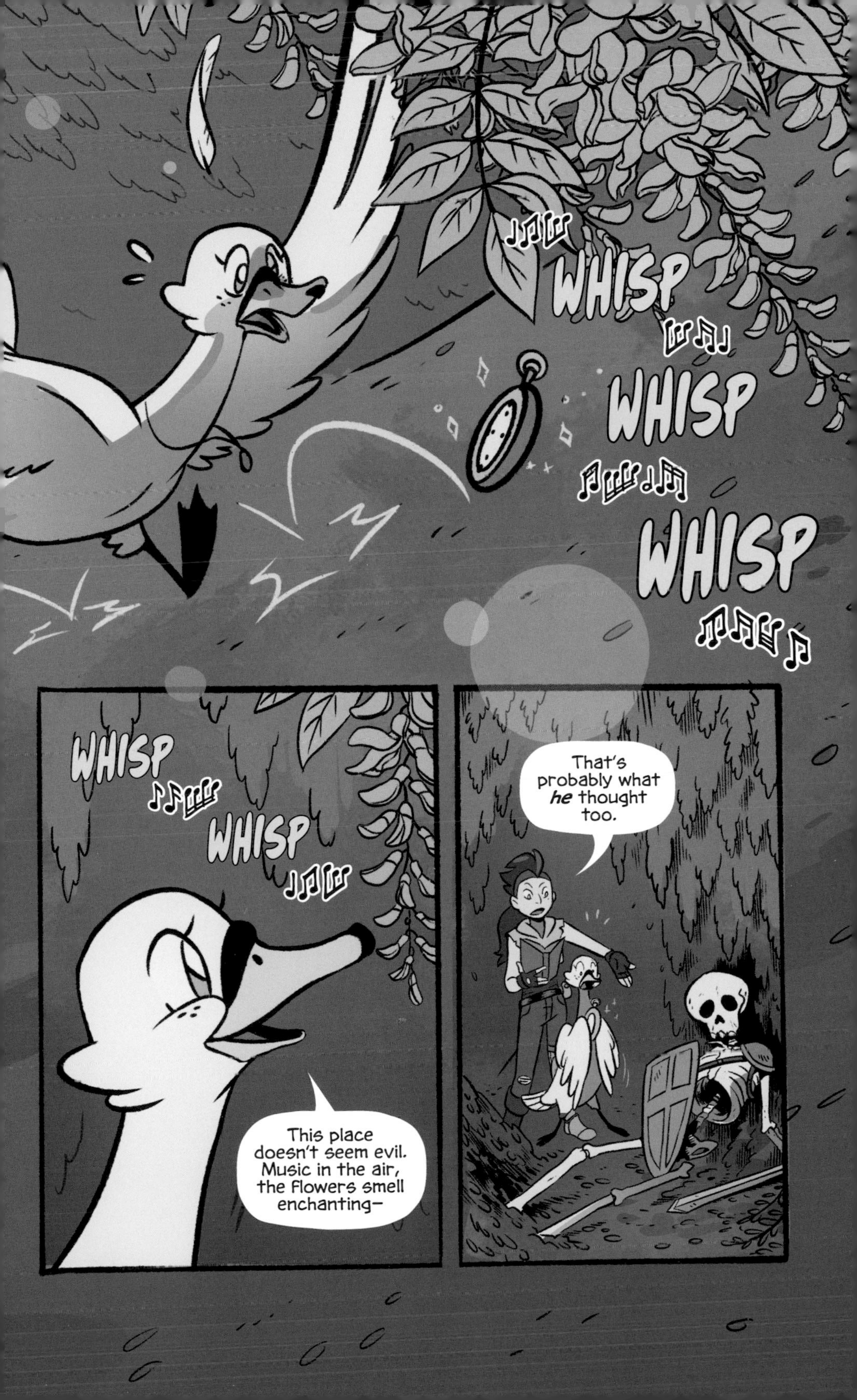

WHISP
WHISP
WHISP
WHISP
WHISP
This place doesn't seem evil. Music in the air, the flowers smell enchanting–
That's probably what *he* thought too.

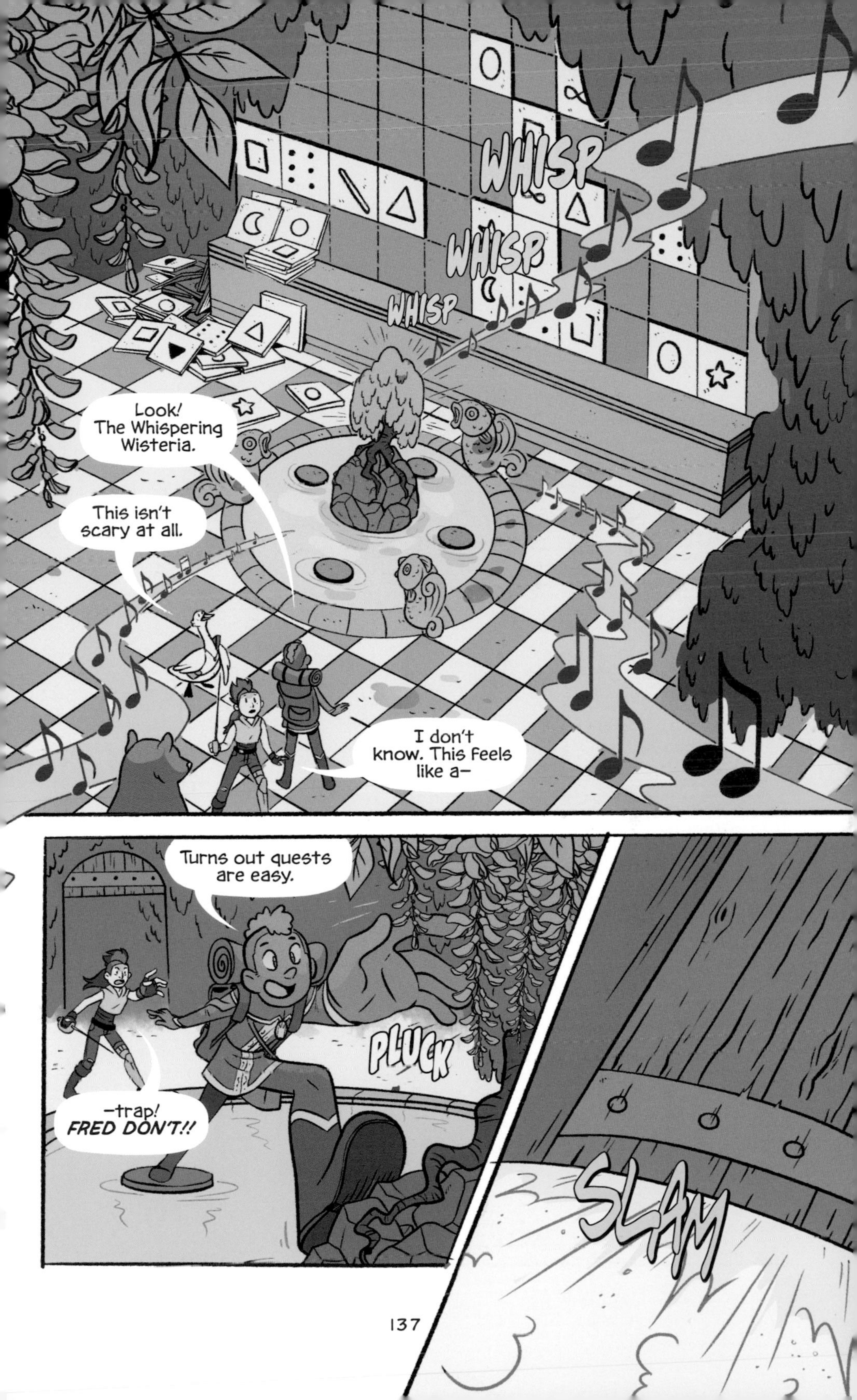

WHISP
WHISP
WHISP
Look! The Whispering Wisteria.
This isn't scary at all.
I don't know. This feels like a–
Turns out quests are easy.
–trap! FRED DON'T!!
PLUCK
SLAM

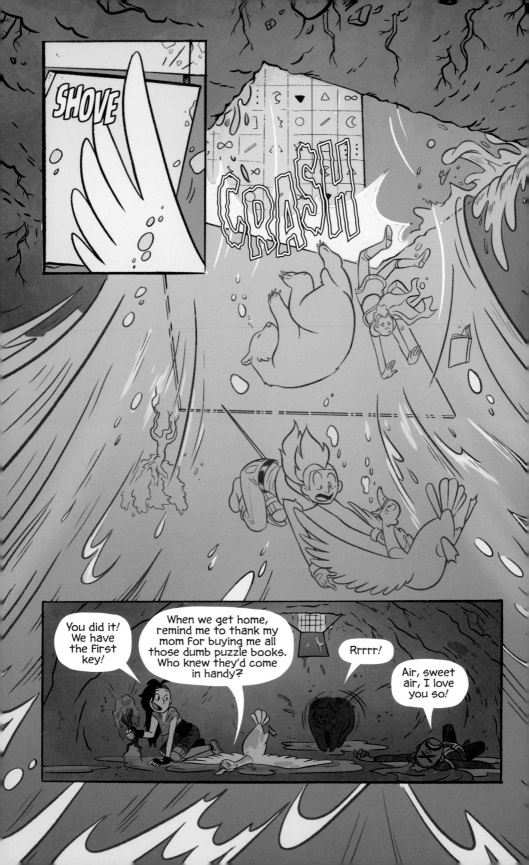

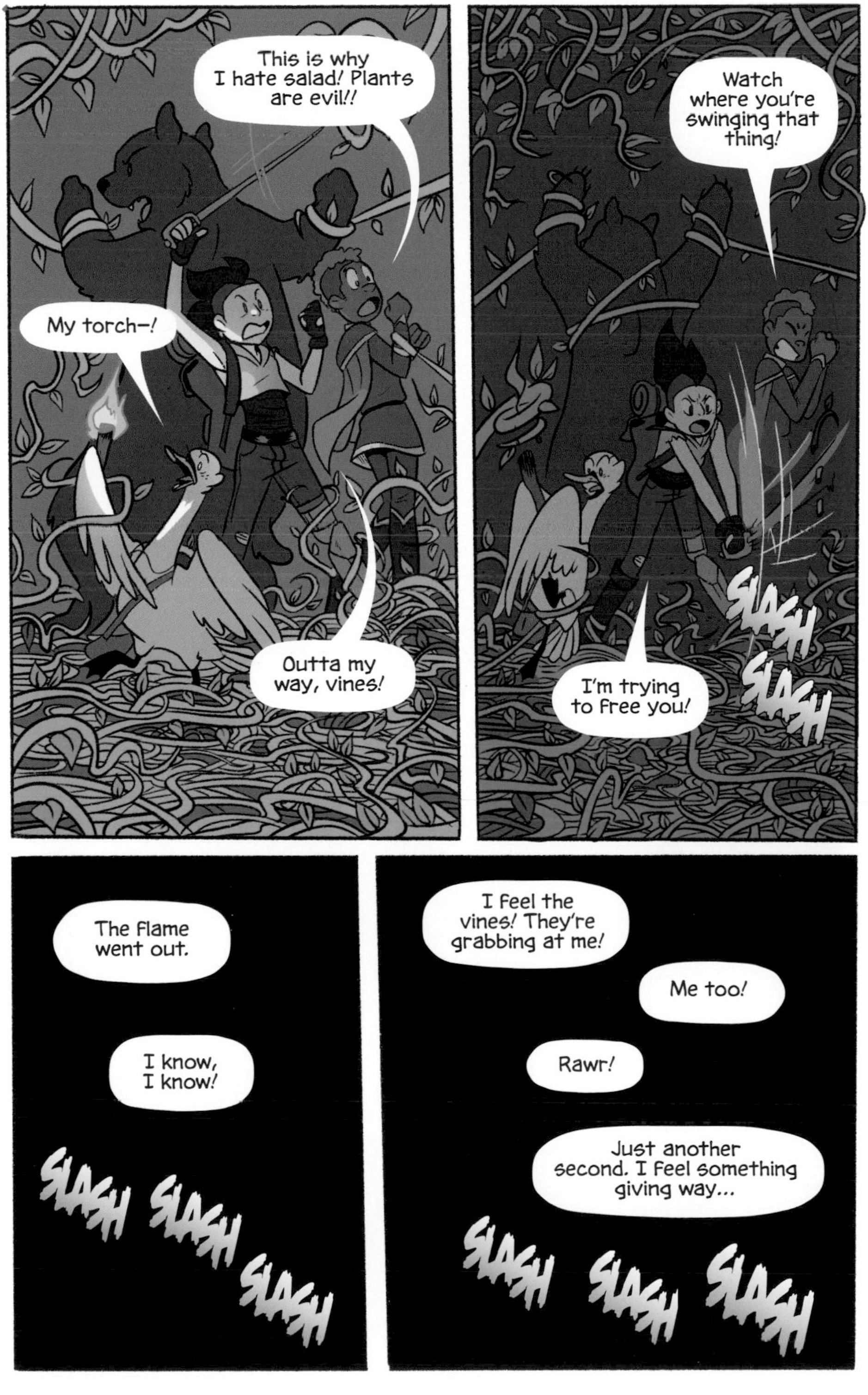
This is why I hate salad! Plants are evil!!
My torch—!
Outta my way, vines!
Watch where you're swinging that thing!
I'm trying to free you!
SLASH
SLASH
The flame went out.
I know, I know!
SLASH
SLASH
SLASH
I feel the vines! They're grabbing at me!
Me too!
Rawr!
Just another second. I feel something giving way...
SLASH
SLASH
SLASH

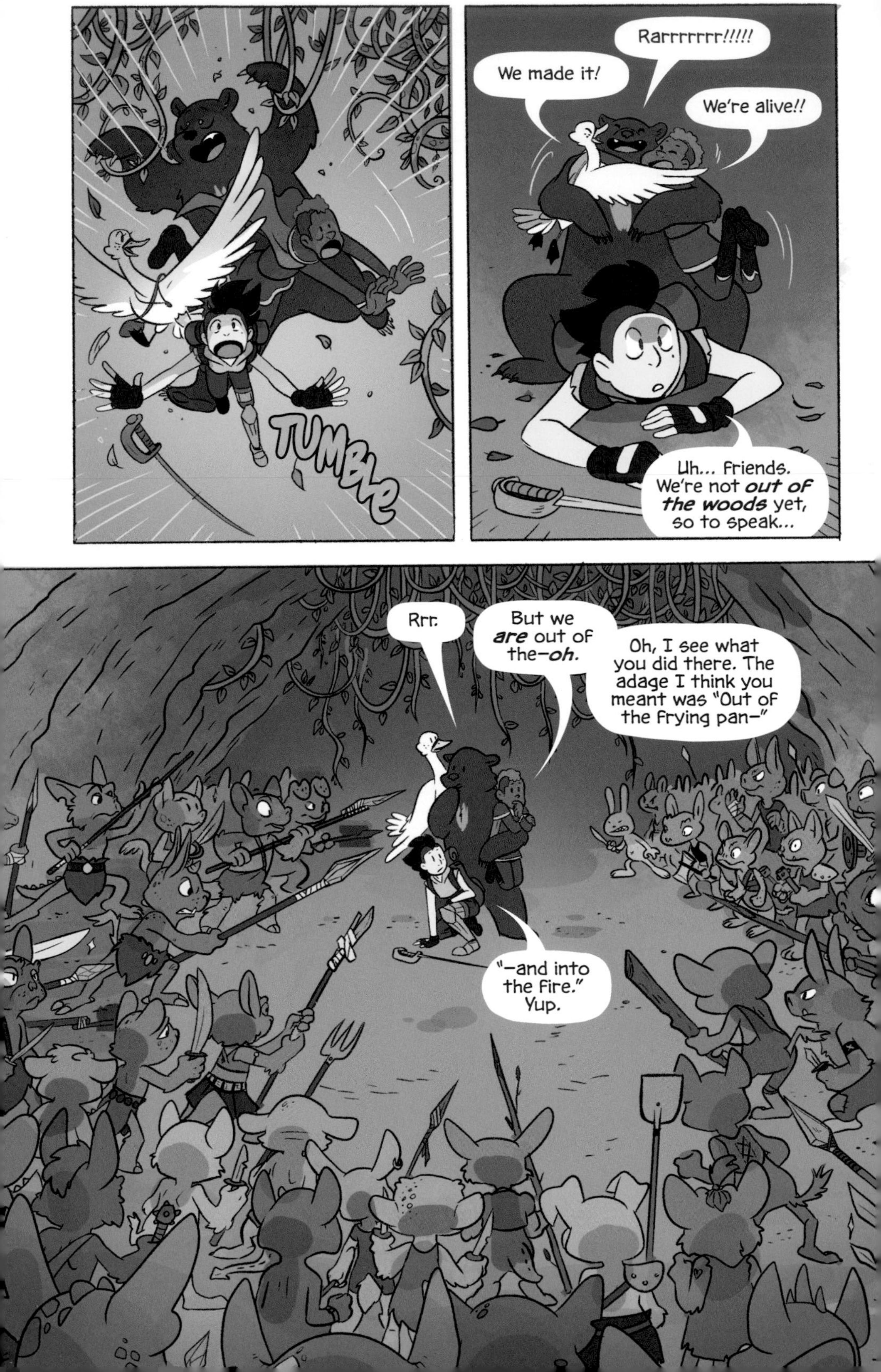
TUMBLE
We made it!
Rarrrrrrr!!!!!
We're alive!!
Uh... friends. We're not *out of the woods* yet, so to speak...
Rrr.
But we *are* out of the–*oh.*
Oh, I see what you did there. The adage I think you meant was "Out of the frying pan–"
"–and into the fire." Yup.

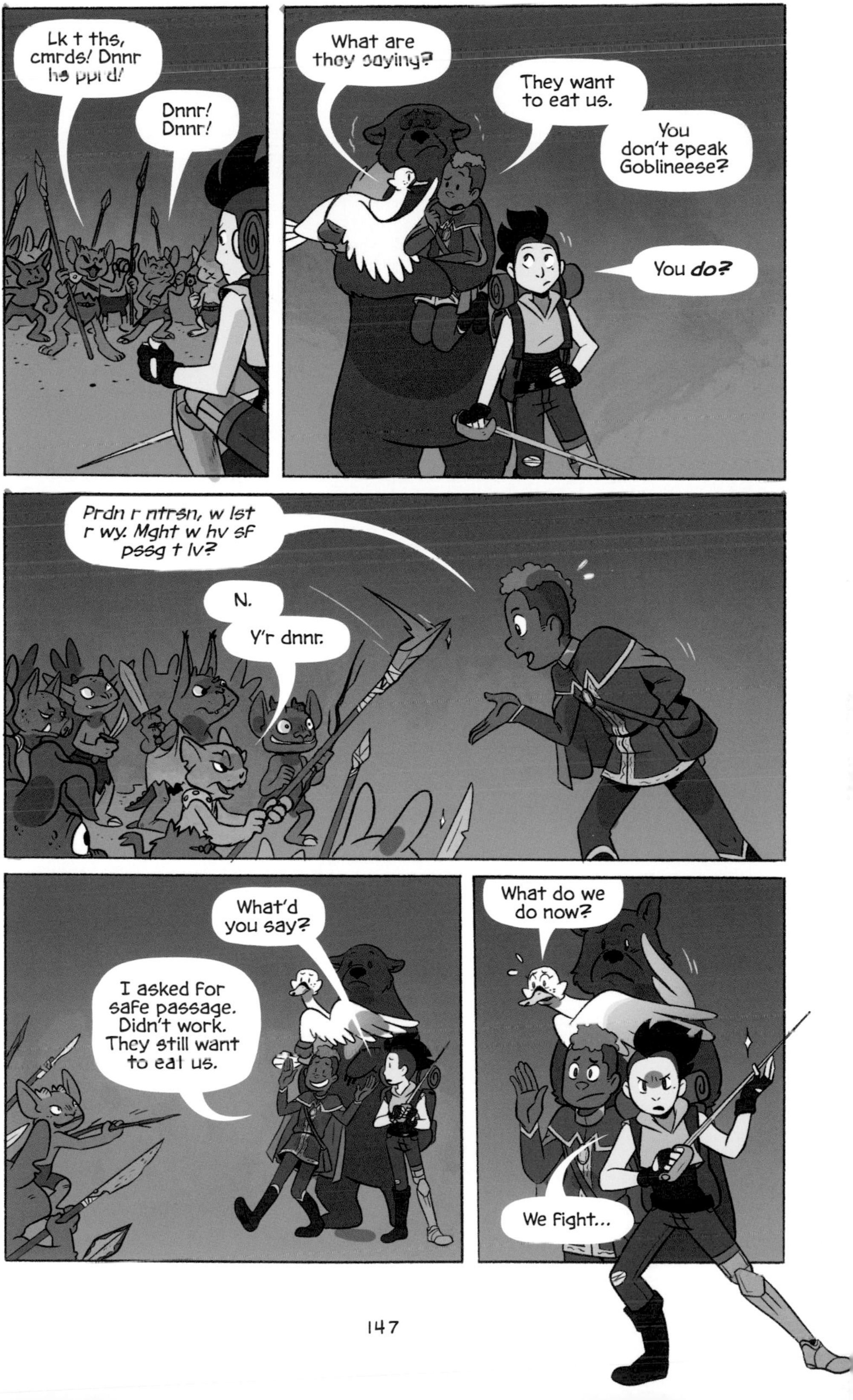

Lk t ths, cmrds! Dnnr hs pprd!
Dnnr! Dnnr!
What are they saying?
They want to eat us.
You don't speak Goblineese?
You *do?*
Prdn r ntrsn, w lst r wy. Mght w hv sf pssg t lv?
N.
Y'r dnnr.
What'd you say?
I asked for safe passage. Didn't work. They still want to eat us.
What do we do now?
We fight...

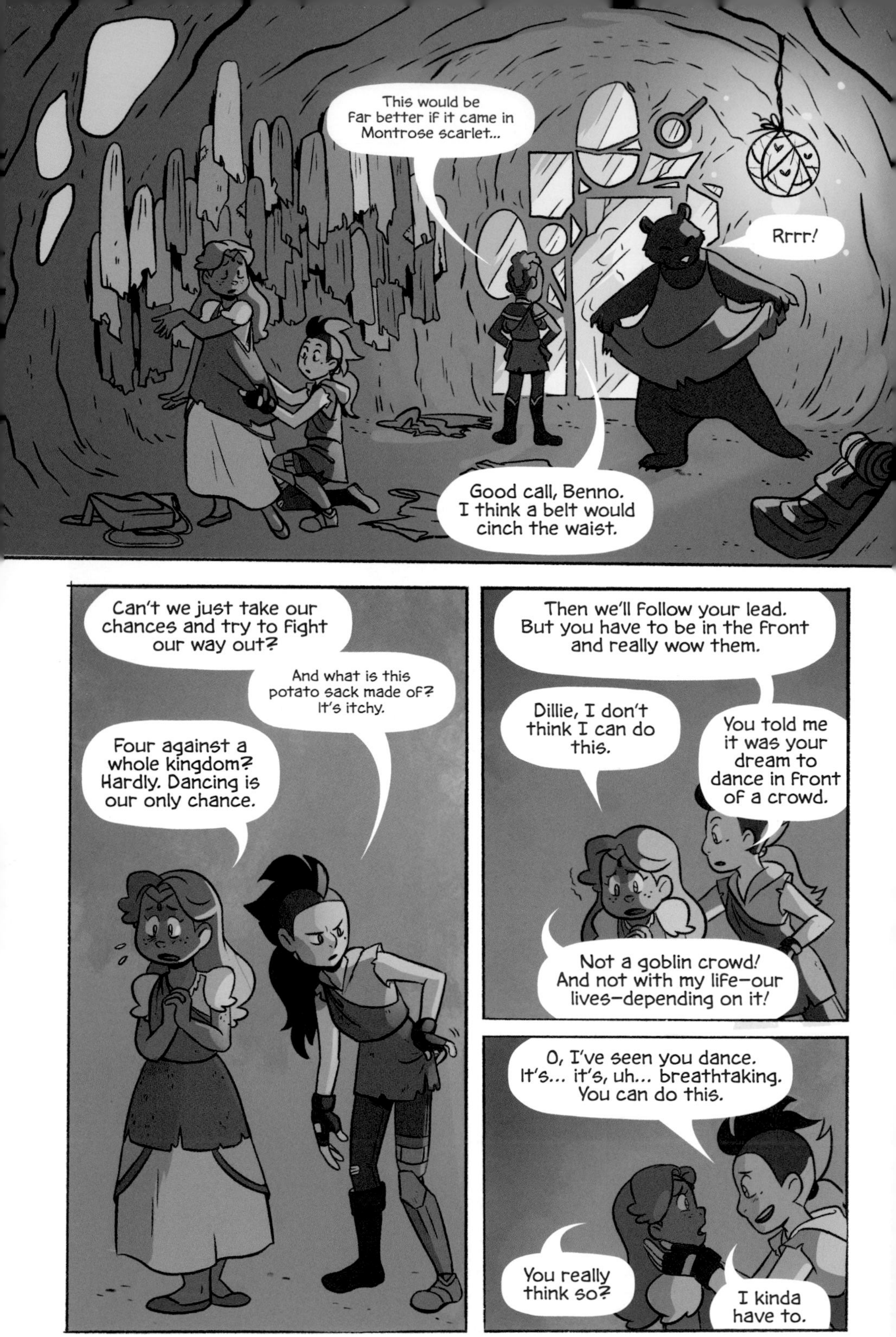
This would be far better if it came in Montrose scarlet...
Rrrr!
Good call, Benno. I think a belt would cinch the waist.
Can't we just take our chances and try to fight our way out?
And what is this potato sack made of? It's itchy.
Four against a whole kingdom? Hardly. Dancing is our only chance.
Then we'll follow your lead. But you have to be in the front and really wow them.
Dillie, I don't think I can do this.
You told me it was your dream to dance in front of a crowd.
Not a goblin crowd! And not with my life—our lives—depending on it!
O, I've seen you dance. It's... it's, uh... breathtaking. You can do this.
You really think so?
I kinda have to.

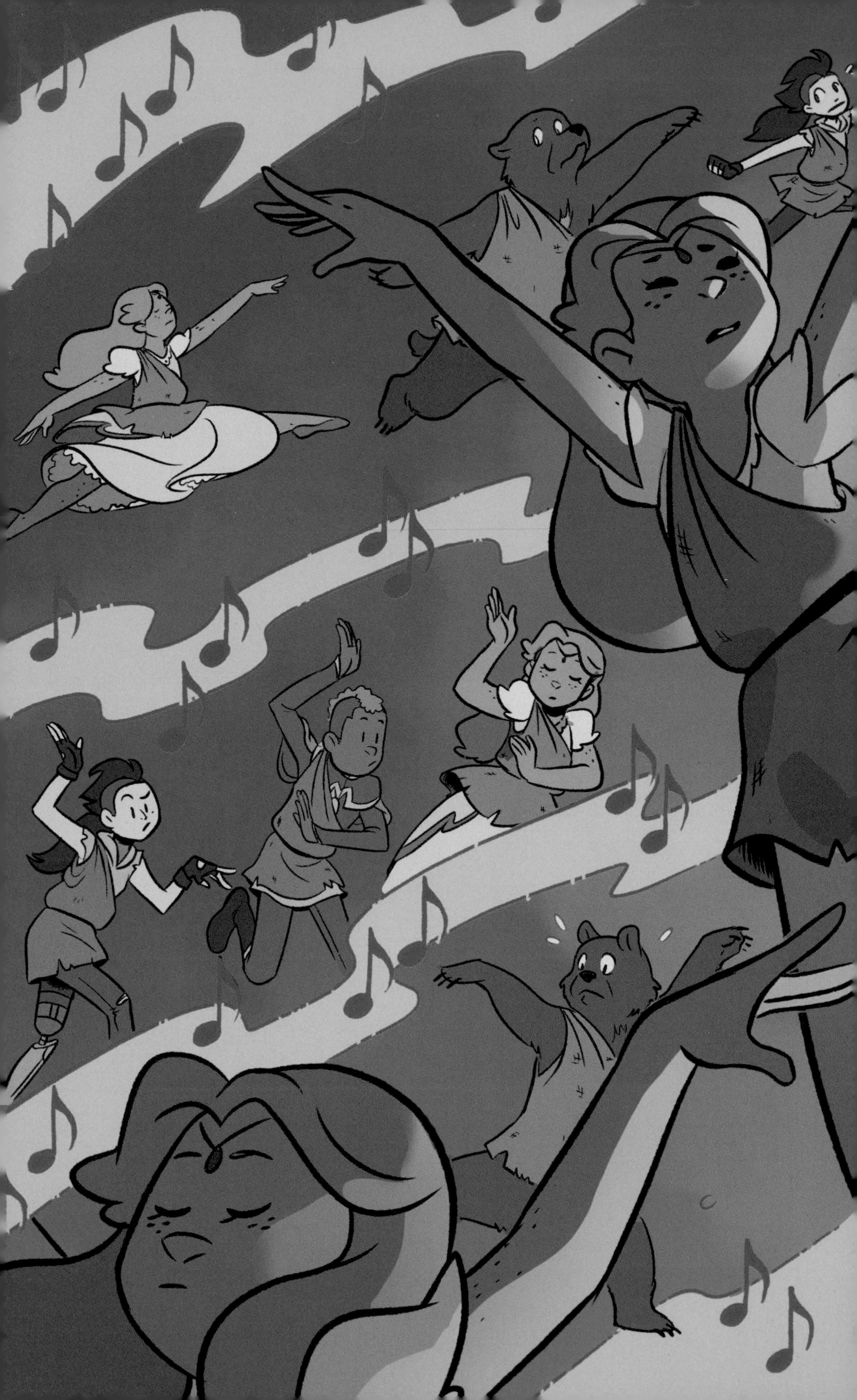

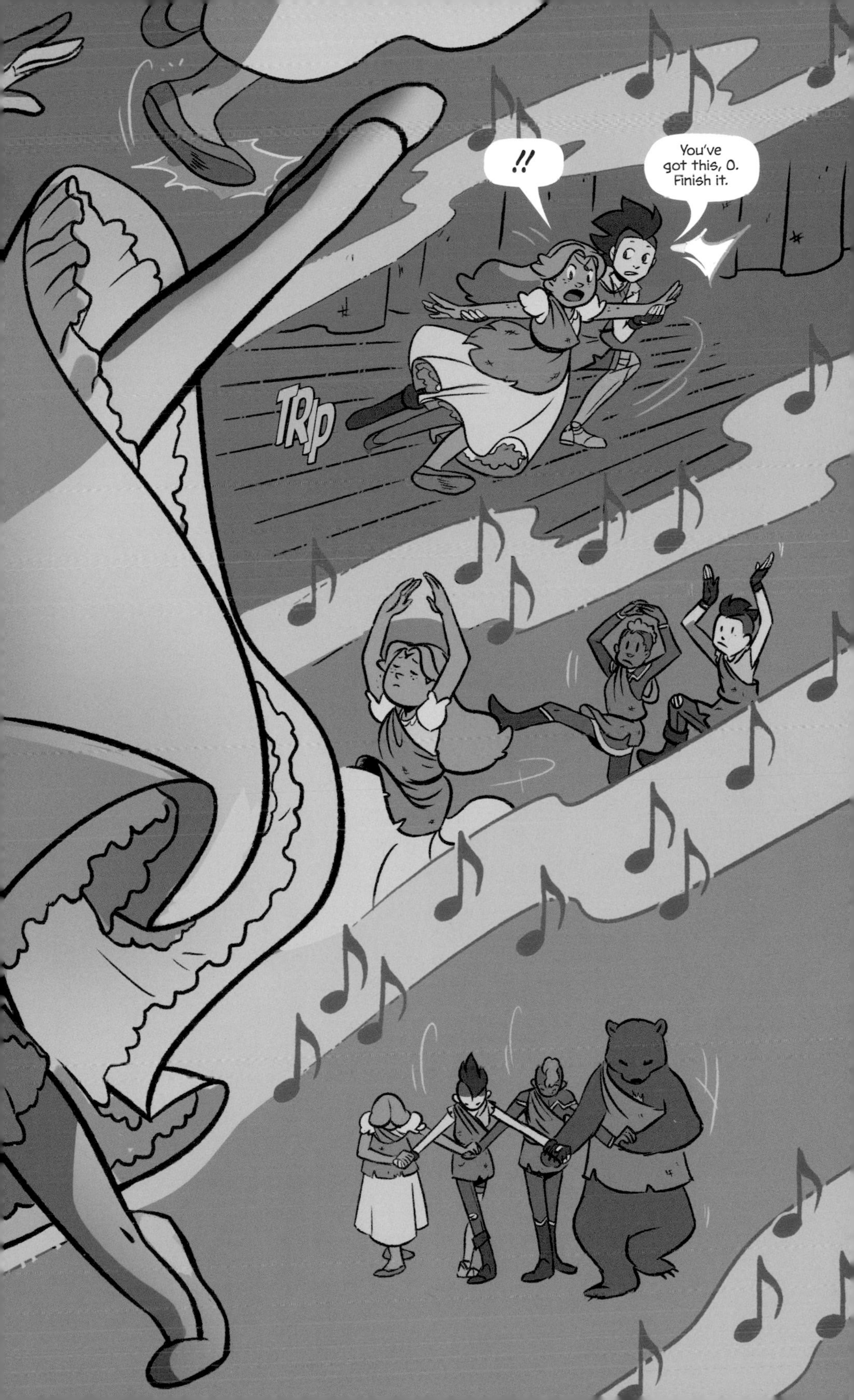
!!
You've got this, O. Finish it.
TRIP

157

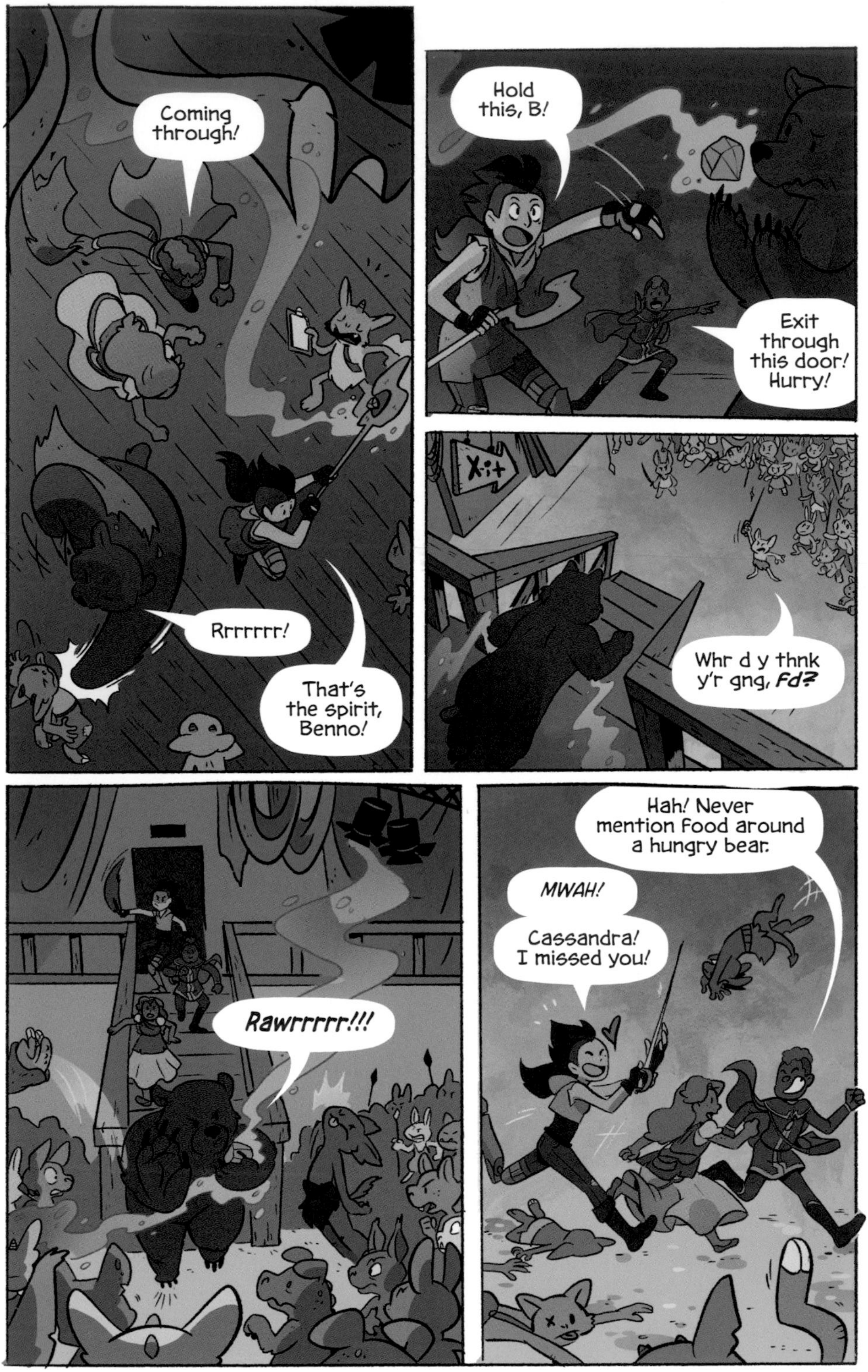
Coming through!
Rrrrrrr!
That's the spirit, Benno!
Hold this, B!
Exit through this door! Hurry!
X-i-t
Whr d y thnk y'r gng, Fd?
Rawrrrrr!!!
Hah! Never mention food around a hungry bear.
MWAH!
Cassandra! I missed you!

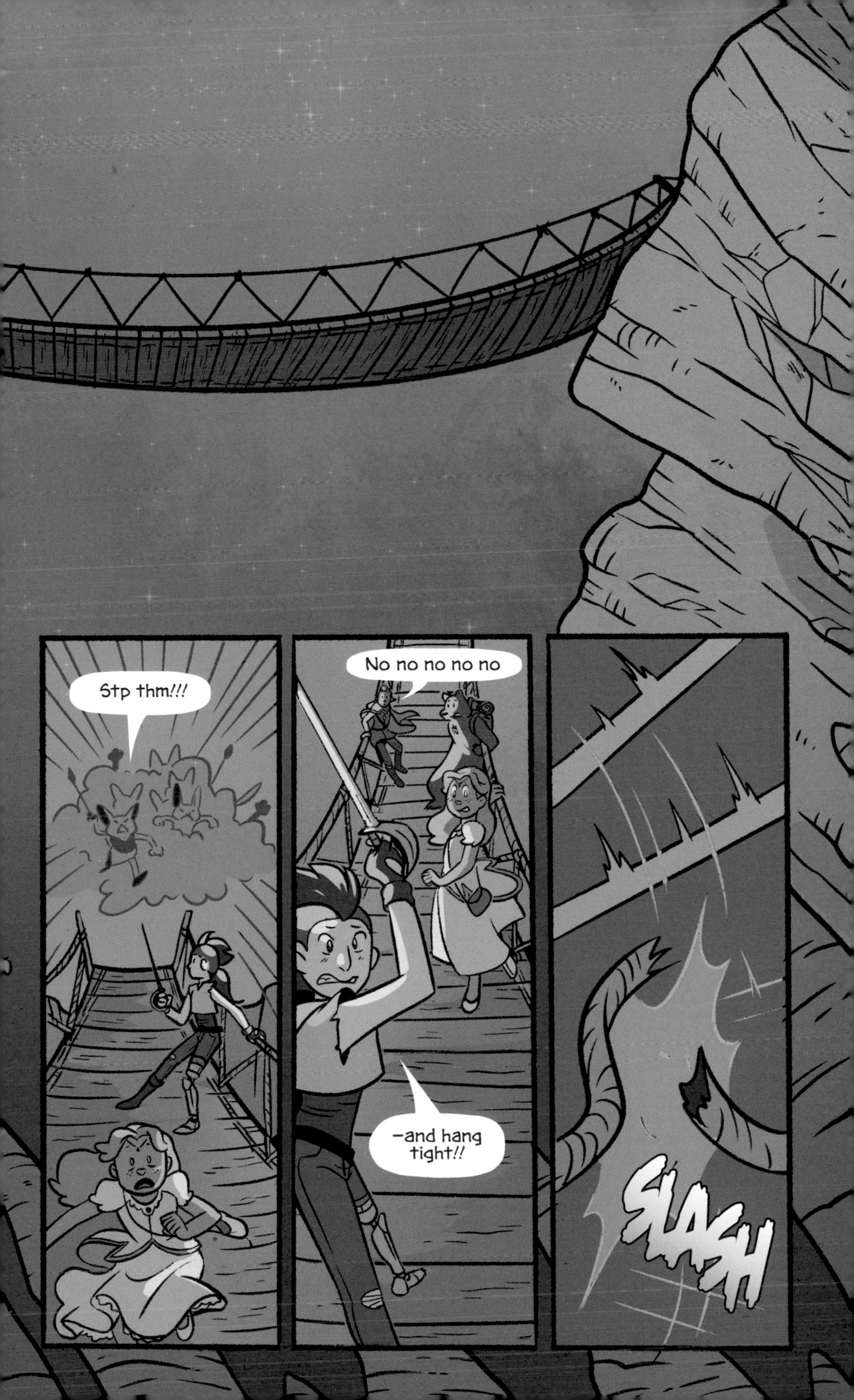
Stp thm!!!
No no no no no
–and hang tight!!
SLASH

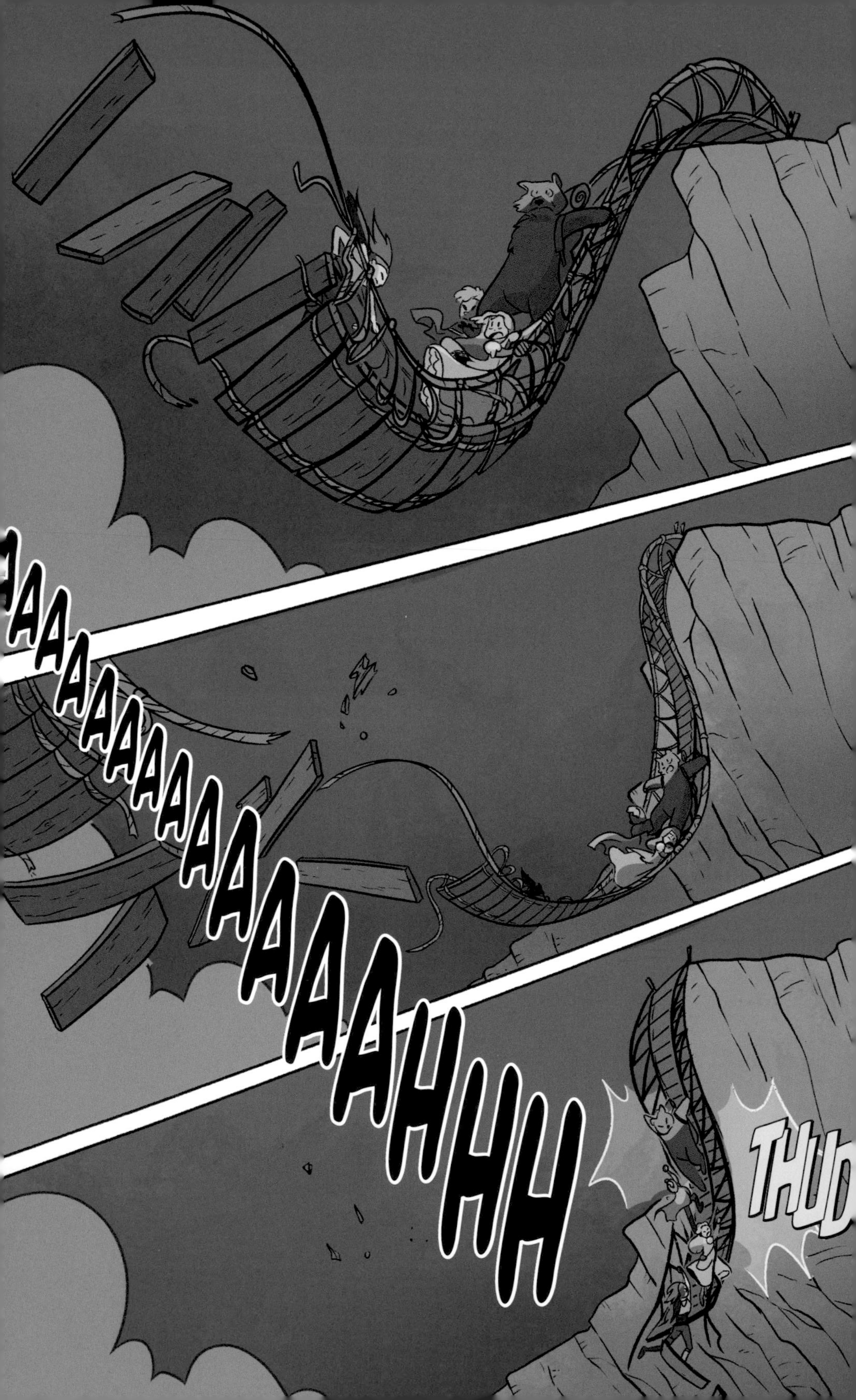
AAAAAAAAAAAAAAAHHHH
THUD

163

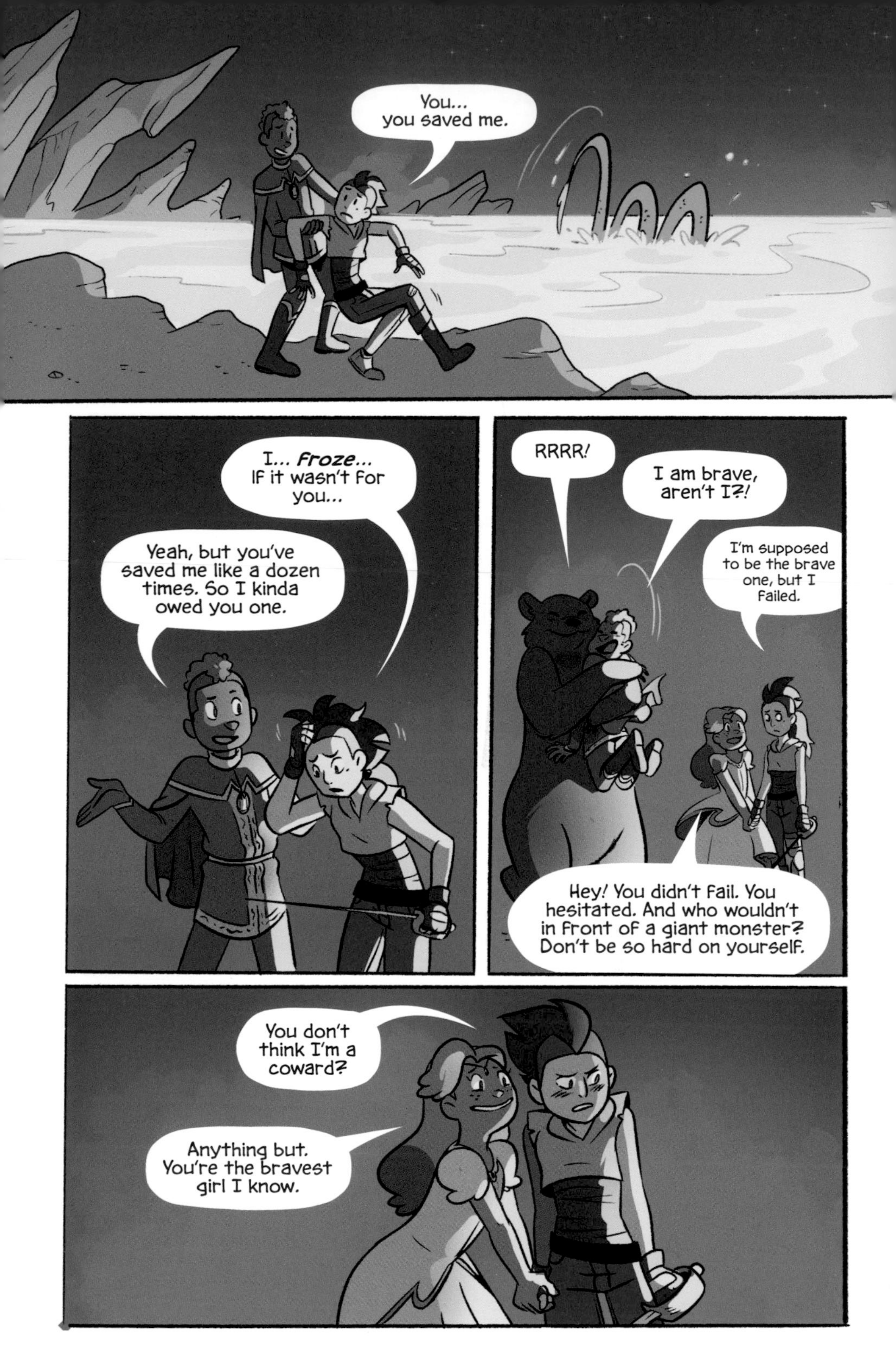
You... you saved me.
I... *Froze*... If it wasn't for you...
Yeah, but you've saved me like a dozen times. So I kinda owed you one.
RRRR!
I am brave, aren't I?!
I'm supposed to be the brave one, but I failed.
Hey! You didn't fail. You hesitated. And who wouldn't in front of a giant monster? Don't be so hard on yourself.
You don't think I'm a coward?
Anything but. You're the bravest girl I know.

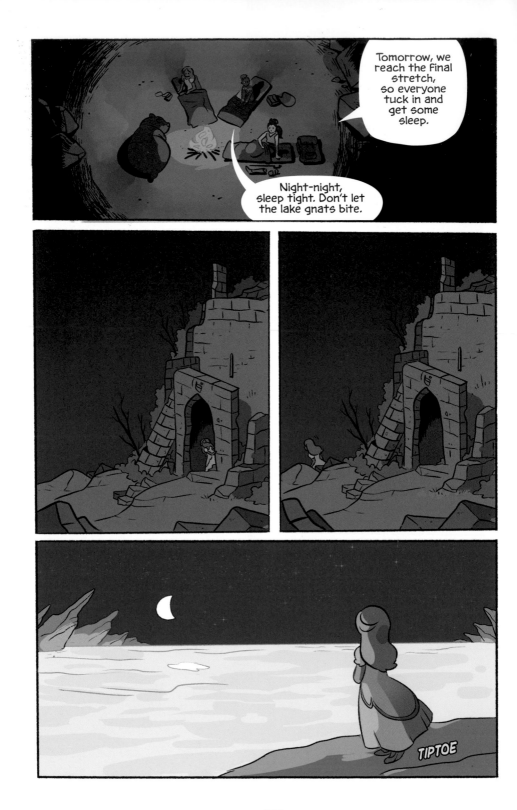

173

The next day...
So those are the *Night Mountains?* Nope, not scary at all.
It does look a lot more ominous than I thought—and I thought it'd be terrifying.
Dillie and I have a stake in this, Fred, you don't. We'd understand if you want to turn around.
If I bail now, I don't deserve the Montrose throne. So I have something to prove too. Let's do this.
Rrrrr.

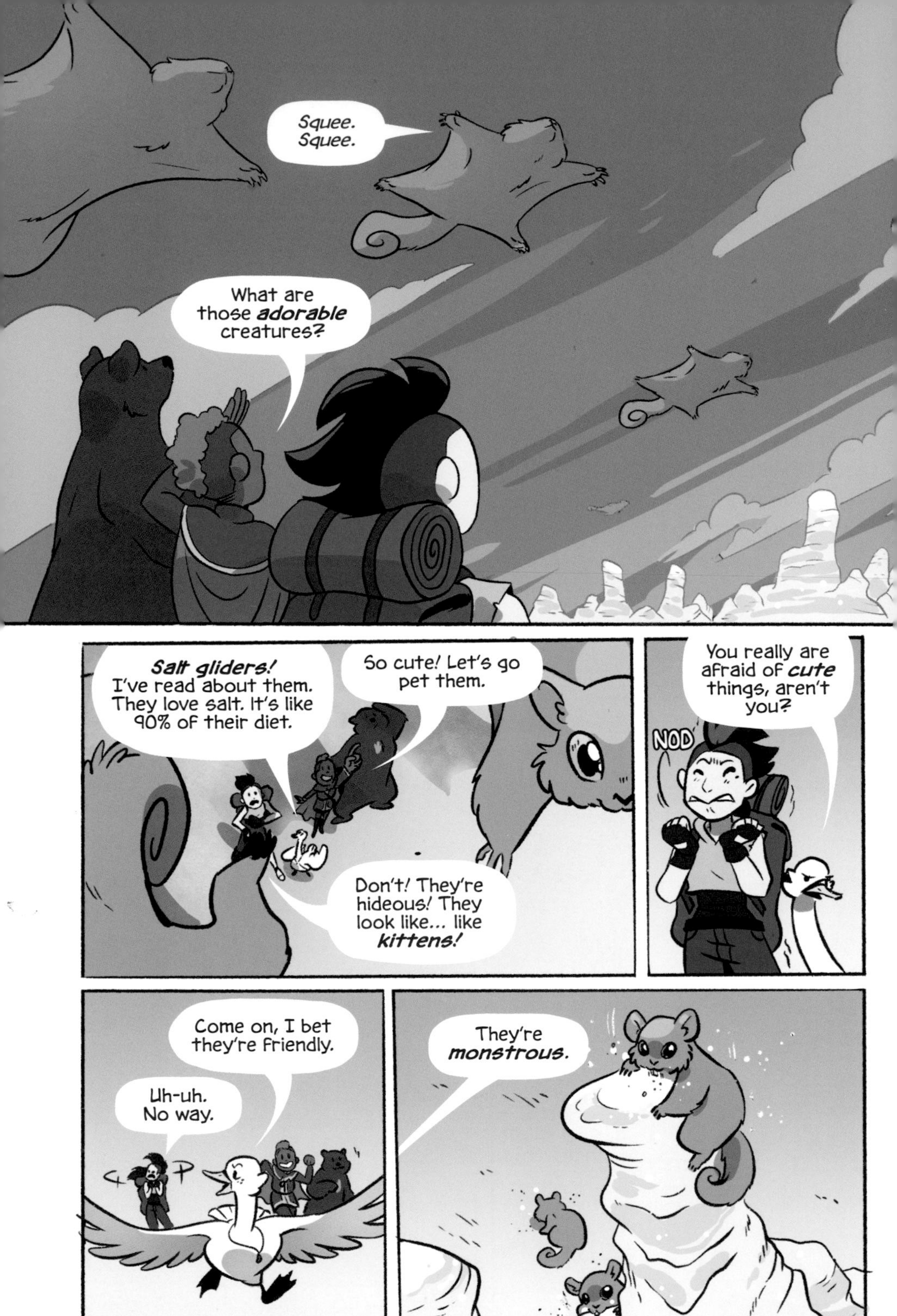
Squee.
Squee.
What are those ***adorable*** creatures?
Salt gliders! I've read about them. They love salt. It's like 90% of their diet.
So cute! Let's go pet them.
Don't! They're hideous! They look like... like ***kittens!***
You really are afraid of ***cute*** things, aren't you?
NOD
Come on, I bet they're friendly.
Uh-uh. No way.
They're ***monstrous.***

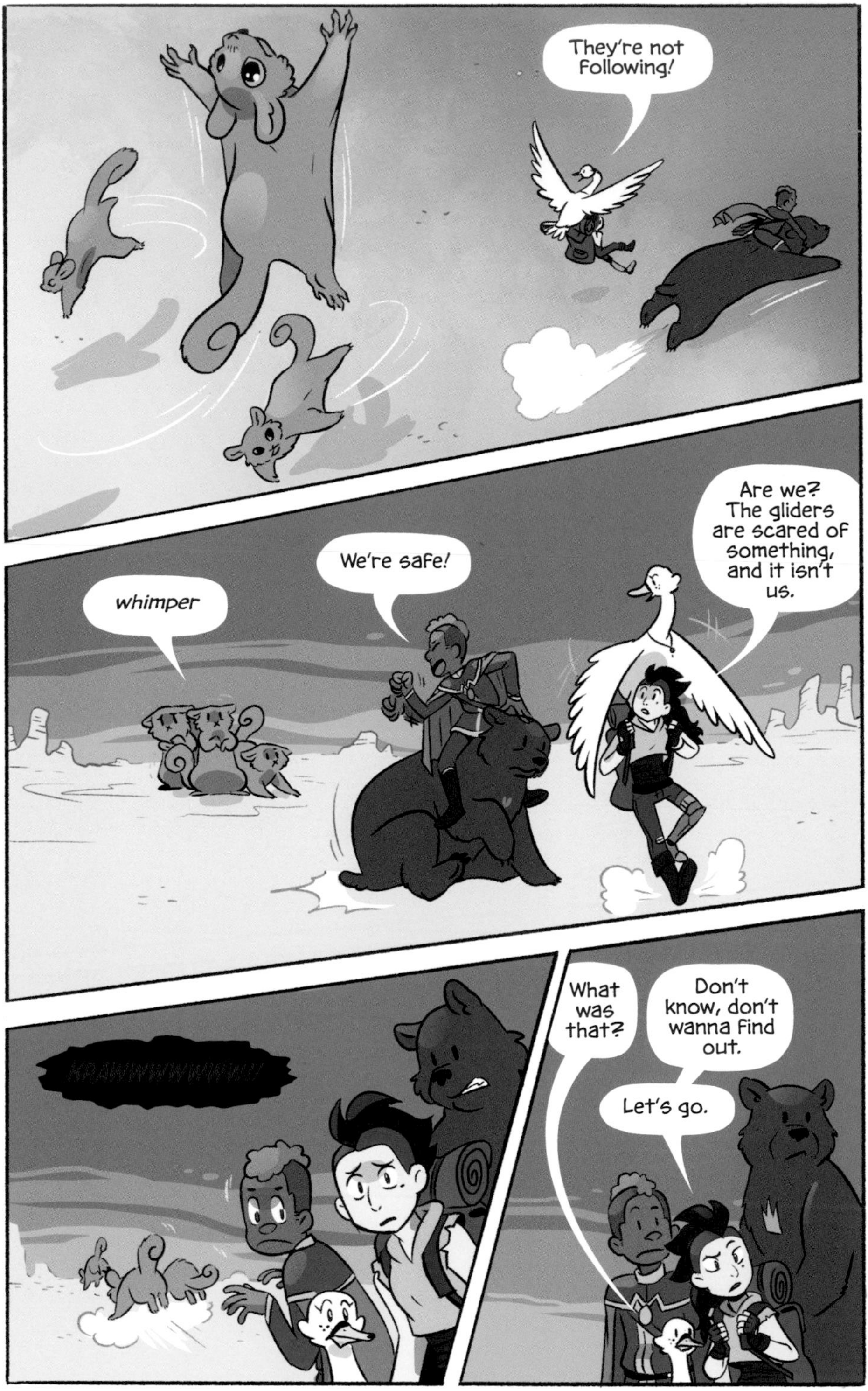
They're not following!
whimper
We're safe!
Are we? The gliders are scared of something, and it isn't us.
What was that?
Don't know, don't wanna find out.
Let's go.

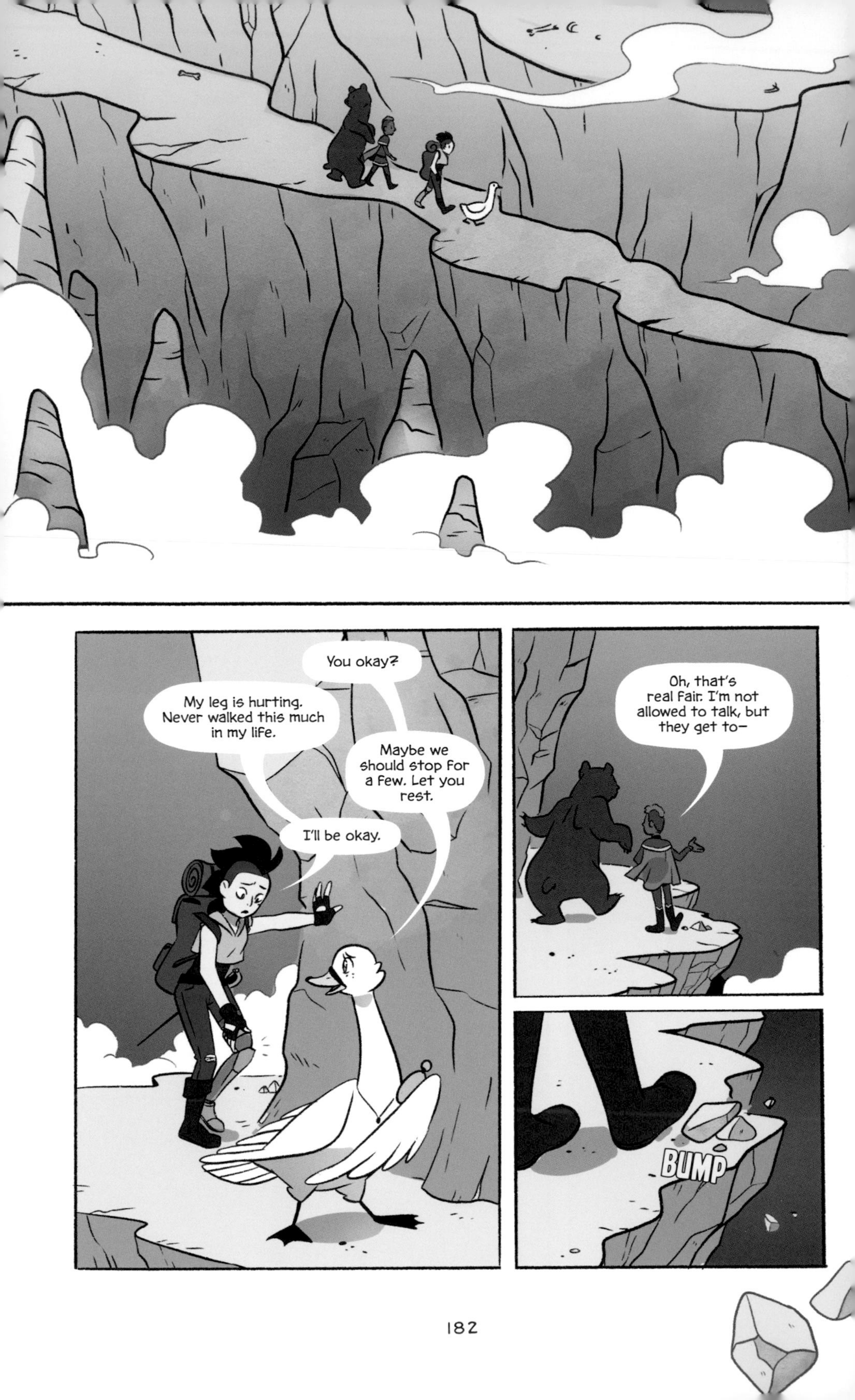
You okay?
My leg is hurting. Never walked this much in my life.
Maybe we should stop for a few. Let you rest.
I'll be okay.
Oh, that's real fair. I'm not allowed to talk, but they get to—
BUMP

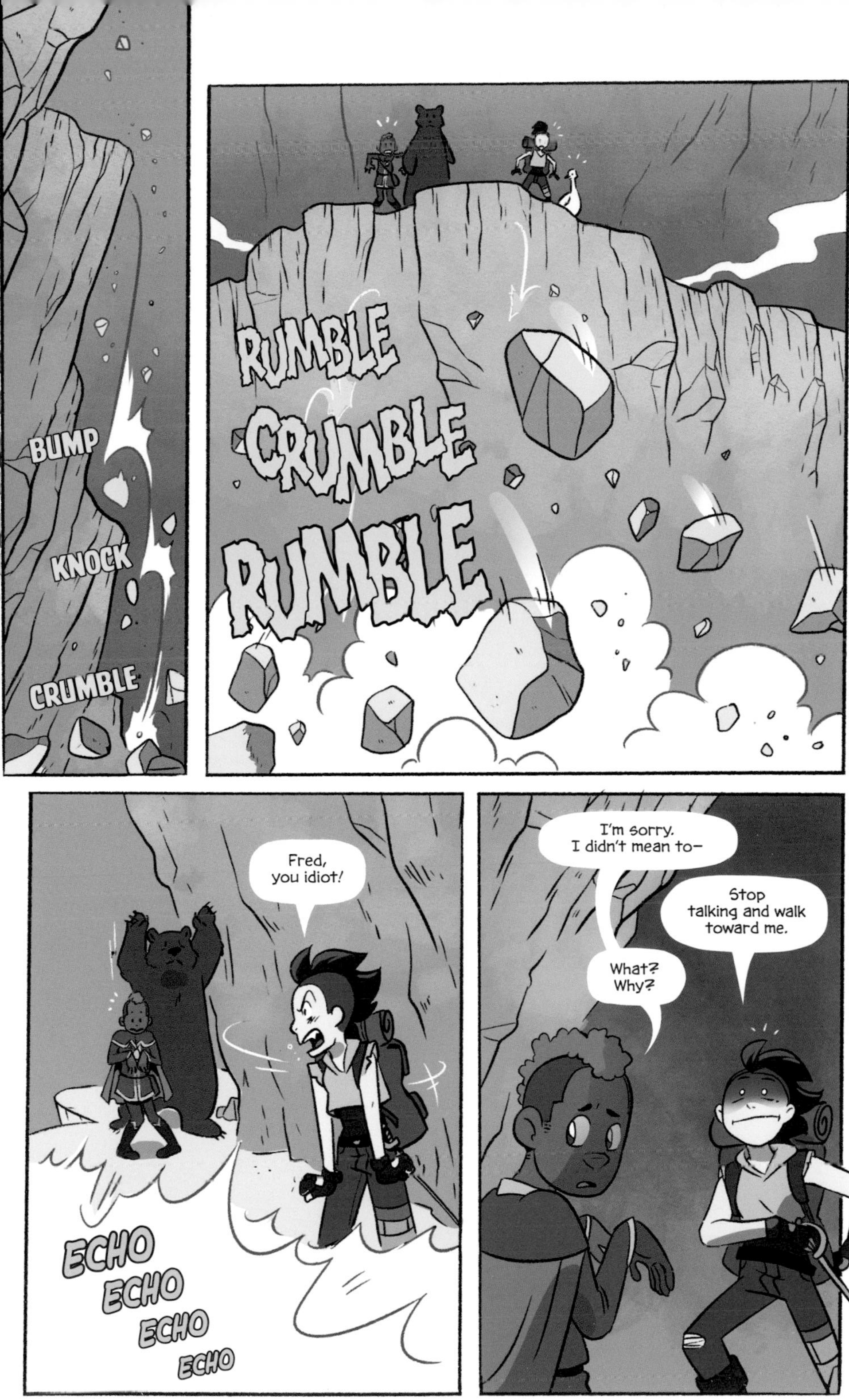
BUMP
KNOCK
CRUMBLE
RUMBLE
CRUMBLE
RUMBLE
Fred,
you idiot!
ECHO
ECHO
ECHO
ECHO
I'm sorry.
I didn't mean to—
Stop
talking and walk
toward me.
What?
Why?

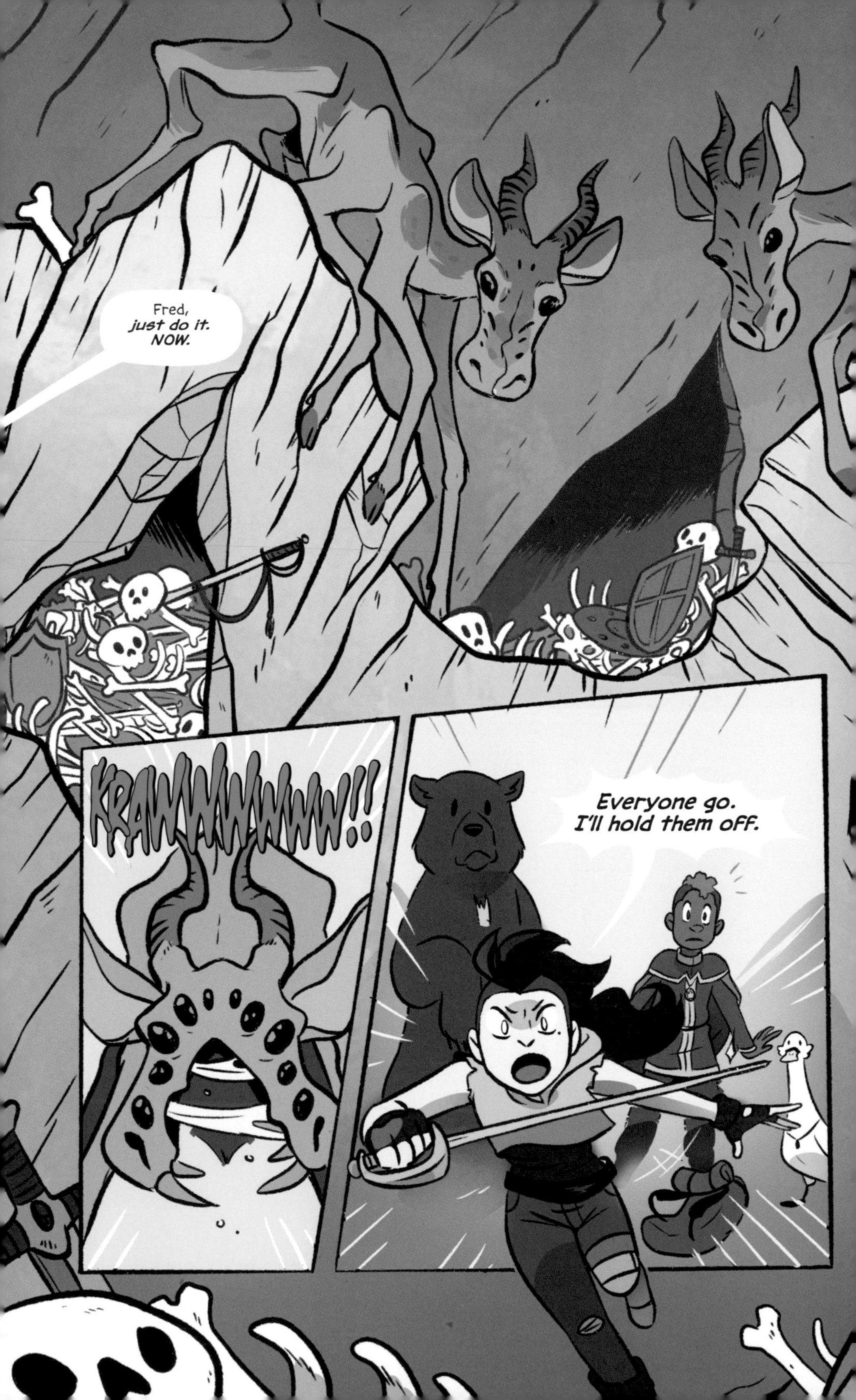
Fred,
just do it.
NOW.
KRAWWWWWW!!
Everyone go.
I'll hold them off.

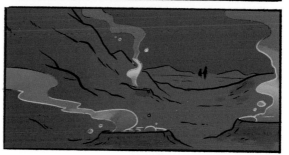

Worry not, my friends. It is always *darkest* before the *dawn...*

PART III

MONTROSE

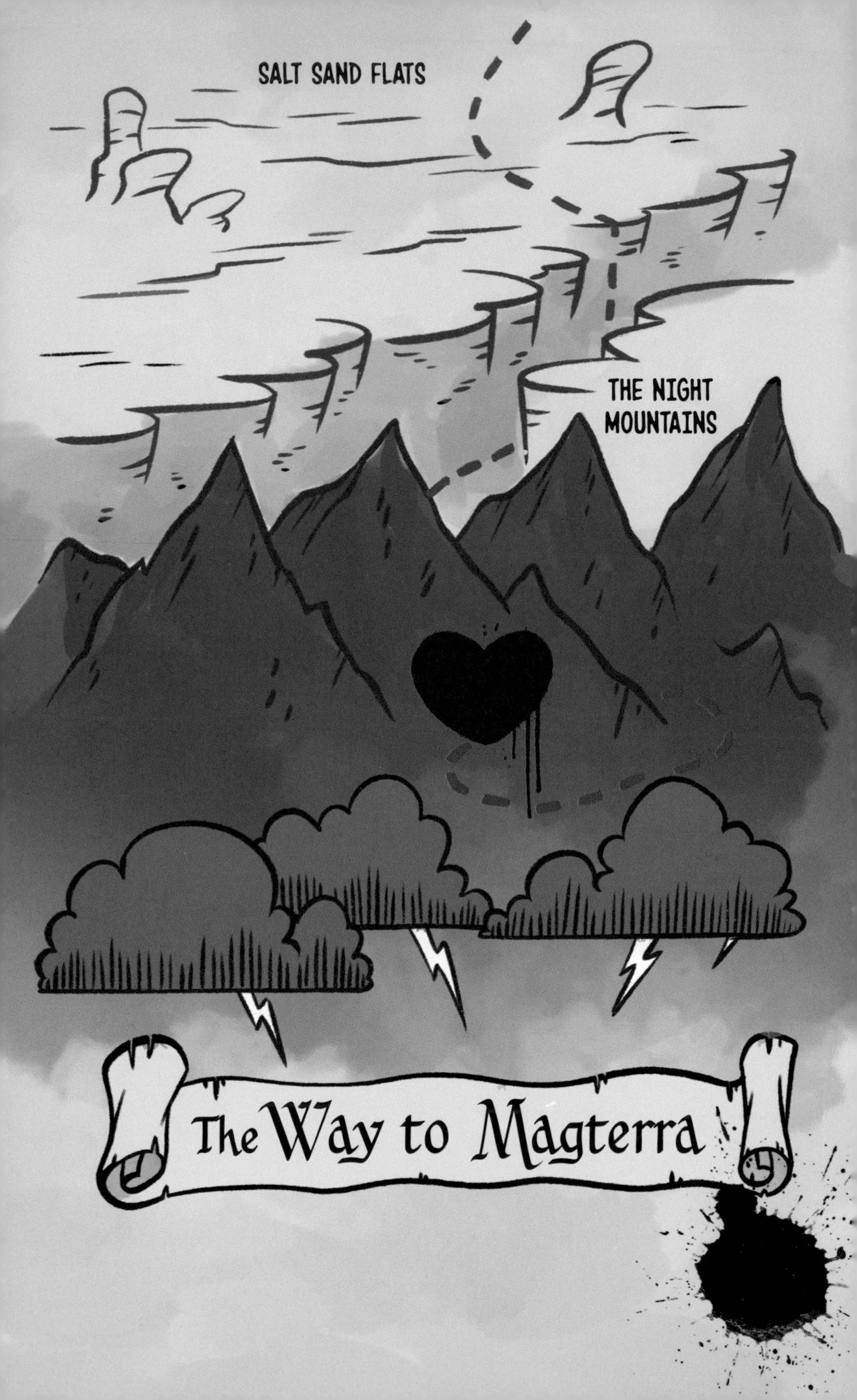
SALT SAND FLATS
THE NIGHT MOUNTAINS
The Way to Magterra

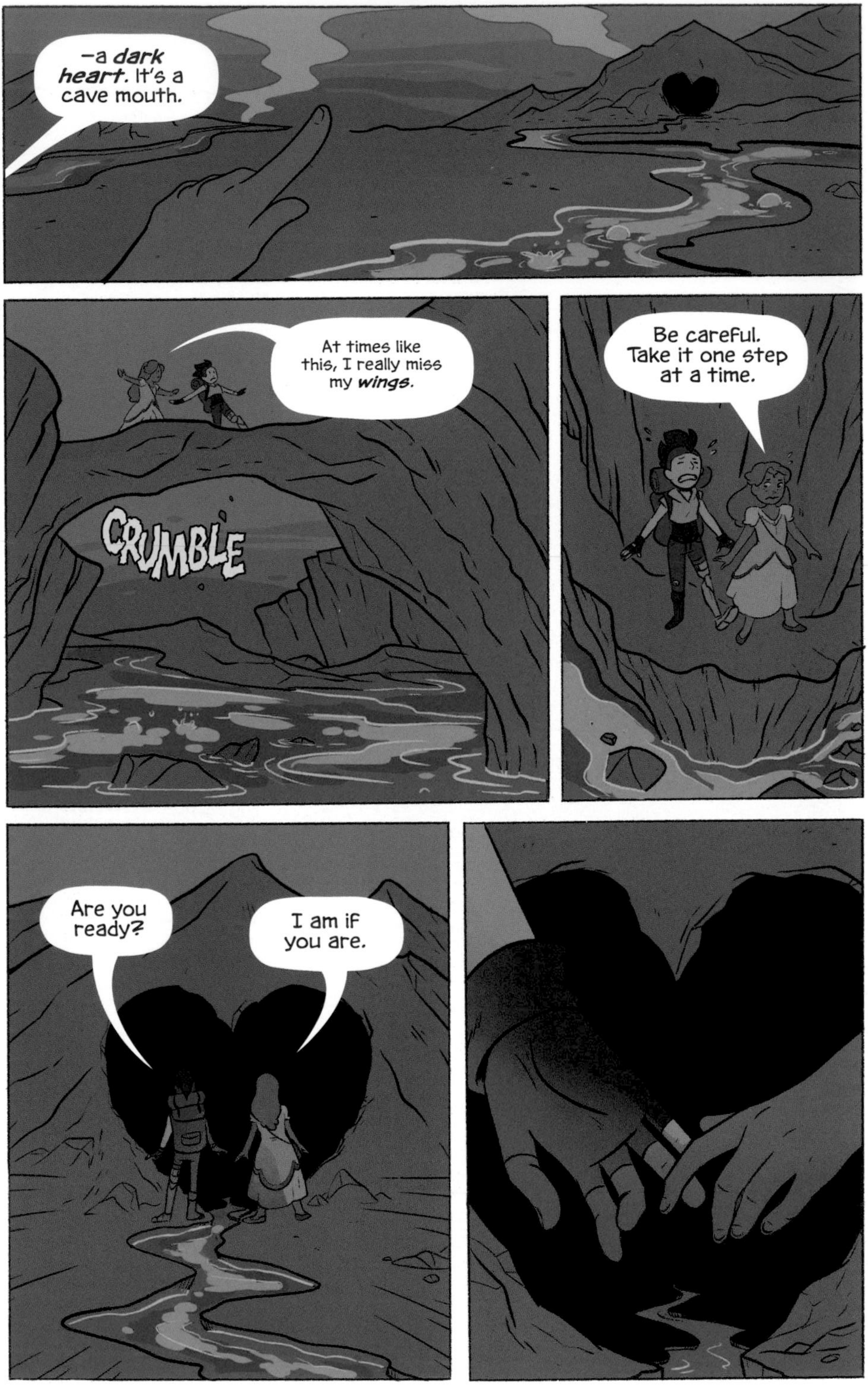
—a *dark heart*. It's a cave mouth.
At times like this, I really miss my *wings*.
CRUMBLE
Be careful. Take it one step at a time.
Are you ready?
I am if you are.

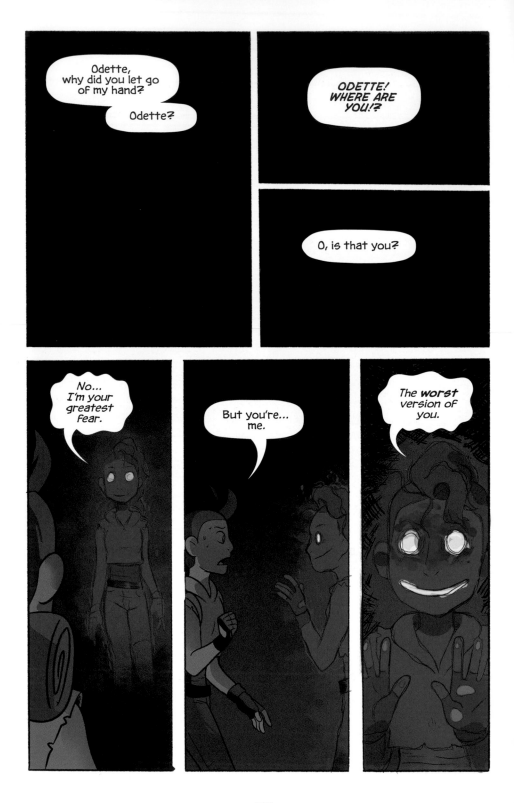

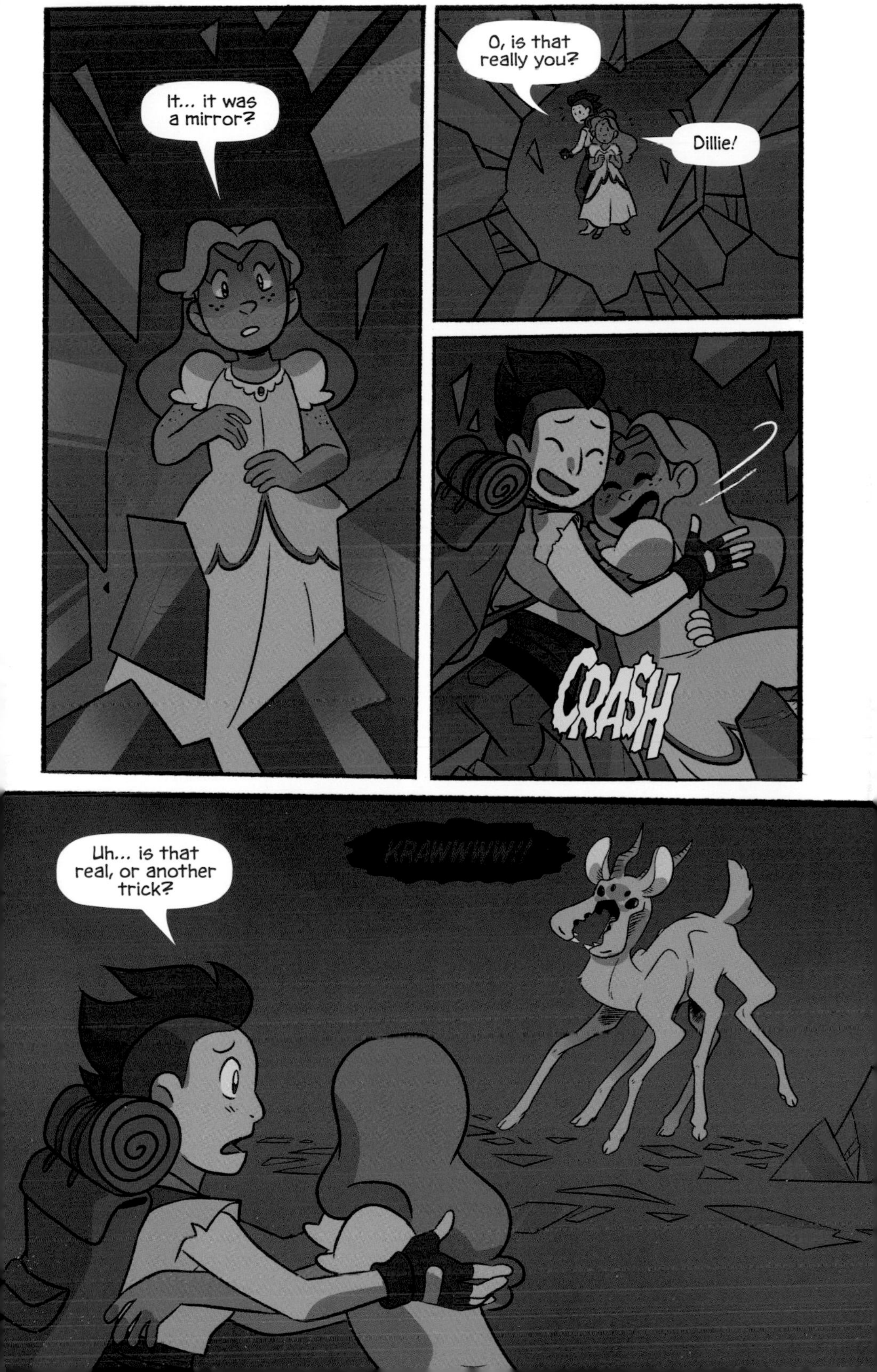
It... it was a mirror?
O, is that really you?
Dillie!
CRASH
Uh... is that real, or another trick?
KRAWWWW!!

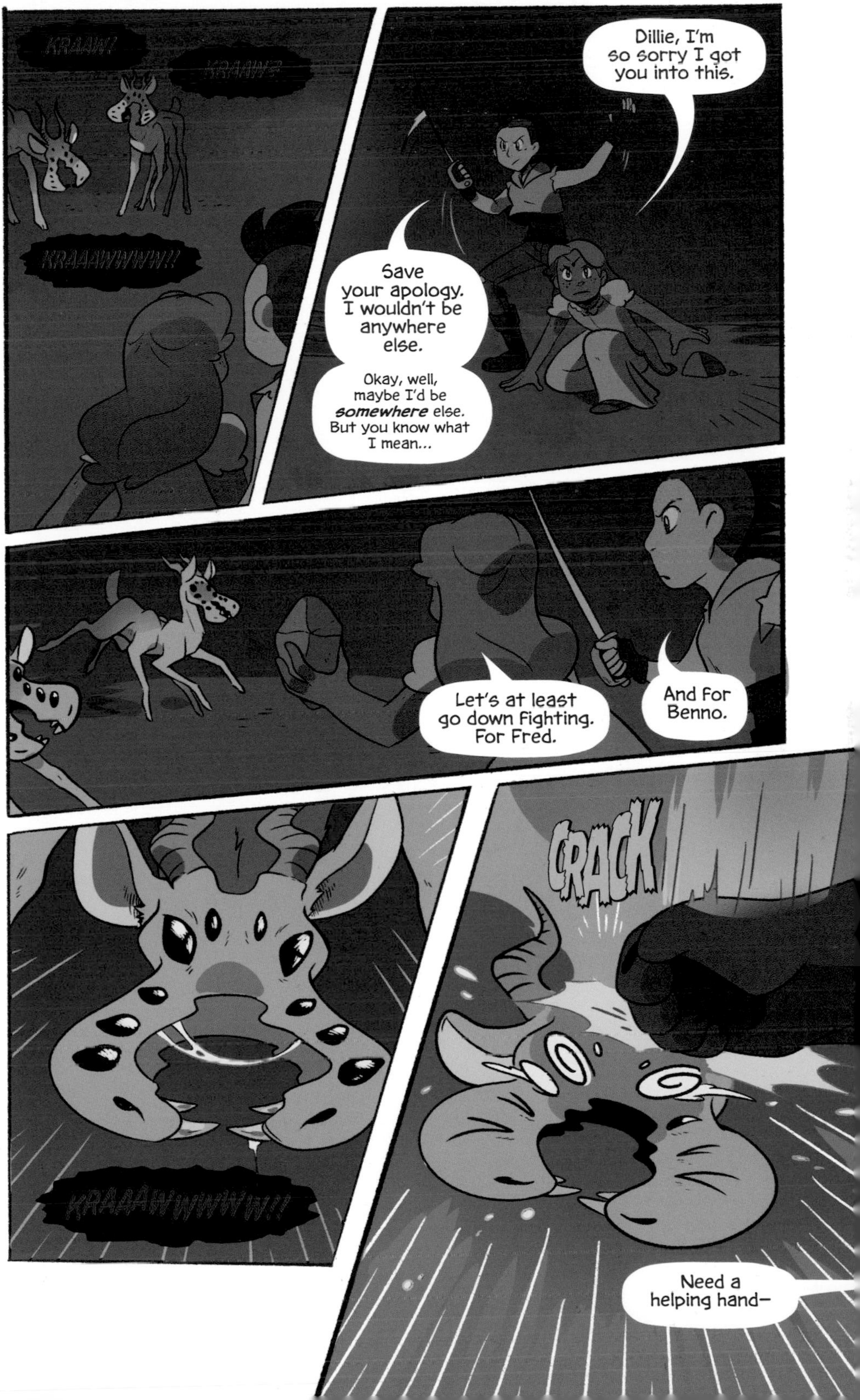
KRAAW!
KRAAAWWWW!!
Dillie, I'm so sorry I got you into this.
Save your apology. I wouldn't be anywhere else.
Okay, well, maybe I'd be *somewhere* else. But you know what I mean...
Let's at least go down fighting. For Fred.
And for Benno.
KRAAAWWWWWW!!
CRACK
Need a helping hand—

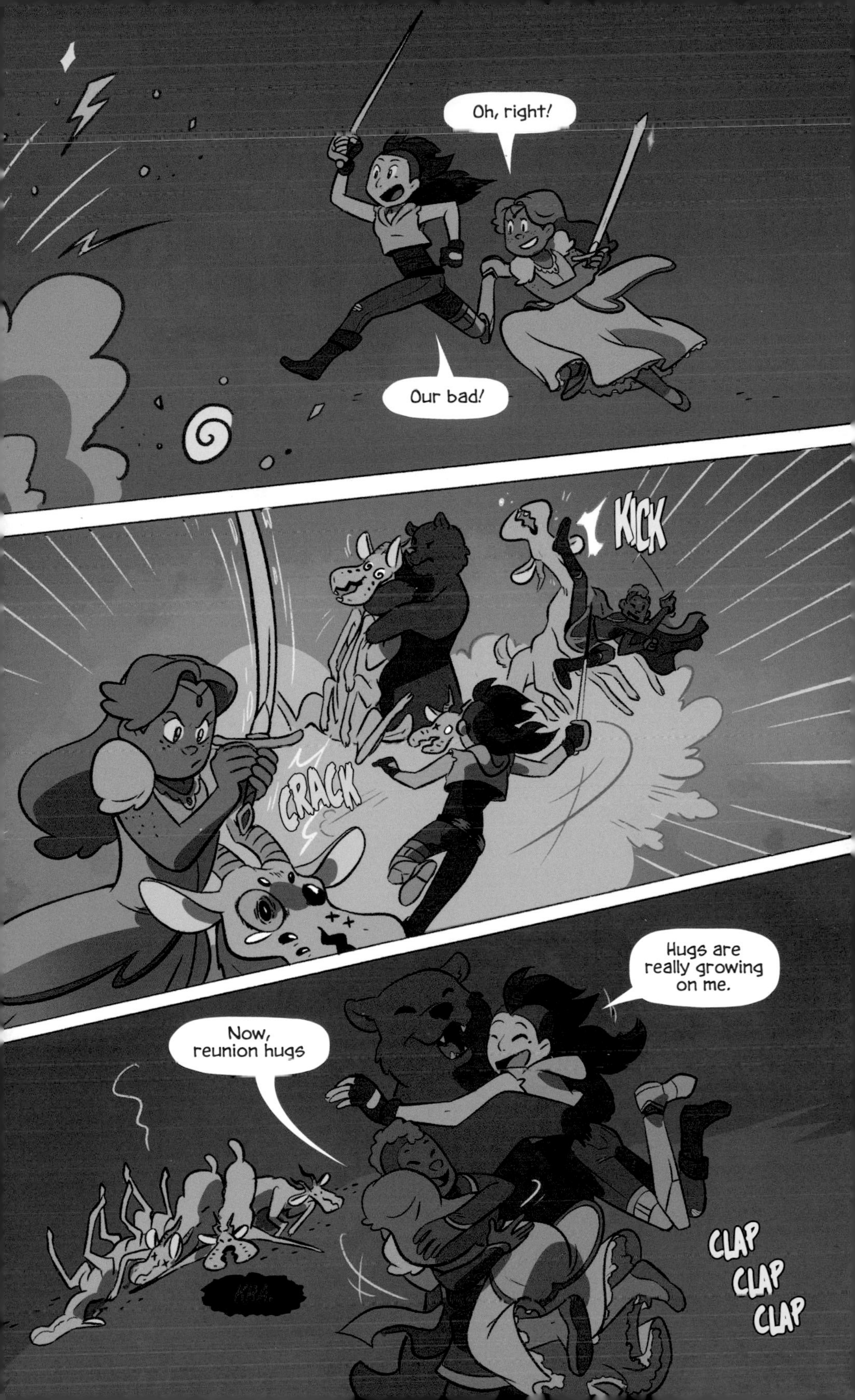
Oh, right!
Our bad!
KICK
CRACK
Now, reunion hugs
Hugs are really growing on me.
CLAP
CLAP
CLAP

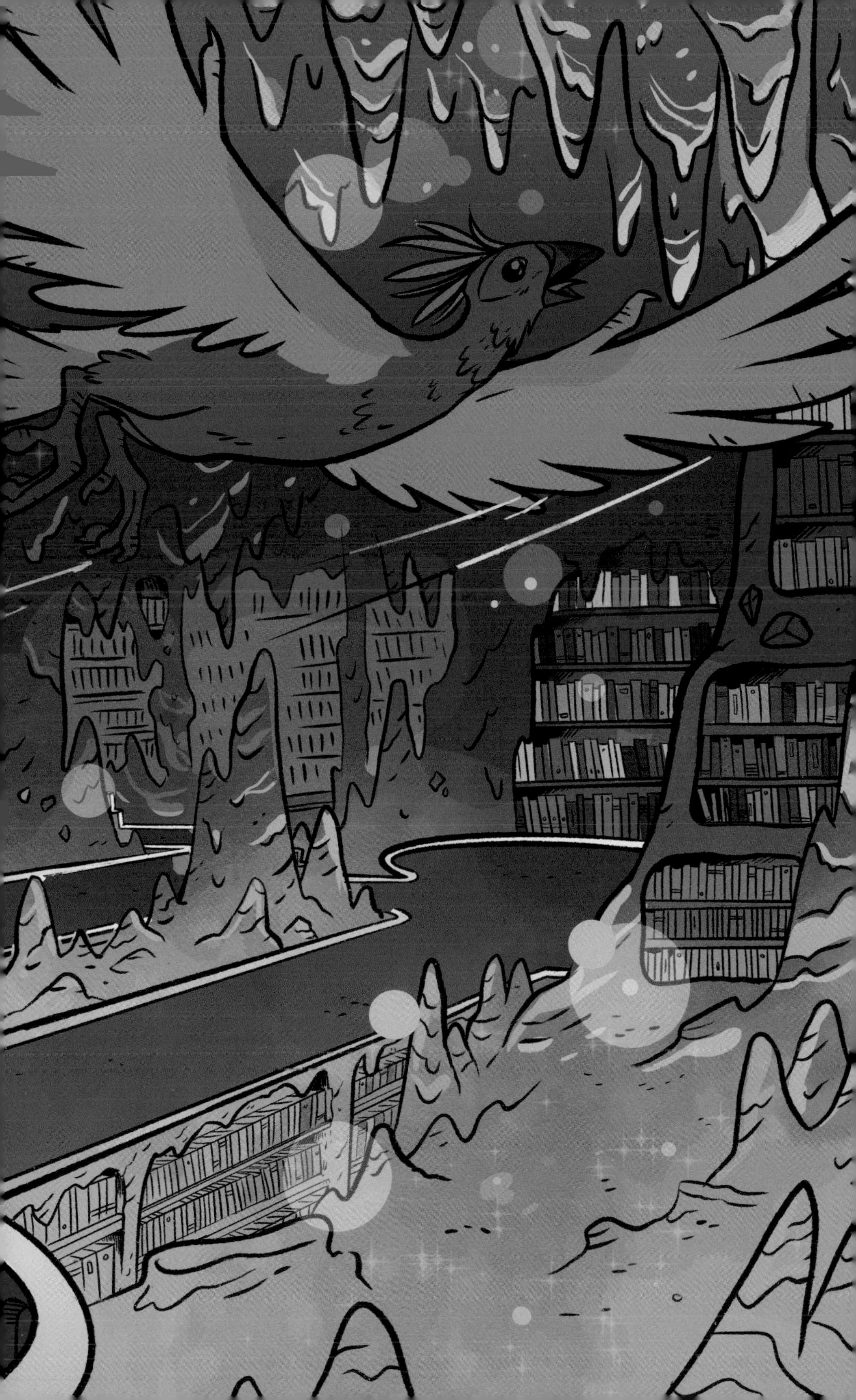

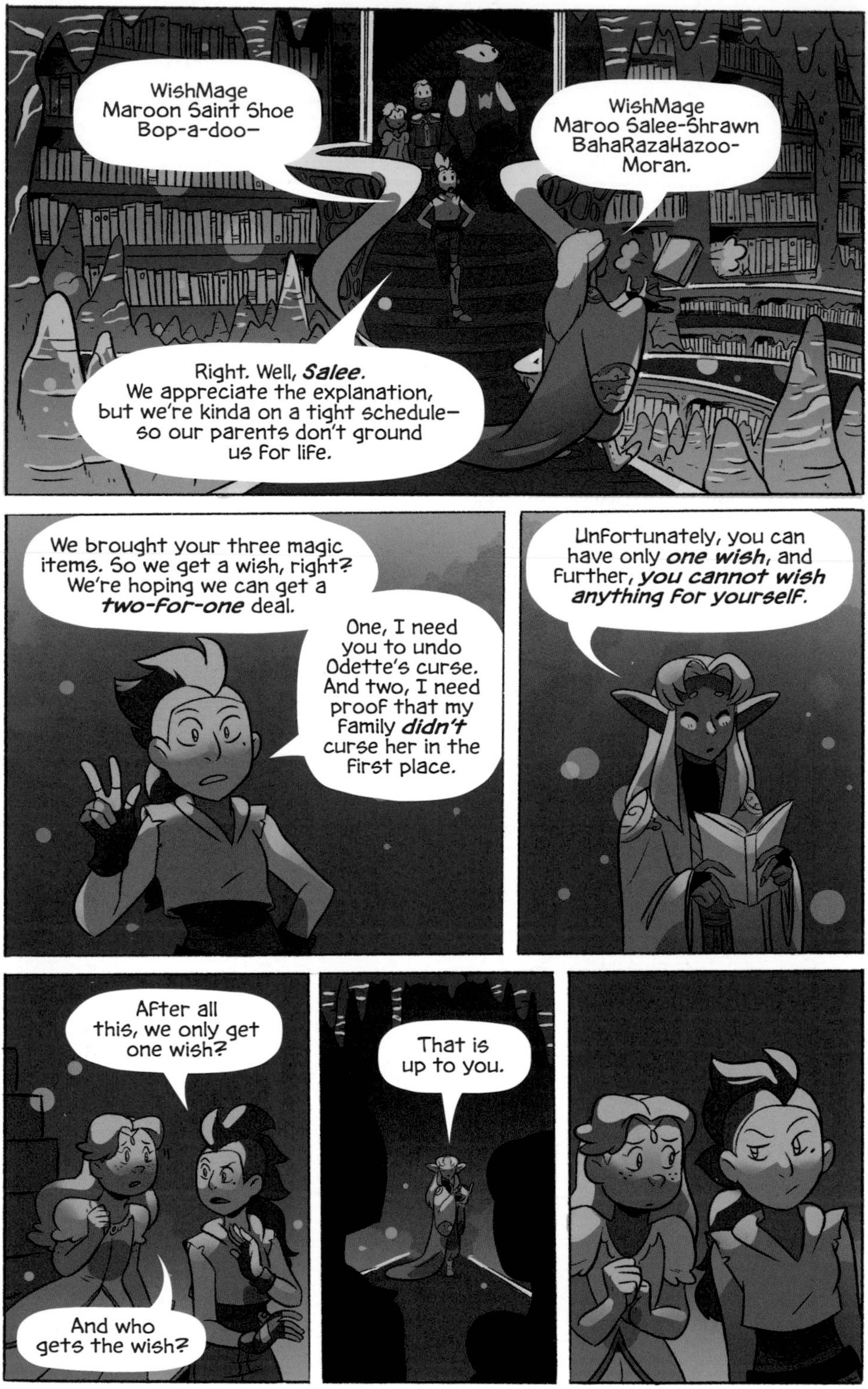
WishMage Maroon Saint Shoe Bop-a-doo–
WishMage Maroo Salee-Shrawn BahaRazaHazoo-Moran.
Right. Well, ***Salee.*** We appreciate the explanation, but we're kinda on a tight schedule– so our parents don't ground us for life.
We brought your three magic items. So we get a wish, right? We're hoping we can get a ***two-for-one*** deal.
One, I need you to undo Odette's curse. And two, I need proof that my family ***didn't*** curse her in the first place.
Unfortunately, you can have only ***one wish***, and further, ***you cannot wish anything for yourself.***
After all this, we only get one wish?
And who gets the wish?
That is up to you.

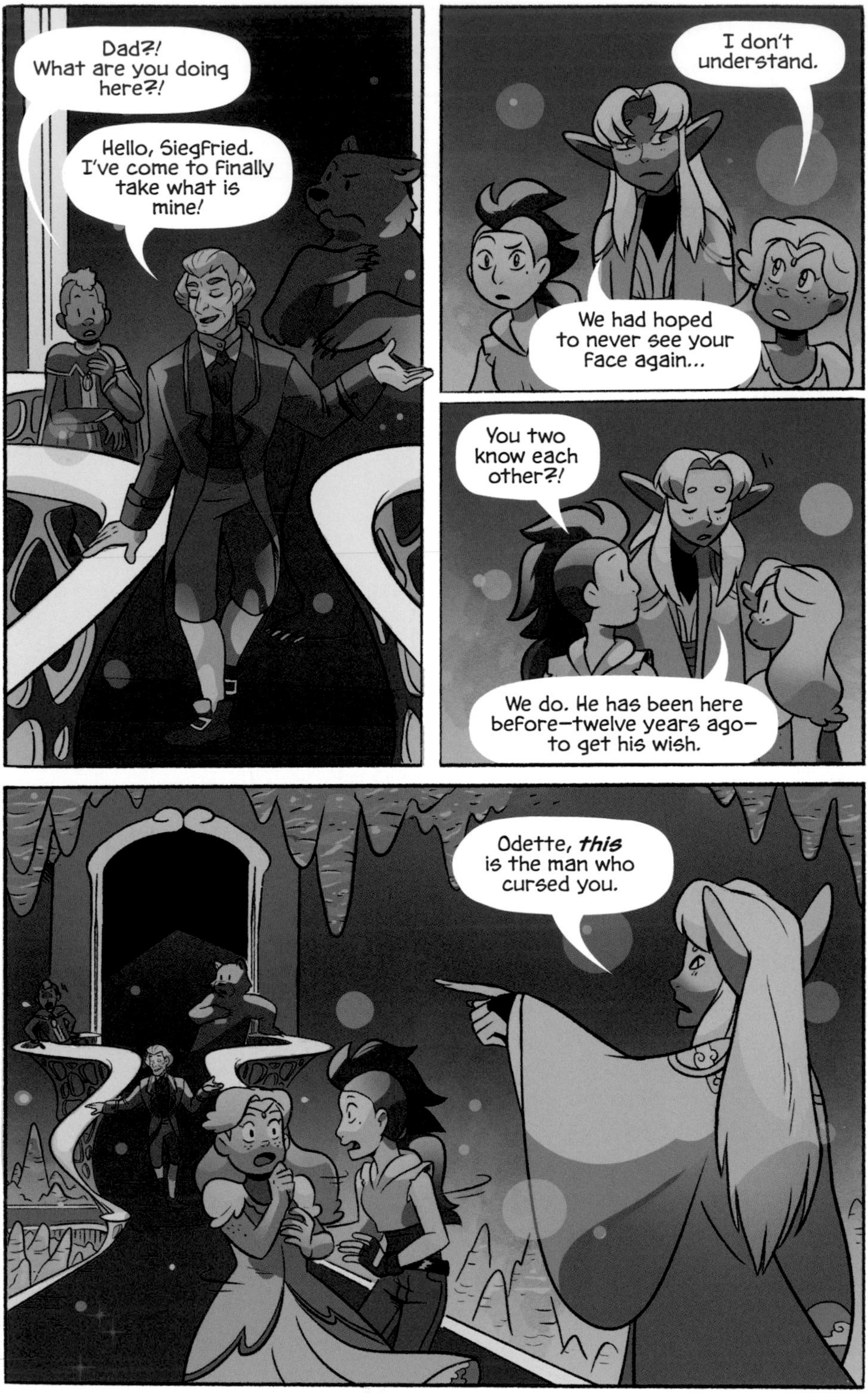
Dad?!
What are you doing
here?!
Hello, Siegfried.
I've come to finally
take what is
mine!
I don't
understand.
We had hoped
to never see your
face again...
You two
know each
other?!
We do. He has been here
before—twelve years ago—
to get his wish.
Odette, *this*
is the man who
cursed you.

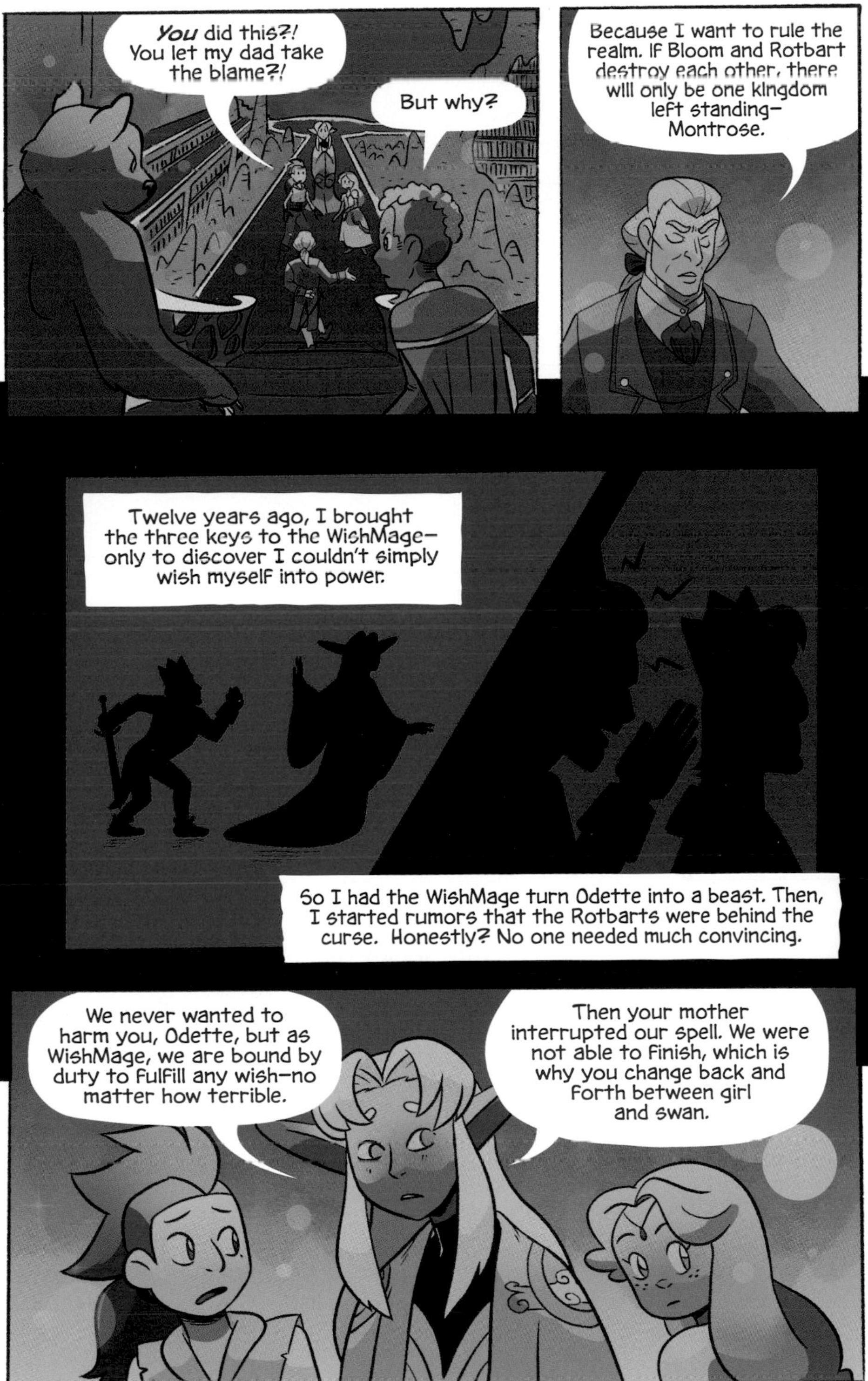
You did this?! You let my dad take the blame?!
But why?
Because I want to rule the realm. If Bloom and Rotbart destroy each other, there will only be one kingdom left standing—Montrose.
Twelve years ago, I brought the three keys to the WishMage—only to discover I couldn't simply wish myself into power.
So I had the WishMage turn Odette into a beast. Then, I started rumors that the Rotbarts were behind the curse. Honestly? No one needed much convincing.
We never wanted to harm you, Odette, but as WishMage, we are bound by duty to fulfill any wish—no matter how terrible.
Then your mother interrupted our spell. We were not able to finish, which is why you change back and forth between girl and swan.

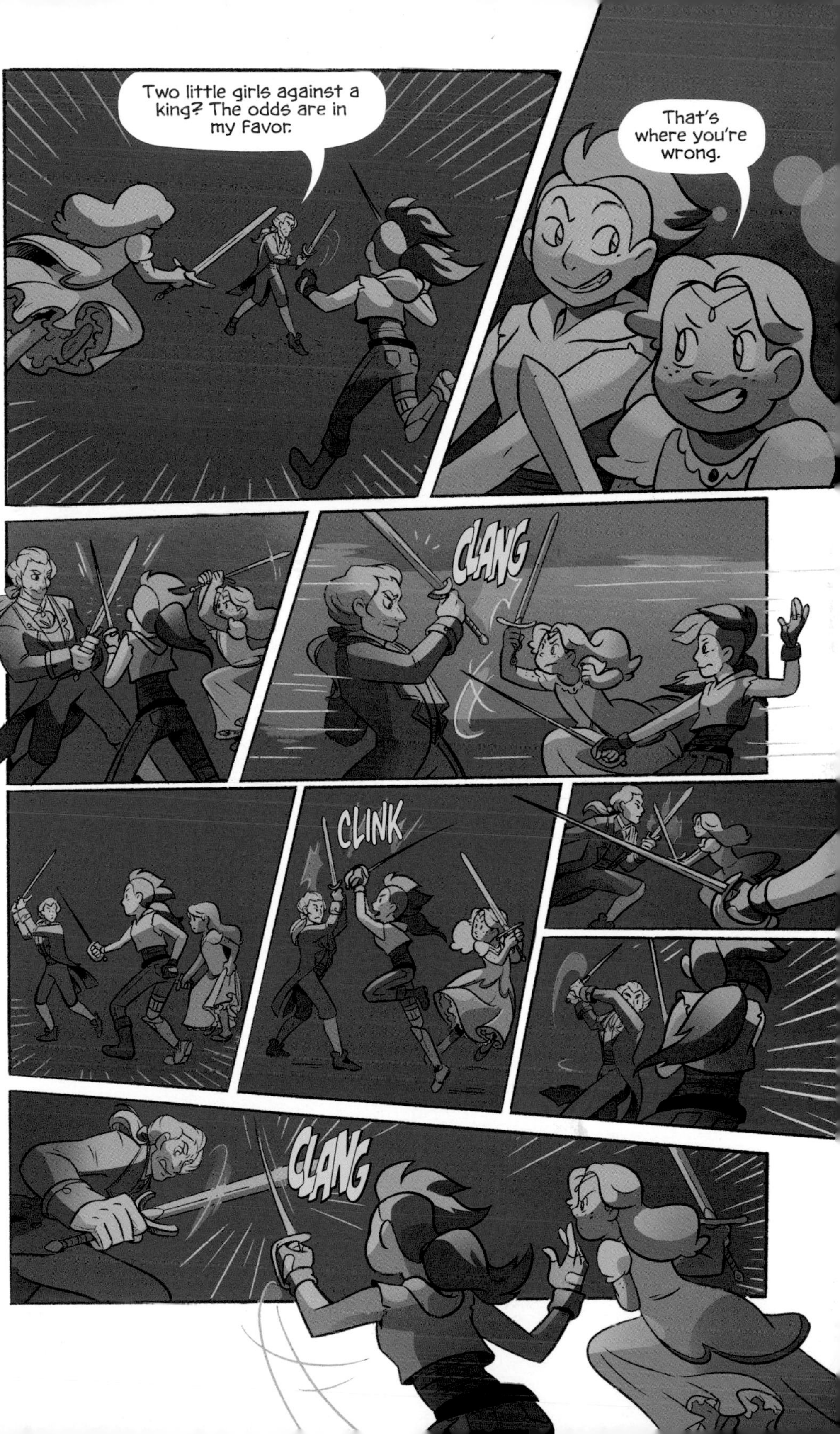
Two little girls against a king? The odds are in my favor.
That's where you're wrong.
CLANG
CLINK
CLANG

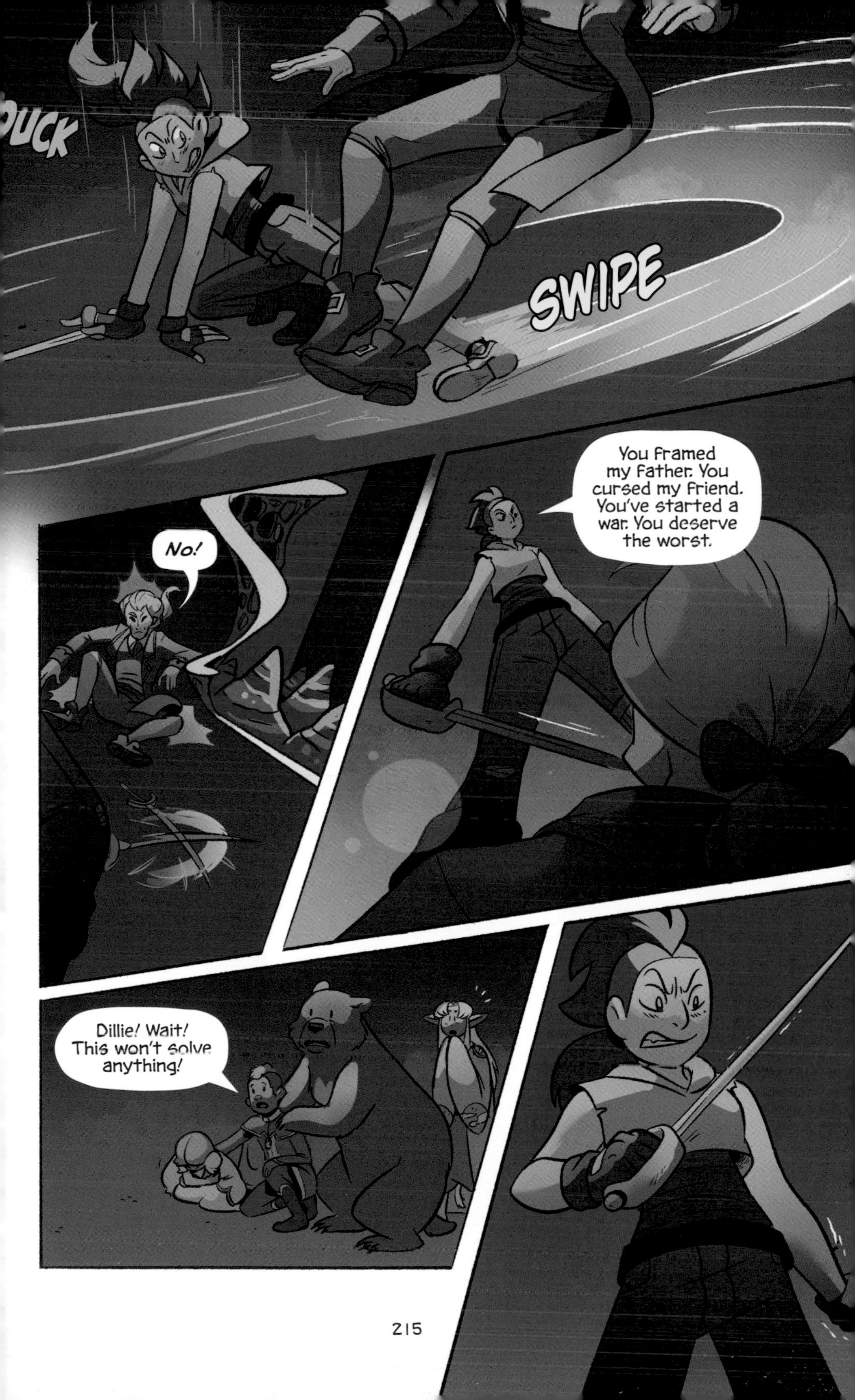
DUCK
SWIPE
No!
You framed my father. You cursed my friend. You've started a war. You deserve the worst.
Dillie! Wait! This won't solve anything!

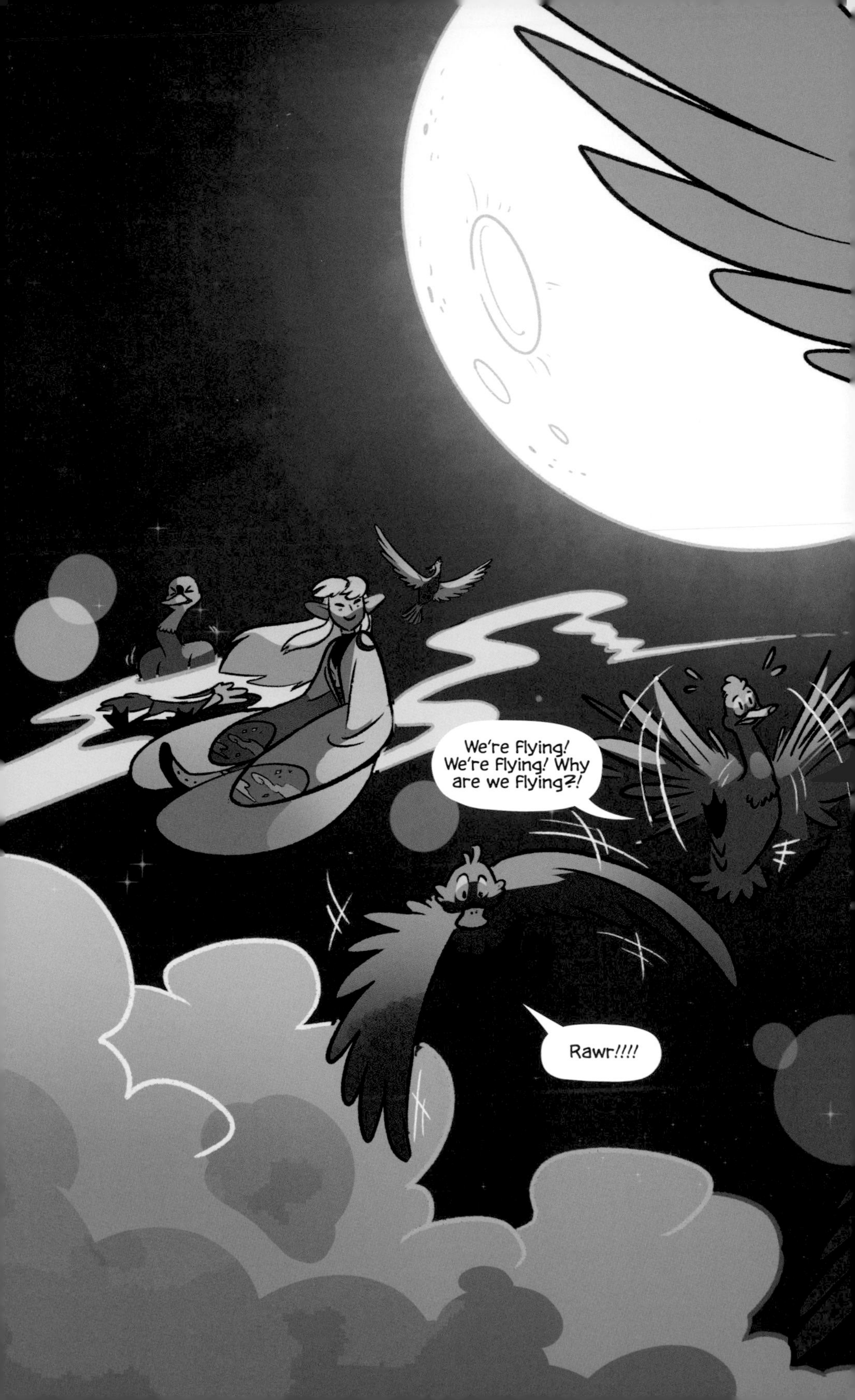
We're flying! We're flying! Why are we flying?!
Rawr!!!!

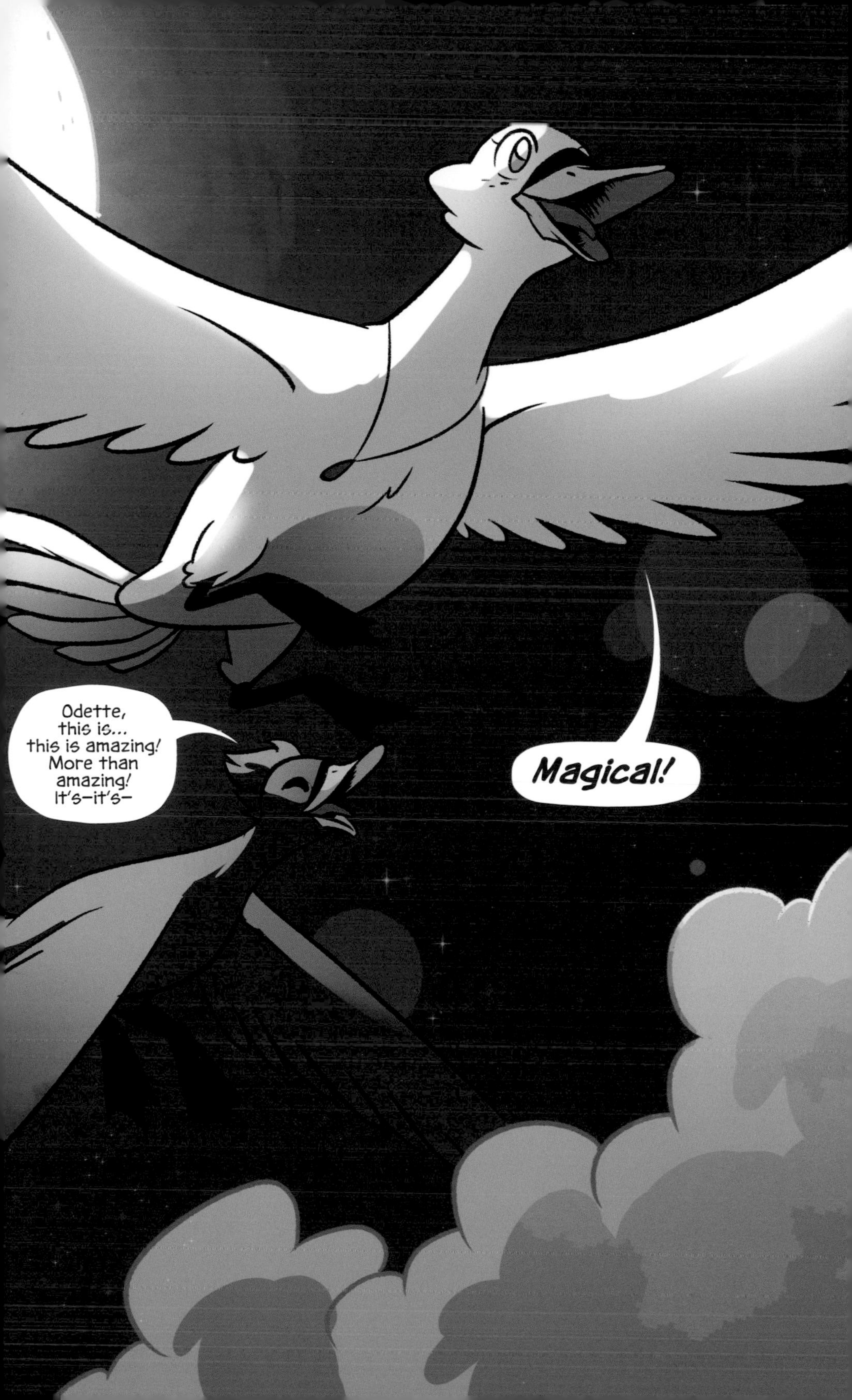
Odette, this is... this is amazing! More than amazing! It's—it's—
Magical!

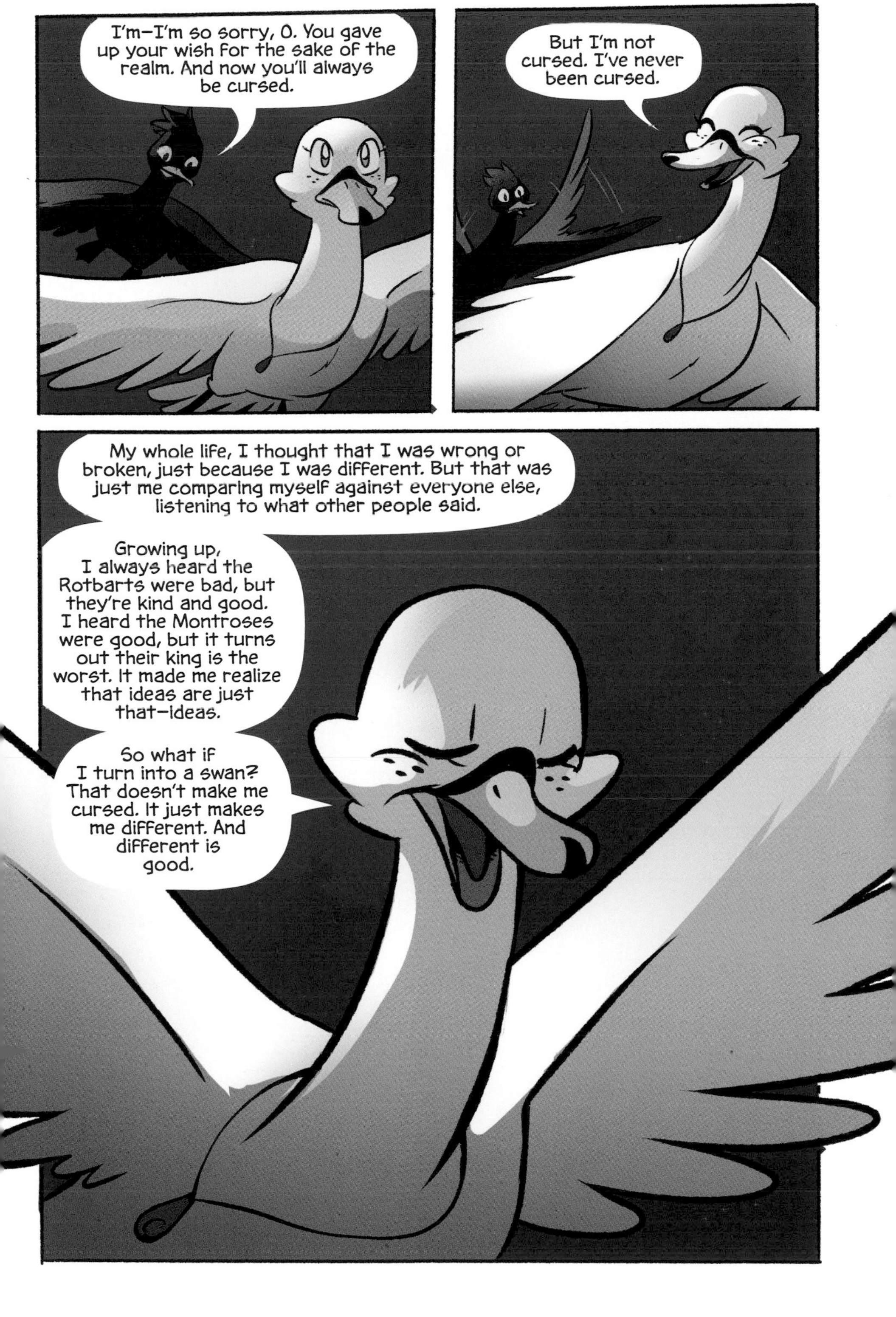
I'm—I'm so sorry, O. You gave up your wish for the sake of the realm. And now you'll always be cursed.
But I'm not cursed. I've never been cursed.
My whole life, I thought that I was wrong or broken, just because I was different. But that was just me comparing myself against everyone else, listening to what other people said.
Growing up, I always heard the Rotbarts were bad, but they're kind and good. I heard the Montroses were good, but it turns out their king is the worst. It made me realize that ideas are just that—ideas.
So what if I turn into a swan? That doesn't make me cursed. It just makes me different. And different is good.

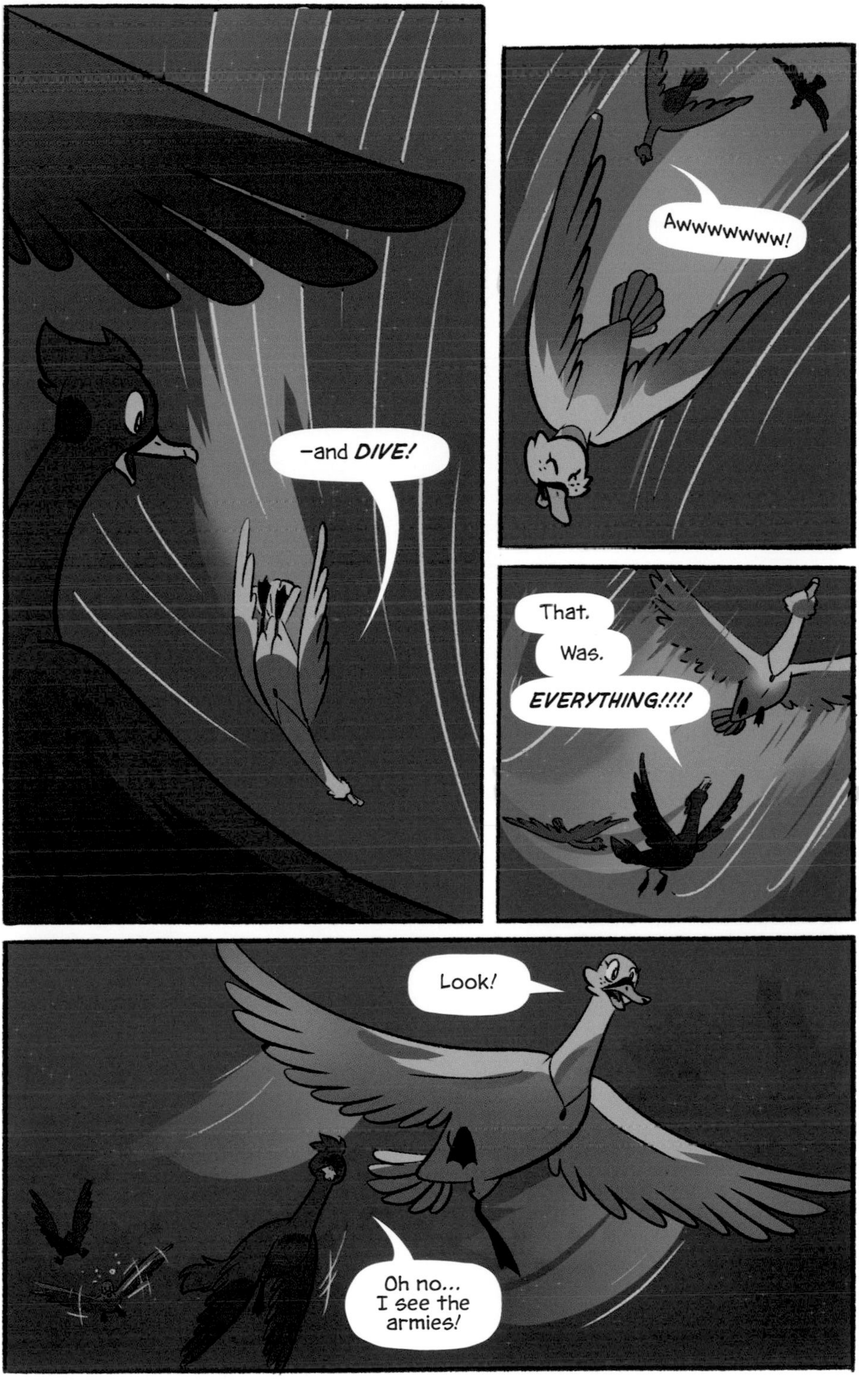

–and *DIVE!*
Awwwwwwww!
That.
Was.
EVERYTHING!!!!
Look!
Oh no...
I see the
armies!

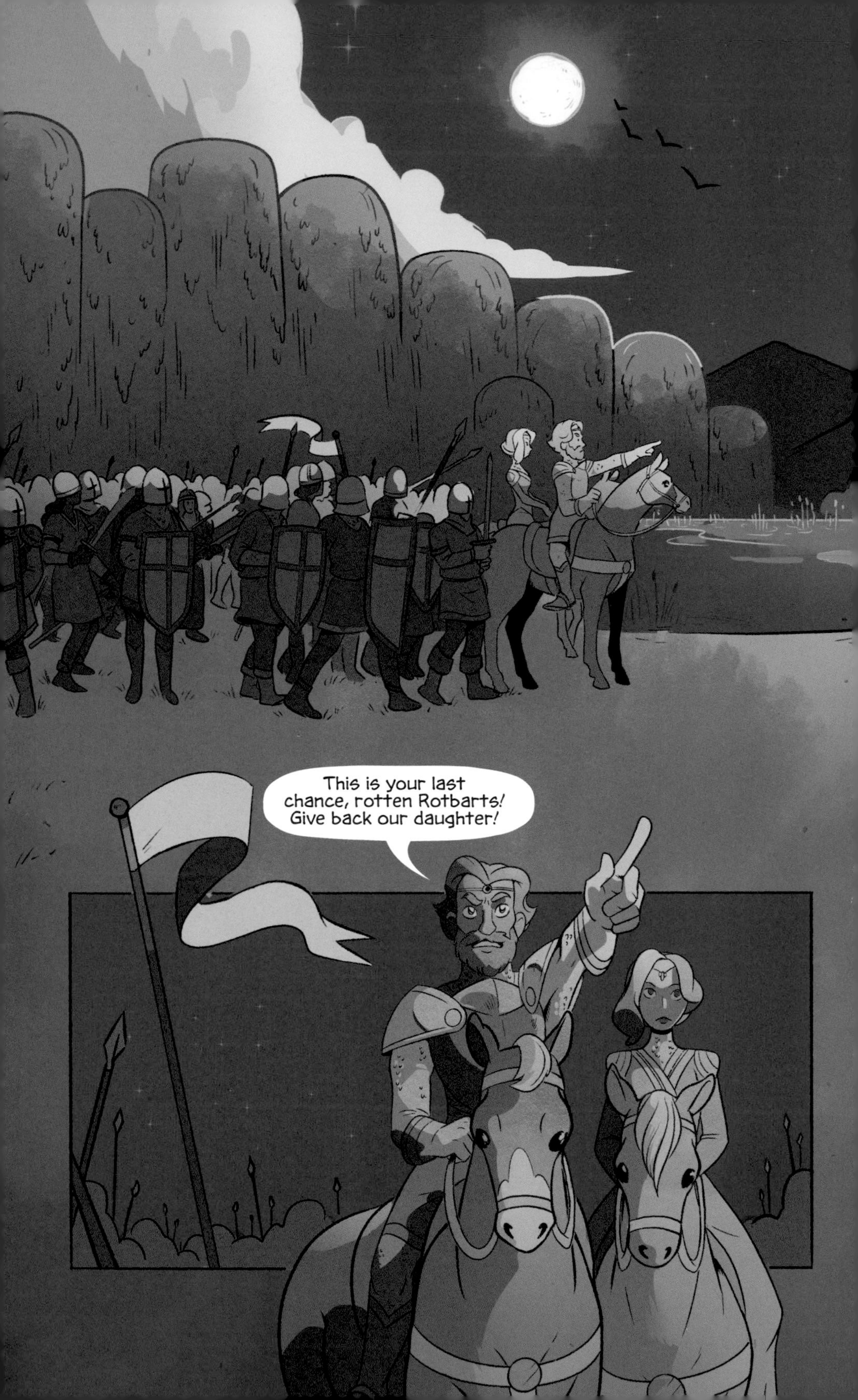
This is your last chance, rotten Rotbarts! Give back our daughter!

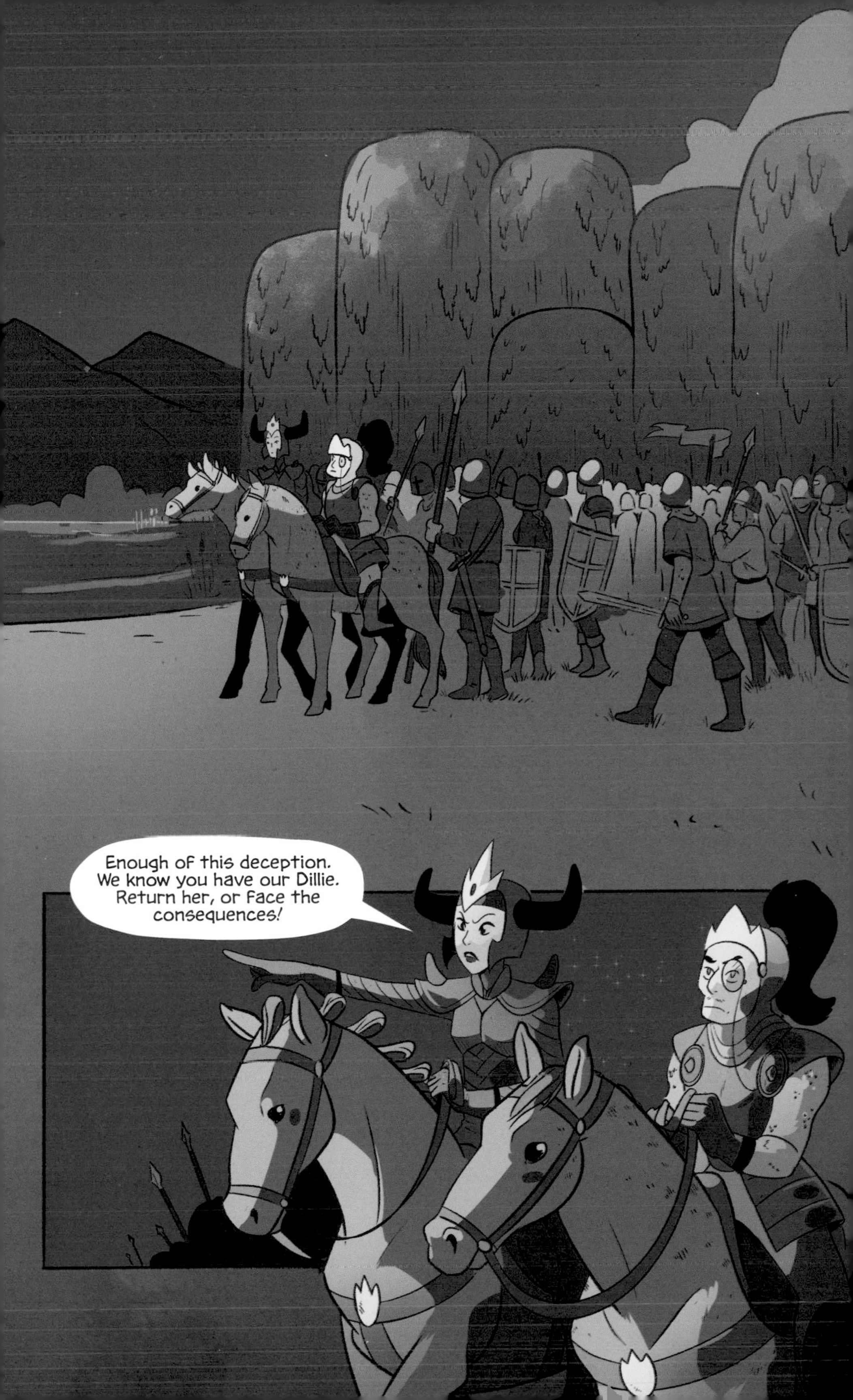
Enough of this deception. We know you have our Dillie. Return her, or face the consequences!

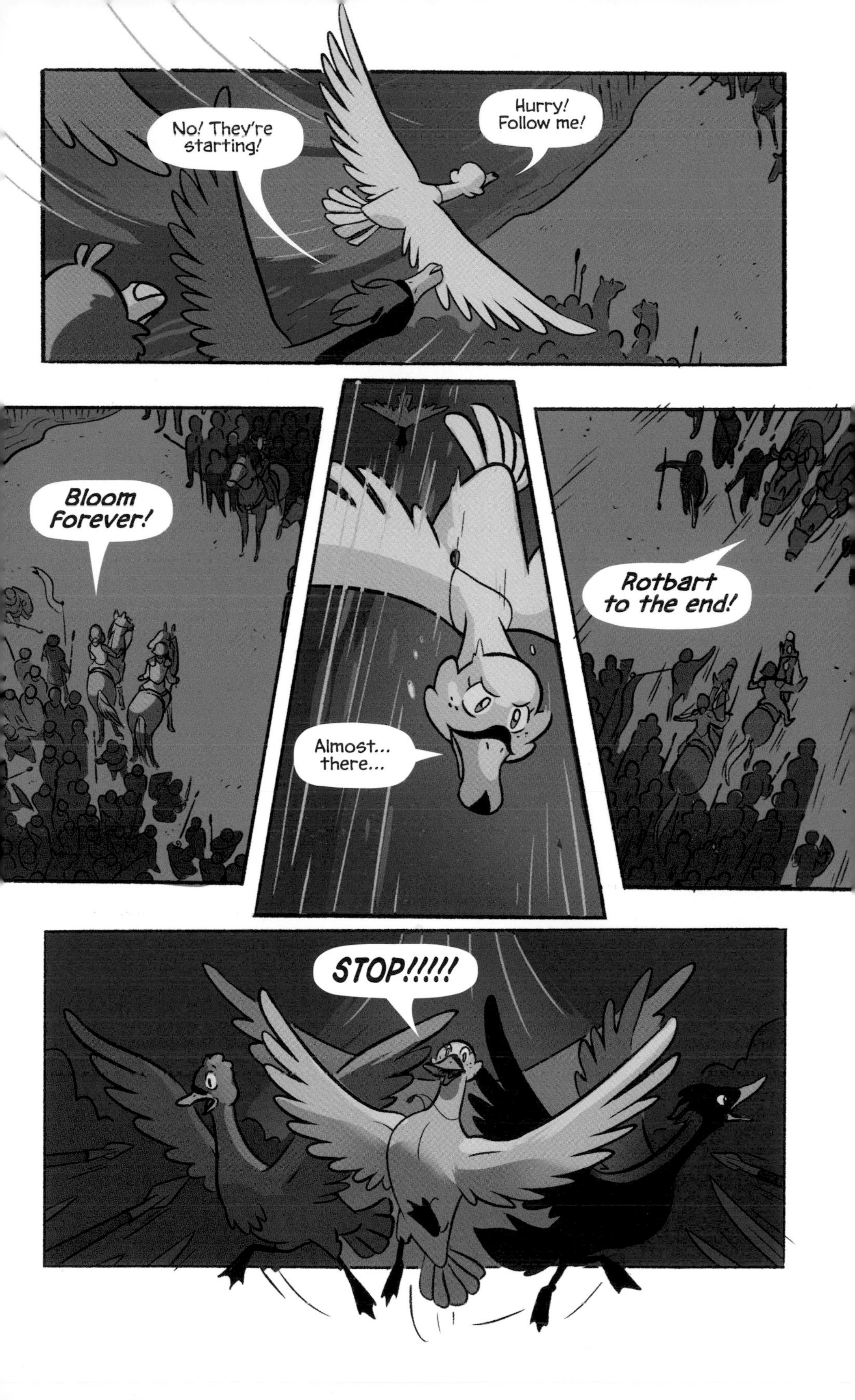
No! They're starting!
Hurry! Follow me!
Bloom forever!
Almost... there...
Rotbart to the end!
STOP!!!!!

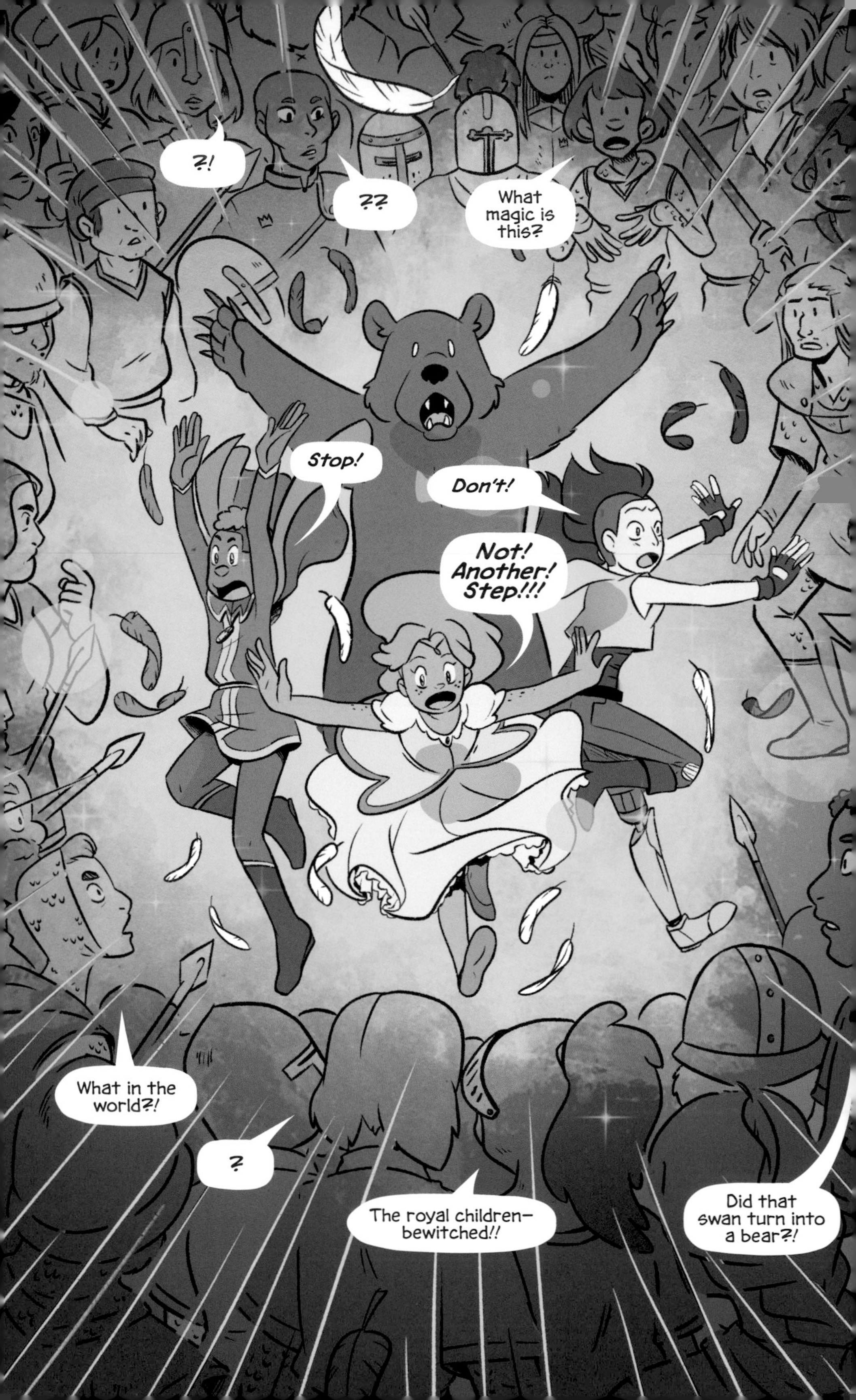
?!
??
What magic is this?
Stop!
Don't!
Not! Another! Step!!!
What in the world?!
?
The royal children—bewitched!!
Did that swan turn into a bear?!

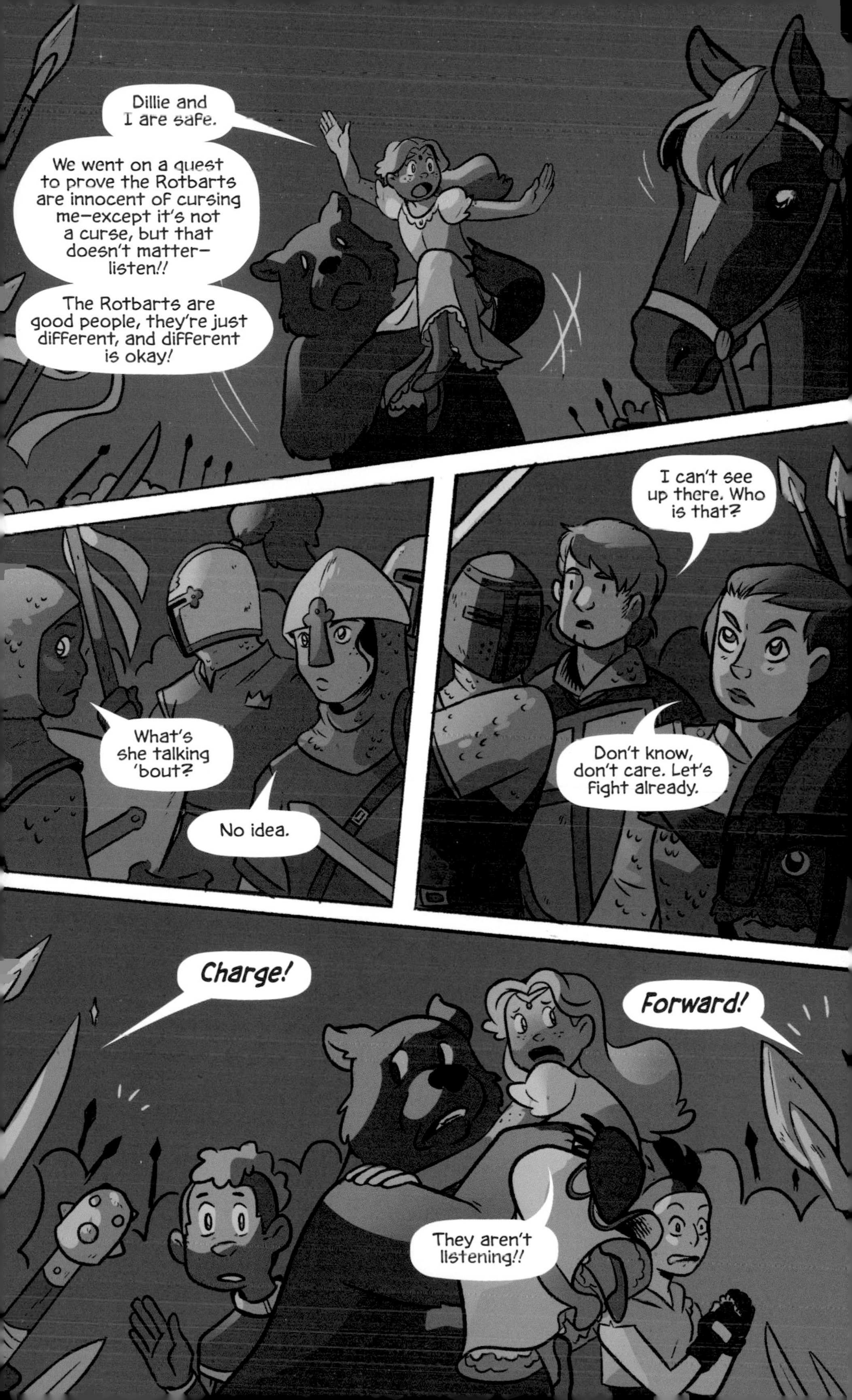
Dillie and I are safe.
We went on a quest to prove the Rotbarts are innocent of cursing me—except it's not a curse, but that doesn't matter—listen!!
The Rotbarts are good people, they're just different, and different is okay!
What's she talking 'bout?
No idea.
I can't see up there. Who is that?
Don't know, don't care. Let's fight already.
Charge!
Forward!
They aren't listening!!

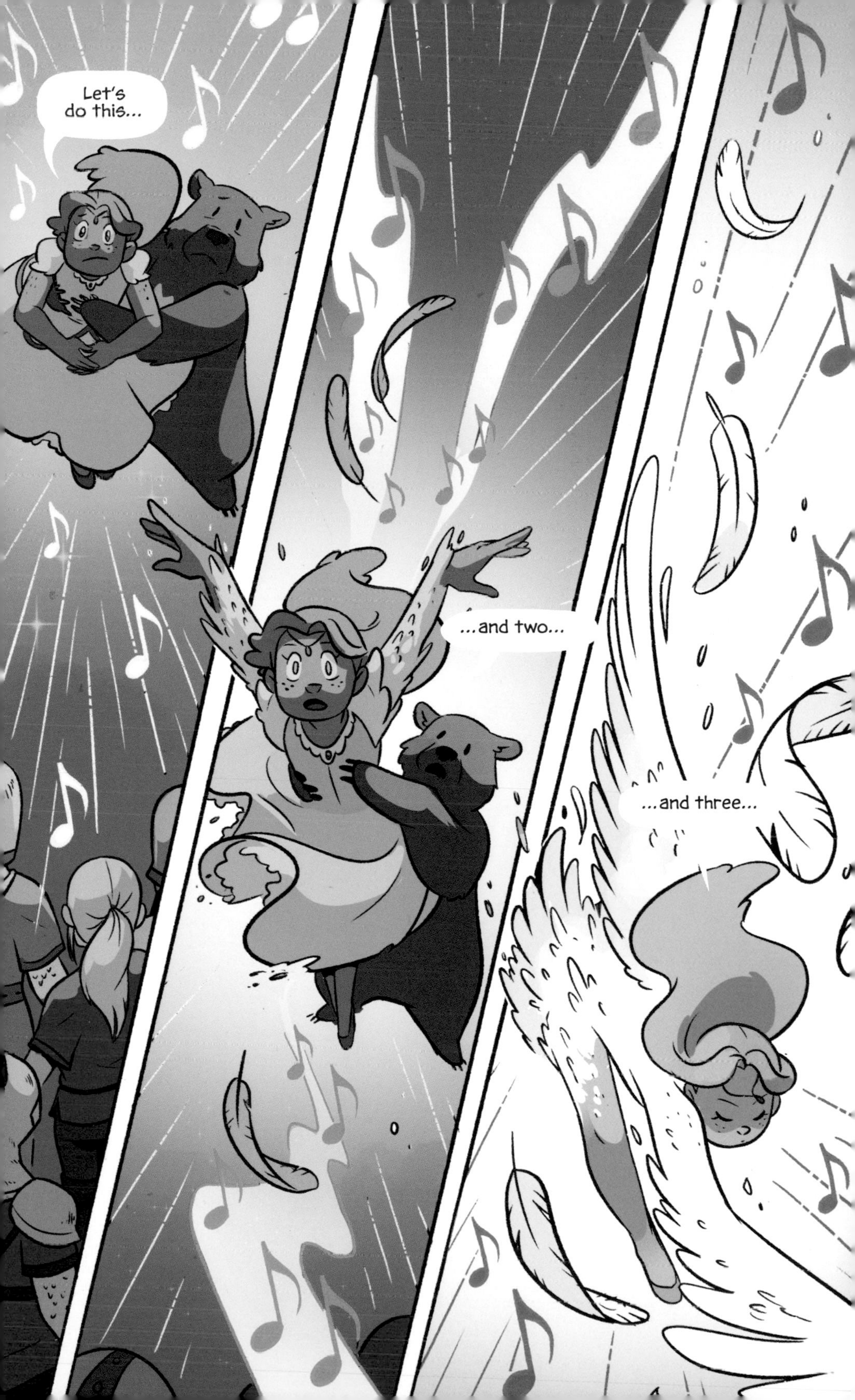
Let's do this...
...and two...
...and three...

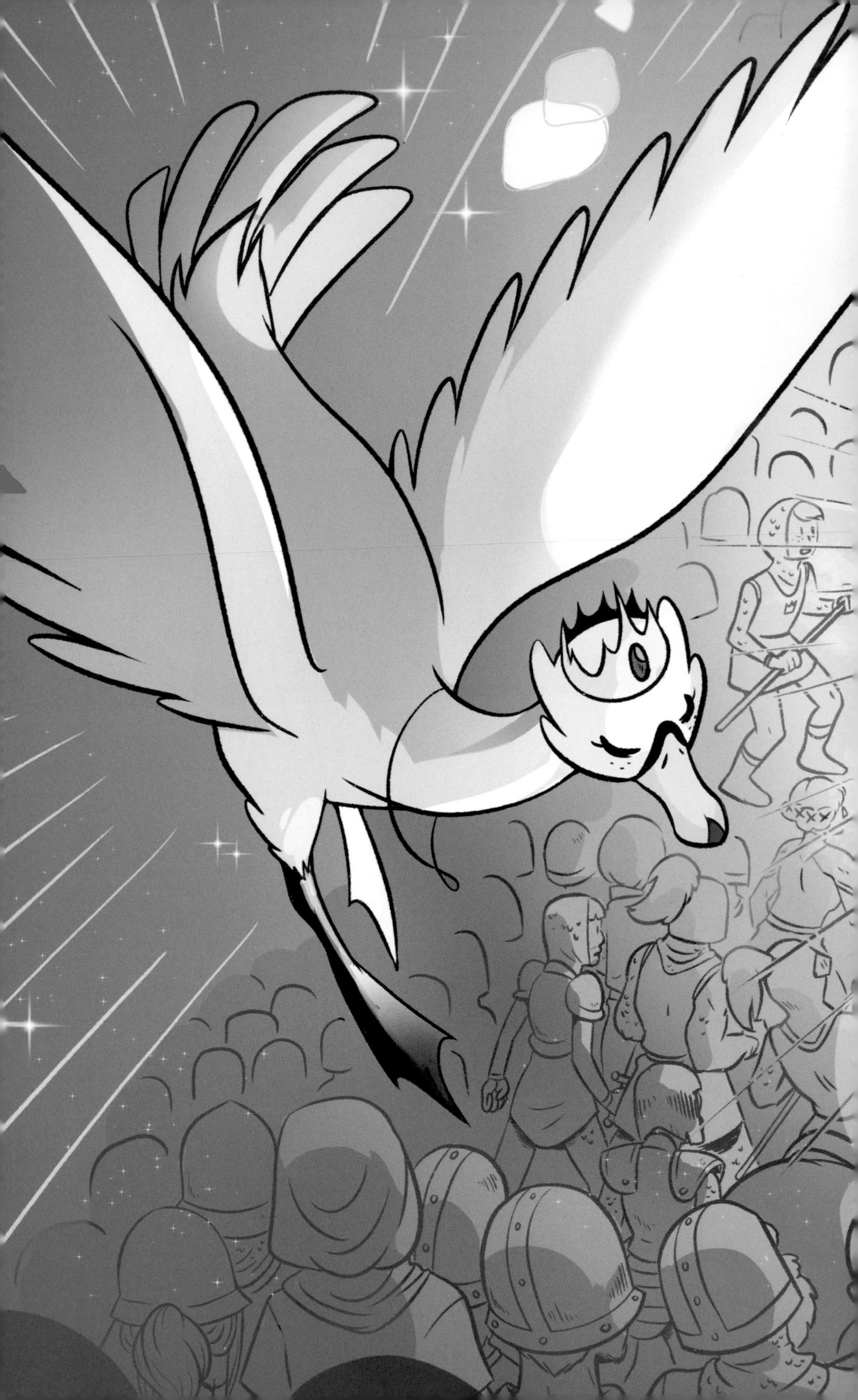

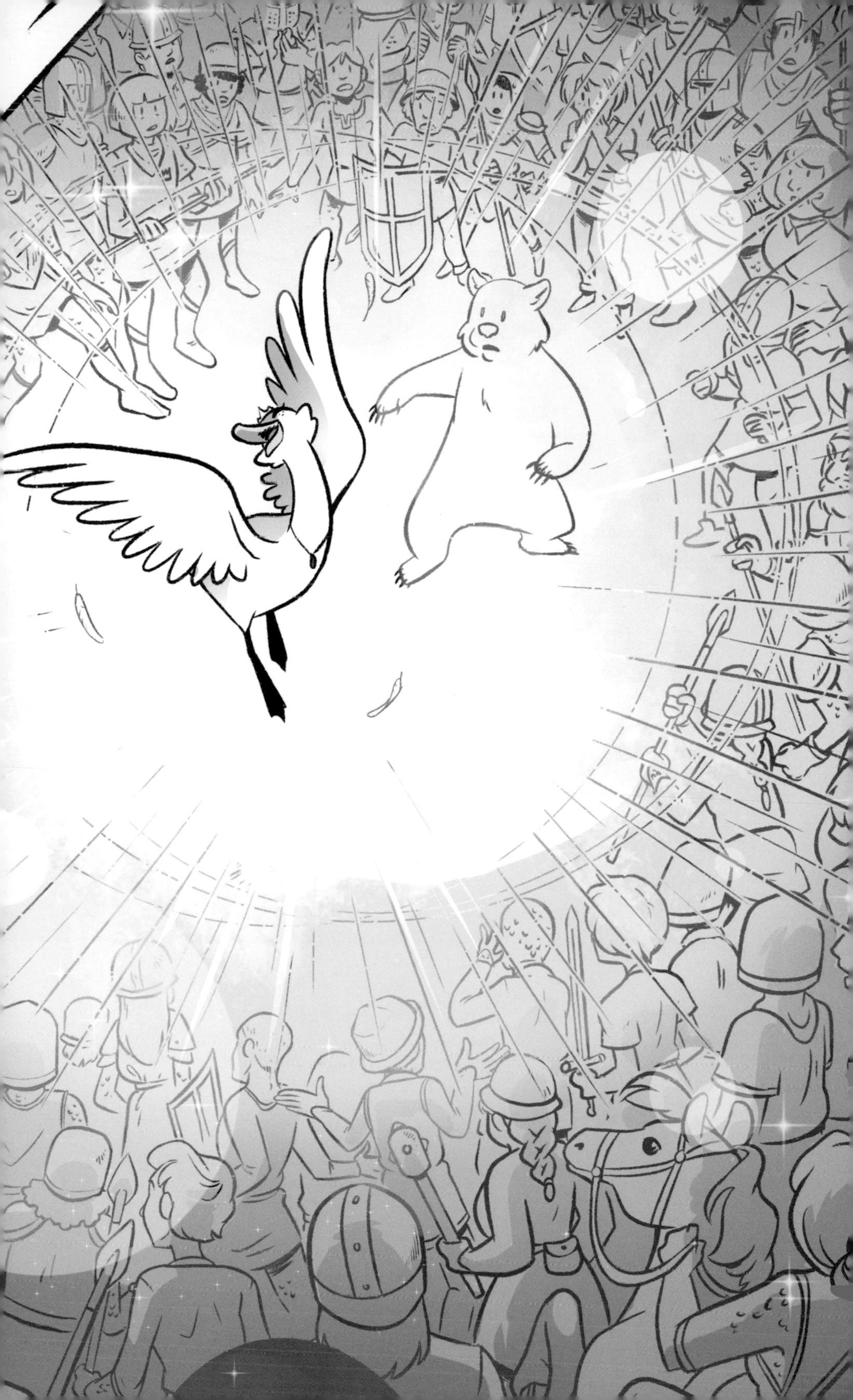

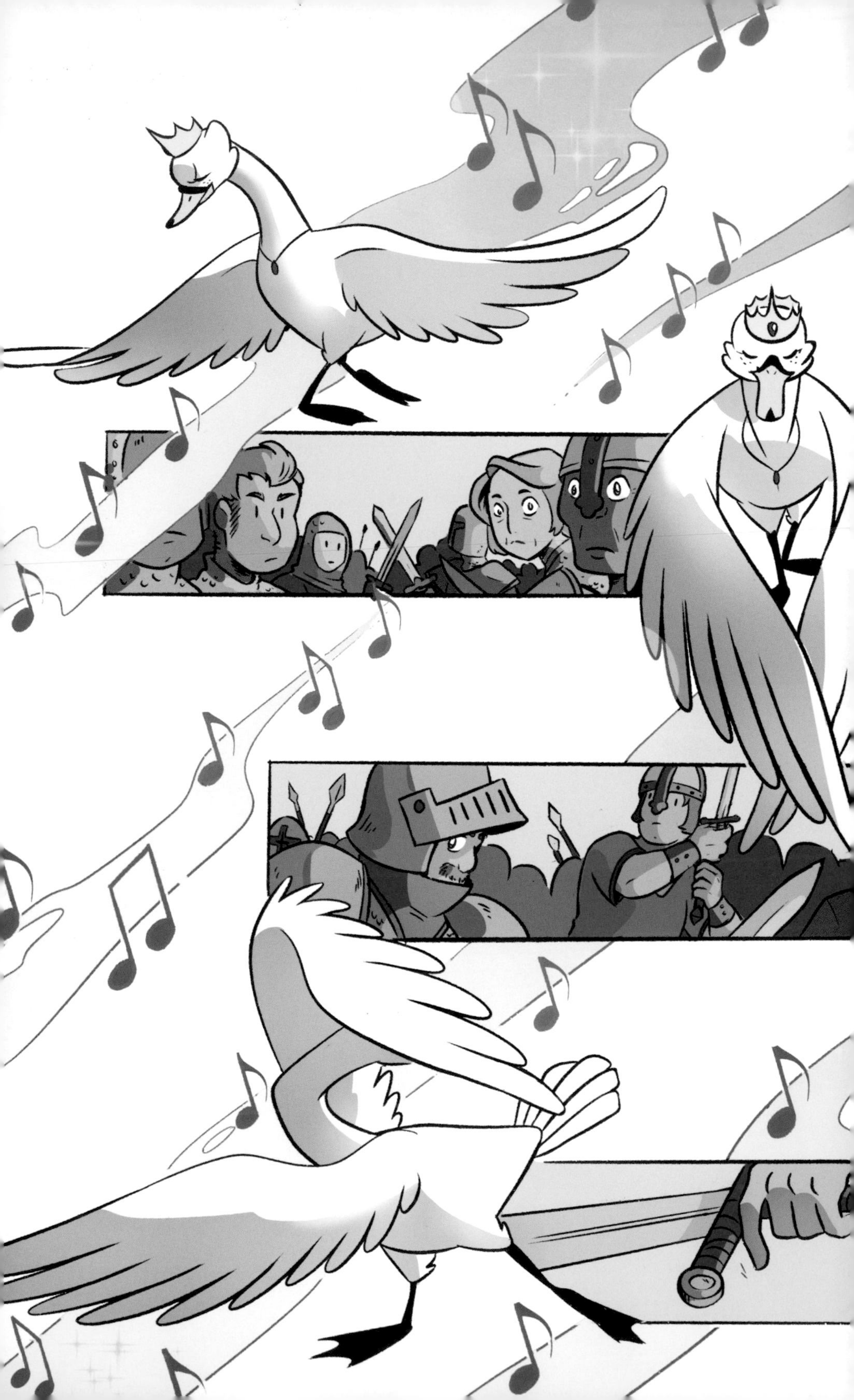

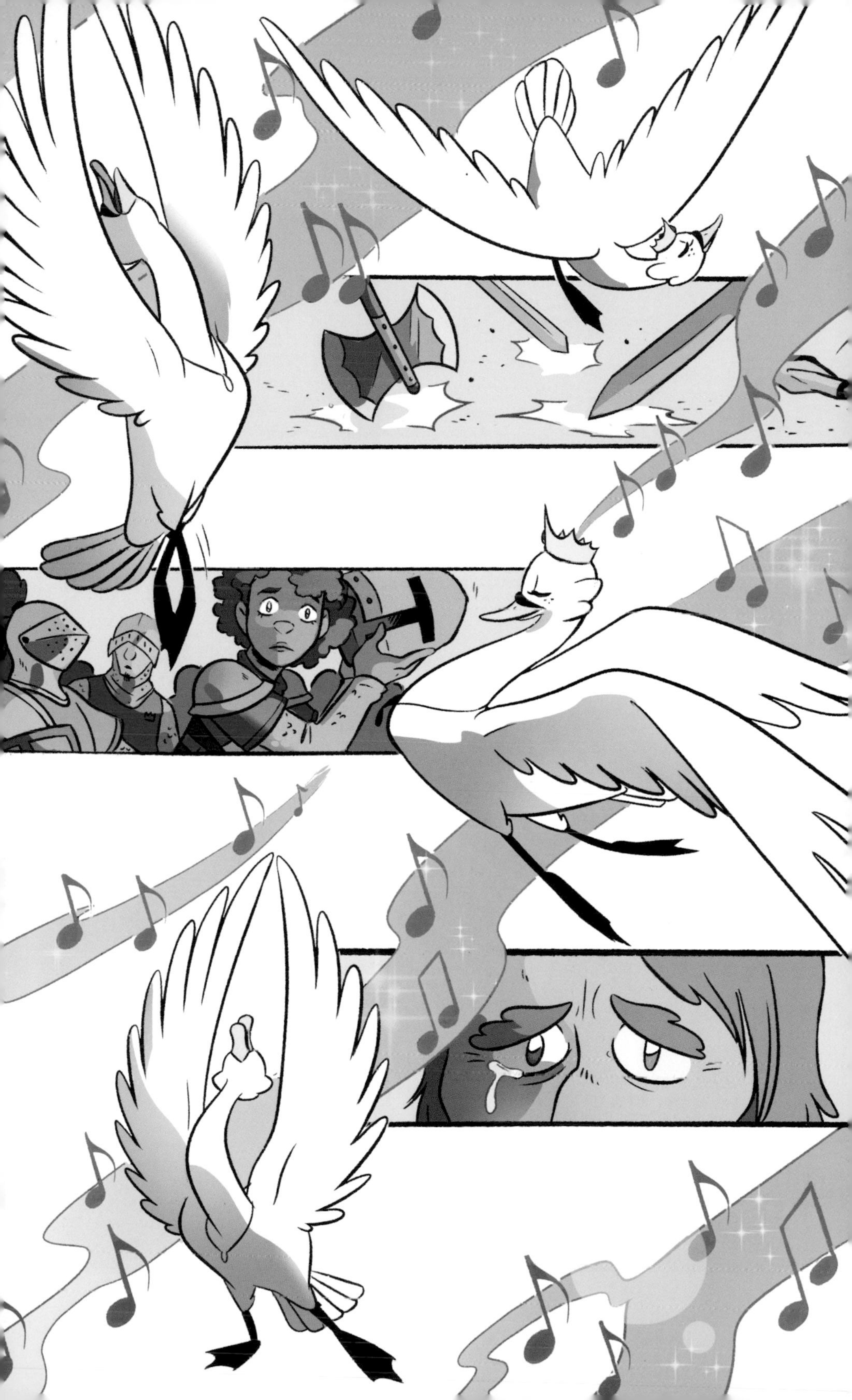

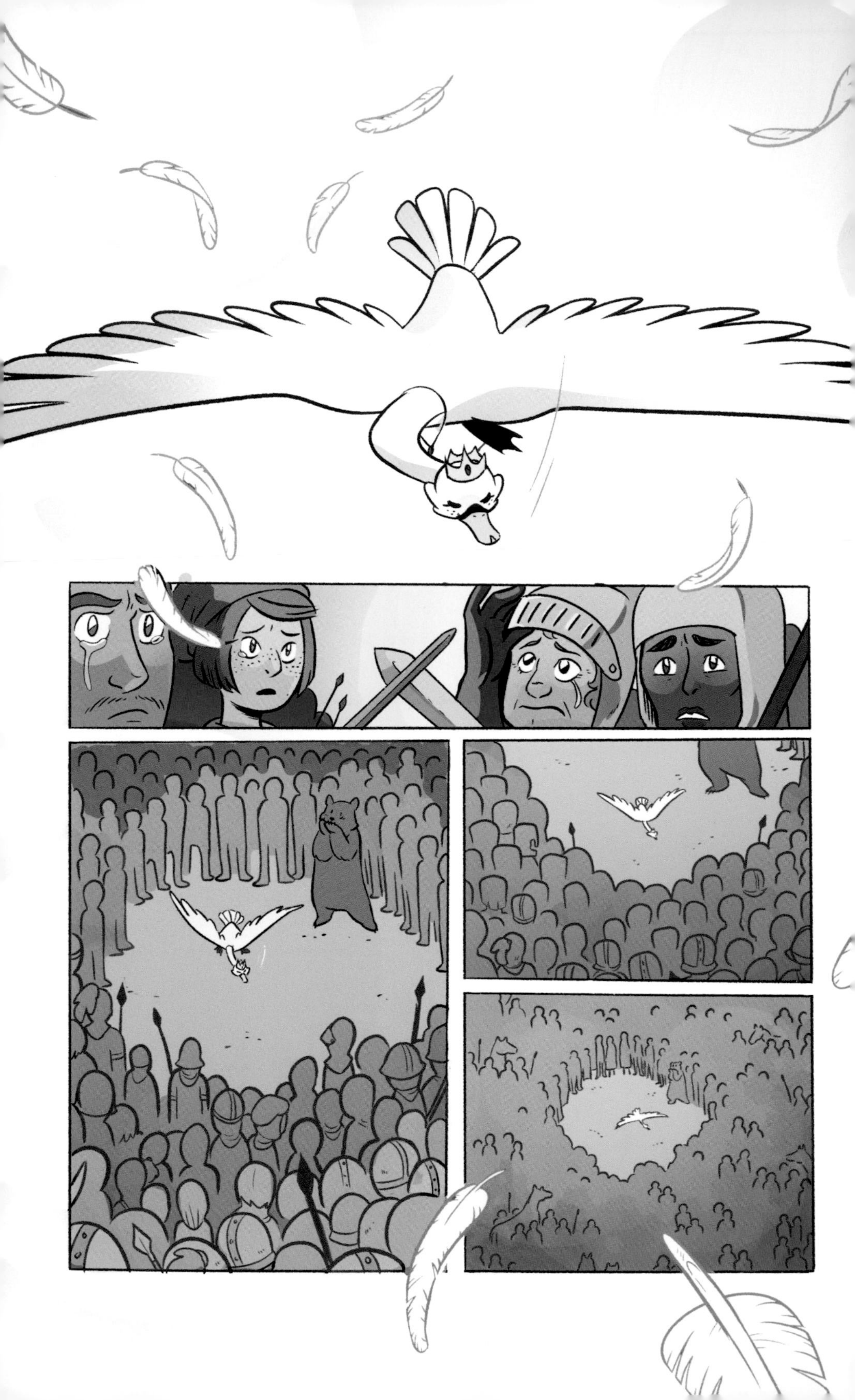

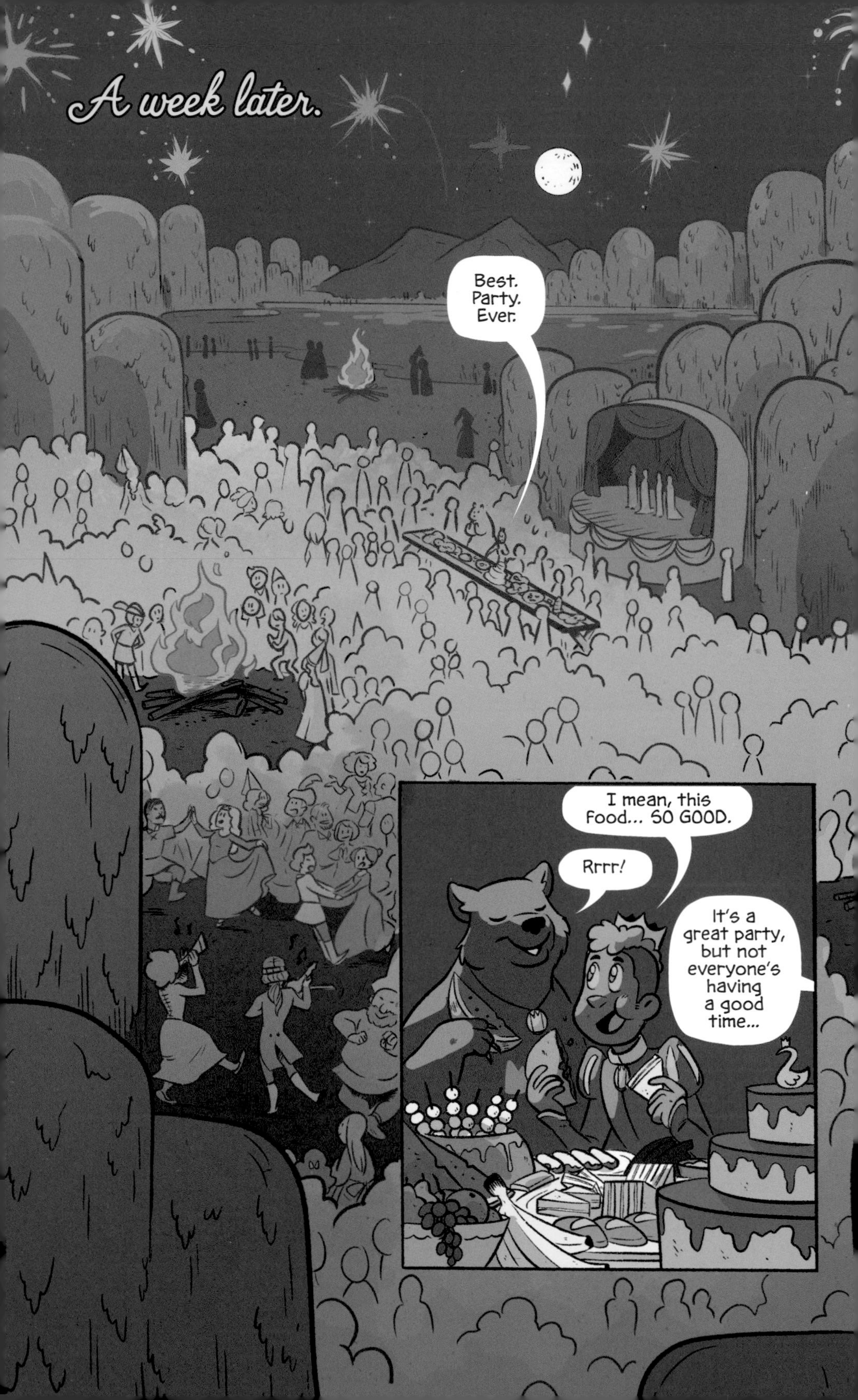
A week later.
Best. Party. Ever.
I mean, this food... SO GOOD.
Rrrr!
It's a great party, but not everyone's having a good time...

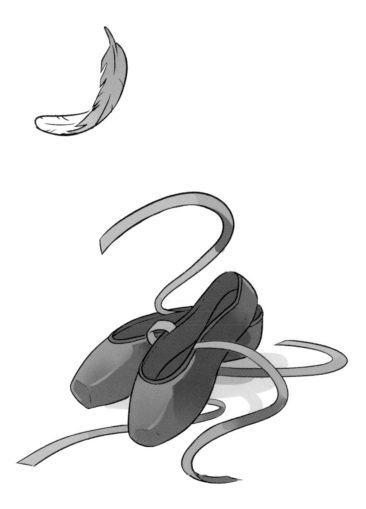

The End

Curses, Cowboys & Ballet

AUTHOR'S NOTE

I was a boy in Texas in the 1980s, and boys were supposed to be cowboys or army soldiers or astronauts. We were not supposed to be into ballet. But in first grade, Mrs. Hamm wheeled in a TV and a VCR and played us **Swan Lake**, and I was mesmerized. It was the most beautiful and graceful thing I'd ever seen. And even cooler? Mrs. Hamm explained that it was a story about a princess turned into a swan by an evil sorcerer's curse. It sounded like my favorite cartoons: **He-Man** and **Dungeons & Dragons**.

OF course, that weekend my mom's boyfriend found me dancing around the living room, trying to leap, and fly, and bounce on my tippy-toes,

and—the hardest part—spin and spin and spin and spin (I'd later learn this was called a **pirouette**). My mom's boyfriend took one look at me and sneered, "Quit acting like a dang sissy." I didn't know what a sissy was, but his tone suggested it wasn't a compliment.

I honestly didn't understand what I'd done wrong. On Saturdays, I knew he and my mom dressed up in tight jeans, plaid shirts with pearl